Library of Congress Control Number 2008943468
The Publishing Place   www.thepubplace.com

underthebridge.com

by Paul Martin

For Debbie, for today, for tomorrow…..

# ACKNOWLEDGMENTS

Writing novels is an act of faith…on both the part of the writer and of those who love him. I have been honored by the faith in me that so many people have shown, and to them I owe more than these few words will express.

Too many times to count, I shelved this work and the idea behind it. Had it not been for the encouragement and commiseration of my writing group, it may have remained nothing more than what everyone seems to have: an unfinished novel in the back of a desk drawer. So, thank you Marie Manilla, Laura Bentley, John Van Kirk, Shannon Butler, Zoe Ferrarris, Mary Sansom, and Leslie Birdwell, hearty Rogues all, and excellent writers whose books you must also read.

A special thank you to the West Virginia Division of History and Culture whose financial support and recognition helped bring this project to fruition.

To Kramer, who was there at the beginning, and to Lainey, who was there at the end. I don't exaggerate when I say that the companionship of a dog is an immeasurable comfort to any writer sounding out dialogue to an otherwise empty room.

The first gift I ever remember receiving from my mother Louise, besides love, is a book; and though I don't remember its title, I do remember that it has ever after been followed by many more. Her love of books became my own, and I hope she is proud of this one.

For their love and patience with a stepfather whose silences often indicated he was writing in his head during our raucous family Sunday dinners, I honor Mark and Barclay, and their spouses Jessica and Jamie, too. They have respected and been proud of me when I did nothing to deserve it.

Perhaps I had a reason to write before they were born, but now that they are here, I can't imagine a writing life, or any life, without my blessed grand-children: Holley, Luke, Harrison, and he-who-will-be-Jake (I think). My goodness, I love you.

This novel's publication is the result of winning a contest sponsored by the publisher, Avant Garde Publishing, and the powerhouse of a woman behind it—Jen Pemberton. Her shepherding instincts and gentle nudges have brought the book to fruition. I thank her so much, and would be remiss if I did not also thank those people who voted for this novel. I'd name them if I knew them!

And finally, Debbie, my wife. She knows I am no handyman; that the house might fall down around us if it were left for me to repair. But she kept telling me that in spite of those inabilities, there WAS some-thing I could do—I could write. I needed those words from her. But more than that…I needed her. For giv-ing me all her irreplaceable gifts, I thank and love her.

## CHAPTER 1

I could use *egregious* in a sentence. I could discuss Hegel, Kant, and Kierkegaard with equal facility, though I thought most of it was self-pitying drivel disguised as dispassionate profundity. One summer I read all of Shakespeare's thirty-some plays, including that dreadful *Pericles, Prince of Tyre*. My knowledge of architecture was not limited to Frank Lloyd Wright. I had taken to drinking single malt Scotch and knew what wine goes best with Kobe beef. And I could afford that Kobe. I could expound at length on the relative merits of ISDN hookups, broadband Internet access, and the future of global computer networks.

But for several months I lived underneath an Interstate 81 bridge in southwestern Virginia.

It wasn't so bad really. It was very rural and the bridge went over a little creek, so it was quiet enough, once I got used to the rush of cars and trucks on my "roof."

I slept in the V formed where the bridge's underside met the concrete slab beneath it. There was a small, level place that stayed dry and protected, and I stuffed some blankets there, which I assiduously folded every morning. I was a neat freak. The term was not mine, it was Corinne's. It used to drive her crazy, but that trait wasn't the only one that annoyed her. Three years ago, when I began showplace.com, she described me as "focused" and "driven." I was intent on achieving financial success, huge success really, and that, too, was a source of conflict. Not the financial success — I'm sure she had no problems with that — the drive.

I also had anger management problems, though I think that the slower lifestyle forced me to learn new methods of handling conflict.

I had trouble handling both business and Corrine, and when I spent one too many nights working late, or maybe it was one too many nights at home trying to explain leveraged buyouts, or the need for more liquid venture capital, or the relevance of an IPO to her future and our happiness, she began having an affair of sorts with my business partner and best friend. I don't know for sure how long the affair went on. I'm not even sure that it was technically an affair, but I do remember how I found out about it.

Things got ugly, then.

I really don't have to wonder about why I lived underneath that bridge.

If I followed the creek north about a mile, it bent back toward the interstate and actually flowed behind a service plaza. I spent a great deal of time there because I lived off the proverbial kindness of strangers, though they never knew it. I was surprised at how much food was wasted, thrown away. I didn't gain weight by any stretch of the imagination, but I also wasn't some emaciated poster boy for the disenfranchised lower class.

I flew beneath the radar. I visited the plaza at different times so no single worker could see me that often, sometimes skipping a day or two entirely. I could have been a commuter or a traveling salesman. But I didn't think that caution was even necessary; no one gave me a second glance. I was just another traveler.

A few weeks into my exile, a Wal-Mart truck overturned a couple of miles north of my bridge. The clean-up crew loaded the scattered contents onto an open bed trailer and parked it in my rest stop until Wal-Mart sent somebody after it. That's where I got my blankets. I could have gotten a great many other things.

Here's something else that was surprising: food wasn't the only thing wasted. I found clothes tossed in trash cans, shoes, and once someone left a toiletry bag on the shelf over one of the restroom sinks, with a nice razor, shaving cream, deodorant, comb, even a bottle of CK One cologne. I'd been using the cheap toiletries from the vending machines, but how many decent shaves are there in disposable razors? And let's just say that any financial outlay exceeded my anticipated income. After my discovery, though, I was the finest smelling bridge troll on Interstate 81.

I stayed presentable because I knew appearance was important and because I was sure that one day I'd be arrested, and I didn't want to look like Ted Kaczynski. On that front I was forever vigilant. I scavenged trashed newspapers from all over, including Cincinnati, and as far as I could tell my disappearance was not news. I was not flattered by that.

I wouldn't steal. Anything I borrowed, including my blankets, I intended to some day pay for. When I reached into a parked car for the apple on the front seat, I'd make a note of the license plate number. When I unzipped a soft-sided car top carrier and pulled out an overnight bag, I made sure to keep the ID tag. These kind strangers would be most surprised when a check for their "misplaced" items appeared one day in their mailboxes. And I promised myself that some lucky Wal-Mart would be the recipient of an anonymous donation, though

I hardly thought it needed it.


Life has a rhythm and one of the keys to happiness lies in matching your rhythm to the lifestyle which chooses you. You can get terribly out of sync if you fight that, so I knew I had to acquiesce to my enforced cadence until I felt a little more control.

The most difficult aspect of life under my bridge, at least at first, was losing track of time. My watch did not make the trip with me, whether I lost it somehow or simply failed to put it on before I left. I had always prided myself on my clear sense of time. I could wake up one minute before my alarm sounded; I could gauge a 15-minute conference call within seconds, and a half hour lunch without looking at the clock. I didn't really need a watch when my company was steamrolling its way into dot-com prominence.

For the first few weeks here, though, I was never sure whether it was 7 or 9 in the morning when I woke up. Later I learned to judge by the traffic overhead: busy early, as commuters worked their way toward Bristol or Abingdon; then a relative midday lull filled by the immoderate whines of big trucks bulling down the long grade in lower gears. Passenger cars, by contrast, seemed almost inconsequential as they passed, skimming rather than cleaving their waters.

These distinctions also allowed me to guess about the days of the week, indisputable points of reference that I never considered I wouldn't know. Even as a child during the interminable summer breaks from school, I knew every day had its own feel. Mondays were separate from Wednesdays, Tuesdays from Fridays, Saturdays and Sundays from all the others, especially Sundays, even though every summer day for a kid could be filled with precisely the same activities.

There, though, the sounds from atop the bridge let me know the weekends from the weekdays. Weekends were dominated by automobiles, filled with, I assume, happy/squabbling families rushing to or returning from the vacations of their lives, probably some cheesy, filthy beach littered with cigarette butts and dog shit half submerged in the sand, and globular matrons waddling around in K-Mart swimsuits strangling the circulation from their legs. I much preferred the great trucks, greasing the commerce of the country, the exclamation marks of the weekends.

Weekends, however depressing otherwise, were the best times to be at the service plaza. Vacationers, especially those returning home, discarded the most trash, often quite usable, as they emptied their cars of every superfluous snack item they thought they couldn't travel without. It was amazing how that 20-pound bag of Cheetos, which little Johnny couldn't live without during the pre-trip grocery store binge, lost its cachet after being lugged from car to the top of the refrigerator in the rental condo and back to the car at week's end. Orange fingers leaving parallel orange veins on the minivan's cloth upholstery sealed the Cheetos fate, and thus they ended up in the trashcan in the plaza's parking lot. They weren't brie-tos, but damned if they didn't hit the occasional spot.

*     *     *

Only once, early in my tenancy under the bridge, did I think about stealing a car. I had just gotten to the plaza on a Saturday, having left my car a few miles up the road a few days earlier, and a couple of guys, early twenties, stood stretching beside a late model Mustang. One interlocked his fingers high over his head in the loose-limbed insouciant pose of an athlete, perhaps a swimmer. Both were severely tanned, the kind that spelled a future of skin lesions, and they wore two-day beards and Oakleys. They weren't related, that was obvious, but damned if I could tell them apart in their faded, baggy University of Auburn/Tennessee/Notre Dame tee shirts with carefully cultivated rips. They wore sandals. Men should not wear sandals.

I disliked them immediately.

The taller one, the swimmer, finished his stretch and grinned over the top of the Mustang at his Tonto, who was busy tugging at his shorts and arranging the ragged sleeves of his tee-shirt to showcase ropy arms. Tonto grinned back. I imagine the last hundred miles had been filled with stories of sexual conquests.

I sat in the picnic area doing my best impersonation of the inattentive wayfarer intent only upon the map I had taken from inside the plaza during an earlier visit. Swimmer and Tonto scrunched their toes firmly into their sandals and laughed loudly at some indistinct remark, then scuffed across the sweltering blacktop and into the plaza.

I was not really predisposed to stealing their car. I had skipped the last two days of coming to the plaza and my visit was just routine—some food, a check in the mirror about the state of my hygiene and appearance (I was beginning to wonder what I'd do about a haircut), and the opportunity to read a newspaper or two or three. I also wasn't even sure what I'd do with a car. I already had a Porsche. I just didn't know where it might be by now. I had begun this "adventure" with $94 in my pocket and by this time had only $70, so what would owning a car help me accomplish? I couldn't park it under my bridge, there being no road leading to it, and though I knew I wasn't living there forever, it was there I had found myself, and there I would be until I formulated a more viable plan.

In fact, the theft idea occurred to me only incidentally. Once the plaza had swallowed Swimmer and Tonto through its electric doors, I ambled in the Mustang's direction, pausing beside the passenger door, placing my hands on the small of my back and feigning a stretch of my own, though no one was looking. I was searching for snacks, hoping for an apple, banana, something reasonably healthy. I've always been fairly in tune with my body and its needs, not obsessed with health, not the kind of person who would look down my nose at someone for eating a Big Mac, but let's say I am intrigued by the body's potential, mindful of its requirements. And just then, to reach any sort of potential, my body needed something healthy. I'd have settled for Fig Newtons. To be frank, I hadn't had a decent crap in days. Stealing their car was not the first thing on my mind.

The passenger door was not locked. I knew it wouldn't be. They either didn't plan to be inside very long, or they simply didn't care. Anyway, the J. Crew crew had only a can of Diet Pepsi in the front seat. A flash of something shiny on the driver's side floor caught my eye—an empty, crumpled pack of Marlboros, and beside it, a key ring.

Still, I had no use for a car, though it seemed that fate was trying its best to provide me with one. I'd go back to Cincinnati some day, I was sure, but not just now and not in a stolen 2005 Mustang GT.

Instead, I decided to make my rounds through the plaza. If nothing else, I'd pick up a couple more brochures to read back under the bridge. I had scabbed discarded magazines whenever I could, but in their absence there were plenty of unread brochures and free travel guides to be had in the racks. I found myself rationing them, the way I used to slow myself down when reading a novel I loved. Since I couldn't bear to get to its end, I'd limit myself to maybe twenty pages a night. I did *Cold Mountain* that way. Now, laughably, I did the same thing with "Things to See and Do in the Blue Ridge" and "Southwestern Virginia's Charming Bed and Breakfasts."

I stood inside the air-conditioned plaza, blinking until my eyes adjusted to the darkness, then headed for the restroom to clean up. Travelers rarely gave me a second glance as I "bathed" shirtless and with paper towels at the sink. I was simply a guy on the road, freshening up during a long drive. They were just passing through and had probably done the same thing, or had seen it done, or admired me for being conscientious about my appearance. We would never see each other again.

I was brushing my teeth when Swimmer and Tonto came in. They saw me but just as quickly glanced away. I was, as always, invisible.

"I've had to piss for twenty miles," Swimmer said, unzipping and positioning himself in front of a urinal.

Tonto considered himself briefly in the mirror above the sink next to me. "You and me both," he said, lightly touching in several places his close-cropped dark hair, as if each quick touch put his appearance an angstrom closer to perfection.

What I wanted to say was "I thought you had to piss." What I did, though, was spit toothpaste loudly into the sink and get my shaving cream and razor out of another toiletry bag monogrammed HST, that I had previously "borrowed" from an unattended car.

By the time Tonto stood before the urinal, Swimmer had already made a great show of sighing as if a giant burden had been lifted and pantomiming a slow shaking of his penis as if it were too heavy for one person. Tonto snickered.

Swimmer took his turn at the mirror to review his blonde hair, cut exactly like his friend's. Difference was, he didn't touch it. Perfect as it lay. He smiled broadly into the mirror, rubbed his forefinger in a brushing motion up and down his teeth. Our eyes met in the mirror but just for a second.

He stepped away and farted.

"Let's go fuck with the natives," he said.

Minutes later, I left the restroom feeling refreshed, presentable, though the mirror had not lied to me. My life under the bridge was beginning to alter my appearance. Certainly I wasn't sleeping well. I may have been dry and protected, and the unexpected largesse of Wal-Mart blankets provided warmth during the nights that were surprisingly cold for late spring, but the ground was still hard and the unaccustomed night sounds kept me wary. This was showing up first around my eyes, which seemed to lack some inner light. I had never slept much but always slept well.

My hands, too, never felt clean. I'd wash them in the creek, which I'd learned from a map posted on the plaza wall was called Sinking Creek, but they still felt sordid. I thought that if I could just keep them clean and my teeth brushed I'd cope much better. At least I was clean now.

And I was hungry. The plaza housed a gift shop that sold local crafts and cheap souvenirs, and several fast food restaurants that spoked off the main welcoming area. I tried on my visits there to spread myself thinly, never going into the same restaurant area twice in a row. When I did enter a restaurant, I'd saunter about, reading material in hand, then sit at a table that some inconsiderate traveler had recently left but had not bothered to clear of refuse. I'd push the garbage aside with a small scowl to indicate my disgust to anyone who might be watching and spread out my map, or paper, or brochure and lose myself in thought. After a time, when anyone near me had moved on, replaced by the next set of faceless motorists, I picked through the wrappers and ate.

Today it was Taco Bell. Someone had been unable to finish his Super Macho Mucho Grande Supremo Nacho Tower. I dined not well but heartily, all the while picturing the path this crap was taking down my alimentary canal and wondering just where in my colon it would bunch up. I had to get some roughage, but none of these joints could risk the lawsuits attendant to having an open salad bar along an interstate highway.

The gift shop had some bags of trail mix that contained fragments of ancient dried fruit. They were, I'm sure, soaked in artificial coloring and preservatives bearing as much resemblance to real cherries as motel pictures do to Monet, but at this point I didn't really care.

I was passing through the lobby on my way there when I saw Swimmer and Tonto at the information desk. Swimmer had a map spread out on the desk, and he and the old guy who manned the kiosk had their heads bent over it while Swimmer gesticulated and traced something on the map with his finger. The old guy, who wore a nametag that read    "I ♥ Virginia" and proclaimed him to be Summerset Hundley, had a bewildered look on his face, occasionally glancing up and around as if searching for help. I wandered over to a brochure rack near them.

Tonto stood a foot behind Swimmer, peering over his shoulder at the map, losing his broad grin only when Summerset Hundley looked up from the map and frantically into their faces, speechless as a puppy. Swimmer, I could see now, wasn't really tracing a coherent pattern on the map; in fact, he seemed to be outlining a slightly different path each time he put his finger to it, with different beginning and ending points. He was speaking in French. He was fucking with the natives.

But it wasn't until I came even closer, by now just a couple of feet away, that I discovered the nature of Summerset's distress.

"If ...you'll...just...wait...here...sirs — Mon-soors —

I'll…," he pointed at himself, "see…if I…," again he pointed at himself, "can get…someone…to help you," and on the word "you" he pointed carefully at them. He spoke slowly and a decibel too loudly, enunciating each word as if talking to a child or a dog.

He put both hands, palms out, in front of his chest to indicate that he wanted them to sit tight, that he'd be right back, but Swimmer touched one of his hands as if in fear of being left alone, turned to Tonto, and continued the conversation in fluent French.

*"I believe this product of incest thinks he is Marcel Marceau."*

*"Yes, but with a smaller vocabulary."*

Swimmer nodded gravely, then returned to the old man. He again pointed at the map. *"I simply want to know where we could find some mountain whores. You know, like Daisy Duke or Ellie Mae Clampett."* He ran his fingers across the map again while Tonto's shoulders shook with silent laughter.

*"Do you suppose he has a daughter,"* Tonto managed to say.

*"Not one who's over thirteen and still a virgin."* They shrugged and sighed. Swimmer began to refold his map.

"I'm so sorry," Summerset Hundley said slowly. "I can show you where you are. You're right. . . here," he placed a thick round fingertip on his map under the glass top of the kiosk. "But, mon-soors," he paused and looked up at them, proud this time of remembering his lone French word, "if I could just understand where you want to get to…"

"Perhaps I can help, sir," I stepped to the kiosk. "I couldn't help but overhear of your problem in aiding these. . ." I paused, "gentlemen. I speak French. At least the dialect from the region of France from which these two young men hail."

Summerset Hundley looked as if an arbitrary god had

opened the door to his cage. Swimmer glowered. Tonto struggled briefly with an urge to walk away but settled into the comfort of his partner's cold eyes.

"Here's a bigger map if you can figure out where they want to go. I couldn't never get that part. They never understood what I was asking, and I never understood what they were . . ."

I waved a hand of polite dismissal to stop the poor man's rambling. "It's okay. I can help them from here." I faced Swimmer squarely. We were the same height. He was maybe five years younger. For Summerset's benefit I froze a smile and tilted my head beatifically. *"Listen, assholes. Don't say a word to me during the next sixty seconds. Just nod your heads occasionally to make Mr. Hundley here think you understand me. Let's start now, understand?"*

Swimmer did not move. Tonto nodded but caught himself immediately in the gravity of his partner's anger and stopped abruptly.

I went on, still in French. *"Don't fuck with me. I want you guys to politely thank this gentleman, mosey into one of these hamburger joints, choke down some road food, hop on your horse, and get the hell out of here."*

Tonto seemed ready to bolt, the gig having lost its pleasure.

*"Who the hell do you think you are?"* Swimmer said. His French and his indignation were excellent.

My answer was one I'd held in reserve for an occasion I thought I might need some other time. I broke eye contact for the first time.

Summerset Hundley rustled behind me, fervently wanting to be of some help.

*"I'm an off duty Virginia State Trooper, and what I really don't want is a ream of paperwork to do on the first day of my vaca-*

*tion. You can understand that, can't you? So why don't you guys quit fucking with my natives* — (I stressed the phrase) —*and get on back north to your summer home in the Hamptons."*

Summerset understood the word Hamptons. "Oh, Hampton," he said. "That's near the coast, just beside Norfolk. They've got a long ride ahead of them. I can highlight the route on their map, if they'd like."

"They'd like, Mr. Hundley." I took the map from Swimmer's hands and unfolded it before Summerset Hundley who with great pleasure drew a bright yellow writhing snake from Here to There and handed it to him as if it were a gift.

Tonto's body language indicated he was already elsewhere. Swimmer accepted the map but never stopped looking at me, taking me in whole, top to bottom. He focused on the unkempt hair vining over my ears, then broke his gaze on me.

"Thank you," he said to Summerset with heavy French intonation then wheeled toward Wendy's with Tonto a half-step behind.

"*Oh gentlemen,*" I called calmly, still in French. Tonto turned, but Swimmer merely slowed. "*If you're still looking for whores, go home to your sisters."*

I smiled quickly at the old man and started again for the gift shop and trail mix, but he spoke brightly.

"Do you think I could get them boys to sign our guest book after they eat? It's not every day we get people from overseas in here. It'd be a real kick for me."

I had no desire to get into any extended face-to-face conversation with anyone, so without turning fully, I told him I thought they seemed to be in a hurry to get on the road.

"I forgot to thank you for your help," he said to my receding back. "By the way, what's your name?"

But there was enough hubbub in the area for me to pretend I hadn't heard him.

 

Out in the parking lot with my trail mix, I thought I'd move their car. Not steal it—as I've said, I wouldn't steal—just stow it on the other side of the building in the overflow lot. I'd put the keys back in the exact place on the floor mat. After they'd call the cops, initiate the paperwork and some radio calls, they'd spot their own car and have a helluva time explaining their carelessness. Or stupidity. There would be one vacation truth they would file behind all their lies, one genuine story that would not get told in the college bars.

I hopped in, put my toiletry bag, or rather HST's toiletry bag, beside me, and inserted the key. The car leapt forward like a startled rabbit, the front tires bumping violently against the curb.

It was a standard. I can't drive a standard, and I didn't have time to learn the intricacies of clutches and gearshifts.

But what I could do was keep turning the ignition until the front tires hopped the curb, and leave the boys wondering what giant had lifted their Mustang just enough to rest it on the sidewalk.

And this is what I did.

# CHAPTER 2

That night I built a fire on the creek bank beneath my bridge. It wasn't cold and I wasn't scared, but the creek's sweep was more a sigh than a sedative and sleep just wasn't coming. Fact was, I missed Corinne. Hunched beside the fire, I drew an outline around my foot with a stick, scraped away the length of my heel and redrew it, shorter this time. Now it was Corinne's foot. I missed her perfect little feet with bubblegum toes. I missed the wet imprint of her feet on the bathroom floor when she'd step from the shower — the wet ball and ridge with the narrow curve down to the solid round circle of her heel. Five tenuous dots at the top. It was the shape of Florida. Her feet were Florida and reverse Florida. Florida with crowns.

I tried to think of the last time we had made love or if we had ever done so outdoors, but I could recollect neither.

Then some sticks in my fire shifted and collapsed, spitting a universe of sparks into the sky, a mesmerizing screen saver. The fire flared, pleased with its new configuration, and soon became too hot to sit near, so I moved from its circle of light closer to the creek.

Something, a frog probably, peeped and splashed into the creek, and after a few moments of relative silence, the night sounds began again. Insects chattered. I always had the picture of crickets sawing their legs together to make that sound, like playing a fiddle. I don't know if that's true or whether it's another fallacy I adopted as a child and accepted as true. I heard or read somewhere, too, that some animals mate for life, but I could never remember what animals did this. So for now, it pleased me to think that every animal or insect noise I heard was a mating call, a plaintive cry for companionship with a concomitant promise of fidelity and shared dreams. This constituted the sum of my knowledge about the wild kingdom.

I couldn't imagine Mrs. Possum, for instance, screwing Mr. Possum's business partner, Mr. Raccoon.

Other, larger, things shuffled in the brush on the other creek bank. Deer, maybe. Maybe a dog. If it was a dog, though, I didn't need him sniffing around here. I picked up a rock and waited for him to move again. Three, four minutes passed, but there was no more sound.

Okay, then, I hadn't heard anything.

Then, I did, more loudly this time, though further off. I thought I saw the brush move up the opposite creek bank and 20 yards downstream, though that might have been shadows from my dying fire. The sound crested the hillside and slipped over, and I did not hear it again until, at length, I climbed the bank on my side of the creek and settled in the blankets under the roaring traffic.

I think most people misuse the word "dream." They "dream" of becoming a doctor, of wealth, of a cabin in Aspen. They talk of "dream" vacations, dates, and boats. They act like any good fortune is less the result of hard work than it is a fortuitous accident, a cosmic intersection of right place and right time. In real life there is far less of this chance, circumstance, and happenstance than they think. I worked hard and set goals. I met them or didn't; I don't credit or blame anyone else, and I certainly don't believe that fate either smiles or frowns on anyone. Fate gets way too much attention. Those who feel otherwise are simply lazy.

Corinne may have shared this worldview, but I had no way of knowing that when I first encountered her.

I met her outside the Westin on Fountain Square the day before the Browns game. It was the inaugural game in the new Bengal's stadium, and downtown was packed. Corinne was helping senior citizens off her tour bus from Lexington and wore a badge on her crisp navy blazer that announced, "I Have Bengal's Tickets—Ask Me." I didn't need any; after all, showplace.com had its own skybox in the stadium purchased expressly for sucking up to corporate clients.

But there was a sweetness to the way she used both hands to steady the old folks down the bus steps. She looked each of them in the eye, spoke to them by name—and how she could know all their names after only an hour's bus ride, I'll never know—and managed, too, to know which stubborn, prideful old men not to offer a hand.

It was that sweetness, that I know could not have been affected, that drew me to her. After the last polyester-clad geezer had entered the Westin, and she was issuing instructions to the bus driver, I approached her.

"How many do you have?" I said.

She smiled a megawatt. "Twenty-six."

"I'll take them," I said and reached into my pocket for my wallet.

Her smile stiffened. The mouth stayed open, two rows of perfect Chiclets bordered by full, red lips; but the eyes blinked rapidly three times, auditioning expressions before they settled on incomprehension. "You'll take them?"

"Yes. All of them. How much for all twenty-six?" I thumbed through my bills until I got to the hundred's section.

Corinne looked down at her clipboard. "I'm not sure I understand. No, yes, I *am* sure I don't understand. These are people. People on a weekend trip to Cincinnati, part of a tour that includes the zoo, Eden Park, and Krohn Conservatory to-day, and tomorrow they'll go to the ..."

She stopped. Slammed on the brakes as if she'd just noticed a red light. And then, I swear, she blushed. I hadn't seen a girl blush since high school because in my business no one blushes. They can be caught unprepared, unknowledge-able, or even in a lie, but they will attempt to weasel out of any situation with jargon or obfuscation. But also in my business, I sometimes have to pretend that they are not doing this. It's an elaborate ritual—they bullshit me and know that I know it. Neither of us acknowledges this, however, because I might have to do the same sometime.

Not Corinne, though. "I can't believe I went on like such an idiot." She touched the badge on her chest. "Of course, you mean the tickets. I have four. I'm afraid they're not very good seats, though..."

I bought all four at face value and later sold them to a scalper at a slight profit.


Later that day I positioned myself among an impres-sive stand of bromeliads in the Tropical House of the Krohn Conservatory in Eden Park overlooking downtown Cincy. I'd been there an hour, listening to the pool's tinkling and sur-rounded by the plants' heady, peppery perfume which I was to later realize was not unlike that which wafted up from the nameless weeds down on my creek bank in the afternoon's steamy heat. The seniors from Corinne's bus were being led on a tour by a wrinkled woman docent who was probably older than most of her group's members and whose voice alternated between squeaky excitement at a prized exotic "capture" and a brittle rasp like very old papers being shuffled while she pointed out the more pedestrian species. A few tourists, mostly women, huddled near her cupping her words while the men near the pack's rear lost focus and touched leaves beside signs that begged them not to.

Corinne was not among them, and so I assumed my calculated gamble had not paid off, but as I left, I saw her seated on a bench in the shady lawn beside the Conservatory. Her shoes lay on the bench beside her, her little Floridas were scrunching the cool grass. She ate a peanut butter sandwich, and an apple lay on the brown paper bag beside her.

"Not a plant lover?" I said from behind her.

She twisted around, smiled. "I love them. I can't count the times I've been through the Krohn with and without a group. I'm just hungry, is all." She scooted her bag and apple closer to her so I could sit. "You aren't going to use those Bengals tickets, are you?"

"No," I admitted. "Fact is, I already have seats for the game, and I'd like for you to…"

She interrupted. "I can't, or rather, I won't. I need to make sure all my charges can find their seats, and believe me, there'll be some trouble getting up to them."

I understood, I told her. "Then how about …"

Noise from the Krohn's exit caused Corinne to turn and stand. Her group was heading toward the waiting bus. She dropped her apple into the sack with a thunk and said "Seafood 32, 8 o'clock. If I'm a little late, have a drink and don't worry. Make mine their house red; I like it room temperature anyway. My schedule is not always precise."

At dinner that night I discovered Corinne's definition of dream mirrored mine because neither of us used the word at all when we talked about the future.

The morning after my encounter with Swimmer and

Tonto found me ravenous. Hungry, because, well, I simply wasn't eating enough. Life had been reduced to a few essentials: food, water, and shelter. I had shelter, and since I was a scavenger of food rather than a predator, I had a great many hours of enforced leisure to deal with. The prospect that all this "spare" time might not be good for me suddenly reared its ugly head.

Eons of cultural evolution tell us we have progressed beyond mere survival needs. I needed stimulation. Brochures weren't getting it. I was learning the area's flora, fauna, geography, topography, history, prehistory, attractions, fairs, festivals, places to stay, things to do, hidden treasures, where I could buy fire station apple butter, Granny's quilts, pick my own apples, blueberries, blackberries, try the Sinking Creek Women's Club's recipes for peach cobbler and buttermilk gravy (though it seemed I would need more advanced kitchen equipment than I had readily available), even a hotline to call if I felt I was beyond redemption and considering suicide. This, of course, raised the Zen question: if one is considering suicide but has no phone, is it still considered suicide, or a murder by an unresponsive but complicit society?

No matter, I wasn't considering suicide. Too many people might take enjoyment from that. Or worse, my body might never be discovered.

I needed something to do, desperately. I even practiced typing on an air keyboard in the same manner that teenagers and aging hippies will play an invisible guitar and smile at the invisible groupies who toss their invisible panties to them as they dance in their invisible arenas. I needed a mouse to click or a software problem to solve. Those things I could fix.

I was disappointed in myself, too. It had been foolish to bail out old Summerset Hundley. He was nothing to me and would have suffered no ill consequences from his encounter with the assholes. Now, he might recognize me, and I was forced to alter my plaza visitation patterns, though I didn't know how much more random I could have made them.

The area was open 24 hours, but the crowds were so sparse and fewer of its restaurants were open after midnight that I risked becoming a familiar to the workers, or worse yet, recognized by troopers who routinely patrolled that stretch of interstate.

I thought it best, then, to go a day without eating and I'd just wash in Sinking Creek. I had done it before and the hunger pains eased as long as I could keep my mind busy. But the problem was I had nothing to read, nothing to work on. My "home" required no maintenance, and so I found myself in a catch-22: the act of going to the plaza would give me something to do, taking my mind off my hunger, thus I wouldn't need to go to the plaza to get something to eat. But since I couldn't go, all I did was sit there and think about food. My world continued to shrink, and today, it seemed, it would consist of about 300 square feet with a shitty view.

I watched a squirrel eye me a few feet away. I did not think of him as food. I was no modern Robinson Crusoe, creative enough to fashion a microwave oven out of twigs. Nor was I a Thoreau, there to learn more about myself or my society. But it was there I had found myself. The squirrel, then, was safe, and I think somehow he knew this. He wandered closer to pick up some sort of nut, sat back like a Buddha on his haunches, and ate in his rapid, peripatetic fashion, grasping the nut and twirling it in his paws until his teeth found entrance.

After a minute or two he bounded off in graceful parabolas toward the south until he disappeared in the thickness of the Jo Pye weeds (I'd seen illustrations of them in the brochure "Edible and Non-edible plants of the Southeast"). And what a dumbass I felt like as I realized this. I had a veritable encyclopedia of salad information in brochure form stashed with my blankets. I'd reread it with an eye toward its information rather than its entertainment value later this afternoon.

Watching the squirrel head up the creek gave me another pause. I had worn a path north to the rest area, but the God's truth is I had never considered following the creek in the opposite direction to see what lay within my forested kingdom that way. What kind of businessman doesn't explore not only all the alternatives at his disposal, but also those that are not so readily visible? It's Business 101. Three months lying low under a damn bridge and I had confined myself unnaturally to a 3-foot swath of path that lead from my bedroom to my kitchen/bath/ living room a mile away. What a floor plan.

Traffic was heavy on the bridge, so I knew it was somewhere between 8 and 10 a.m. I folded my blankets, and fished through my current brochures (outdated information about a summer camp for boys—"Mom and Dad, you won't recognize your young MEN when you pick them up in August"—and a color pamphlet outlining the role of the Corps of Engineers in the area's flood control) until I found the edible plant booklet and put it on top of the stack. I checked how dry some t-shirts were, folded them, and put them neatly into a tan suitcase. I would someday repay Mr. Henderson S. Turner for both the suitcase and tacky vacation clothes I borrowed from his car during my first week here, so I didn't feel guilty. I already left his camera, personal valuables, and a $20 bill of mine in his back seat, and though I would have preferred other ways of shopping, my options at the time were limited.

I changed into a pair of plaid Bermuda shorts, and a bright—no, loud—Hawaiian print shirt because they looked hilarious and because I certainly wasn't going to see anyone I knew. And I headed south.

Along the creek in this direction, there was the faintest remnant of a path, neither wide nor distinct enough to have been recently human-created. I was sure it was a highway for the animals I heard at night. In moments, the mid-summer humidity had me sweating and the horseweeds made my bare legs itch, and I realized that I would soon have a monumental headache from thirst. But for that moment, I was Columbus, De Gama, Pizarro, Armstrong, blazing my way into a new world.

The creek was lined on either side with knobby sycamores, their roots grabbing the bank like knuckles, and their upper trunks bare of bark and bone-white through the canopy. It seemed to be a damn fine day somewhere out there.

After an hour or so, the headache I predicted hit. I was not one to take much medicine, preferring to allow my body to use its natural defenses to heal itself, but my one weakness was aspirin. I swallowed it like candy, doing so often during meetings with pain-in-the ass clients who thought I was eating Tic-Tacs, and probably wondered why I didn't offer them one. Sometimes I'd take them prophylactically before a meeting I dreaded. Sometimes the aspirin helped; sometimes the headache wouldn't be derailed. The one approaching then had the potential to be a bastard, so I sat in the creek's shallows to cool off a bit.

Leaning over the creek was a willow tree, and I remembered reading in a brochure that the Indians would chew willow bark for pain. In fact, the same chemical compound in the willow is the active ingredient in aspirin. Problem solved, then. I stripped off a chunk of bark and chewed. It was, of course, bitter as hell, but no more so than the aspirin tablets I had often swallowed without water.

I didn't know how long it would take for relief to come, or if the feeling of well-being that I got from aspirin tablets would be duplicated by this bitter bark, but I simply couldn't keep walking just then. My head throbbed and the act of walking was going to make me vomit. In my former life (as I had begun to think of Cincinnati) I would have closed my office door, closed my remote controlled window shades, told Essie to hold all calls, swallowed four aspirin, and laid siege to the headache. Here, though, I had no such luxury. I had to have some clean water, and Sinking Creek did not fit that description.

I lay back into the creek's margin, no more than six inches deep that near the bank, cleaving the water's flow with my head and allowing it to run down the length of my body. It was cool, not cold, and when I closed my eyes, I could picture myself in a refreshing, albeit horizontal, shower. I may have even drifted briefly into sleep, my fingers interlocked corpse-like on my chest. A yoga pose. The water running past my ears prevented my hearing anything but its soft, bright cadence, and soon I no longer thought of my head, and whether it was the creek's rhythm or the bitter willow bark, my headache dissipated.

The wind must have freshened because the treetops above me began swaying and kaleidoscopic patterns of shadows offered nebulous glimpses of sky. This far away from my bridge I had no clear idea of the time, no traffic sounds for orientation, and I felt vaguely uneasy. Reflexively, as I had done so often in the past three months, I raised my left arm to check my watch, which, of course, was not there. Water dribbled onto my face.

The water, my thirst, the shifting shadows, the dispersal of time, all became a bit much. I closed my eyes and conceded. I can't say I slept, but I did dream, and though I rarely can recall my dreams with any accuracy, it seemed pleasant enough and seemed to include Corinne and someone who might have been me.

When at length I opened my eyes, the wind had died, no shadows wavered, and the severe slant of light told me that, though there was still plenty of daylight left, some significant time had lapsed, and I needed to get home. I was stiff, chilled; my neck felt heavy and locked, so I drew my knees up from the water first. They made a sucking sound as they pulled loose from the sand that had been piled against their length by the current.

On the bank, not ten feet from my head, something emitted an unearthly shriek. I covered my head with my arms thinking first that it was a wild animal, a bobcat or something, that had seen me as prey, and my best reaction would be to protect my head. Then I drew my legs into my chest forming a dizzying ball of soaked plaid shorts and Hawaiian print shirt. I could only hope the beast would choose not to eat something with such hideous fashion sense.

When the attack did not take place, I peered cautiously toward the scream which continued, but seemed to be receding. It was, as was its author. And though I could tell nothing about her age or facial features, I could tell her long hair overspread and slapped her naked back like a tangerine fan.

For the next three days it rained. And rained. It rained as if all the heavenly hosts were pissing on me. Sinking Creek rose and rushed, its volume dial ratcheted up until I heard only its roar instead of the traffic overhead. Rivulets of water like whipping silver threads traced their way down paths on both banks. I might have found the whole scene picturesque if it weren't disturbing the feng shui of my living quarters and making my progress to anywhere slippery and, if not truly dangerous, at least annoying. A simple trip down to the creek side became an Olympic gymnastic routine.

I made a daily visit to the plaza, uncharacteristically but purposely during the busiest time of the day, and went straight into the restroom because I was, of course, soaked and muddy. I cleaned up as best I could, changing into clothes I carried in a plastic trash bag I had borrowed from a janitor's cart on a previous trip, then put my soggy head beneath the bank of hand dryers until I felt precariously close to conspicuousness. I wasn't going to appear on the cover of Forbes, but there was nothing else I could do. I stayed on the margins of the crowded halls.

The first day I ate at a burger joint, the next day at a pizza place, the third at a cafeteria. At the first two I ate remnants of other traveler's mistakes. At the cafeteria, however, I spent $5.75 for the "Vegetable Lover's Plate." It was the best meal I'd had in a while — overcooked spinach, a wilted wedge of iceberg lettuce with a spoonful of glutinous Thousand Island dressing (though the only island where this might have come from was Three-Mile), mashed potatoes with a gravy imposter, and something called creamed peas, which I gather is a local delicacy because the counter girl let out a low, almost erotic, "yummm" and threw a knowing smile at me as she plopped them in my little bowl. The coup de grace, it seemed, was a crumbly dildo of cold cornbread.

I sat at a table beside a rain-spanked window. Out on the interstate, cars shot silver flukes behind them. For the first time I thought about how fast they were moving. In one hour they would go farther than I had walked in the months I had been here. And though I didn't care where they were going, their sheer speed intimidated me. This represented as profound a change in me as any I was beginning to see in the restroom mirrors. I was never the type to be frightened by speed; in fact, I courted it.

In the world of internet portals, speed was king, and I don't just mean microchip processor speeds or even broadband dumping speeds, though these were numbers I could quote in my sleep to clients. No, Raccoon and I used old business clichés like "strike while the iron is hot" and coined new ones like "first-mover advantage." We talked, worked, thought, ate, and—like those cars outside the window—we drove fast. We slept little and saw things, openings, we were sure others weren't seeing. We communicated in hastily typed half-sentence emails, not even bothering to capitalize i. Emoticons replaced emotions. We thought in zeroes and ones.

And right now as I looked out at a wet world of rain-bright cars and trucks with slobbering, grinning grills, I thought again in numbers, and counted my dwindling funds, because now that I was satiated, I resented those costly vegetables so overcooked as to be devoid of nutrients, so bland as to be indistinguishable from one another. I let out the shortest laugh, a snort really, as I realized that the forty dollars and change I was hoarding represented some tips I'd left after big-client dinners.

I felt a woman at the table opposite me look up at my noise, so I blew my nose into my napkin and avoided eye contact.

I thought, too, of the tangerine-haired girl on the creek bank. Sitting under the bridge for the past three days, huddled in Wal-Mart blankets against the damp chill, I had thought much about her. How long had she been watching me lie in the creek? I didn't think she was a real threat to discover my home. After all, I had traveled up the creek for a good mile before stopping, so she wasn't going to trace my movements.

Besides, her shriek indicated her fear of me. I had nothing to worry about.

But, too, for the last three days I had cultivated other questions about her. Once I convinced myself that she herself represented no menace, I dismissed her presence as an unfortunate, but unlikely to be repeated, encounter. But had she been alone? And why had she been naked, or at least topless? Was she bathing there? Living there, like me? I had seen her dart through dense undergrowth like a deer, nimble and practiced, and even in fear she moved like she was accustomed to the surroundings. Moments later, I had followed her zigzagging course for a good hundred yards. There was no pattern, no discernible footpath. She left no clothing behind, and I had seen none in the fists of her pumping arms. I had gone back to the creek and sat, still dripping water, on a log and asked myself the most existential question of all: had she really been there?

Now I went to the cafeteria's condiment cart and grabbed a handful of napkins. There was a cheap black ink pen in HST's toiletry bag. Together, the pen and napkins would make an impromptu stationery kit. When I got back to the bridge, I needed to record some things. I needed a mission statement and a business plan with some clear goals. But most of all, I needed to write some things down to make them real.

## CHAPTER 3

Soon, Henderson S. Turner's duffel bag contained not only his vacation clothes but also a collection of napkins, which constituted the sum of my days. Each morning I made a to-do list for the day. Early on, it consisted only of two things — find something to eat and stay alive. I dutifully checked them off when I'd return from the plaza, my day's "work" accomplished.

But the tactile sensation of writing, of seeing words spread from margin to margin, line to line, napkin to napkin became addictive, and I began to write a great many things. It reminded me of the only yard task my parents could get me to do without whining when I was a kid. I loved mowing the lawn because I could see the progress. The results were immediate and the patterns I could make were endless. Sometimes I'd mow in an ever-decreasing rectangle, sometimes simply back and forth. Other times I'd make more intricate designs — interlocking rings or the outline of animals. I fancied our long, level yard my personal Sistine Chapel.

My napkins, too, allowed me to see advancement, each one representing a captured thought, and so my days, even without a watch to mark the time, again became linear. Became purposeful.

I catalogued the plants in my immediate area after cross-referencing them against brochure illustrations. I wrote ideas for new software, though without computer access I had no way of knowing for sure that they had functionality. I wrote lines from poems as well as I could remember them, and thanked some of my junior high teachers who had cruelly made me memorize them. I listed my favorite restaurants and Corinne's favorite artists. In the evenings I chronicled my day's activities. I wrote on napkin after napkin, stuffing my pockets full of clean ones each time I visited the plaza.

I folded my blankets first thing each morning, washed in the creek, brushed my teeth, then sat down on the log I had dragged to my fire ring near the water and wrote. If it rained, I wrote under the bridge. In the same way that I'd never leave my office without my PDA, I never left my bridge without my pen. If I couldn't think of anything original to say, I simply copied brochures word for word until my writer's block crumbled before my determined onslaught of words, my flood of words. Those napkins, the ones on which I copied brochures, I threw away. Everything else was filed into the duffel bag. After my evening writing sessions and before dark, or around a fire on the few nights I built one, I reread everything I had written that day.

I wrote, too, while I ate at the rest stop, but for those sessions I saved my "business" writing. Being around people, around trade, inspired me to work on less personal things than I did under the bridge. Something about this felt like going to a job.

There, amid greasy, crumpled burger or taco wrappers, in a rectangle I'd clean off with a damp napkin, I composed sample mission statements and outlines for business plans, organizational flow charts, and cost estimates in which I factored in a 7% capital cushion because I was sure the cost of doing business had risen during my absence. I thought of catchy names for useless new dot-com services: *slab4u.com* for a virtual tombstone site, *luvgrooms2.com* for a marriage registry for men tired of getting bath towels and place settings for wedding gifts, *lucyblooms.com* a database that matched buyers and sellers of rare wildflowers. I knew, of course, that whimsical or esoteric sites like these were fads, were not comparable to showplace.com and served no useful function in the business world. I thought of them as practice.

      One afternoon I stood in front of the large bulletin board just inside the plaza's foyer looking for anything new. The board was an eclectic mix of lost and found notices, advertisements for work-at-home jobs (I had to laugh at that), religious tracts, local announcements, just typical small town detritus that seemed out of place on an interstate highway. As if someone zipping through from New York to Florida gave a shit that Myrtle Flycatcher had lost her precious Brittany Spaniel somewhere near Dunwoody after the Spring Trillium Festival.

      I had seen most of them before, but there was one new one.

      It was a regular sheet of typing paper with large, clear hand-printed letters asking for four people to serve free coffee and soft drinks to motorists during the upcoming 4th of July weekend. The first thing about the sign that gave me pause was that it forced me to think about the date. It was now the middle of summer, and I had been out here since…when? Corinne's birthday, in late April, I guessed. I had seen spring wildflowers come and go, the nights get progressively and thankfully warmer, the days muggier, the forest canopy thicker. I had marked these things without giving much thought to the calendar.

      What then got my attention, though, was that the gig paid $5.00 an hour. If I worked the three 12-hour shifts from

Friday through Sunday, I'd be able to restore some of my seriously depleted funds. The sign told me to inquire at the service desk.

Turning, I looked directly into the beaming face of Summerset Hundley. Before I could look away, he motioned for me to come to the desk. And right then, for the second time in my life, my stupidity, my inattentiveness, my awareness of my incredible carelessness and self-absorption washed over me. The first such episode had cost me my business and, ultimately, my wife; this one cost me my anonymity. What else it might prove to cost me remained to be seen. My note-taking, my writing, my new "job" had enveloped me lately. I had sat too long in the restaurants and out on the picnic tables of the service plaza. I had always looked at people just before they looked at me, so no memory of eye contact would linger with them. I saw them, evaluated them, then dismissed them before they even realized they were sharing a hallway, restroom, or gift shop with me.

There was no question he was talking to me because no one else was near the bulletin board.

The acrid taste of adrenaline, a purely visceral taste remembered from grade school when a teacher might too loudly call my name while I daydreamed, filled my mouth, my soul. For the briefest moment, I thought of bolting out the door; I thought of another flight.

But I didn't. Instead I composed myself and sauntered over to him thinking all the while that I had been in countless boardrooms to give presentations to some of the most ruthless, brilliant, and wealthiest venture capitalists in America, so a two minute conversation with a rube who surely wore bibbed overalls when he wasn't in this snappy Virginia Department of Highways-issued uniform couldn't be that much of a challenge.

Summerset maintained the same high-magnitude grin the whole time I walked toward the service counter.

"Yes sir, what can I do for you?" I said.

"Two things really," said Summerset Hundley, his smile never dimming. The top of his head was perfectly smooth, a lustrous tan as if it had the lightest sheen of shoe polish, and tonsured with close-clipped white hair. It was a head that had seen a lot of sun.

I set my expression to reveal neither curiosity nor surprise.

When it was clear I didn't seem curious, he went on. "Well, first I want to thank you for helping out with those foreign boys a couple of weeks ago. I surely was out of my water with them." He chuckled at the memory. "But they seemed to take to you. What was that they were talking? French?"

"I don't think I know what you're talking about," I said.

He acted as if I hadn't said anything. "You were gone before I could tell you thanks. Anyway, that's one thing. The second thing is —" he pointed back toward the bulletin board, "you'd be perfect. Just what we're looking for."

I knew, of course, he referred to the notice about selling concessions next weekend, but I needed to know what else he might mean. "Why am I just what you're looking for?"

"It's just that you're in here all the time, or a lot, anyway, so I figured you must live close by." He lowered his voice and leaned over the counter. "And I suppose I thought you could use the money."

It wasn't my imagination that just then he looked at my clothes with greater intensity before our eyes snapped into each other's again. I thought of a time not so long past when I might wear a casual weekend sweater that might cost a week of Summerset Hundley's salary.

He reached a coarse, thick hand that looked like a wad

of dried tobacco leaves across the countertop to shake, and tugged at his nametag with the other. "I'm Summerset Hundley, as you can see. Can I ask who you are, young fella?"

I shook his hand perfunctorily, tried to match his strength and felt foolish in doing so. His hand seemed intrinsically firm, earth-strong. My grip, I'm sure, felt forced. "I appreciate the offer, Mr. Hundley, but I'm just passing through."

We dropped hands and I think that, though his smile didn't waver, a light in his eyes faded. I turned to leave.

"If you change your mind, just tell me. I'm working all week."

"Sure thing," I said over my shoulder, "but like I said, I'm just passing through."

"Or if you're in after 5, ask for Della in the gift shop. She'll give you the skinny."

I waved with the back of my hand as the automatic doors whooshed open for me.

********************

Sometimes at night under my bridge I could hear the universe breathe. Huge sounds, rhythmic and regular, punctuated with an occasional sigh, then an apneaic pause before it picked up again. I don't think I was hallucinating, and I don't think this was the figment of an overactive imagination; my creativity manifests itself in much more concrete ways. And don't think for one moment that I lapsed into the realm of the poet and mistook the cars overhead for the respirations of a great oversoul. No, I sometimes heard the universe breathe, plain and simple.

This "contact" with the universe did not inspire me or

make me feel any closer to a great truth. It felt both ancient and vernal, like I had always been able to tap into it and yet had never done so. But frankly, I saw it as merely another thing to hide. Who would believe it? Who would care? And why, as its great chest heaved and collapsed, had it chosen me? Because I was quite sure that no one else could hear it. I had less use of this sound than someone who was searching for it. In fact, I would rather have been left alone. It sometimes kept me from sleeping.

What else kept me from sleeping this night, though, was what to do about Summerset Hundley. The old bastard had been perceptive enough to notice things about me that I'd fought so desperately to conceal.

I reached into Turner's duffel bag and pulled out a handful of napkins and the pen. The nearly full moon promised a few more hours of useful light. I could pull an all-nighter if I had to; I'd done so countless times from college on. It was a sound business tactic that had often provided the basis for a great many solid decisions throughout showplace.com's meteoric rise. Adrenaline might have been my best business partner, was, in fact, my most dependable. I'd make a list of the pro's and con's of accepting Hundley's offer. I knew, of course, that this was about more than dollars and cents, but that was always — always the best place to start.

An hour or so later, after a series of false starts and misfires, I had an enormous pile of napkins, which I hoped to separate into two piles that would offer me a definitive, quantitative direction. It seemed simple enough — put each napkin into either the "positive" or "negative" pile. What I found, though, was that some napkins resisted these neat, narrow demarcations.

Where to put the "working with strangers" napkin, for instance? Or the "appallingly low pay" one? Some, such as the "might require identification for payment" were obvious negatives; "need the money" an obvious positive, but so many others defied easy cataloguing.

I did my best, shuffling some from pile to pile and back, and in the end, the piles were relatively even, the delineation between some of the napkins, I finally had to admit, being arbitrary and forced and could just as easily have been reversed.

I scooped up the napkins and unzipped HST's duffel bag to file them, then stopped. I became aware of the night's sounds, of the crickets and the creek's chuckle, and I realized what I'd been doing wrong all along. The napkins would have been more accurately divided into three piles, and I saw clearly where those categories originated.

Corinne and I spent much of our honeymoon getting to know each other. I suspect all couples do this, even those with long courtships or engagements. That we loved each other and were not merely infatuated is beyond question, but only three months had elapsed between our meeting at the Cincinnati Westin in September and her acceptance of my very public proposal on the Bengals huge scoreboard at their last home game.

The entire stadium applauded during the break between the 3rd and 4th quarters as the scoreboard flashed "Corinne, will you become Mrs. showplace.com, aka Mrs. Duncan Post?" and zeroed in on the seat number I had provided them. The seat was empty — Corinne was helping an elderly woman from her tour group to the restroom — so the old woman's husband leaned into the camera shot, vigorously shook his head, and mouthed "yes" with toothy exaggeration.

From my seat in showplace.com's skybox, I endured the hoots from my business partner, Richard, and the coterie of clients and potentials we were hosting. The stadium's fans roared with laughter. The scoreboard operator flashed "Will she or won't she? Stay tuned!" and phoned up to the skybox to ask when, or if, I wanted him to try again.

"It's an omen," one of the drunker clients said. Or maybe, now that I think of it, Richard said.

I told the scoreboard guy to try during the two-minute warning. The game was laughably lopsided; maybe this would keep fans in the stadium, I told him.

"I'll have to check with the team's officials," he said. "But for you, Mr. Post, I'm sure it won't be a problem."

It wasn't. At the two-minute warning, while the TV audience watched a handful of commercials, the stadium crowd stood as one and again watched the huge video screen. Accompanied by the theme song to Final Jeopardy, the same message as before flashed brightly, and suddenly Corinne was onscreen. Corinne, two stories tall, was beaming, looking up at herself and saying yes with no less exaggeration than the old guy had.

Again the stadium erupted, just before filing out. We had, indeed, kept them there.

Richard was the first to shake my hand. "I like her, Duncan. I liked her the first time you introduced us. She'll be good for you." He leaned toward me. "And what's good for you is good for business," he had said, then turned to the twenty or so people in the suite and raised his glass. "To Duncan and Corinne." That bastard.

Three weeks later we were sitting under a bright red market umbrella on a stunningly white beach in Aruba, our marriage less than 24 hours old.

"How many times a day to you think about me?" she said.

I didn't look up from my laptop. "One."

"That's it, one?"

It's like tic-tac-toe when you know the other kid hasn't learned the one move that can keep him from ever losing. I had her.

"Yes, one. But it lasts all day," I said, still without looking up.

She didn't melt; Corinne wasn't a melter. She just seemed quietly satisfied with that answer, and this began our real courtship. One of us would begin a conversation with the most seemingly innocuous of questions or declarations, and we constructed elaborate labyrinths into each other. I don't think some couples who have been married fifty years ever dug as deeply as we did in those first six months. It was superficially Socratic and yet as profoundly personal as a caress. These conversations might begin without warning anywhere or at any time, and I immediately recognized the difference between "how was work?" and "tell me about work today."

One evening, not long before our honeymoon ended, we left a harbor side restaurant and stepped into an evening breeze redolent with clean brine and papaya, with that ancient smell of old wooden boats and the aged brown fisherman tying them up, of jasmine maybe, of rum drinks topped with hibiscus blossoms, and behind this scene and through this air we saw the last half of the shimmering red sun dissolving into the sea. We stopped our hurried walk to our cabana to watch, and we saw other evening walkers stopping to do the same. Each new couple who emerged from a shop or restaurant along the pier uttered a sudden gasp and hung suspended with the rest of the crowd. Cooks and dishwashers taking breaks in the little gardens behind their cafés leaned over white fences, motionless except for the smoke curling from their cigarettes, and faced the sun in silence. An aproned waiter stood on the front step of another restaurant. Clerks from gift shops did the same. A child holding her father's hand asked what he was looking at, but the father simply knelt to her and pointed, and the girl fell quiet, too. Only the boats creaked as they bobbed softly on mild waves.

Not until the last tip of flame was doused by the burnished, razor-edged horizon did people begin moving again, and it seemed they moved more slowly, as if it would take some small time to pick up speed, to find their former rhythm.

I don't know what it was, but Corinne and I slowed our pace, too. She knitted her arm through mine. "What made that happen?" she said.

"Well, you see, the earth spins on an axis, and since the sun is stationary…"

She pinched me on the forearm. Hard.

"Why, I oughtta…" she imitated Moe from the Three Stooges and raised her free fist. "Seriously, now. What made everyone just stop and watch the sun go down? Do you suppose the people here watch it each time, or is it just a tourist thing, like at Key West?"

I reminded her of the Aruban workers.

She went on. "But I don't think I would have stopped if I hadn't been with you. How many sunsets have I seen in 27 years, and how many did I stop to watch? I might have thought briefly that it was pretty, but I wouldn't have parked my car and looked at it. What's that say about me? About us?"

"You love plants, flowers," I said and recalled our meeting at the Krohn Conservatory.

"Plants are different. They're alive. They need tending. In most ways they're like people who eat, breathe, require the right environment to thrive. They'll grow anywhere, but they won't flourish without the perfect conditions. But a sunset isn't animate, just, I don't know, picturesque. It doesn't need us to exist; it just…is. So, why did we stop? Is picturesque enough to do that?" She was hungry for my answer.

I had none to give, at least not one that could have sat-isfied what suddenly seemed such an appetite. We continued strolling down the pier in the general direction of our cabana. Though the dusk infiltrated and the wind freshened, it wasn't noticeably cooler, yet Corinne's hold on my arm felt tighter, needy. Saying "I don't know" was just too easy, or maybe too difficult for me, I'm not sure which, so I said nothing for a bit.

"Would you have stopped if I hadn't been with you?" she said.

Yes should have come from my mouth. "No."

Corinne wore a sheer lavender sarong that flirted around her tan legs. Her midriff was bare, just as tan, and her bathing suit top was white with purple flowers of a type she knew the name of, but that I had forgotten. This was what I wanted to admire just now. And I told her so.

She was adamant. "I had a sociology professor tell us about a species of monkeys somewhere — Africa, Central America, somewhere — that would stop their swinging around and chattering and just sit on a tree branch and watch the sun go down every evening. *Every* evening. He said that animal behaviorists, the more feeling among them, at least, argued that they could only be doing so as an expression of awe. That they in some way had the capacity to appreciate beauty."

I looked over to see if she were kidding. I'm afraid my smile was more solicitous than empathetic. "I don't know about that," I said.

"I don't either." Our walking pace increased through Corinne's impetus. "But I want to believe it. Don't you?"

I said I couldn't really make a comment on the motiva-tions of monkeys.

We had reached the back porch of our cabana and sank into the deep seats of the side-by-side Adirondacks that looked over the bay crackling with captured drops of reflected moonlight. I just wanted to hold her hand. She just wanted more. I didn't feel inadequate or frustrated as if I were unable to satisfy a client with a legitimate business concern. This was altogether different, more akin to fear.

At length I rested my hand on hers, and we settled into moments of restless peace listening to small waves rattling across the countless beach shells. Her toes, at first wiggling from the ends of her beaded sandals, stopped their frenetic dance, and I thought it might be time to lead my bride into our cool cabana and into the open-sided bedroom where trade winds kept the doorway curtains in constant, graceful motion like waltzing ghosts.

Before I could do so, however, Corinne broke the stillness. "Gordon wouldn't have stopped to watch that sunset, Duncan. Would your father?"

I laughed. We had never really talked about our parents. I knew only that her father, whom she called by his first name, was a small-time gambler who was absent for long stretches, and had been found dead in his car of a heart attack in the parking lot of a seedy casino on the outskirts of Reno. Her mother still lived in Indiana or Iowa, I think, one of those roughly rectangular states in the Midwest. I don't mean to sound callous. I gave them little thought because Corinne spoke of them just once.

"My Dad? I don't honestly know. Dad would be tough to figure." My father was the neighborhood jolly guy, ruddy-faced and sociable. A porch-sitter, a lean-over-the-back-fence-and-talk-for-hours type. "If the person he was talking to made note of it, he would," I said.

Corinne smiled to acknowledge this. "When I was twelve, just sprouting breasts, Gordon took me to the mall to buy some school clothes. I don't remember where Mom was, but it was Gordon this time. He was driving along and with-

out ever looking over at me, and without any preamble what-
soever, he just said 'You know, Corinne, man really has only
three motivations for anything he does...'" She slipped her
hand from mine. In profile, only the small, rounded tips of
her nose and chin extended past the confines of her curls. "At
first I thought, here we go, it's The Talk, and shouldn't Mom
be the one, and shouldn't he have said 'boys' instead of 'man'?
But apparently this was where I was going to hear about pe-
nises and vaginas, only he'd call them Willies and Secrets, here
in the bucket seat of his old car on the way to the mall."

I wanted to smile. No, I wanted *her* to smile. The story
was so Corinne, full of detours and overly scrutinized details,
but her voice wasn't light. It continued to carry that same ra-
pacious tone that had infused the 'what made that happen'
question that had originated this conversation. I shifted in my
chair and settled in for the long haul.

She continued. "I turned the radio up a couple of
notches hoping to derail Gordon, but he just spoke louder. If
this annoyed him, he didn't show it. 'Just three, Corinne.' I
could tell he wanted me to ask what they were, so I did, with
as much boredom as I could muster. That didn't bother him
either. Finally, for the first time since we'd gotten in the car,
he looked at me. 'Greed, loneliness, and guilt,' he said and
grinned a big loopy grin like he was revealing this huge, cosmic secret, and I was supposed to nod sagely and ponder and
pronounce his wisdom."

"What did you say?"

"Nothing. I gave him my what-are-you-talking-about
look until he focused on the road again. Greed, loneliness and
guilt. What a goddam thing to tell your 12-year old daughter." Corinne exhaled as if she had been holding her breath.
"I hope to God he was wrong."

Greed, loneliness, and guilt, then, were the three piles into which I divided the napkins, and I thought that the more comfortable I could become with these three companions, the more comfortable my life might be. I was going to take Summerset Hundley's job, I knew. There is one undeniable truth in America, even under the bridges of America. You need money. Of course I knew that before I ever began writing that night.

The funds would support me as I moved on. Not back to Cincinnati yet—I had some more thinking to do about that, and I still wanted to return on my own terms.

And something else: sudden flight from Hundley would give him more reason to remember me than if I stayed, worked, and then gradually allowed him to see me less frequently. No, I would work the weekend and, like the best waiters, be friendly but not familiar, then disappear by degrees through the rest of the summer until one day the old man would realize he couldn't recall exactly the last time he had seen me. I would simply recede from his life like the dot on a turned-off monitor.

## CHAPTER 4

Della, the gift shop girl Summerset told me to talk to about the job, had a face like a custard pie. Smooth, round, expansive, it looked like it might jiggle if you touched a mounded cheek. It was a younger face up close than from the distances I was used to maintaining, though. Her hair was what had made me think she wasn't young. It was so fuzzy as to mask individual hairs and looked to be in perpetual motion, like a swarm of bees. From my perspective across the counter I was reminded of the mist at the base of a waterfall, of an ethereal, unremarkable brown fluff with indistinct patches of auburn. I thought if I touched it my hand would either come back stung or wet. But I could see now that she was probably close to my age and had just taken bad hair advice. If she dropped forty pounds, discovered the miracle of make-up, and tried a hair-do from someplace other than a 1950's Redbook, she might not have been half bad.

It had been my habit to avert my eyes when dealing with anyone in the plaza, but doing so now would have made Della think I was either autistic or embarrassed to look at her altogether. So I matched her every look, head tilt, or smile with one of my own, then I asked her about the job.

"I thought you might be coming by," Della said in a voice that surprised me a bit. It was perhaps a register higher than I anticipated coming from so robust an instrument, and she spoke rapidly. Very rapidly. It is not a stretch to say that each sentence consisted of one long, multisyllabic word, punctuated by metronomic eyelid blinking.

"You did? How's that?"

"My dad said to be looking for you. He said he had a good feeling about you being able to help us this weekend. Everybody says he can see into the great heart of people and I've never known him to be wrong about anybody," Della hadn't drawn a breath.

I stopped her by holding up a hand. "Hold on a moment, Miss…" I looked again for her nametag. It just said Della.

"Monroe. Della Monroe. Mrs. Daylon Monroe, actually. Married my high school sweetheart. People in Sinking Creek can't say Daylon without Della and vice versa and et cetera. We'll be married twelve years this November. Peas and carrots, it doesn't seem possible, twelve years. Just yesterday, Daylon, my husband — but of course I already told you that — was saying that…"

I had to hold up my hand again. Good God, this woman could prattle. "First, who's your father and how does he know me? And second, how would he, whoever he is, know I'd be asking about a job?"

"Second question first, okay, Mr. Truman? About everybody who works here at the I-81 Sinking Creek Travel Plaza figured you'd be asking about the work, so Dad's no soot-sayer, no David Copperfield, for sure. Not about that, at least, though he does know a lot about a lot. You know people like that, don't you; people who can answer nearly anything you ask them, irregardless and irrespective of the subject matter? Dad's that way. In fact…"

I put both hands on the counter. I wanted to put them around her throat. "Who's your father?" I said slowly. I had no time for this.

She was like a wind-up toy with one click left. "Oh yes,

question one. Summerset Hundley, of course. You've met him he said."

Summerset Hundley, of course. At one time I could step into a room and within moments, in the time it took to nurse one Belvedere martini, have scanned the assembled sheep and calculated the relative social status of everyone there. Body language—a lean here, a shifting there—eye contact, posture, the tenor and volume of a person's laugh, all would have given me the topography of the room. I would know who owned whom, who was financially stable and who in a precarious position, who was buying and who selling, even who was fucking—literally and figuratively—anyone else in that room. It wasn't something that required practice; it was intuitive, the most useful skill not taught in any MBA program.

And yet, here I had not been perceptive, for if I had, I would have at once distinguished old Hundley's hawkish nose and arrestingly gray eyes, the color of winter twilight, in the epicenter of his plump daughter's pie face. Too, I should have connected their huge, guileless smiles. I could not afford to let my guard down, even now, but whatever else these people intended, harming me didn't seem to be on their agenda.

"Yes, I've met Mr. Hundley," I admitted.

From behind me a kid in a South Park tee-shirt asked Della how much the Gummi-bears were. I stepped aside, allowing him to approach the glass-topped counter. Della looked apologetically at me. I nodded that the interruption was okay. And it was because I needed to absorb some of Della's avalanche of words. Her relationship to Summerset Hundley wasn't necessarily shocking, though it did make me wonder what kind of spider web this plaza was. Was the girl who spooned up my mashed potatoes a daughter, too? The creaky old night-shift janitor who I'd seen mopping the restroom a brother? How about the teens grinning behind the Taco Bell,

Pizza Hut, and Wendy's counters?  Nieces and nephews, grandkids?

Della had said that several workers had predicted I'd be asking about work.  I was not, apparently, as stealthy as I had imagined myself to be.  And she had called me a name, simply slipped it into one of her inane soliloquies as casually as if she had known me for years.

The Gummi-kid paid and scurried toward his impatient mother who shouted from the gift shop doorway "I swear your Dad will leave without you."  I didn't feel sorry for the brat or any parents who would let their kid eat such crap and watch such cartoon drivel.  Ten miles down the road they'd be Heimlich-ing one of those bears from the kid's trachea — if they even noticed he was choking.  And ten years down the road they'd wonder why the kid had no respect, no attention span, and no goals.

"Sorry 'bout that.  Now where were we?  You want to sign up for a shift or two and for which days?  We'll start with free coffee on Friday morning, actually coffee's free all through Sunday, but also on Friday, the hot dog booth will start serving the hot dogs, pop, chips and stuff like that that aren't free. Only the coffee's free.  The state of Virginia actually provides that as a safety thing for drivers to stay awake and stay alert. Can't drink it myself.  The caffeine makes me jittery.  'Zit bother you?"

I reached into my pocket for a willow strip.  Della wasn't giving me the headache — I'd had it since this morning — but she wasn't helping it either.  I started chewing on the end of the bark.

"Eeewww.  What's that?" she said, compressing her face as though I'd just munched a turd.

I wasn't about to explain the pharmaceutical effects of the willow to Della.  It was clear her Mensa application had been denied. "Nothing. Listen, Mrs. Monroe, you just called me a name a few moments ago. What was that?"

Della looked quizzically at me, rewinding the tape of our conversation, but before she could answer, something behind me caught her eye and she smiled broadly.

"I'm afraid that name thing is my fault," came a basso profundo from over my shoulder just as a massive hand clamped it. Unmistakably Summerset Hundley's voice and grip. "I kind of nicknamed you Harry S Truman on account of the monogram on the shaving kit you bring in here sometimes. I guess Della assumed I really knew your name."

Summerset was not in his usual Virginia DOT garb. He wore, of all things, khakis and a navy golf shirt, his bare arms the same chestnut color as his pate.

Della let out a short peep, and we both turned to her. "Mea cupid, so stupid," she sang. "I'm afraid I've told near everybody around here that was your name. If it's any consultation, everybody thinks it's cute."

This was an opening I could not pass up. I lowered my eyes and smiled at both of them in turn and thought how strange it felt to smile. Though this particular one was as artificial as any I'd forced in the business world, it was still a set of muscles I hadn't used lately. They felt stiff, atrophied. In short, I saw the smile as a business tool.

"You're not going to believe this," I said, "but my dad was — is — a huge admirer of Harry Truman. That is my name." Hell, I wouldn't have believed that, and I don't care what kind of yokels old Hundley and his dimwit daughter were, this story might strain even their credulity, so I amended. "Actually, it's Harold, and my last name is spelled T-r-u-e-m-a-n. But I've been called Harry since grade school." I had to stop myself. I was beginning to prattle like Della.

If either doubted my bullshit for a second, it didn't show.

Summerset Hundley extended his hand again. "Well, it's good to properly meet you, Mr. Trueman."

I knew better than to match his grip this time, so I settled for not allowing my hand to disappear into his, then turned to Della and offered a shake. She was not accustomed to this. Her hand was small and doughy, like fresh bread. Her nails were ragged from being chewed, with irregular flecks of pink polish.

Hundley nodded toward the willow strip in my left hand. "Headache?"

"A little one," I said, not at all surprised that he would know about willow as remedy.

"You can make a tea from that, mix in a little sugar. Won't be near as bitter."

The small talk was starting to get to me. My headache was gaining steam, and maybe I was a little too hungry — I had noticed lately that I wasn't a very good judge of hunger any-more — and I just felt generally miserable. "I thought I might take you up on that concession stand job offer, Mr. Hundley."

Della busied herself with a man in a business suit who bought a pack of mints to cover up the onions on his breath that I could smell from several feet away.

"That's great, it really is. I was hoping you would. Let me explain the shifts," said Hundley.

I interrupted. "That's not necessary. I'll work them all."

"You don't have to do that," he said as though he were gently reigning in an eager child. "We have plenty of people to work. The Sinking Creek Baptist Church Thursday Women's Circle is working the bake sale stand, and the Volunteer Fire Department is selling hot dogs. You'll just be part of the table between them giving out free coffee to drivers. I have three four-man shifts from 8 'til 8. Why don't you just sign up for one of those each day?"

   I thought quickly that this setup must be one of Dante's conceived but unwritten rings of hell — three days sandwiched between the blue-haired womenfolk and the rawboned, deer slaying men of Mayberry.

   "Really, I'll be fine," I said. I needed to sit down, so I leaned a hip as casually as I could against the glass counter with its colorful columns of Snickers, Hershey Bars, and Paydays. I wondered how many I could eat just now, and the thought itself just as quickly nauseated me. I suddenly felt as though I were hovering a few feet above this scene, watching three people with only mild interest.

   "It's supposed to be in the 90's all weekend, Mr. Trueman, that's all I'm saying. All we have is a canvas umbrella to shade the tables. It gets mighty uncomfortable, all that hot asphalt."

   "I'll be alright," I said, hearing an edge creep into my voice. I wanted to get back under my bridge with some cool water and suck on this willow bark.

   He took me in whole, uncomfortably so, and in a baleful tone Summerset Hundley said, "Okay, then. I'll leave it up to you."


   That night I lay awake much later than usual. After my ridiculous "job interview," I was too unnerved by what old Hundley and his Chatty Cathy daughter had known about me to stay around for anything to eat. I did buy a Slim Jim, though, and pocketed a bag of chocolate-covered peanuts when Della's back was turned. They owed me that much, I reasoned, for spying on me. Besides, one day I'd pay them back, too. I wrote the peanuts' cost on a napkin and filed it in the duffel bag with my other yet-to-be-paid receipts.

It was hot, just like Hundley had said, and I had real trouble getting to sleep. The creek was nearly juiceless from lack of rain, and except for the paths that fanned out in a few directions from my bed — to the creek, toward the plaza, a little way into the woods for latrine purposes, and to a lesser extent, south down the creek — the whole area was covered in dense, vegetable profusion. Some of the Jo-Pye weeds were head high by now, and all that plant life kept things humid and tropical. For the most part, the early wildflowers were gone, replaced by impenetrable, shadowy growth. The only break from the varying shades of green were the feathery white tips of the tall, thin-stalked fairy candles which, in the moonlight, neither flickered nor offered illumination.

I looked at my bare arms and legs. They were covered with bug bites, red welts that I mindlessly scratched until the blood smeared like wine stains. I gave a mirthless laugh. Weeks ago I remembered smacking at any mosquito brave enough to enter my air space. Soon I was waving only at those who buzzed near my face or ears. Later I struck at those that actually landed. I don't really recall when I quit doing that and simply permitted them to feast on me. And I sure as hell didn't remember not noticing them at all. It occurred to me that I hadn't really put my best interviewing skills to work that afternoon at the plaza. I ran my fingertips slowly across my cheeks like a Sioux warrior applying war paint and felt small lumps on them.

Something dropped in one of the pools that remained of the dying creek. Just one loud plunk that I figured to be a hickory nut. The universe was in one of its dormant states, breathing irregularly, like the creek conserving its own resources, marshalling its meager forces, but as I lay waiting for it to resume, there was another plunk in the water, the same weight as the first. Then another; then a spray of plunks. I sat forward and heard something run up the opposite bank, rustling the weeds with a sound like airing a bed sheet. It was bigger than the raccoons I had heard, but if it were a bear, I was simply too tired to be frightened just then.

After a short, soundless time, the crickets and peepers sang again, and I lay back on my blankets. People getting a Thursday night jump on the long holiday weekend kept the interstate whirring above me, and minutes later, I heard the universe inhale and exhale infinitely deeply, and I fell into a rough sleep.

I woke with the sun, feeling like shit. I expected this, though, because I never slept well the night before a new job or a big meeting, but here I had no tea to enliven me nor any breakfast to settle my stomach, and certainly no mirror to check for professional appearance. Why I worried about this prior to pushing free, watered-down coffee at people on their way to crowded campgrounds or outlet malls, and then to diminutive fireworks "displays," I don't really know. But I did.

Too, the thought crossed my mind that someone from my past could conceivably pass through here, but it was a transient thought. No one I knew well would be traveling this distance by car, and I couldn't envision them stopping with the herd, when there was a Starbuck's inside, if they had. I worried only about the state police, but they would be too busy patrolling the crowded highways.

My skin felt stretched too tightly across my cheeks and jawbones, like plastic wrap, and I felt distracted and disconnected. Yesterday's headache had not left but only subsided to a dull rushing behind my eyes, like the white noise in libraries. I wanted to wash up in the clean, cold water of the plaza's restroom which I knew would be nearly deserted at this hour, but I couldn't risk the perusal by Summerset or any of his minions. Instead, I tramped down from my perch to the creek and splashed water from the largest pool. It wasn't cold and it smelled of algae that reminded me somehow of the scavengers of the wild rather than the noble predators at the food chain's summit.

I labored back up under the bridge and dry brushed my teeth, folded my blankets, and tidied up from last night's writing. I'd had nothing to say, nothing to reveal, but the habit had become so entrenched that I couldn't go to sleep anymore without just a few napkins. I saw now that I had simply written my name, Corinne's, and our address several times. I didn't remember that's what I had done. I filed them on top in Turner's duffel and removed the pair of blue walking shorts and white knit polo shirt I had "ironed" by hand-smoothing last night. His lone pair of jeans was noticeably too loose for me now, so I couldn't cover my scabbed legs. I figured I'd preempt the questions by attributing their damages to some ill-advised barelegged brush clearing. It was a brand new set of interpersonal skills I would employ this weekend, but the underlying foundation of deceit remained the same.

The effort of cleaning my "house" fatigued me, and I was shocked at how I felt. Once the blankets were folded and duffel packed, I stuffed them snugly into the bridge and platform V and stood to catch my breath. From the creek below, someone would have to intentionally follow my thin path up through the thick undergrowth to find the blankets and bag, my only two possessions. The bridge's height, this stretch of the interstate's Arcadian setting and speed, and my stealth insured that I couldn't be seen from the roadway. It was a fine waystation, I congratulated myself, and I would be hard-pressed to find a suitable replacement when I had to leave. I'd like to have stayed here today to rest.

Neither Summerset nor Della had said anything about getting there early to help set up, but I needed to get a feel for the whole arrangement, and the walk there was going to take some extra time, the way I felt, so I folded some willow strips into my pockets, put one in my mouth, and took off. Twice, I leaned over to retch, but nothing came up, and what was ordinarily a thirty-minute walk took an hour.

I went straight to the restroom, doused my head with water, shook it like a dog's, and stooped beneath the hand dryers. No one came in. I didn't give a shit, anyway.

The strip of grass at the far end of the parking lot looked like a traveling circus had encamped. Two trailers with red and white striped awnings, their scalloped borders curling in a faint morning breeze, had been pulled onto the lawn. Framing the left side of the big center window of one of the trailers was a hand-lettered wooden sign announcing that the trailer belonged to the Sinking Creek Volunteer Fire Department and that all proceeds from its sales would go to purchase a new pumper. On the right side of that window was the trailer's menu, which consisted of hot dogs, hot dogs with sauce, hot dogs with sauce and mustard, with relish, with kraut, with ketchup, with combinations of any or all of the condiments. Chips, too, for a quarter.

The astounding thing about the sign was that all the hot dogs cost a buck, regardless of the toppings. I hoped these guys were better firemen than they were businessmen. The Sinking Creek VFD was going to have to sell a helluva lot of hot dogs to get a pumper. Men I took to be volunteer firefighters hopped in and out of the trailer, their every step causing it to wobble, and shouted in brassy voices about whose sauce recipe was the best and what exotic ingredients might be in them.

"Can't tell you," said one. "My grandmother would kill me."

"Your grandmother died before you were born," another said.

A third hooted, "It was her own sauce killed her." The trailer roared and rocked. The derided fireman jumped out, laughing. He was early thirties, maybe, with long loose arms, all wrists and elbow, a swatch of sunburn across his cheekbones. His sun-blonde hair flapped as he landed.

"I'm sorry," he said when he noticed me standing in front of the trailer. "The dogs won't be ready for a while yet. We're supposed to start at eight. Though I can't imagine anyone wanting a hot dog at eight in the morning. You'd be surprised, though. Some kids will come through here and make Mom and Dad get them a couple for breakfast. And I suppose if you don't like breakfast food—"

"Thanks, no. I'm not here to eat. I'm going to be passing out coffee." I pointed to the coffee kiosk. Sandwiched between the two trailers were three folding tables each supporting a restaurant-sized urn and impotently shaded by yellow market umbrellas. Regiments of nested white Styrofoam cups stood at attention across the tables' fronts. The brewing coffee already smelled rich and strong. I had always like the smell of coffee better than the taste. Caffeine for me came from chocolate and Mountain Dew.

"Oh, you're Harry Trueman. Maybe later, then, when you get a break. I guarantee you'll like the sauce. It's my grandmother's recipe."

"I heard."

He looked puzzled, then not. "Oh, the guys. Don't pay them any mind. Trust me, you like hot dogs, you'll love these." He stuck out his long-fingered hand. "So you're sloshing coffee, Mr. Trueman? Got a long day ahead of you. I'm Daylon

Monroe, Della's husband. She's told me all about you. How you're a friend of Summerset's."

I shook the offered hand. Maybe it was because I wasn't feeling well, or that I needed a solid meal, but I truly was not surprised that the first person I met that morning would be someone connected to Summerset Hundley. I was a bit startled, however, that this long, lean man, built like a marathoner was married to Della, as soft and rounded as a freshly plumped pillow. I somehow envisioned her husband as a laconic, beer-bellied rube, cheeks stuffed with tobacco, whose communicative talents would consist of pressing a finger to one nostril while deftly blowing snot from the other. Daylon's speed of speech was equally mystifying. It nearly matched Della's, and I couldn't imagine much air being left in the room after one of their conversations.

Again, whether it was weakness from hunger or lack of sleep, I found myself in danger of liking this Daylon Monroe, and before I could censor myself, I said, "Cincinnatians put cinnamon in their chili. You either love it or hate it."

He didn't make a face like most people do when they learn this. "Cinnamon, huh? I'll have to try that. You from Cincinnati?"

"No," I said because that was all I could come up with. I despised myself at that moment. I despised myself because I was breaking every rule I had ever devised about the art of negotiating. I was revealing rather than concealing. I was showing my cards before I understood my opponent's hand.

Daylon waited as if I would continue, would, in fact, tell him where I was from. It was the next logical conversational progression. At the coffee tables, two women were setting out bowls with packets of sugar, fake sugar crap, and creamer. I looked reflexively at my watchless wrist and said anyway and ludicrously, "Better man my post, Daylon."

The two women introduced themselves as Betty and Edna, or Martha and Jean, or some other pair of equally non-descript heartland names, and said they'd be occupying the Sinking Creek Baptist Church's Women's Thursday Circle trailer next to mine. They said the complete name, too, except it came out:

"sinkingcreekbaptistchurchswomensthursdaycircle."

One word, as if none of the component parts could have existed without the others. "Honey, we'll open up our bake sale about ten, but we'll be in the trailer working till then, so if you need anything…" said Edna/Jean.

"We'll keep an eye on refills for the coffee urn," Martha/Betty chirped. "All you have to do is pour and smile." With that, they disappeared into their trailer.

I sat down at the middle of the three folding tables and waited. The sun was just poking over the leafy mountains, not high enough yet for the umbrella to shade me, and it was already uncomfortably warm. Laughter erupted sporadically from the firemen's trailer. Between those raucous outbursts I heard a soothing, steady cooing issuing from the sinkingcreekbaptistchurchswomensthursdaycircle trailer. Fifty yards away, the early traffic whooshed by, quieter than when it did so directly over my head, so much so that its rhythm urged me to lay my forehead on the table.

"Looks like you could use a cup of your own java," a firefighter in full garb said in my dream. I tried to answer, but my head felt like a bag of bullets and lifting it to respond seemed like more trouble than it was worth.

"Well, then, do you mind if I draw my own cup?" the

dream voice insisted.

I rolled my head to one side and opened an eye. It was no dream. I've never dreamed of a 250-pound trucker grinning at me. Behind him the line of travelers drawn by free coffee stretched six deep. I shook the bullets in the bag and stood.

"Sorry, really sorry," I mumbled and began dispensing the first of what must have been two hundred cups of coffee before noon. There was never a lull. In fact, at 10:00, when the SCBCWTC opened the bake sale, several people stood around sucking down a free second cup to go with their muffins or doughnuts.

Freda/Billie seemed clairvoyant about the coffee urn's status, refilling them before I realized they were nearly empty. On one trip she placed a paper plate with a lemon Danish wrapped in a napkin beside me. I devoured it, without bothering to pick out the bits of napkin I ingested with my larger bites.

At noon, old man Hundley appeared from the fire department's trailer, which by now was as alive with activity as the stock exchange trading floor. I hadn't seen him enter it. "Why don't you take a break. Go inside, get a cold drink and get out of this heat for a spell," he said. " I can spill coffee for an hour."

"A protest would be useless, wouldn't it?" I said, hoping so.

"Would."

I rose stiffly, but as I turned toward the plaza, Summerset Hundley grabbed my hand. I thought at first how odd it was that he wanted to shake hands again just then, but this wasn't the same powerful grip he used for shaking. This was gentler, more a sliding motion across my palm, and I realized he was handing me a slip of paper. I looked down at a

$50 bill. Before I could register surprise, however, he was drawing coffee and asking a man in a Virginia Beach ball cap where he was from.

That afternoon was a steady blur of variations on the same "hot enough for ya?" question to which I finally didn't feel the need to respond. Thelma, or Lottie, or Lois materialized to refill an urn, deposit a muffin, a cupcake, a brownie, a slice of peach pie, then vanished. Close to 8:00 Daylon brought over a hot dog and soda.

"Didn't know how you get your dogs, so I slapped a bit of everything on it. That okay? If not, I'll eat it and fix you another. Swear to goodness, I've already had six or seven today. One more won't matter much. Della'll be happy she won't have to cook tonight. Reminds me, I've got to wrap her up a couple or three." With that, he set the hot dog and soda on the table and bounded back into his trailer.

Betty/Edna poked her head from the other trailer's window and told me to go on, they were in charge of cleaning the urns and closing up.

I popped open the can of Mountain Dew, and, when I made sure Daylon wasn't watching, dropped the hot dog into the trashcan. It was going to be difficult to get home before dark. It was going to be difficult to get home at all.

Saturday was hotter still. Traffic went by with the rapidity of film frames, and, in spite of the swelter, drivers stood in line for hot coffee while their car mates got hot dogs or baked goods. And above sat the sun. It did not seem to move. Waves of asphalt heat shimmered until everything at a distance looked to be underwater. The paper tablecloth that covered my kiosk was splotched with my dripped sweat. Purblind motorists who had just stepped from their air-conditioned carapaces into the wall of heat remarked with a frivolous, bemused air, "Man, you look hot." The umbrella couldn't keep my face from burning. I searched the colorless sky for clouds and saw none. Always that sun sat in the same place.

Again Hundley spelled me at noon, this time exiting the bake sale trailer, and drawled, "Gracious, son, have you had anything to eat or drink?"

"I had a cup of coffee or two," I said.

"Nothing cold? No breakfast?" His tone was uncomfortably solicitous.

I stood and suddenly realized I'd been pouring coffee from an awkward seated position for some time. In fact, standing just then made me a bit light-headed. "I'm not really a breakfast person," I said.

"Go inside; cool off. Tell you what, have Della get you one of the clean t-shirts I keep in the storage closet." He pointed his chin at me. "Yours looks a little wet."

"Appreciate it," I said, and like an athlete who doesn't want his coach to know he's hurt, I walked away deliberately, adjusting to motion in a skin of heat.

Inside the plaza, I gulped from a water fountain until a child tapped on my back. In the restroom I locked a stall door behind me, removed my shirt, and spent my lunch break sitting on the toilet, my bare back pressed against the cool wall tiles.


The new shirt Della gave me, handed over the counter with maternal clucks, was navy with the white state outline surrounding the ubiquitous "I ♥ Virginia" slogan. Twenty minutes after I replaced Summerset Hundley, who then went into the bake sale trailer, it was drenched, the first puddle flooding where I supposed Richmond to be.

The onslaught of travelers did not subside, but at midafternoon Daylon came from the VFD trailer with a can of soda and a hot dog covered, as yesterday's, in every conceivable condiment. He winked at me, looked down at the sandwich to draw my attention to it, then comically lifted his eyebrows twice, as if to say, "now that's some good eatin'."

Before I could say thanks, he announced to the throng that he could pour them some coffee from another urn. More than half of my line shifted over, apparently drawn by his greater pep. Part of me resented this theft of "business," and I perked up my efforts. Again, when I was sure Daylon was engaged, I covered the hot dog and slipped it into the trashcan beneath my table. Don't betray me with a hot dog.

At length, the sun hiccupped into motion and started its descent. The traffic, too, lightened, and Daylon went back to his trailer. Freda/Jean poked her head like a gopher from the bake sale trailer's window and said, "Fifteen minutes left, hon. Looks like near everybody's got where they're going. Before you leave, come on over and get some goodies to take yourself home." With that she disappeared again, her trill melting into the soft murmur of the other workers.

I put my elbows on the table and rested my face in my hands. Within moments, though, and without looking up, I sensed a knot of people moving toward my tables and I reflexively began pouring coffee.

"Where do I know you from?" a low male voice said.

My hand lightened perceptibly on the coffee urn's lever. No avenue of escape seemed available just then. I would try to lie my way out of this, but if I couldn't, well, that would be that. I suppose on some level I had assumed this day to be inevitable. But first, I would ignore him. I finished pouring the first cup and began a second.

"You look familiar to me, too," said a second voice.

They were directly in front of my table now. I would have to look up, and when I did, I would be fully prepared to say no, no I don't think we know each other, to open with that gambit and see where it might lead. I needed to be at my most sincere and have no small measure of luck, too. I even thought I might slightly alter the tenor of my voice.

Drawing the second cup was like drawing a measure of resolve, so I prepared to verbally parry and thrust until I was cornered. I would not run, but perhaps a blank look, a small twist of my head and puzzled narrowing of my eyes would make them think I was struggling to remember them from somewhere. If they weren't sure — and their 'where do I know you from?' indicated they weren't — I might pull this off.

I pushed the two coffees forward and looked up to see they were neither looking at nor talking to me. They faced each other as if they faced a mirror, displaying the same head jousting and gaze mimicking I had been prepared to do. Simultaneously they pointed at each other. "Roanoke Galleria," said the first.

The second agreed. "That's right, that's right. I work at the Border's there, and you…" I quit listening. There was no need to hear them chatter about their dreary retail jobs at the mall, and what a small world it was. Frankly, it wasn't that small a world; they were merely the recipients of coincidence. There was plenty of that to go around. Besides, I had coffee to pour for the sheep behind them, and I needed to catch my breath.

It was neither dark nor light by the time I stumbled home, and I was angry with myself for having lost the path once through inattentiveness. The detour cost me fifteen minutes and an expenditure of energy I couldn't really spare. When I got to the creek, I couldn't yet face the steep climb up to my sleeping area, so I sank heavily onto my creekside log. I had a bottled water and a pocketful of homemade doughnuts, but some of the jelly filling had leaked through the pastry and the napkins, and the pocket's entrance was sticky and flecked with chips of the glazing.

The water went first, then two of the three doughnuts. They were cloyingly sweet, and by the third one I realized I was crying. I know I was crying as I ate the third doughnut, but what I wasn't sure of was when the crying had begun, so I mentally retraced my proverbial steps. It turned out I may have started about the time Betty/Jean handed me the doughnuts and told me to go home and get some rest.

I remembered thanking her. I remembered her telling me to drive carefully, then I remember being puzzled about how I could carry all of this food home. And I remembered being so confused by the logistics that I stood behind the plaza before plunging into the woods shifting them from hand to hand, their uneven number bedeviling me, until it struck me that I could cram them into my pockets. That's when the crying had started, I was sure.

This certainty, this working through a problem until I reached its source, comforted me, and I stopped. I tossed the remnant of the third doughnut into the weeds across the creek and trudged up the bank to my blankets. I thought that fatigue would prevent my writing this night, that maybe I'd read some tracts about what animal had been coming around lately, but a napkin and my pen sat on top of the duffel bag. I was sure I had straightened up before I left this morning; I always did. But there they were.

I unfolded a blanket and, like an arthritic, settled onto

it with sighs and groans, then picked up the pen and napkin to put them away.

The napkin, though, had already been written on, but not in my hand. In sloppy, canted printing, the napkin read, "mersy of Lord is everylasting to everylasting. Womin at my church says so."

There was nothing written on the back, and nothing else in the duffel had been disturbed. For the next half hour, my head periscoped from side to side and I sat so still that I could hear my own racing pulse. Soon the twilight was nearly imperceptibly swallowed by darkness. The surrounding woods handed over the hush of day to the unruly night insects and birds, but I was accustomed to every layer of sound I heard.

I had no idea, none, who could have written on the napkin, nor did I have any clue about the message's meaning. Was it a new-age psychobabble warning? A prank from local kids who stumbled on my stuff while looking for a place to swill their first beer? I hadn't really been myself lately — could I have done it and simply forgotten to file it? None of these scenarios felt right. There was a flaw in every theory.

Ultimately, that night represented a great paradox. Apparently someone knew where I was, and yet, as I hugged my knees and rocked on my haunches throughout the sleepless night, I had never felt more alone.


Sunday's daybreak began the final day for the concession stands. I was sure Summerset Hundley would pay me, minus the first day's $50 advance, at the end of my shift, and I planned to take as much food and water as I could carry home with me this evening. I would rest up for a few days and figure out my next step, which would, I now knew, require my moving on. Yes, after some R & R, I would hitch a ride farther south or west from a trucker. This was a far, sad cry from my former grand designs for stardom in the Internet constellation.

I rummaged through Henderson Turner's duffel for a pair of shorts cleaner than the sticky navy ones from yesterday. Everything was wrinkled and musty from the dampness but a pair of plaid shorts — this guy had to be single — camouflaged its untidiness best. Summerset had asked everyone to wear his or her "official" Virginia t-shirts for this final day. I meant to rinse the perspiration stains out of mine before I left the plaza last night but forgot. Powdery salt lines snaked through the state's outline like shifting geopolitical boundaries, as if Virginia were at war with itself.

I stood, stiff and graceless after a sentinel's night, dressed, and thought ruefully that this was not how I envisioned spending my 30th birthday. Instead of dinner with Corinne at La Maisonnette and drinks after with friends, I'd be surrounded by trailers filled with the carnival smell of hot dogs and funnel cakes, and peopled by volunteer firefighters and dowdy women whose names I didn't care enough about to recall. All day long, people in tank tops would stand in front of me gulping hot coffee in 95 degree heat simply because it was free.

Well, then, that's what this day would be.

I raised my arms in mock celebration and shouted as loudly as I could, "Happy fucking birthday!"

The birds and summer cicadas stopped. I realized those were the first words I'd spoken under my bridge. It wasn't much of a birthday present, but it felt pretty good, so again I raised my arms and yelled, "Happy fucking birthday, Duncan Post!"

Just then a truck roared overhead, and I traced its unseen progress with my eyes as it crossed the bridge then rattled across the joint that marked its arrival back onto solid ground.

My eyes scrolled the length of the giant girders, and there, across the gully formed by the creek, in the space between the bridge and sloping platform, in the twin to my home, crouched a figure. It was so inert that I only knew it was alive because I recognized it. Though I had never seen the long tan t-shirt or the cutoff jeans, I would have recognized her tangerine hair anywhere.

We were at least a hundred yards away from each other, but fear sent electricity from my stomach through my shoulders. Our eyes locked and, though I've never hunted, I imagined the look to be the same measuring gaze shared between hunter and prey, both waiting for the immediate surprise to be replaced by the tumbling into place of their roles in this new milieu. She rose slowly out of her crouch, unfolding upward like a paper doll. Her hair, brilliant even at this distance, hung in a solid sheet down to her waist, divided only by her shoulders.

She cupped her hands to the sides of her mouth and shouted, "Today your birthday?"

"Who are you?" I answered.

She cupped her hands once more, but traffic on the bridged drowned her voice.

"I said, who are you?" I tried again.

"Happy birthday, Duncan Post," she shouted, then giggled as light and liquid as a lark's trill. With feline facility she disappeared into the thick forest on that side of the creek. I couldn't have caught her if I'd been a deer.

* * *

When I got to the plaza, Summerset Hundley was placing the cardboard boxes filled with Styrofoam cups under my table and gift shop ashtrays on the paper tablecloth.

"Morning, Mr. Trueman. Going to get a little weather this afternoon," he said. "These ashtrays'll hold the paper down, but if it starts to get rough, you just toss the sugar and stuff in the boxes with the cups and get on inside."

"It's going to rain?"

"Oh son, it's going to do more than rain. We're in for some serious stuff. A gully-washer, a tub-thumper, as the old-timers say. Rain. Lightning." He drummed his fingers on the top of my table, "Maybe even some hail. Yes sir, when it comes down, you close up that umbrella and get your tail inside. I'll pay you for the whole day, no matter."

I looked up at another clear sky, already hot and air-less. "No offense, Mr. Hundley, but I don't see it. What makes you think it's going to rain?

He turned serious; the wrinkles that bordered his gray eyes deepened. He loomed in front of my face. "Blood red dawn, wind shifting from the east, caterpillars all balled up. Ducks swimming upside down, their soles to the sky. Nature, son, nature tells me," he said ominously.

I unrolled a sleeve of coffee cups. "Well, I certainly won't argue with Mother Nature," I said, though I thought that duck shit sounded a little crazy.

"Won't do no good," he said. "Besides, guy on the Weather Channel says there's a 100% chance of afternoon thun-dershowers." He laughed, deep and virile, and put his hand on my shoulder. It was just there an instant, but it seemed to force my whole carriage downward. It was weightier than a hundred boardroom backslaps. He went on. "Tell you what. If it's all right with you, I thought I'd just pay you in cash this evening. I figure you're already doing your bit for Uncle Sam, keeping his highways safe and all, so there's no need for him to bite into your pay. That okay?"

He wasn't looking at me, just busied himself tidying up my tables and arranging the ashtrays that he had already ar-ranged.

I didn't know if he was ashamed of cheating the government or honestly trying to do me a favor. I didn't care; either way worked to my advantage. No taxes and no sticky moments trying to cash a check made out to someone I wasn't. "Yeah, that'll be fine," I said, hoping I didn't sound too eager.

The morning wasn't so busy. After an hour with few travelers, Daylon came out of his trailer and sat at the table next to mine. "Won't pick up till afternoon when everybody's on their way back home. You'll be busier than a one-eyed traffic cop for a few hours, then it'll settle. Maybe we can visit again then."

I told him that would be fine, but the truth was I couldn't keep up with Daylon's conversational pace. I was having trouble simply focusing on drawing cups of coffee and keeping my dizziness at bay — this from a guy who prided himself on his ability to multi-task.

The heat was even worse. It came at me in progressive waves with no breeze. Sometimes I'd look over at Daylon as he talked and I heard nothing, but I could swear his voice increased the temperature, could see heat issuing forth. I used what discretionary thought I had remaining to pray for Summerset Hundley's weather forecast to be right. The emotional lift I had gotten that morning about my pay could no longer sustain me.

After a time it dawned on me that Daylon was saying my name, and may have said it several times, but I wasn't listening, and besides, I wasn't used to answering to "Harry." He seemed alarmed when I didn't respond quickly. "What's that?" I said, my voice bubbling slowly up from a depth.

"I said, do you want me to get you a bottle of water? You don't look so hot. No, that's not right — you do look hot. Incredibly hot. How 'bout a Coke?"

I know what he asked me. He asked me if I wanted

some water or even a Coke, but this is what I said: "Sure, I'll get you some water. Or would you rather have a Coke?"

He looked at me with the same quizzical look a dog gives at hearing some distant and foreign sound.

I tried to make it right, to rectify my mistake, but now I couldn't remember what he had asked. "I'm sorry, Daylon, did you want some coffee?" I reached into the box for a cup.

"Listen, Harry, let me go get Summerset. He can have someone sit in for you today. I suppose I probably can," he said.

Daylon Monroe rose, but as he did, a voice from the VFD trailer hooted, "Uh-oh, Daylon, here comes trouble. Must not have finished your honey-do list this morning."

"Nope, left without kissing his sugar-booger good-bye, and she's coming to collect one," said another, and the trailer roared and swayed as it had all weekend.

From behind me came the singsong voice of Della. "You hairy-legs mind your own beeswax. You're just jealous, all of you," she said and hugged Daylon like he'd just returned from war. He seemed genuinely glad to see her and unembarrassed about a display of affection in front of a chorus of men who simultaneously whistled and smacked hands.

"I wuv ooo, Daywun," one of the younger firemen mocked and hugged a partner, eliciting still more catcalls.

From the sinkingcreekbaptistchurchswomens-thursdaycircle trailer Lena/Thelma leaned out at the sound, saw the couple, smiled beneficently, disappeared again. This removal of direct attention on me gave me time to gather my faculties. I didn't feel as placid as the bake sale trailer nor as boisterous as the firemen, so this moderation grounded me.

Della sat a plastic cooler down on my table. "Dad wanted me to bring you some water, Mr. Trueman," she said and opened the cooler to reveal several bottles of water with ice up to their necks. I wanted to bury my face there. Reaching in, she plucked out a Dr. Pepper. "And this is for you, baby. I know you don't really like Coke," she said to her husband.

"The baby doesn't weawwy wike Coke," the youngest fireman repeated.

Neither Daylon nor Della responded to him. In fact, they acted like they hadn't heard at all. Daylon was only a couple of inches taller than she, but her girth made her seem as large. He was all sharp angles, she ovals. Both wore their navy Virginia t-shirts, the sharply ironed shoulder creases contrasting with my shapeless, filthy counterpart, and Della wore denim shorts with hemmed legs rolled up once and constricting the ample flesh just above her knee. There was no discernible difference between her calves and ankles. Her hair buzzed around her face. She looked like a stack of folded blankets with a beehive on top.

A woman poked her head from the bake sale trailer. "Is Tessie going to come help us today, Della?"

"'Fraid not, Mrs. Hamm." She pointed to her packed shorts. "I'm going to help outside today. Tessie's off again."

"Dear Lord. How long this time?"

"Week or so. You know, it's summer," Della answered.

The woman tsked. "I don't know how you and your Dad handle that. Goodness knows, I couldn't."

"You get used to it, Mrs. Hamm. Been twenty years now."

Mrs. Hamm looked at the distant hills. "Twenty years." She shook her head. "I guess so. I guess that's right," she said and busied herself again.

Della, who I'd noticed spoke more slowly than I'd ever heard during the exchange with Mrs. Hamm, turned her attention to me. Her face opened like a hope chest. "I've got something else for you, Mr. Trueman," she said as though I were a child and she had saved my best Christmas gift for last.

She rummaged through her purse, then pulled out a closed hand. "Hold out your hand and close your eyes, I'm going to give you a big surprise," she sang.

I did so and felt her drop something there. I waited.

"Well, open it, silly goose," she said. There in my hand was a tie-tac shaped bar with my name in black against a white backdrop. Except it wasn't really my name. It read "Harry Trueman."

"Go on, put it on; I've got to see how you look in it. Dad had me make you one even though this is your last day working here, but who knows, maybe you'll find something else to do, Dad appreciates hard workers," she said breathlessly.

"Go on, put it on," Daylon echoed.

I looked around, hoping a coffee customer might materialize, might save me from the ignominy of the nametag. No one did. I put it on. They clapped.

Della reached toward my chest, but I drew back reflexively. "Look down, Mr. Trueman, and tell me what's wrong with that picture."

I did. I could have told her of an infinite number of things wrong with the picture of my life at that moment, but all I said was "what?"

She was undaunted. "Your name tag. It's turvy-topsy. You can read it but no one else can. Don't you already know who you are? I would think with a name as extinguished as yours, *you* wouldn't need reminding. Dad and me thought it would tickle the drivers to be able to say they'd been served coffee by a former US of A president." She laughed. Daylon put his arm around her shoulders and squeezed. They looked down at me like pleased parents.

Again she reached toward me to correct my name pin, and this time I let her.

She stood back, admired her handiwork, nodded its acceptability. "I pronounce you....ready to pour coffee, Mr. Trueman. Or should I say, Mr. President?"

"The cup stops here," added Daylon.

"What do you mean?" Della was genuinely puzzled.

Before I had to listen to Daylon explain the allusion, a gaggle of customers came for coffee, forcing the lovebirds to part for their respective trailers. But behind me, I heard Daylon ask in a much more serious tone, "Still no Tessie?" and Della's "no" sounded like a single note from an iron bell.

Daylon was wrong. It was busy, even before noon. I was thankful for this, though, because it took two seconds to fill one of the Styrofoam cups, and I marked each cup as that much closer to the end of this day. Frankly, the end of this day was all I could think of just then. And as wrong as Daylon had been, so too was Summerset Hundley's prediction of apocalyptic weather. Between cups and inane questions about how far a motorist was from Point A, I scanned the sky for just one cloud. By the time old Hundley came to relieve me at noon, I was as wrung as a sponge, and the white sky still simmered.

I was irrationally angry with him for this and wanted to say something, anything, a snide remark that would cut into his smug, self-assured attitude.

"What do you think about the caterpillars and ducks now?" I said, scarcely able to control my frustration.

"You mean do I still think it's going to storm?"

"Yeah. What's Mother Nature telling you now?" I wished I could click on weather.com and catch some live radar and print out a forecast from somebody with a degree and not rely on some Andy of Mayberry bullshit.

Just then a truck rumbled loudly on the interstate causing me to look up. There was no truck, of course, and I turned
back to Summerset Hundley's broad grin. He had the civility
to avoid an I-told-you-so, but he did point toward the top of
the high ridge that framed the horizon. A solid mass of black
clouds, wide as a continent, was just cresting above the hills.

"Go take your break. We got some time before it gets
here," he said and dove into conversation with a traveler as if
they'd known each other their whole lives.

I turned toward the plaza, but it didn't seem solid from
where I stood, shimmering surreally through waves of asphalt
heat. Though I'd been swilling water all morning, I was still
thirsty and that seemed reason enough to head inside. That
and I simply had nothing else to do with the next thirty minutes. So I put my head down and walked, focusing on the
painted lines of the vast parking lot because, otherwise, the
distance to the oasis was overwhelming.

When at length I looked up, I found myself nowhere
near the plaza's entrance. Instead, a woman gestured comically on a huge television screen not two feet in front of me.
Startled, I stepped back to see that she had nearly piloted her
minivan into me. Though I couldn't fathom why, it seemed to
have been my fault, so I lip-synced an elaborate apology and
moved aside.

I located the plaza, laughed at my own inattentiveness,
and struck off again. The plaza's shimmering disconcerted
me, flickering like a mirage, in fact nauseated me, so again I
looked only at the hot pavement and walked and made a game
of stepping on the parking lines. I walked the perimeter of the
implied squares for cars and thought of the functionality of
the modern parking lot, how a little white paint, inexpensive
to produce and to apply, could induce in otherwise indepen-

dent people a nearly Pavlovian response, forcing them into conformity as incontestably as if there were concrete walls around them.

And I thought how illogical it was to be thinking this just now, when what I most needed was a drink of water, and I was having my own Pavlovian response at the image of the condensation on the stainless steel housing of the plaza's water fountain.

I was lost.

Each time I looked up from the lines to avoid a parked car, I was further away from the plaza. Even the concession tents and trailers were no longer within walking distance. I was in the furthest regions of the parking lot, an area I had never had occasion to visit. I had never seen the lot full enough to warrant cars out here, and for the first time since I'd left Cincinnati, I was scared.

A simple five-minute walk from my coffee station to the plaza had become an Olympic event, and I had no strength for the effort. In the hot distance I saw both the plaza and, to its right, the concession area, alive with people like yellow-jackets around the bright umbrella I had recently manned. The whole scene, even the ribbon of busy highway in front of that, seemed like a television on mute from this deserted corner of the parking lot.

I sat down squarely in the middle of an empty parking square, secure in the knowledge that I possessed it, but sure of nothing else. No one would dare park here. How dare they question my claim, as undeniable as if I were a car? The asphalt was hot, hot enough to burn through my — no, HST's — plaid shorts, and I thought I should get up very soon, but I simply could not. I rested my head on arms across my bent knees and waited for the scalding to stop. But there was something about this pain that belonged to me.

And then the rain came. I didn't have to look up. I heard it advancing across the parking lot like spilling gravel. It did not come gently — I heard it, then felt it. With my head still down between my legs, I saw the pavement sizzle then steam like a million pistol barrels. The rain battered the back of my head, and the wind raised quick chill bumps on my arms. I thought it would feel good to cool my face, too, and to drink. I looked up and saw, barely through the spirit waves of rain that chased themselves across the lot, the wooden shutters of the fire department's hot dog stand and the SCBCWTC's booth closed tightly. The umbrella of my coffee stand had been folded; the table emptied. I thought, but could not be sure, that I saw the outline of Summerset Hundley standing still in the rain's belly, shielding his eyes against the downpour and slowly scrolling his head around the parking lot.

I lay back then, my face to the boiling sky and opened my mouth to drink. It filled quickly and I swallowed and choked, swallowed and choked. Lightning ripped and arced. Thunder dwarfed the rain's beating and echoed up and down the valley like marbles settling in a wooden bowl.

Through it all, through the bullying wind and the spanking rain, and despite the chill bumps on my skin, the heat behind my eyes didn't cool. At length I closed them and hoped for a stray lightning bolt or for two fat raindrops to land squarely on my closed lids like coins on a dead man's eyes. The clatter inside my head was indistinguishable from that above it.

I gave in to the thunder that seemed close enough to destroy with just its sound and thought: T. S. Eliot was wrong — the world, at least mine, was going to end with a bang, not a whimper.

## CHAPTER 5 — *CORINNE*

Corinne crossed, uncrossed, recrossed her legs within seconds of sitting down. She repeated this several times, finally pulling her skirt down to her knees and settling back in the chair before answering the question.

"What you see with Duncan is not always what you get. It will take you awhile to learn this—it did me, anyway. This makes him no less interesting, and really, it didn't or doesn't change the way I feel about him. In fact, I think it's endearing that he's so willing to become different people for different situations.

"The problem is you'll think there's more to him than there really is. I think *he* thinks there's more to him than there really is. But you know those people who are much deeper than they first appear? The kind that, the more you talk to them, the more layers you discover? They're like onions because they have layer after layer? Duncan is not that person, though he'd desperately like to be."

Corinne seemed more comfortable now that she'd begun to speak. Gone were the restless leg movements. Her arms lay motionless on the chair's leather arm rests. She paused, waiting for the man to write on his canary yellow legal pad. But he didn't.

"The summer I met him, Duncan tried to memorize the names of all the plants in the Krohn Conservatory so we could talk about them. I'd notice he'd point something out and not just say 'isn't that a stunning flower?' No, he might remark about the difficulty of maintaining proper light requirements for this species of bromeliads or that variant of the agave. And not just their common names, either. Scientific names. Latin tongue twisters.

"It was cute, but I finally had to tell him I liked them because they were pretty, because they were exotic, because their smell took me somewhere away from Cincinnati for awhile." Corinne hesitated again, sure the man would record some of this.

"I see," he said when it became apparent that something needed said.

She leaned forward and put her long, thin, wing-like fingers on the edge of his desk. "He often did things like that. He had a client who golfed, so he took two weeks of lessons, expensive lessons from some pro, then practiced for hours every day of those two weeks, just so he wouldn't feel lost when he took this guy golfing. He was still terrible — Duncan is no athlete — but at least he could speak the guy's language. He's tried to learn the names of constellations and the myths that created them, of trees, of dog breeds, obscure politicians. It was like a kid learning the capitals of all 50 states: he doesn't know anything substantial about Vermont, probably can't find it on a map, but by God he knows that its capital is Montpelier. That's Duncan. He needs to appear to know things. Duncan's not an onion; he's an apple."

Corinne sat back. She felt tired from revealing. Tired, and saddened.

The man across the desk drew in a deep breath, picked up a pen. "Mrs. Post, perhaps you misunderstood my question. When I asked you to describe your husband, I meant what he looks like. If I'm to find him, I need a physical description. I'm not going to be very effective if I go around asking people if they've seen someone who reminds them of an apple, now am I?"

Corinne's hands fluttered back to perch on the chair's armrests. Her body followed into the deep seat. "I'm so sorry, Mr. Daugherty," she said, closing her eyes for a long moment. When she opened them, she could not look at the private investigator. Instead, she looked at the back of the picture frame on his desk. She knew the picture would be of the man standing astride a freshly killed elk or buffalo or grizzly bear, its neck twisted unnaturally; or of the man holding a stringer of dripping fish, their scales glinting in the sunlight and their mouths vainly gulping for water. Either way, he'd be grinning broadly. To break the silence she pointed at the picture frame. "May I?"

"It's alright, Mrs. Post. There'll be time for me to learn the other details about Mr. Post, things I can't learn from newspaper articles. I'm sure these things are important and may, indeed, later prove useful." He nodded his head toward the picture frame. "Of course."

Instead, she dug into her purse. "Here's the most recent photo I have of him. Of us." She tried to reach across the broad desk to hand it to him, but her hand trembled slightly, and just as the man touched the photo's edge, she dropped it.

"Not your fault; it's a big desk," he said.

On its flight back, her hand picked up the picture frame. Both Corinne and the investigator studied the pictures they held. Corinne was surprised. The frame from his desk held a ticket stub to a 1978 Eagles concert. Across the bottom was written "First Date! Who knew??? Love, Tina'." She gingerly replaced the frame into its outline in the desk's thin film of dust.

Daugherty's perusal took much longer. He traced the photograph's surface with his index finger as if he were reading Braille. He seemed to be sketching shapes, and Corinne wondered if he were sketching her face, too. He jotted something quickly on his pad, then drew in a breath and did not immediately exhale, making her think he were about to speak. He said nothing, though, and returned to his inspection of the photograph.

"You were recommended to me because of your discretion," Corinne said.

"I'm like a priest," said Daugherty with no crumb of sarcasm and without looking up. "What's said here stays here. I report only to the client who signs my check. And it will be a large one, Mrs. Post, whether I'm successful or not."

Corinne looked around his office. A large mahogany hutch held a few books, a crystal decanter set filled with Scotch, and trophies of football players in various heroic poses: Bronze men frozen as they reached for an unseen football or stiff-armed a vanquished tackler; bronze men with forearm veins like lightning bolts, forever inches away from glory. She rose from her chair and walked toward those men, the slender heels of her shoes barely catching the carpet's nap with an electric snap. As she knew they would, each trophy's plaque was engraved with Daugherty's name.

"I didn't mean for that to sound so mercenary. I'm sorry," Daugherty said, when he finally placed the photograph in a file folder and looked up.

Corinne turned from the hutch. "That's fine. That's okay. I know that discretion isn't cheap, and I know this may not be an easy task. I'm afraid you won't have much to go on. I can't be of very much help."

"Oh, it's my experience that folks can often be much more helpful than they might think they can. But I have to tell you something about this profession. When you get right down to it, I'm nothing more than a snoop. Most of my work involves lurking around catching some neglected housewife in a Harlequin moment by a suburban Motel 6 pool with her 'soulmate,' or a bored husband banging — pardon my expression — trysting with his secretary during a sales convention in glamorous downtown Detroit. Occasionally, I'm hired to trap a poor sap who's been funneling petty office cash to plunk down on a trifecta at River Downs. It's good money; I'm not complaining. My technology has changed, but the human fascination with the seven deadly sins has not." He leaned back to assess the impact of this wisdom on Corinne, his thin red silk tie riding the wave of his belly like pulled taffy — the jock gone soft.

When Corinne had no reply, he went on. "I have to start with this question, though: why not the police, Mrs. Post? That's how most people begin a missing person's search."

Corinne turned again to the hutch, leaned forward and pretended to be engrossed in the trophies' inscriptions.

Daugherty continued. "That has no bearing on the tenacity of my search, but often I find that law enforcement can provide me with helpful information. I have contacts."

At this, Corinne picked up the Scotch decanter, held the heavy cut-crystal toward the sunlit window, and swirled the amber drink. Heels snapping again, she walked back to Daugherty's desk and placed her palms on its edge. "Once you begin, Mr. Daugherty, will you call me every evening at 7:00? Even if you don't have anything new to report?" She sat, pulled her long blonde hair from the sides of her face, and tucked it behind both ears. "I'll answer any question I can. But remember, discretion is a two-way street."

\*     \*     \*     \*

Not until the elevator had deposited her into the brilliant marble and chrome lobby 37 floors below Daugherty's office was Corinne able to take a breath she could characterize as normal. She had not lied to Dexter Daugherty, though she felt he had lied to her. Not lied, really, but misrepresented himself. One doesn't occupy 15,000 square feet of prime office space overlooking both the Ohio River and downtown Cincinnati simply by embarrassing cheating insurance salesmen and their hausfraus. Daugherty would find Duncan, and she had the money to pay him.

No, Corinne had not lied, but she, too, had misrepresented herself, she acknowledged. She had been vague, perhaps, and had tried to seem composed, even tough. She had thought an interview with a private investigator (these guys still existed?) should be conducted like a scene from a Bogart movie and was unprepared for the office with its muted lighting, handsome, imposing woods and tasteful art, the efficient, smiling receptionist and hushed waiting area — more like a plastic surgeon's office than what it was. She had played her part in spite of this, however. She wished she were her best friend, Ariel, who, though she wasn't any more a film noir heroine than Corinne, could have given a much better imitation of one.

Now, she stepped blinking from the lobby into the harsh July sunshine, walked the block to Fountain Square, and slumped heavily onto a green metal bench, scattering pigeons like shrapnel. *Discretion is a two-way street.* She cringed at the memory of saying that and hoped she had delivered the line like the callous bitch she had tried to steel herself to be. A panhandler approached her, and in anticipation, she reached into her purse for both a five and her sunglasses. The bum thanked her with feigned obsequiousness, while behind her sunglasses, Corinne cried.

## CHAPTER 6

I've always thought life would be better lived if accompanied by background music. Little flutes—what are those called? piccolos?—accessorizing my tie selection each morning. A slow tinkling of upper register piano keys tracing the sweet, melancholy path of autumn leaves drifting around Corinne and me as we walked through Eden Park in oversized cable-knit sweaters. Strings swelling during bittersweet, emotional goodbyes. A low, steady tympani to fortify a successful workday, the march of commercial progress. Cymballic crescendos and bass drums signaling the triumphant moments when prized clients signed on the dotted line.

Movie moments. Danger announced, then averted. Even during the most mundane days, days of errands or waiting, of hours in airplanes or limos, there should be some sublayer of rhythm to heighten existence.

I even know with certainty that I could have marched into war, Civil or otherwise, if I'd had piped into my ears "The Battle Hymn of the Republic" belted out by a purple-robed choir of massive black women gospel singers, their sincerity and lethal fervor causing them to sway and sweat. I always loved their big, soul-rattling sounds and syncopated body motions that built up like a rogue ocean wave you can see from a great distance and still not avoid. I'd have charged into any battle with only crazed fury as a weapon if fueled by that song thus sung.

I never wanted my own motif, though—no sprightly identifying little ditty like, say, Peter and the Wolf. Music wouldn't be a substitute for living, just an adjunct. If there were a heaven, I always assumed, it certainly would have background music.

I guessed, then, that I had died because before I opened my eyes to see my heaven, I heard music. In fact, hearing it so softly played is what kept me from opening them. I knew the piece and wanted to identify it before I saw the orchestra responsible for it. My chunk of heaven must be big, I decided, because there were a great many instruments at work.

It came to me in bits. First, I remembered that it was Corinne who had introduced me to this, had taken me to the Aronoff Center initially against my will. "You're a water person, Duncan," she'd said. "I'm water, too, and Scheherazade's sea section is perfect. I cry as soon as the cellos open that movement."

I laughed at her, I recall. But I recall, too, that when I stole a look at her as the movement began, I cried because she cried. Just a touch, mind you, but I couldn't have answered a question with a full voice. She would have known.

So, Scheherezade, then, would be the background music for my introduction into heaven, perhaps even with Rimsky-Korsakov conducting the orchestra. Surely he was dead, too. This choice of music seemed appropriate, I thought, and I thought something else before I was ready to open my eyes.

I thought my heaven was pretty damn comfortable, though with a quick twinge, I nearly simultaneously realized I shouldn't use the word "damn" to refer to my comfort level. Perhaps I had some celestial indoctrination period ahead of me. A time to rinse out the remnants of earth. After all, the last memory I had was of lying on my back on a searing asphalt parking lot, staring into the face of a thunderstorm, parked directly over me with obvious malevolent intent. Swing low, sweet chariot, I expected my royal-robed Aretha Franklins to sing just then. Scheherazade continued, however.

Really, I knew I was not dead, that this was not heaven, that the down pillow and crisp sheets I felt enveloping me were not clouds, but that I was not opening my eyes because I was scared shitless about where I really was. I was most certainly no longer flat on my back in the travel plaza parking lot with a thunderstorm pummeling me. I was no longer under the bridge that had served as home for the last three months, and to which, strangely, I wanted to return; and I was not in any kind of hospital I could imagine with classical music piped into the room and what must have been 600 count Egyptian cotton sheets.

Tentatively, I sent my hands out to explore either side of me. Lewis and Clark splitting up. The terrain was quilted, the frontiers too vast to fall over the edge where there be monsters...

"Be careful," said a voice I'd heard before but couldn't place. "You'll knock Flopsy off the bed, Duncan Post."

Then, of course, I *could* place it. It had to be the only person who had recently heard me reveal my real name. Who had heard me wish myself a self-pitying happy birthday. Who had seen me beneath my bridge.

Opening my eyes felt like pulling apart an envelope flap. A girl stood silhouetted between the two tall canopy posters at the foot of my bed. The unshaded window behind her prevented my focusing on her features at first—I kept blinking like a mole—but the long tangerine hair was unmistakable.

"I'll go get Poppie and Della; but first, do you like Flopsy?"

Before I could ask the relevant questions—where am I? who are you? how did I get here?—something rustled on the pillow beside my ear. Something with fur.

"It's okay. You don't have to answer now," she said,

coming to the side of the bed and scooping up what could have been anything from a gerbil to a newborn dingo. Its eyes, like mine should have been, were still closed. I recoiled reflexively, as quickly as my stiff neck would allow. She laughed, that bright trill I'd heard in the woods. "It's just a baby rabbit. I found it down by the creek and never could find the nest. We're feeding it milk with an eyedropper."

"Who is?" I said and tried to sit up. The voice was mine, but I didn't realize how much effort it was going to take to produce it. And I couldn't even push myself up into a sitting position.

She was coming into focus for me, and though her high, quick voice and animation seemed like an early teen's, her face, pretty enough in a plain, unpolished way, had some lines. She had to be twenty, maybe older, maybe close to my age. She wore, if not the same outfit I last saw her in, one in the same spirit: cut-off jeans and a faded blue tee-shirt with a white rubberized oval on the chest. The bleached white script inside the oval read "Harvey's Groceries" but now missed the "H" and "G," darker blue fabric shadows replacing them.

She looked at me as if I had Alzheimer's, scooting closer until her face loomed only inches from mine. Slowly, she said, "All…of…us. Me…Della…Poppie…even Daylon," she picked up speed again, apparently crediting me with understanding, "though he said he'd rather eat rabbit than keep them for pets. I think he was just fooling with me, though. But with Daylon you never really know. He'll eat just about anything that won't eat him first." She sat on the edge of my bed and picked up what must have been Flopsy. Before I could protest, she placed the squirming dab of fur on my chest. "Keeping a pet teaches you responsibility. They're so helpless. As far as they know, you're their mother. You have to feed and protect them. It really is a big job. You can name him whatever you want—

Flopsy doesn't have to stick; I just thought…"

"Tessie, please. Take your rabbit back outside and leave Mr. Trueman be for a bit. He's not ready for any conversation just yet." The voice coming from the doorway to my right was unmistakably Summerset Hundley's, and I was simultaneously overjoyed and terrified to hear it.

Tessie leaned over me and scooped up the rabbit, her hair spilling forward over her shoulder and draping my face. I fought the urge to sneeze. Before turning to leave, she whispered, "Need to see Flopsy, Mr.….*Trueman*….just let me know." She kissed Summerset Hundley on the cheek as she passed him in the doorway. He tugged her hair.

"Get downstairs and help Della with supper, girl," he said to her back.

Summerset picked up a straight-backed wooden chair from just inside the doorway and carried it over to my bedside. It seemed no heavier to him than picking up a magazine. Again I struggled to push myself up, but my arms wobbled with the effort.

"It's not worth it, Harry; just relax," he said. "You're not ready to go anywhere just yet."

Though I surely was ready to go somewhere, I collapsed back onto the mound of pillows beneath me and looked down at my traitor arms. The inside crook of my right one was bruised badly.

"Dr. Baker gave you some fluids," said Summerset, nodding toward my bruise. "You were a bit under the weather, pardon my pun, there for a while, but you're looking a touch more spry now."

There was only one thing I could say to him that would get me out of here — wherever "here" was — and back to, well, back to the bridge where I could think about my next move. This was a mistake I'd learn from.

"Mr. Hundley, I'm sorry about this morning. I hadn't eaten any breakfast, and I guess the heat got to me. There's no sense telling you it won't happen again since today was the last day of the holiday, but I just want you to know this is not the way I handle my business." I felt for a moment a quick surge of humiliation at referring to my three days of serving coffee under an umbrella at an interstate rest stop as "business." In fact, I felt humiliated by having to apologize to Summerset Hundley at all.

Until my partner Richard Rice screwed me figuratively, and Corinne literally, we were on the verge of taking showplace.com global, anticipating a huge IPO, becoming a real player in the universe of virtual headhunting. No more baby steps.

Summerset looked at me as he might a babbling child. "No sorry's necessary. What say we take things one at a time? You need to know it wasn't this morning you took sick, Harry. It was almost a week ago, now, that Daylon and I got you into my truck and brought you here. This is my family's house. You've been here since last Sunday. This is Friday."

I opened my mouth to protest, to tell him that couldn't be true, he must be mistaken, or worse (for me), lying, but I was too weak to accuse just then.

"It's okay, son. Doc Baker says you'll be fine." He laughed. "And Doc Baker is probably the best veterinarian in Sinking Creek. Has to be, I suppose. He's the only one." He laughed again, more fully this time. I had to admit it was a good laugh, sincerely offered, without derision. It invited laughter that I wouldn't give. He stopped when he had mined all the joke's humor. He didn't notice, or care, that I hadn't joined. "You'll have a bushel of questions, probably already do, I'm sure, and there'll be plenty of time for the answers, but let's first get you in shape to ask them."

He rose, placed his big hands on the small of his back and arched.

"Della and Tessie are fixing you some vegetable soup right now. If you're ready for some, I'll send them up. It's not fancy, but it'll fix what ails you." As if on cue, sounds of silverware and of women laughing issued from downstairs.

Summerset Hundley was right. I had plenty of questions, but I had to weigh my curiosity against the questions they might have in return. And he was right on another point, as well. Some homemade vegetable soup sounded damn good.


Over the next few days, life settled into a rhythm. Every morning Summerset poked his head into the bedroom, cautiously, apologetically, helped me to the bathroom across the hall, waited outside, then walked beside me back to the bed, all the while holding his arm out toward me as if I were a toddler careening toward a sharp-edged coffee table. He'd be followed shortly by Della, with a tray of pancakes, or French toast, or waffles, or biscuits and gravy, or maybe scrambled eggs and sausage, pots of tea, sugar cookies, or some combination of all of these.

At first I tried to refuse the food, telling them truthfully that I was no breakfast eater, had always been too busy for it.

"Well, you're not so busy just now, are you?" Della said after a few mornings of this protest.

I had no immediate answer because I had already stuffed my mouth with biscuit and strawberry jam. I had become a metabolic machine. I had no idea I had been so profoundly hungry.

"Oh, I'm sorry, Mr. Trueman," she said quickly. "That didn't come out the way I intentioned. Daylon tells me I can come across persnickety at times. I usually just lose my temper with Tessie, but she'd try Saint Holy Mother Teresa, you know…" and she was off and running. By the time she'd finished the twenty-minute sentence, the topic was Daylon's cousin's hairdresser's fainting goats or some such shit. I had quickly learned to zone out during one of her "conversations" and continue eating, occasionally nodding like I understood or cared. I used her droning as white noise. The truth was, though, I was beginning to enjoy — no, that's not right — to tolerate it.

She and Summerset would then leave for the plaza after breakfast and the day became infinitely more interesting. Though I was still too weak to navigate downstairs, I was gaining some strength. I didn't want them to know how much, however, because at some point, I'd simply disappear. I was, after all, wanted for murder. This, of course, caused me some basic problems even here.

Summerset had to assume I lived nearby, but he had never asked about contacting anyone for me and didn't seem curious about exactly where I lived or what I did for a living. Neither he, nor Della, nor even Daylon, who visited every evening and engaged in the inane conversations that guys do — sports, weather, the vagaries of the opposite sex — ever asked me any personal questions. What at first had seemed like a blessing, now struck me as odd, perhaps dangerously so.

At the risk of sounding paranoid — and didn't I have every reason to be? — I fully expected they were simply fattening me up for the proverbial kill, that one morning instead of breakfast I'd be served with an arrest warrant by sunglassed FBI agents curtly informing that I had the right to remain silent. A right that I had largely been exercising for three months now. Perhaps they already knew my story, and that explained their lack of curiosity.

I would either return to Cincinnati and turn myself in,

or continue on to somewhere else and start over; and though I could justify either course, the choice had to be mine.

The wildcard in this equation was Tessie. For the bulk of my morning, the downstairs was totally quiet; so quiet, in fact, I assumed I was alone, and this seemed fine because I was unquestionably in need of recuperation. I heard no televisions, no radios, no phones. The only sound came from an old fashioned round-faced alarm clock, the kind with two bells on top and a clapper between them, that sat on the nightstand beside my bed. And though I napped on and off after breakfast, I was never unaware of its ticking. I no longer made use of the length of shadows to tell time, as I had in my kingdom on Sinking Creek. That my life now was being paced off by the maddeningly slow insistence of a wind-up clock rather than measured in gigahertz per second seemed counter-evolutionary. I thought of this alarm clock as about the midpoint on my rise from marking time with shadows until the day I might again wear my Tag Heuer.

At noon, precisely, at just about the time the bedroom became overwhelmed by the clock's stentorian ticking and I was certain that I was totally alone, classical music would dance, or pound, or thunder, or threaten, or tinkle, twinkle, or tidal wave its way up the stairway from the house's first floor. After Corinne had introduced me to Scheherezade, my crash course had included what she called the "absolute necessities": Brahms and Bach, Mozart, Beethoven, Strauss, Haydn and Handel. I even learned to tell some of them apart. Every day the music from downstairs sounded vaguely familiar.

Within a half hour of the music's first notes, Tessie would appear with a lunch tray. More soup, a sandwich — always cheese and lettuce, always cut diagonally — and tea. "Here's your dinner, Duncan Post," she'd say, grinning conspiratorially, and setting the tray on the nightstand. From an apron pocket, she produced Flopsy.

"Thanks, Tessie," I said automatically and always followed with the same request: "Why don't you sit for a minute. I've got a few questions."

The first few days, her cryptic answer remained "Poppie said you would," before she giggled and left the room. But one day, a Thursday, I guessed, she sat confidently on the end of the bed and said, "I knew you'd want to pet Flopsy."

She sat gingerly on the foot of my bed and released the rabbit. With a finger she prodded the squinting animal until it labored its way up the blankets toward me, instinctively moving toward warmth before it exhausted itself. "Summerset's your father?" I said. Casually, I hoped. "And Della's your sister?" The questions were too casual, I guess, because she must have either taken them for statements or she was too engrossed in the rabbit's activity — or lack of — to respond.

"Is that right, Tessie? Summerset's your father?"

She didn't look at me, but tried to lure Flopsy back to her with a piece of lettuce produced from a second apron pocket. "Poppie and Sis, that's right." When Flopsy didn't react to the wilted lettuce leaf, resting instead on the mound of blankets that was my knee, she smiled dreamily and set the leaf down. "I knew Flopsy would like you. Animals know who has a good heart."

"Thanks," I said because I wasn't really sure what kind of reply was appropriate for such an unassuming compliment. I'd have been much more comfortable had she commented on a suit I'd worn or a job I'd done. Only Corinne had ever complimented me on something as intangible, once telling me she'd thought I hung the moon. I was taken aback only briefly, however. Truth was, Tessie didn't, and couldn't, know me, and I wasn't about to pet that half-blind rabbit now just to pacify her.

"Do you like my room, Duncan Post Harry Trueman?" she blurted.

I looked again around the room that for the last few conscious and unconscious days of my life had been my world. It was inconceivable that this was Tessie's bedroom. Besides the four-poster canopied bed, one wall was dominated by a massive oak dressing table, with shelves on either side of a huge oval mirror with an intricately carved frame. The lace curtains around the window on the facing wall had been sewn to match the frame's interlocking pattern that struck me as somehow Celtic. On one set of the dresser's shelves sat an assortment of perfumes or colored waters in Victorian stoppered bottles, and on the other was a delicate ceramic hummingbird captured in mid-flight feasting on the nectar of a pink calla lily. Believe me, I'd had plenty of time to absorb this room, and it simply couldn't be Tessie's. It was too feminine. And something else, too. Though not chronologically so, the room seemed too adult to belong to this woman-child sitting on the edge of my bed. I had assumed it was a guest room, a room furnished with the Hundley's very best. It felt much more like an upscale bed-and-breakfast.

"It's a nice room, Tessie. I'm very sorry, though, to be taking your room. I hope to be…"

"Getting the h-e-double hockey sticks out of here?" Tessie finished, her eyes always on Flopsy.

"That's not what I was going to say." Though a sanitized version of it was.

"That's what you said a lot for the first day you was here."

"I don't think that's right, Tessie."

"Oh, that's right, Duncan Post, and you fought with everybody, too. Especially Doc Baker. Fought and cussed a lot the first day. Then Doc Baker gave you some medicine and you settled and slept most of the rest of the time until you finally woke up again for good the other day. Doc Baker and Poppie said to pay you no mind because you didn't know what you was saying so you couldn't mean it the way it sounded. It scared poor Della; she's fragile, bless her heart, but me, I just laughed, and Daylon did, too, and said 'give 'em hell, Harry,' till Poppie run us out." Tessie seemed to enjoy the memory.

"Well, then, I'm sorry you had to hear that," I said. There are conversational conventions in the business world that dictate what can be talked about and what must be talked around. It's an art form for which everyone knows the rules, and since they do, every statement can be decoded. *I'm sorry to hear about so and so's setback* really means *the bastard had it coming and now there's a little more room at the table for the rest of us.* Tessie's total guilessness, however, demanded a kind of tact, too; one that I was not versed in, though I felt I'd better learn fast.

I went on. "Did I say anything else, Tessie? Anything else I need to apologize for, maybe?" I cringed inwardly at the question's transparency and hoped that Tessie was just too simple to understand my hidden meaning.

Tessie looked up at me only briefly, then continued pushing the pale, limp lettuce leaf at Flopsy's clenched mouth. "You didn't say your name was Duncan Post, if that's what you mean, Duncan Post."

"No, of course, that's not what I meant," I said as sincerely as I could. "I just didn't realize I had said anything at all. In fact, I didn't realize I had lost the better part of four days. I'd appreciate anything you could tell me about that time, Tessie. Anything to help me reconstruct what happened to me. You can understand why I want to know, can't you?"

For the first time Tessie's eyes met mine for longer than a beat, and I could see that she was, indeed, Summerset

Hundley's daughter, as much his daughter as Della was, though they were opposite sides of the same genetic coin. Tessie, with a quick visit to a beauty spa, could have been stunning. Her grey-green eyes, copies of Summerset's and Della's, and arresting citrus hair alone would stop traffic. But her long, lean build, thoroughbred in its fluidity, gave her an ethereal, feline grace of movement, and she radiated a physical power I'd previously associated only with athletic men.

"No, nothing really; you just mumbled some."

"Did you call anybody? About me, that is?"

"Just Doc Baker," she said.

I saw an avenue to the information I was truly after. "Yeah, about Dr. Baker. He'll need to be paid for his services. Did he wonder about insurance, maybe? About notifying my …next of kin?"

"Who we going to call, Duncan Harry Trueman Post? Don't really know much about you, now do we?" She pointed toward my lunch tray. "You not hungry? I can fix something else. Want some popcorn?"

I quickly picked up my cheese sandwich and took a bite. "No, I just thought this Dr. Baker would want to make sure he would get paid. You know how doctors are," I said, hoping she'd agree with the joke.

"I wouldn't worry about Doc Baker. Poppie gives him plenty of business already. You won't make or break him. He's doctored all our animals since before I was born."

"Your animals?"

Tessie's puzzled expression mirrored mine. At first I thought she was mocking me but decided she wasn't capable of this. "Sure. Lots of dogs and cats, a course, and he's helped birth most all our calves and ponies, and lots of our kids— baby goats to you, I guess— and doctored them up when need be. And he's put down more than a few of them, too." She grew quiet, picked up Flopsy and rubbed him across her cheek. Her eyes watered. I saw that, as closely as they matched her father's and sister's eyes, there was, too, a fundamental difference. In that instant, as she both looked at me and at some memory, I saw veil after veil being drawn in their depths.

"So, then. Dr. Baker *is* a veterinarian. Truly a veterinarian. Your father wasn't just teasing me?"

From downstairs, the music changed from something symphonic to a single, mournful piano piece. "Poppie would have called a town doctor if you'd needed one, but I heard him tell Daylon and Della it might be best just to call Doc Baker first. Once Doc Baker told him you was just thirsty and bushed, we figured it was okay just to keep you here."

Tact be damned. I had to know some crucial things, and it was apparent that Tessie was incapable of duplicity. Maybe everyone in this black hole of Sinking Creek was incapable of it, too, at least everyone I'd met since I'd been here, but I was sure that Tessie's limitations would be like a truth serum.

"Tessie, why has no one tried to find out anything about my background? No one's asked me where I'm from, if I'm married, what I do for a living, even where I live now." Strangely, I heard my voice rising, as if I wanted to answer those questions, or at least needed to be asked. "Good Lord, no one even asks me if I like cheese sandwiches."

Tessie stood, put Flopsy and the lettuce shard back in the apron pockets. At first, I thought my brief tirade had frightened her; instead, her voice was even, perhaps affronted. "Just yell when you're finished with lunch, Mr. Trueman, and I'll come back and get your tray." She walked to the doorway, stopped, turned, and said, "Like everybody, you're from someplace, doesn't matter where. You was married, may still be, the tan around where your ring was says so. Right now, you live in my bedroom. You do what you have to to get by—just like the whole world does. And you don't like cheese sandwiches. But we just haven't been to the store to get lunchmeat."

As she wheeled to leave, her hair licked her shoulders like flames.

That evening I learned from Daylon that Tessie had gone to the store for lunchmeat.

"Tessie drives?" I said.

This amused Daylon. "Oh, Tessie *can* drive, Harry. In fact, she handles Summerset's big Deere better'n I can. Drives the cultivator, hay baler, handles a four-wheeler like a TV stunt man, but I know you mean a car, and no, she don't drive cars. State of Virginia isn't going to give Tessie a license."

We were walking slowly in the field behind the house, Daylon having offered me clothes and his services "to show me around." I had told Della and Summerset when they brought my dinner tray earlier that evening that I was certainly strong enough now to be on my feet and gone.

"On your feet, maybe, but not yet gone," Summerset had said, and soon after, Daylon had shown up with some jeans and a loose white tee shirt, telling me that the outfit I'd been wearing when they first brought me here would be washed and ready when I left. Which, according to Daylon, I couldn't do until I'd eaten all of Tessie's lunchmeat and listened to a business proposition from Summerset.

Daylon's admission that Tessie was somehow unfit for a driver's license seemed to be an invitation to ask him what I could not ask her father or sister. Before I could say anything, however, Daylon—a few steps ahead of me—stopped at the top of a small rise and motioned me up.

"Every time I climb this little hill I'm amazed at something, Harry," he said.

I caught up with him, and though the hill couldn't have been more than a relatively gradual ten feet high, the climb winded me.

"Look where we've come from," he said nodding back toward Summerset's two-story white house and massive red barn, receding in the blue half-light of summer's dusk. A single lane dirt road ran in front of the house and beyond it lay parallel snaking lines of trees separated by a thin creek. Sinking Creek, I supposed. "Now, look this way," he said, pointing like a game show host at a new vista on the other side of the hill.

It was impressive, I had to admit, with several wide pastures running up slopes, then giving way to bushy hilltops like broad-faced men with curly hair. Beyond them, hills folded into other hills.

"Yeah, it's nice Daylon," I said, feigning the enthusiasm I could tell he needed. "You live in God's country, that's for sure."

"But here's what I wanted to tell you, Harry. Everything you see on this side of the hill, and I mean every blade of grass and every oak leaf, everything but the sky above it belongs to Summerset."

"Summerset works in a travel plaza, Daylon."

"Oh, he didn't buy this. Who could? No, this land is the old Hundley homeplace. Goes back to before the Revolutionary War. Summerset's great, great, great—I don't know how many greats—grandfather was give the property by some king of England. Called a land grant, or something like that." He paused, apparently contemplating the enormity of history. On the edge of one of the far fields, a deer stepped cautiously from the thick forest. It raised its head toward us, then realized the safety in its distance and grazed warily.

"So, Summerset's rich, then," I said and turned again to face his large house, which from here looked like a bit player in a Turner landscape. My, well Tessie's, bedroom and the opulence (though much too country for my taste) of the little bit of the rest of the house I'd seen indicated some wealth, if poorly used.

"Rich? Rich? Hell, no, Harry. Summerset's land poor. These acres don't do him any good now. Was a time, maybe, when land and wealth was the same thing around here, and I guess in the right circumstances it still is, but Summerset doesn't get squat from this land no more. Keeps horses, some milk cows and beef cattle, goats, some chickens, but it's small time stuff. Just for looks, is my take. Doesn't make much money off any of it. Keeps Tessie interested, though. He worked hard for a lot of years to keep it up, to keep the whole thing running like it had for a couple hundred years before, but mostly it just keeps dragging money from what he's got saved up."

Three other antlerless deer joined the first one in the far field, and the sun just grazed the treetops behind them. "The answer's simple, Daylon. Sell some of it. Section it off for housing developments. Jesus, Daylon, just on these pastures here you could build fifty, seventy-five big houses." I briefly pictured copies of my huge neo-Georgian in Blue Ash that seemed so much more imposing architecturally than Summerset's house, but in fact was no larger. "Offer underground utilities, a gated entrance, a couple of pools and tennis courts for the hausfraus to flock around drinking gin and tonics. You're not that far from Bristol. Bound to be a demand. Market it as the newest utopia — an escape from the hustle and bustle of the metropolis." Had I really called Bristol a metropolis? Didn't matter, I had to admit to a surge of the enthusiasm for commerce, the painting of a dream. I could see the images on a mental screen and was already thinking of a name for it.

I went on, flushed with ideas pent up since my life under the bridge had begun. This wasn't a dot.com business, in fact the ideas seemed too facile, prehistoric even, but they were ideas of a tangible sort. And then, something bigger hit me. "Even better, attract an industrial client to build a park here. That's where there's real money."

Daylon, who I just realized hadn't been looking at me as I built mini-mansions on his father-in-law's ancestral land, now turned to me. He tugged the bill of his faded orange baseball cap, first down, then up off his forehead, revealing his damp blond bangs. "Well, I can tell you now that Summerset won't never sell the land to put up a bunch of houses. People from lots of places have tried to get him to carve this land up for years. Wal-Mart, too. Some country singer even wanted to build water rides — slides and such, and it was a singer that he listened to. You can imagine how polite Summerset was, but he wouldn't budge. But, Harry, you say you could put a park here? And that it could make money? Now, *that* Summerset might go for."

I needed a whiteboard, or better yet a computer presentation screen, just then. Graphs and charts. I had points to make, schematics to illustrate. Instead, I crouched stiffly, and began scratching with a stick in the soft dirt of the hilltop. Daylon huddled with me like kids drawing up a football play. This, however, didn't last long. Immediately after I blocked in the proposed location for shell buildings and electrical grids, Daylon stopped me with a pair of fluttering hands.

"You said a park, Harry. Not a factory of some sort."

I felt as if I'd been punched. I didn't know whether to be angry or amused. My response to either was going to be hostile. These people couldn't be that stupid. I stabbed the stick into the middle of the office complex. It stood like a tomb-stone. "That's what an industrial park is, Daylon. A place where they make things. If this farm is as big as you say it is, I'm sure we could find a piece of it far away from the house. He'd never know it was on the other side of the hill. There's money to be made here."

Daylon unfolded upward athletically and looked out toward the distant pasture, now populated by more than a dozen deer. "I don't know, Harry. Summerset won't even log this place or quarry any of the granite. Those alone would bring in enough to keep this place running for the rest of his natural life, but he won't allow the truck traffic. He wants me and Della to have the farm, and to keep Tessie on it, too. I'm not opposed to that—how could I be?—but I just don't think we can keep it the way he wants us to. Maybe you could talk to him, Harry. He thinks the world of you."

"I don't know how or why, Daylon. He doesn't really know me." I stood, too, though with much more effort, and I realized I wasn't as fit as I needed to be to haul off on my own just yet. Across the pasture the deer began scattering, trotting at first through the open field, then gaining speed and re-form-ing as they neared the woods on the other side of the pasture like iron filings drawn by a magnet.

I heard the reason for their flight before I saw it. It sounded like a coffee can full of wasps, and it burst full throttle from a copse of beech trees, the tangerine hair of its pilot thrash-ing wildly from the back of a black helmet.

Daylon smiled. "Looks like Tessie's back from the store. Took the shortcut. Bet you got pickle loaf. She always gets me plain bologna." He winked at me like he'd just revealed some secret. In truth, both pickle loaf and bologna sounded the same as yak shit to me. "She's got a crush on you, you know."

I laughed reflexively. I was living in the middle of a P. Buckley Moss print. "A crush? I haven't heard that phrase since grade school."

"That keep it from being one, Harry?

The four-wheeler careened down the far pasture slope and disappeared into the valley beneath us, its frantic buzzing decreasing in volume. "I suppose not," I said, and I thought about Corinne. The concept of a crush was archaic but accurate. I had fallen that way for Corinne, and though in the early days I read books about the evolution of relationships, about the development of a "we" syndrome, about a healthy nurturing of interdependence, about a whole shopping cart full of new age psychobabble, somehow Daylon's unabashed use of the word "crush" more precisely captured that feeling I had when we met. Had even now.

"I'm married, Daylon."

"That right?" he said, though there seemed to be no surprise in his voice. "Well, I didn't tell you that about Tessie to make you squirm. Just, maybe, to make you feel good about yourself. There's nothing more to make of it. We know you aren't stringing her along. It's just cute, is all. You've done her a pile of good, and we're all grateful for that. For one thing, she's not took off once since you've been here."

We had begun to move down the hill toward the house, though I couldn't tell you who took the first steps in that direction. Our shadows were long, thin stalks before us, and we walked into them. "How old is Tessie? She seems a bit too old to be running away from home, or to have *crushes*."

"Let me think." Daylon stopped. My shadow got one step ahead of his, making them the same height. "She's six years younger than me and Della. Twenty-eight, then," he said and continued walking. "Maybe you don't call it a crush back in Cincinnati, probably seems old-fashioned to you. But that's what we call it here. I had a crush on Della since seventh grade. Still do, I guess." I expected him to blush at this—I would have—but his wide face just seemed to open a bit more at the thought. Without breaking stride he bent at the waist and snatched a long blade of grass to put in his mouth. "And you're right, too, she's a bit too old to be running away, though nobody in Sinking Creek really calls it that."

"What is it, then, and why does she do it?"

"*What* it is is easy enough to tell you, but *why* is a different animal altogether. And I don't want you to think Della nor Summerset wouldn't talk about it, but it's probably more my job."

Obviously Daylon was trying to tell me something he deemed important. What I wanted to tell him, though, was that I didn't really have the time to care. That's not true—I didn't have the room. "Daylon, never mind. I wasn't trying to pry."

It was as if I hadn't uttered a word. "After the accident, when she was ten, Tessie started disappearing into the woods. At first it would be just a couple of hours, not really long enough for the worry to grow. But then one time she was gone overnight. Summerset and most everybody in Sinking Creek took to the woods. I'm talking about old-timers who had hunted these woods for years, men who could sniff a bobcat fart from a mile away. Me and the whole Sinking Creek football team, too."

By now we were rounding the back of Hundley's barn. Chickens scattered and chuckled impatiently. "Some of us were still out in the woods next morning when Tessie moseyed through the back door into the kitchen, plopped down at the table, poured some milk over her Cheerios, and asked Della why she was crying. A week later she did it again, even though Summerset had blessed her out till a fly wouldn't light on her after last time. Most of us went looking again, though I don't think anybody was quite as worried. Pretty soon she was gone for stretches of a couple of days and more, any season, any weather. She'd be gone; she'd show up again. Never lost any weight or looked any worse for wear. Finally, only me and Summerset made up the search party, but Tessie knows these woods like her own heartbeat."

The whole story seemed harmless enough to me, but what I really wanted to know about was the "accident" he had glossed over—what could have caused her to turn into wood nymph complete with all the childlike naïveté that implied. "You sure it wasn't just some adolescent rebellion, Daylon? I admit ten years old is a bit young and twenty-eight a bit old for her to be playing the happy wanderer, but it's apparently not harming anyone now." I laughed at the surreal conversation I was having, defending a grown woman's right to run away from home, but I was finding it increasingly easy to accept a great many perverse concepts. "Besides, I'm guessing that Tessie…" and it dawned on me that I had no good way to say next what I really meant, "doesn't play by the same rules as you and I."

"If what you mean is she's slow," Daylon said as he opened the gate into the Hundley's back yard, "you're wrong. And you're right."

Just then, the can of bees burst over the hill we had just walked down, went airborne and landed with a springy thud. Tessie flipped up the opaque visor of her helmet and screamed as she sped into the barn. "I got pickle loaf!"

## CHAPTER 7 — CORINNE

Corinne had told Dexter Daugherty to phone her every evening at seven to report, even if there had been no progress in his search for Duncan.  And he did, faithfully, though she sat by the phone from five-thirty on and stayed there for a full hour after her five-minute briefing, just in case he had forgotten to tell her something.

There was plenty she had "forgotten" to tell Daugherty, however, though she was unclear about the effect her full story would have on the tenacity of his search.  Involving the police she saw as unnecessary, embarrassing.  Duncan wasn't really a missing person any more than he was a murderer.  The computer monitor he had hurled at Richard had been as errant as it was deserved, though in fact, Corinne thought it was she who should have been the rightful target of the scare.

She hadn't married Duncan for money.  She hadn't married him for love, strictly speaking either, though she did love him.  She married him for something she saw in him that she never found in herself: Duncan was above the world.  Not pain, not greed, not even the gratification that came, or should come, with achievement drove Duncan.  He simply *was*.  He was fully this moment, and then he was fully the next.  To someone who didn't know him, he seemed driven, perhaps even frenetically so, sometimes to the point of rudeness, but Corinne knew immediately and instinctually this was a function of his ability to encompass life rather than vice versa.  She *surrounded* herself with beauty — flowers, art, music — he *became* that beauty.  It made him seem one-dimensional, unable to grasp depth, while in truth he embodied it. She regretted having described him as an apple to Dexter Daugherty.

He moved fast, thought fast, and acted fast; and if Einstein was right, then at some point Duncan would be able to stop time, to crawl around indefinitely inside a single moment until he was done with it, until he had distilled from it whatever it held that he found useful.

This is who Corinne saw when she got to know Duncan Post. At her suggestion, she and Duncan had their third date outside, to catch some of the late spring warmth. They biked some of the Little Miami River Trail, suggested to her by the sweetest little old man from one of her antiquing tour groups. The biking sounded lovely, gliding along the forested path, a tunnel of green, serenaded by the sliding water, chipmunks scuttling in the underbrush just off the trail.

Their first two dates had been successes, she had told her best friend Ariel, full of conversation and attention. But she had sensed in Duncan an inchoate agitation, a desire to move. He didn't overtly fidget, but there was an energy just below his skin, and his compensation to control this energy made him seem too polite, even stiff. Her first thought would have been that he was inexperienced in dating, but by now she and Ariel had done their homework.

Months before, there had been a profile of showplace.com and its "brash young visionary" in the Sunday *Cincinnati Enquirer*. Apparently he had squired a number of local celebrities to a variety of functions and was most recently linked with the city's highest rated — and cutest, Corinne had to admit — TV anchorwoman and photographed, arms entwined, at the Mayor's Ball.

But by this third date she felt wanted. Though Duncan was nothing if not chivalrous, there was something in his conversation she could only describe as hunger. He wanted to know her, not the where's and when's of her, but the how's and why's, and Corinne knew what that passion to "try on" someone else while still being yourself was like. She suspected it was not possible, but that it was still worth the effort.

There was a difference between them, though, and she learned this from the bike date. It seemed simple enough. Neither of them owned a bicycle, and Duncan rejected her idea of renting one at the trailhead. Instead, he picked her up with two bicycles perched atop the roof rack on a brand new Land Rover.

"If we do very much of this outdoor stuff," he told her, "I figured an SUV might come in handy." Her thought of buying water bottles for the date suddenly seemed Lilliputian. She found out weeks later that he had bought not only the car, but also the bikes, the rack, even the knobby-soled cross training shoes on his feet that morning before he picked her up.

The bikes were identical, except for their frame size, and were equipped with small, computerized speedometers on the handlebars. Within minutes after they had begun riding, Corinne relishing the dappled pale-green light on the path, Duncan asked her what her speedometer read.

"12.6, no 12.8 miles per hour," she said.

He looked down at his speedometer. "How about now?" he asked again.

"About the same."

"About?"

"Well, it keeps fluctuating. Sometimes it's 12.6, sometimes 12.8."

He said nothing for a while, and Corinne got lost again in the easy rhythm, the  tires whirring on the asphalt, and the pockets of cooler air she noticed in the path's dips. Soon, however, she sensed that Duncan was trying to mirror her bike's progress, adjusting his pedaling to synchronize their speed.

At length, as their front tires had maintained a nearly perfect congruence for several hundred yards, she saw him smiling.

"Are you reading 13 even?" he said.

"I'm sorry; I'm going too slow, aren't I?"

He seemed embarrassed. "Oh no, it's not that. I just wondered."

"Well, then, no. I've got…" Corinne looked at her speedometer, and her biked weaved a bit, "looks to be 13.2."

His smile flickered, as if he'd just lost something and didn't know where to look next. "Well, I'll just have to adjust that when we stop for lunch."

Corinne's smiling at this memory flickered, too, because she realized that it was almost 7:30 and Daugherty had not yet called. Dinner could wait. She was rarely hungry anymore, anyway.

But what did this delay portend? Was there progress, perhaps even a sighting just now? She stared at the phone, willing it to ring.

At midnight, Corinne rose wearily and went to bed. Within the last hour her anxiety had been overtaken by fatigue, and her uneasy shifting on the brocaded sofa had been replaced by resignedly laying her head on the sofa's arm and drawing her body into a fetal position. She had quit looking at the traitorous phone. In the floor lay her cell phone, no bigger than a compact, and though she had never given the private investigator that number, she thought it wise to have it near her just in case. Just in case what? Well, just in case…

She didn't bother to draw the bedroom curtains. She stretched out on top of bed, still clothed. She would wait again tomorrow by the phone. Her last thought before she fell into a fitful, dreamless sleep was that this waiting would be her portion.

## CHAPTER 8

Just before Tessie exploded over the hill with something called pickle loaf—which, it turned out, was not ground up pickles in a loaf shape, but sliced bologna with bits of pickle incongruously scattered through it like cymbal clashes in a lullaby—Daylon had essentially told me that Tessie was "slow"… or that she wasn't, I could take my pick.

This was unacceptable ambiguity, especially since she was the one person who knew my real name, so the next morning I thought I'd engage her about some topic other than Flopsy and figure it out for myself.  I asked her if she'd show me around the whole house because, until my first walk with Daylon had taken me down the wide staircase and out the front door and had given me a glimpse of a formal living room dominated by an ebony baby grand piano, I had seen only "my" upstairs bedroom and the adjacent bathroom.  Even with that limited perspective, however, I had sensed the house was much larger than its number of inhabitants required.

"Sure, Harry Trueman," she said.  "What would you like to see?"

"Well, all of it, I guess."  I still couldn't adjust to speaking to this woman as I might a child.  She assumed nothing in conversation, understood nothing of sarcasm or subtlety, and seemed to have no agenda beneath the dialogue's purpose.  In fact, it dawned on me that no one I had spoken to in the Hundley family or in my short stint hawking coffee at the rest stop—and didn't that now seem another lifetime ago?—read anything beyond the literal. Sinking Creek was where irony went to die.

And in some ways I was having more difficulty adjusting to their simplistic, unvarnished method of communicating than they had in deciphering my verbal cues or body language or metaphors or out-and-out deception because they simply didn't get them. I thought it best to maintain my guard, though, in case this was part of some larger, more clever plan. People simply weren't this unabashedly transparent. Not even Tessie.

I followed her down the steps and, oddly, straight out the front door. She closed it behind us, leaving us standing on the full, covered front porch, its painted gray boards squeaking beneath us, a white wicker swing at one end swaying slightly as though someone insubstantial had just gotten up, a ghost. Then she turned again to the door, and pulled back her shoulders like a new salesman about to knock on the first appointment of her career.

Grinning at no one, or at the door itself, I suppose, she pulled open the screen door, twisted the brass lever handle, and pushed the wooden door. "After you," she said.

I went along with her tour guide charade, and thought of Corinne who, even after she knew that our lifestyle did not depend on her inconsequential income, claimed to miss her job shepherding seniors through museums devoted to steam engines, or women's art, or antique dental equipment, or other such shit. *I love that they're never too old to learn,* she'd say, or *it keeps them young,* or *you should see their eyes light up when they see an old pop bottle that reminds them of their childhood.*

It struck me, too, that there was something of Corinne in Tessie just now, just this once—maybe her gait, simultaneously hurried and dignified. Not entitlement, I thought, but a surety that each step was on comfortable ground. Of course,

Tessie knew this house and so I understood her level of confidence here; but Corinne, I knew, would walk here for the first time with the same lack of hesitation. I did ache for her, more now than even those nights under the bridge, and this ache made me resent her more.

Tessie showed me the kitchen, the laundry room, mud room, and some other bedrooms downstairs—though she didn't go in any of them, just pointed toward the doorways and identified them: *Poppie's* or *Della's when she was little* or *Della and Daylon's*.

It was a nice house, and though I told her so, acting as interested as I could, Tessie never really responded to my compliments. "So, where have you and Flopsy been sleeping since I've taken your bedroom hostage?"

My mentioning the rabbit pleased her. She pulled him from her jacket pocket, raised him to her face, and rubbed him across a cheek as she might a tissue. By now Flopsy had doubled in size, looked like he might actually survive, and rather than struggling at this constant handling of Tessie's, hung limply in her hands. He was either resigned to this overwhelming outpouring of interspecies affection, or hell, maybe he loved her, too.

Without provocation, she held the rabbit toward me.

"I really couldn't, Tessie. I've never even held a baby," I said, and as soon as I did, I realized that was true. I had never held a baby, and until now, that thought had never occurred to me in sentence form. Saying it made it so. Not that I had ever cared to, even now. This was not a longing, just a fact. But it also occurred to me that there probably weren't a great many thirty year-olds who had never at least held one, a nephew perhaps, or a friend's kid, even if you just held it while its parent put on a jacket.

I held out my hands as if receiving a tossed ball.

"Relax, Harry Trueman," she said and waited for me to draw my arms back to my sides. "No, make a cradle...like this." With her right hand Tessie manipulated my arms into a shape she deemed appropriate to accept Flopsy. She placed the rabbit into the crook of my elbow.

He lay there, as inert and mute as if he were stuffed with rags. I, too, stood motionless, and I guess it was this tableau that made Tessie begin to laugh. It, like her voice and mannerisms, was the laugh of a child, bright and unaffected. I had told jokes at cocktail parties, in meetings with clients, to open talks to civic groups, but I had never heard laughs to rival this. I hated being laughed at, but this did not seem derisive. And just when it seemed to fade naturally, I started to laugh.

Mine wasn't really much of a laugh, however—more a guttural chuckle that came out in short bursts like prairie dog chatter. It was a foreign sound, and it made my chest hurt at first. These were muscles that had not been exercised in quite some time. At my first bark, Tessie's laugh began again, and this in turn tickled me more. We laughed until mine turned into a coughing spasm, and I leaned into the closed door behind me for support.

The door wasn't latched, and I tumbled backward through it, thudding on my ass because I didn't want to use my hands to break my fall and drop Flopsy in the process. I wheezed now in laughter, able to make only an airless, squeaky noise. I rolled onto my side and released the rabbit who went deeper into the room we had fallen into, moving just away from me by stretching his front paws, then leisurely pulling his back legs forward like a languorous Slinky toy.

I didn't hear Tessie but knew that she must be enveloped in laughter so intense that she, too, had lost her breath. When at length I regained mine, my ribs and cheeks aching, I labored to my feet and poked my head out of the door and back into the hallway. There stood Tessie, no longer laughing, but pale and frightened; afraid, it seemed, even to look around the door facing and into the room I had fallen into.

"Please, Mr. Trueman, get Flopsy and let's go upstairs and I'll show you the rest of the house."

I knew immediately what must be wrong. Another look in the room confirmed it. There was a small twin bed, a scuffed nightstand, a red toybox with a cowboy twirling a lariat overhead stenciled on its lid, and a coat tree leaved in baseball caps. A tall Washington Redskins trash can held several aluminum baseball bats. I had stumbled into Tessie's real bedroom, and she was embarrassed by its puerility. Clearly the upstairs bedroom I had been staying in was Tessie's in name only.

I went back in, scooped up Flopsy, and got out quickly. "Tessie, I'm sorry. I really am. I didn't meant to... I really didn't know this was your bedroom. I......"

Before I could finish telling her that it was a perfectly fine room, that it seemed more like her than the one upstairs, before I could say anything that would erase the horrified look from her face, Tessie snatched Flopsy from me and hurried down the hallway toward the front door.

She turned her head as she walked, and the fear I saw in her face infused her voice, too. There was something else besides, an anger maybe. "That's not my bedroom, Duncan Post Harry Trueman. It's none of your beeswax, but I sleep in the barn."

The carpet muffled her footsteps until she turned the corner, and I heard her tennis shoes squeak on the hardwood of the formal living room. I stood in the middle of the long hallway, the kitchen behind me, the front door ahead, with bedroom doors on either side, and felt as lost as the first night I spent under my bridge.

There I stood, with much more room than if I were between Scylla and Charybdis, yet still unable to go in either direction. Indecision paralyzed me, but just as I decided to go toward the living room, two sounds suspended me again—opposing magnetic fields. At once I heard the back door open—someone coming into the kitchen from outside—and simultaneously the clinking of piano keys from the living room.

I know it was irrational, but I felt guilty for something and hoped that whoever was coming into the kitchen would forgive me, would absolve me of any inadvertent sin I had just committed with Tessie. I hoped it would be Daylon.

The footsteps in the kitchen stopped briefly as if their owner was listening, then picked up speed. Summerset Hundley turned into the hallway as the piano music increased in volume and pace. He stopped, looked at me, then at the open bedroom door I stood beside, and something clicked behind his gray eyes. He slowed when he got to me, and with one hand closed the door gently and patted my shoulder with the other.

"I'm sorry, Mr. Trueman," he said and slid past me down the hall toward the piano's sounds.

What for, I thought. Shit, what for? What had *he* done? What had *I* done, and why didn't I just get the hell out of this loony bin now that I was strong enough?

He disappeared around the corner, his steps slowing as though he didn't want to startle Tessie, and I realized I knew the song she was playing, or trying to play, rather. Though the timing was irregular, halting, Tessie was playing the right-handed half of Chopsticks, the only song most people ever learned on the piano before they gave up and allowed it to become a dust gathering set decoration in their living rooms.

It was the only piece of new furniture that Corinne had put in my living room after we were married. She brought nothing else from her cramped apartment. She played well, at least to me she did, though she denigrated her ability whenever I complimented her. "You know music like I know computers," she'd said. Maybe she was right, but we would both learn, I told her. So, I taught her how to set up and access an email account; she taught me the left-hand part of Chopsticks. Both of us were fascinated.

I didn't feel comfortable going into the kitchen alone — this would have seemed a guilty gesture, a hiding — and going upstairs to my bedroom required that I pass through the living room to get to the staircase, but that was the better choice.

I eased through the broad doorway into that room whose sterility stood in sharp contrast to the warmth of the rest of the house. The furnishings were expensive but sparse: a claw-footed divan with a muted brocaded pattern, and two matching chairs, the kind that are much more handsome than comfortable, arranged in a sitting area around a cold marble fireplace, a couple of occasional tables. The piano, behind the divan and facing the picture window, was the only other piece of furniture in the room, so it didn't take long to survey it.

Flopsy was winding his way through Summerset's legs while the old man stood behind Tessie, whose right-handed playing of Chopsticks had taken on a manic pace while her body rocked forward and back, out of time with her notes. Her tangerine hair flew with her rocking, erratic as a tossing kite, and on one such soar, Summerset caught a palmful, covered it quickly with his second hand, as one might gently capture a butterfly, and patted it. "There, there, Tessie girl. It's going to be okay. It is okay. I'm here, I'm always here for my little girl," he said, and repeated "I'm here, little girl" over and over again.

At length both her playing and rocking slowed until her half of Chopsticks was not only recognizable but infectious. Summerset let his palmful of hair sift sandlike through his fingers, and quietly turned to me. Though, of course, he had known all along that I had been there—and though on some level I knew he knew this—his facing me made me feel voyeuristic, somehow dirty. He smiled, though, a grim, resigned smile, and mouthed *she's okay*, and nodded slowly. I don't know which of us the nod was to assure.

He turned back to the piano and slid onto the bench. Tessie took no note, simply continued playing the piece. As it came back around to its beginning, Summerset placed his left hand on the keys and began playing the other half. He missed a note here and there, and occasionally his rhythm didn't match Tessie's, who by now was playing perfectly, but within a few rounds they were in synch.

I caught myself moving the fingers of my left hand and playing my half of the music. I may have missed a note or two, too, but no one hears an air piano.

Summerset slipped his right arm around Tessie's shoulder. I expected this child-woman to tilt and rest her head on her father's arm, exhausted by whatever trauma she was feeling, but she didn't. She continued her robotic playing, and I wondered why her hand wasn't cramping when mine already was.

I shook mine to loosen the tension, half expecting Summerset's portion of the song to falter because I'd quit the motions, and looked again around the room. Out of the corner of my eye, a long tube of fur oozed languidly toward the fireplace. Flopsy seemed as aimless as air, intent only on getting away from the piano's noise, but in no real hurry to do so. After what seemed like an hour because of the rabbit's torpid pace, he reached the fireplace's opening, crawled in, and nestled himself into a ball, presumably to sleep.

By some silent consent, the music slowed, became almost elegant. The whole scene was a perverse fairy tale, and if it were a painting would have seemed wholly pastoral: the dutiful daughter and doting pere at the piano, enjoying an evening diversion, the family pet (albeit a rabbit) curled cutely inside the fireplace. The thought of this as art made me sense something else about the room, something not so readily apparent at first glance, though I'm sure it would have been Corinne's first comment. The walls were bare. For such a formal room, there was no art of any kind on the walls, nothing that identified or defined the tastes, beliefs, or hopes of the inhabitants of the house. The tables had no vases or figurines either, and this was not in character with the rest of the house as I had seen it—cluttered with knick-knacks of indeterminate, but assuredly little, value.

Then Flopsy inadvertently led me to a quaking discovery. He shifted positions, and as I watched him resettle, I looked up at the mantel above him. I've no idea why I didn't notice it before, but I guess because I expected a picture on a mantel it simply didn't register the first time I had scanned the room. I had been more taken with what *wasn't* in here than with what *was*. It was a horizontal 11 x 14 inside a simple gilt frame: the family portrait, I could tell from here. But something didn't add up. I walked over toward the fireplace. Flopsy opened her eyes at my approach but closed them just as quickly. Behind me Chopsticks continued.

In the picture stood Summerset in a navy blue suit and blue and silver striped tie, smiling broadly. His winter gray eyes were exactly the same, and his hair, though a few shades darker than now, could still be called gray. He rested his hands on the shoulders of a seated woman who was obviously Della and Tessie's mother, with Della's round face and, incredibly, the same tangerine hair of the younger daughter. The daughters flanked her, Della probably fifteen and Tessie's freckles and missing-toothed smile betraying her as nine or ten. All this is what I would have expected from a family portrait made in a church or a mall, but here was what startled me: standing with Tessie, arms linked with hers, was a boy whose freckles, open grin, and buzz cut shadow of citrus was the mirror image of the girl.

That evening after dinner, a dinner that I rushed through and that Tessie took out onto the front porch to eat in the swing, I initiated the walk with Daylon.

"If you reckon you're up to it, I reckon it'll give me an excuse not to help red up the dishes," he said and winked at Della.

Della, though, had already begun to clear the table and fill the sink with water. The kitchen had a dishwasher, was, in fact, a very modern kitchen with gleaming, seemingly new, electric appliances, but I'd never seen them used. She did not respond to Daylon's playfulness, a first in my brief tenure here. Summerset, too, had been preoccupied at dinner, making inane conversation about travel plaza business. Both got up from the table often to "go see if Tessie needed anything," and seemed relieved whenever they heard the porch swing's high-pitched squeaking. A shrink would have been my suggestion, but no one asked.

It was the first time I had not felt like a guest.

"I guess you've got some questions," Daylon said after I huffed my way to the hilltop behind the house. I leaned forward and put my hands on my knees. I could only nod assent just then, so he continued. "I want you to know first off that I wasn't trying to hide anything from you, Harry. It's just that you dropping into our laps like this has caused some questions, too, and I didn't have any inkling how long you'd be sticking around. But Summerset told me, Della too, not to go poking around in your business, and I trust their intuition."

I regained my breath and straightened up. I wasn't prepared to turn this into a quid pro quo interrogation, I had too much to hide, but I had been lulled into believing that these people were so fundamentally different from me that they simply lacked the curiosity about others that was common in my circles. This, I had come to believe, was just a "country" trait, and I supposed it was called trust, or gullibility, depending on which side of the pasture you called home. I confess, it had been a gift to me, but Daylon's admission told me the gift might come with strings.

"Summerset has this ability to look at a person and see something about him that he might not even see about himself," he said, ominously, I thought.

I could tell he was about to launch into one of his Summerset-as-myth homilies, and ordinarily I would have allowed it to run its course, but I had gotten the point already in the last few weeks. Admittedly, I found much to admire in the man, but right now I just didn't have the patience for it. I interrupted. "What's Tessie's story?"

"You're ready to separate the cream from the clabber, aren't you?" he said, and though I had no idea what the hell that meant, I nodded.

We had crested the hill. Daylon paused and turned back to face the house and barn far below us. Instinctively, I did the same. "Let's keep walking then," he said, and we slipped over the hill and toward the shade of the forest at the far end of one of the broad hillside pastures. Daylon's pace was not hurried, but the natural length of his stride caused me difficulty in keeping up. "Watch the manure," he said once, as if I hadn't already been doing so. And then, pointing at a particularly impressive pile, "That's worth ten cents of any man's money."

I wanted to tell him that for every ten times somebody simply clicked on the startup.com website, I made ten cents without having to shovel anything.

When we reached the forest's fringe, I could make out a worn path snaking into the gloom. There was room for us to walk abreast, and Daylon slowed to allow me to do so. Within a few yards the forest's cool air raised chill bumps on my arms.

"Tessie's 'story' ain't just hers. It belongs to Summerset and Della, and me, too, I suppose, and I figure all of Sinking Creek holds some claim to it if you was to ask them," he said as prelude and continued walking, treading nimbly over roots and sticks that cluttered the path. "And, yes, she does sleep in the barn, but that's not exactly how it sounds."

I didn't care how it sounded, other than as cruel punishment, perhaps, for her occasional running away, and it surely didn't square with the patience I had seen the family exhibit for her eccentricities. I could only assume, then, that it must have been Tessie's choice. "Don't you think that's carrying this Tessie, girl-of-the-woods, act a bit far? Seems to me, it borders on sadism."

"You're going to have to give me some space to tell it right, Harry. It don't go in a straight line."

I felt chastised, though Daylon's voice hadn't really displayed irritation.

"The bedroom in the barn is nice, every bit as nice as any in the main house, and with a bathroom. Me and Summerset built them especially for her."

"But why?"

"Not a straight line, remember?"

With my thumb and forefinger, I made a zipping motion across my lips. A breeze stirred the treetops, though we couldn't feel it. No longer chilled, I was starting to sweat again. The path kept bending and rising.

"Tessie had a twin brother, but I figure you know that already from the picture in the piano room. Name was Andy. They were as alike as any two kids could be, their hair, features, voice, everything. Both loved ketchup but hated tomatoes. Neither of them scared of thunder or snakes. In fact, I'm not sure neither one of them was scared of anything. School lets out in spring, both of them heads out into the woods all day and come back in the afternoon for lunch with crawdads in their pockets and baby critters of every kind. Once brought home a skunk so young it was still blind and not old enough to spray them. Loved school, too, and had plenty of friends there. Used to make Della proud because, well, because Della wasn't so popular."

He paused long enough to jab a finger into my ribs and chuckle. "Me, neither, truth be told. Navy's what give me any education I got. Touched up my mechanic's skills to where I think I can open my own shop pretty soon."

I would have broken my oath of silence and said something socially appropriate, but I didn't want to be admonished again. And the path was steepening.

"Anyway, only real difference between them was a natural one. The summer they turned eight, somebody at school asked Andy to play organized baseball, some kind of peewee league before Little League. Didn't ask Tessie, though girls were allowed and she was probably as good an athlete as any boy in her grade. She wasn't hurt, didn't pout, or didn't show it if she did. She just asked Maude — Mrs. Hundley — if she'd teach her a song or two on their piano while Andy was away at practice. This piano was Maude's pride and joy, and she could play. Played for the Baptist Church on Sundays and Wednesdays and always wanted Della and the twins to show their own interest in it. Della's fingers were a bit too chunky, though, and the twins wouldn't light long enough."

I felt the quick stab of a need to say something chivalrous, to defend Della from a truth delivered by her own husband, but there was so clearly no trace of malice from him that I dismissed it as nothing more than a lack of varnish on Daylon's part. In fact, I could envision Della saying the same thing about herself.

He went on. "Wasn't long, Tessie had outgrown what Maude could teach her. She wasn't better than Maude, not yet anyway, but Maude was self-taught, too, so she didn't really know how to answer some of Tessie's questions, or teach her how to read the notes. And more than anything, Tessie wanted to know what the notes meant. Maude told her, 'Girl, you're wearing me out. I hear a hymn enough, I figure out how to play it. That's all I can tell you.'"

To the left of the trail, some small animal scuttled. Daylon picked up a fallen branch, broke it in half by stomping on it, and handed me one of the halves. I had a fleeting, ridiculous thought that he wanted me to play pirates and cross swords, or chase down the scuttling animal. It was, however, a makeshift walking stick.

"So she quit after learning Chopsticks?" I said.

"Goodness, no. Summerset hired the music teacher at the high school to give her lessons. She outgrew him pretty soon, too. Told the Hundleys they had a prodigy on their hands, and they was doing her a disservice if they didn't find her a better teacher than him real quick. Chopsticks was what Tessie taught Andy to play. Summer evenings they'd play that for what must have been hours on end. Me and Della was courting then, probably tenth grade, so we sat with Mr. and Mrs. Hundley on the porch and listened to the twins play it on and on. It's like they used it to catch up with each other. Andy would tell her how baseball practice went—who swung like a girl, who cried when he got hit by the ball—and Tessie'd tell him what she'd learned to play, and all the while, Chopsticks went round and round. Sometimes they'd speed it up, sometimes slow it down, all by some unspoken signal. They could make that one simple song sound like a dozen different ones."

I needed to rest, my lungs sang in my ears, but Daylon showed no effects of the exertion. When I pointed to a downed log, though, he nodded.

The log was more comfortable than it looked, having become spongy with time. Daylon noted that we were in a stand of beech trees and motioned upward with his chin at the canopy, alive with squirrels. Looking up at them made me dizzy, and I wished for a cool drink. The uniform green tunnel that had led us up to this height was now broken by some yellowing leaves in the understory, and it occurred to me that I didn't know today's date, just that the Fourth of July now seemed like a long time ago. Cincinnati even further. "Fall's coming," I said, hoping that might make Daylon mention something to indicate the date. Asking him would have seemed a weakness.

"Always does."

I wanted to hear more about Tessie, but his earlier admonition about impatience prevented my asking for it. I couldn't ask for the date, couldn't ask for him to continue, I couldn't ask him what he really knew about me — I was as impotent as a child. In fact, if he were to suddenly disappear, I'm not sure I could have found my way out of these woods. Our path had intersected a number of others, and only Daylon's surety of step had guided me. Like a backseat passenger, I hadn't paid attention to any landmarks along the way.

"So, Tessie's an autistic savant?" I said, thinking this was surely an innocuous way to recharge the conversation, to redirect Daylon, who seemed to have forgotten that he was in the midst of a story. I was sorry now that I'd needed to rest. It was as though he could only talk while walking.

He frowned. "I don't know anything about that, Harry."

"Did you ever see *Rain Man* with Dustin Hoffman?"

Daylon's eyes lit up, and in a flat voice that belied the animation of his expression, he said, "It's definitely not my underwear," and then "Of course I'm an excellent driver."

"You got it. Is Tessie like that, a genius at the piano but a little…slow, I guess in other ways? How about Andy, was he the same?" By now I knew the story would include something tragic about both Andy and Maude—they weren't around and had never been mentioned, so I assumed their absence was a painful presence in the lives of this family. But we all lose people, so I wanted some insight into those who were still here, those people who had some impact on me.

Daylon stood up and arched his back. "Let's get going, Harry. You've got it all wrong. Tessie's story takes a turn."

If he had been a book, I'd have turned to the last page.

"I told you Tess and Andy were as normal as any other kids, probably smarter than most. Not straight A's, but good enough. Better'n Della, she'll tell you," he said. Then his voice strained slightly and became more deliberate. I liked his voice, even found his poor grammar acceptable, almost endearing, but now his tone plummeted with gravity. "One day, the summer they was ten, Andy come home from baseball practice all upset because he hadn't played so good, I suppose. Anyway, he was moping around and Maude made him go lay down in his room until he could quit bad-mouthing hisself. Neither Maude nor Summerset let their kids feel sorry for theirselves, never. Told them there'd be enough people in this world who could make them feel bad without doing it to theirself. Summerset was out cutting hay, or he'd a busted Andy's butt hisself.

"Well, Maude got to feeling bad for being hard on him,

and she saw that Tessie was upset for him, too, so she went into his room and laid down on the bed with him to pet on him and talk him out of his mood. Awhile later, Tessie looked in and saw them both asleep and thought she'd make some chocolate chip cookies cause now everybody was happy and cookies was a way to celebrate that. That's how a ten-year-old thinks, ain't it, Harry?" he said.

I thought the question might not be rhetorical, but really, I didn't know how they thought, so I babbled. "Ten year-olds might be onto something, you know. Nothing wrong with using cookies to make you happy."

"Dog shit, Harry, happy people don't know they're happy," he said, not harshly, but I felt slapped nonetheless. I had heard him curse around some of his fire department buddies, but rarely around his family, or me, for that matter. "It's not 'til you ain't happy that you ever knew you were. The cookies ain't the point."

There it was. I knew this little burg held something besides ice cream socials, July Fourth parades, smiling home-coming queens, apple butter recipes. I wasn't upset by Daylon's words. No, in fact, I relished that hint of anger, even of darkness. These were emotions I could fathom. I was on my turf again.

"Sorry," he said, thinking I might be offended, and took off his baseball cap as though the apology needed a more formal gesture.

I waved my hand in a no-harm-done signal.

"No, really," he added.

I patted his shoulder. It was the first time I had initiated a touch on any of these people. "It's okay. Go on."

He did.

And when he finished, when at length we stepped from the black woods into the lighter night of the open pasture with the distant lights of the farmhouse and barn as beacons no bigger than fireflies, I knew I'd be staying in Sinking Creek a while longer, and I knew, too, I couldn't have articulated why.

## CHAPTER 9 — CORINNE

Corinne's subsequent interviews with Dexter Daugherty, either by phone or in his imposing office, took on a guarded sameness. He probed, gently at first so that she was capable of parrying any overtly intrusive questions, but he soon became more aggressive. It was then that she claimed other appointments or lack of knowledge to end the questioning.

His exasperation would reveal itself only in what became his standard parting words to her: "It's your money, Mrs. Post."

Corinne knew that Dexter Daugherty knew a great deal more about her and Duncan than he let on. Much of their married life was lived in the public eye. How could it not be? They weren't Brad and Jennifer, but Duncan was a local celebrity at least, and their marriage and philanthropy had often made the social section of the Cincinnati Enquirer. And when dot-coms began flaming out at an alarming rate, both Duncan and his partner, Richard Rice, had been interviewed several times about how showplace.com was doing.

Fine, just fine; in fact, business is increasing — not at last year's rate, but hey, we'll take it, given the climate, they had always said. Duncan had been wrong. Richard had been lying. Corinne simply didn't know. She was having enough trouble in this new world where her job was to attend "functions."

Duncan hadn't told her he wanted her to quit her job

guiding tours, but she felt that "retiring" was something she could contribute to the marriage. Odd that doing nothing would be seen as a contribution, but Duncan's pleasure with her decision was obvious. It was true, as he'd said, they didn't need her financial portion, and the job took her away for a couple of weeks a month, so she saw the wisdom in her decision.

Her hope had been to be a partner in Duncan's life, personally of course, but surely there could be a professional role she could play, too. Richard Rice seemed to think so. At every turn he encouraged Duncan to increase Corinne's visibility. "Allow her to do some presentations for us, Dunc. She's a helluva lot better looking than you, and almost as pretty as me," he'd said often.

Once, at dinner, when she mentioned in passing that she was a bit bored, Duncan relayed Richard's idea.

"Eye candy? I don't think so," she snorted.

"I don't think you give yourself enough credit."

"Do you want me to?" she said. She had thought Duncan was being facetious, not about the idea, but about Richard's reasoning behind it; that Duncan, too, saw Richard's idea as patronizing.

"I think you could be a real asset," he said, echoing a favorite phrase of his partner's.

Corinne held onto his eyes for an extra beat. "I'll think about it," she said. But it was that word, "asset," that she thought about into the night.

Like her interviews with Daugherty, her life since Duncan left had settled—and wasn't that a paradox, she thought—into a routine. Cincinnati's Julys and Augusts were exercises in dampness. A haze rose from the Ohio River and spread like a wet tissue over the towns along its banks. The sky was wrung of its blue and adopted the color of the river's concrete floodwall. People reading summer romance novels in the shades of their weekend backyards found the pages sticking together, warping slightly. No one stayed dry. Summer heat didn't so much blaze into Cincinnati as it wept on it.

At their twice-weekly lunches, which Corinne both anticipated and dreaded, she knew exactly what Ariel would say. And she did, as soon as they were seated: "We'll be sweating like hogs before the salads get here, honey. Why don't we eat inside today?"

Corinne smiled weakly and traced a line through the condensation on her water glass. Ariel was her longest-standing friend, if she didn't count anyone from high school.

"It's not so bad today," Corinne lied. "It's nice here in the shade. I don't like feeling cooped up in the summer."

Ariel wet her napkin, then picked her long blonde hair off her shoulders and rubbed the nape of her neck with the cold cloth. "Oh, I don't mind, Rinnie, not at all. It's just like dining al fresco on the front porch of hell." She laughed then leaned forward and rubbed the condensation on Corinne's glass, too. The streams she caused pooled on the glass's base like Corinne's had, then soaked into the white tablecloth. "You know you're the only friend I'll suffer heat rash for, don't you?"

This was why Corinne loved Ariel. No judging, no coddling, no prying. They both knew Corinne chose to eat here so she could scrutinize the passing parade on Vine, hoping ludicrously that Duncan would walk by. Too, they both knew that before the shared cherry cheesecake, Corinne would tell her the latest non-news from Dexter Daugherty. They had known each other for six years, having met as novice tour guides and had bonded as they fretted over what to do about the old guy in the back of their first bus together who had urinated in his pants and was too embarrassed to disembark.

Corinne loved her because she had not laughed about him later. She loved her because Ariel had told the rest of the group that Mr. Pimminy was a retired navy mechanic and he was staying behind to help them with some engine trouble. Mr. Pimminy, it turned out, had lost his wife six months before. The trip had been Mrs. Pimminy's idea, and she had made him promise he would go even if she couldn't. And Ariel loved Corinne because she had cried with Mr. Pimminy.

The waiter brought their salads, refilled their water glasses.

"I'm sabotaging the whole search, I suppose," Corinne said after the waiter left. "I answer his questions as vaguely as possible; I don't volunteer any substantial background information—certainly not about Richard—and the one thing Daugherty seems to want to know most—*why* I want Duncan found if it's simply a case of marital discord—I don't answer so truthfully either."

Ariel speared a grape tomato, its splatter nearly reaching Corinne's plate. "It's getting expensive?"

"I'm sure it is; it would have to be. I'm not necessarily worried about it yet. Showplace.com is dead—it was dying when this whole mess began—but Duncan was a great money manager, so we have plenty. Plenty of …assets," she said and scrunched her nose at hearing herself use that word. "I could go back to guiding again, just to stay busy, if you guys would have me. In fact, I wish I'd never stopped."

"Love to have you, love," Ariel said. "The Amish Country Ramble's just not the same without you. What is that, a smile?" She went on. "You know me, Rinnie, I don't want to know anything you don't want to tell me, but I've got the same question as Daugherty: why do you want to find Duncan? Seems to me, he's just taking some time to himself, and he'll either come back to try to reconcile or to divorce you. Either way, the next move is really his, isn't it?"

"I wish it were that simple. And I don't mind the waiting; it's not that." As soon as Corinne said this, she wondered if it were really true.

"Do you want him back? Is this a Harlequin Romance?" Ariel said. "I know you well enough to know you didn't marry him for money, and I know you don't want him back because you think this is a fairy tale, so the marriage — like mine, honey, like everybody's — was something in between. Good and bad, up and down. Yours was just lived at a little faster pace, and in a little better neighborhood, than most people's."

Corinne said nothing. She would let Ariel throw out more options until she, Corinne, felt that one of them was correct.

The waiter returned with their club sandwiches. Since Corinne had only pushed her salad around on its plate, he hesitated, stumped about where to put her sandwich on the café table. She made no move to make room for it. "Was there something wrong with the salad, Ma'am?" he said, the sandwich plate still poised expectantly.

To Corinne this suddenly seemed the most difficult question she had ever been asked. All she could do was stare blankly at the poor boy. Had he simply asked if she was finished with the salad, she could have nodded, and he would have replaced the plate and left. But now she would owe him some explanation. *The salad was fine, I'm just not very hungry*, she could say, but then he might ask if she really wanted the club sandwich. Or he might wonder why she had ordered anything at all. He could take the sandwich off her bill, he might say. Lunch had become a minefield. Answering this question was fraught with danger, yet it seemed to hold a key to what may follow.

"She's finished," Ariel said, rescuing her, and once the

waiter left, she leaned forward to grab Corinne's gaze. "I thought I'd lost you there," she said.

Corinne straightened her posture and smiled animatedly. "Sorry, I just kind of zoned out for a second. Not getting much sleep," she said. But a part of her wanted to go back in time—just a minute back—to see how she would have answered the question about the salad if she had a second chance.

"I know, hon. You need company. Want me to come spend the night? A couple of nights? Thyme won't mind. He can leave his beer can on the end table without a coaster, and I won't be there to nag him. He'll love it."

"Ariel, don't lie to me. Does what I did count as having an affair?"

Ariel didn't immediately answer. She continued chewing, even taking another bite of her sandwich before lowering it back onto its plate. Corinne wasn't looking at her, looked instead at the busy street. Finally, Ariel dabbed her napkin at her lips. "So that's it, isn't it, Rinnie? It's guilt. That big, bad monster, Guilt, has crept into your psyche. That's a good thing, I suspect. It means you love Duncan."

Corinne's eyes broke away from the noonday downtown sidewalk. The writhing crowd, like carp squirming for dropped popcorn, dizzied her. Everyone looked like Duncan, then didn't in the same instant. "I never did *not* love him," she said.

Her friend held her palms up. "I'm not implying that you didn't; I'm just saying this reinforces it. But I have to tell you, I'm the worst person in the world to ask about relationships. I've always felt they're like everything else in this world: they have a beginning, a middle, and an end. Don't you remember mine and Thyme's vows? We had that till death did us part crapola taken out. He believes the same way I do, thank God. We just hope we recognize the end at the same time, but we're cool with it even if we don't. *That's* love." Ariel picked up her sandwich for a bite and motioned for Corinne to do the same.

Corinne did, though the sandwich seemed bland, the act of eating an inconvenience. She did not see herself as a romantic, nor did she view Ariel as calloused. Had she been wrong about both? As a bridesmaid in Ariel's wedding, she had indeed noticed the non-traditional phrasing of the ceremony, but her friend was decidedly non-traditional anyway. Corinne supposed it was Thyme's macho idea of hedging his bet, or maybe it was a way for both of them to assume immortality. She didn't ever connect it to a shared philosophy.

The waiter was conspicuously less attentive since the salad plate confusion. She would leave him a bigger than average tip to make up for it, but for now she'd love to have him interrupt this conversation to see if they needed anything.

Ariel went on. "Thyme and I are children of flower-children, Sweetie. Hence our names. Didn't you ever wonder? We don't necessarily subscribe to the idea of good karma/bad karma, or communal living and shared bathrooms, but maybe that free love concept is in our genes. Not that we actively look, nor are we swingers—that's too '70's, too disco—and we won't screw around with anyone else, at least not physically..."

*Where was that waiter?*

"...but when either of us decides that it's not still working for us, that it's keeping us from maximizing our life potential, then we'll split."

Corinne interrupted. "Then why..."

"Get married? I knew you'd ask that. Of course you would. But you know something? I could have asked you the same thing. You're as unconventional as I am, just in different ways," Ariel's voice was without derision or sarcasm or judgment. It encompassed all tones and none. It didn't preach, but Corinne felt mildly deprecated, nonetheless.

"Maybe I didn't buy into the white picket fence, the Pottery Barn kids, and the golden retriever myth, but I married Duncan Post thinking it would last until, well, until death did us part," she defended.

At last the waiter appeared, and Corinne could see the wariness in his slouch. "You ladies ready for dessert, or should I get your checks?"

He was, she noticed for the first time, exceptionally good-looking in a dark-haired, skater-punk way. His tongue was pierced—how could she have missed the clicking sound when he talked—and she wondered how many tattoos his crisp white long-sleeved shirt hid.

Ariel scooted one of the two empty chairs away from the table with her sandaled foot. "Sit down for a second, can you…" she squinched her eyes to look at his nametag, "…Brian?"

Corinne fired a warning look across Ariel's bow. She chose not to notice.

"Well, you see, that kind of puts me in a bind," he said.

Ariel placed both elbows on the table and clasped her fingers for a chin rest. Her eyes fluttered, reminding Corinne of a doe. "How so?"

"On the one hand, we're not supposed to sit down on the job. On the complete opposite hand, we're all about making sure the customers achieve a kind of dining nirvana. So, we're supposed to honor all reasonable requests." He clearly enjoyed her flirting.

Ariel knew she had already won this spar. "I can assure you we won't have reached nirvana until you give us a couple of minutes of your time."

Brian didn't know if the two women were taking the

first step towards fulfilling some Mrs. Robinson fantasy, or they simply wanted detailed dessert information. Either way, it was both a justifiable way to sit for a second, a slight thumbing of the nose at authority.

Ariel unleashed an assault of body language in the waiter's direction. If it were possible to make-out with someone without actually touching them, then Ariel was doing so. And immediately Corinne knew why and what it meant.

"You go to college?" Ariel said.

"Xavier."

"What's your major?"

Corinne wanted the foreplay to stop. *Just get on with it, girl.*

"Undecided, right now. I'm looking at something in business." Ariel made a sour face. "Or philosophy," he added.

"I guess you college kids know a lot about computers, don't you? I mean, you have to use them for schoolwork and games and all that riding around on the, what's it called, the interweb?" Ariel's eyelid fluttering increased. Corinne thought her head might levitate.

"The internet," Brian corrected.

Under the table, Corinne stretched her leg to kick her friend. Ariel did not jump. Ariel was as facile on a computer as any hacker. Much of the work both of them had in the tour business involved computer time.

Brian, obviously comfortable now, continued. "Dude, I spend half my life on a computer. It's my generation's entertainment center."

"What do you do on it?"

"Well, besides school stuff, stuff any typewriter can do, I buy things, blog and read blogs, email — you know what that is, right?" he said without waiting for a reply, certain of the term's ubiquity, "go places, check out cool sites about my favorite bands, IM my friends.  Just generally stay connected."

"Stay connected?  Without ever really talking to or see-ing another person?"  Corinne was certain Brian didn't catch Ariel's sarcasm.

"That's right.  It's a brave new world out there," Brian said and sat back in his seat as if he'd just won a debate.

Corinne looked back out onto Vine Street at the jostling crowd, then up into the air.  How did Brian's concept of con-nection take place?  Was there a vaporous world just above the tangible where these charges, these impulses of people, fit better than in a face-to-face world?  No need for vanity in an online world.  But if that were true, why would Brian pierce his tongue or tattoo his body?  Eventually would anyone ever need to "see" anyone?  Was this the brave new world?

Meanwhile, Ariel was having a great time.  She leaned forward, chin still cupped in her finger nest, until she was well inside Brian's personal space.  He didn't seem to mind.  "I've heard you can have sex on the internet," she purred.  "How is that possible?"

"That's not only possible, that's preferable.  I can name ten, twelve, sites off the top of my head where you can go en-gage in the pleasure of the virtual carnal world.  Some are just chat room fluff, full of perverts and predators.  Twelve year olds or 50 year olds; not much in between.  But there's some software out there that let's you actually do it.  Virtually, that is. Some of it is very, very realistic. Connoisseur stuff."  Brian looked around to see if a headwaiter might be looking for him.

Corinne wanted to stop this train wreck.  But she knew she'd have to see its conclusion.

Ariel was deft.  She could have kept the poor waiter in his chair until he lost his job, but she had guided the conversa-tion toward its intended target.  She would let both Brian and Corinne off the hook very shortly.

"Why do you say it's *preferable* to physical sex?"

Brian looked at Ariel, then to Corinne and back. "Just think: no risk of STD's, you can be whoever you want, have sex with whoever that person wants to be, whoever they've created on the screen, and believe me they're always hot looking, then say goodbye without having to call tomorrow. No muss, no fuss."

"But it's not really sex, is it? Two people aren't really touching, are they? And please don't give me the mental picture that you're sitting in front of a computer screen masturbating. You're not, are you?" Ariel said.

Brian grinned. "I'm not a pervert. It doesn't replace sex; it's just a different kind. But no, you're right, there aren't two people touching each other."

Corinne stood to excuse herself to the restroom. There was something like sex in this very conversation.

Ariel released Brian from her gaze, untangled her fingers, and sat back in her chair, too. Before Corinne could take a step toward the restroom, Ariel said, "So, it's just pixels having sex with other pixels."

Brian seemed surprised that a computer novice had used the term pixels. "I suppose that's one way you could look at it."

"I suppose," Ariel said, looking pointedly toward Corinne. "I think we'll have a piece of cherry cheesecake now. Two forks."

## CHAPTER 10

The morning after my walk with Daylon, Tessie left. No one, except me, seemed particularly surprised, and though Summerset and Daylon bent over backwards to assure me it wasn't my fault, I felt responsible. Della wasn't quite so magnanimous, and as I came down the stairs for breakfast, I was sure I had heard her say the word "snooping" to Daylon.

It was Della who had discovered Tessie's absence. "I knew as soon as I come into the kitchen to fix breakfast she was gone," she said, setting a plate of biscuits in the center of the table with a bit too much vigor. The plate spiraled a bit before settling. "And it's not a good time to be gone, neither. Nights are getting cold."

I didn't know what to say, or whether to say anything at all. Neither Daylon nor Summerset spoke either, just passed the biscuit plate around the table. I noticed, though, that instead of taking two or three biscuits, as was their custom, they each took only one. I followed suit.

"Gravy's lumpy. I didn't stir it enough. But it'll eat," Della said, continuing her trips from the stove to the table and back, putting bowls and plates on the wooden table with force. Each clack sounded like a judge's gavel. "Apple or peach, Mr. Trueman?"

"I'm sorry?" I said.

Strands of her brown hair had worked loose from Della's normally tight beehive. Dark half moons pooled under her eyes. "Do you want apple butter or peach jam?" she said slowly, as if I were incapable of understanding the words.

"Della," Summerset warned.

She turned from me immediately and brought a jar of each from the refrigerator and set both directly in front of me.

Daylon looked intently at his plate, studied his food, and ate with such a singularity of purpose that he might have been alone at the table. I thought of a scolded child who would have to clean his plate before being allowed to play outside. Summerset ate vacantly, chewing methodically, as if the regular rhythm might conjure a meditative state.

Della, meanwhile, did not sit down. With her back to us, she stood before the sink, staring out the kitchen window, picking chunks out of a biscuit, and mumbling softly.

Though I could no more understand her mumbling than I could have deciphered Mandarin Chinese — or reindeer, for that matter — and Daylon acted oblivious to it, Summerset apparently grasped its gist. "That's enough, Della," he said. "Tessie will be fine. This is no different than any other time she's been gone."

Della turned from the sink to face us. "It is, Daddy, you know it is." The biscuit in her hand looked bullet-riddled by now. "You're worried, too. This time."

Summerset didn't respond. Daylon was seated at the end of the rectangular table with his back toward the sink and thus his wife. He didn't turn to face her when, through a mouthful of biscuit and gravy, he asked, "How so? How is it so different?"

Della looked at the back of her husband's head as if it had just sprouted horns. Her round face grew subtly pinched, and she spun back around again to the sink and the window above it, then moved to the counter that flanked it. Using a water glass, she pressed its rim into some rolled dough and placed the disks onto a baking sheet. "Who'll want more biscuits?" she said. "Oven's still on."

Summerset and Daylon looked at the plate in the middle of the table still piled with biscuits, then looked at me. I shook my head. Summerset stood, pushing his chair with the backs of his legs, walked over behind his daughter, and placed his hands on her shoulders the same way he had done to Tessie at the piano yesterday.

Unlike Tessie, who had had no response to Summerset's touch, Della turned and allowed herself to be enfolded by her father. Summerset said, "I'm sure it won't last any longer than usual, but if it'll put your mind to ease, I'll get the four-wheeler and go looking. Maybe I can get some other folks to help."

"I'll start right after work," Daylon offered.

"I'll do what I can," I heard myself say. "Maybe I could try to follow the path that Daylon and I took yesterday evening." It wasn't much, but I had no idea how far up or down the creek I was from my bridge, and that really seemed to be a more useful tactic since I had encountered her at least twice in that area: once when I surprised her while swimming in the creek, and then the time she had overheard me yell my name on my birthday. I still wanted to guard those meetings from disclosure, afraid of the questions the Hundleys might ask.

Della did not try to escape the haven of Summerset's hug, and I don't know whether our offers of help soothed or agitated her, but when her shoulders started quaking, I looked away.

I looked instead toward the oven, still hot, still awaiting a sheet of raw biscuits and wondered if this electric version sat in the same place as the old gas stove that Maude Hundley had used for years because "it just cooked better'n one of those heartless electric things." The whole kitchen had been redone, indeed the entire house had been made over,

Daylon had told me yesterday, and yet nothing could convince Tessie to ever again sleep within its walls. It seemed important for me to know if that was where the old stove had stood. I can't say why.

I wondered, too, if, this morning before I joined them at the breakfast table, Daylon had told his wife and father-in-law that he had at last told me Tessie's story, and how Tessie's act of love for her mother and her twin had killed them.

I think now that Daylon knew he would tell me Tessie's story on one of our walks, and I think, too, that he made sure we were in shadow, either darkened woods or dusk, because it would be a hard story to tell.

It was a hard story to hear.

While Andy and Maude napped after making up, Tessie, spirits buoyed by their restored harmony as any kid might be, rummaged through the cabinets and refrigerator gathering ingredients for chocolate chip cookies. Maude and Tessie baked together often — birthday cakes, Christmas cookies — and Maude bragged about her daughter's talent, calling her "my little Betty Crocker," so Tessie knew her way around the kitchen.

No, Daylon told me, the problem wasn't that Tessie didn't know what she was doing, or that she was irresponsible. The problem was that she was ten years old and that her heart was too big. Tessie opened the oven door, lit the long kitchen match and turned on the gas jet, but just as she did, she heard her little shepherd dog chasing chickens in the yard. She did what any kid would do who knew the trouble her beloved pet would be in if any of the chickens were harmed — because she loved them, too, all forty of them — she ran outside to protect both the dog and the frantic chickens. The oven door stayed open, the jets stayed unlit, and of course the gas poured out.

She was ten, Daylon said again, as if to simultaneously comfort himself and to keep me from judging Tessie, so when she got distracted by capturing all the chicks, then soothing the scolded dog's hurt feelings, and finally following the progress of a pair of ants hauling a dead wasp to their colony, you can understand that, can't you, Daylon had asked me; you can understand that she didn't know what her act of compassion had done?

Because you can imagine, too, he had said without waiting for me to acknowledge that truth, what she must have thought when she finally, finally went back inside and wondered why her brother and mother wouldn't wake up when she shook them, why they just looked asleep, Andy curled into his mother's cupped body.

When Della came home from playing hearts up the road on a friend's porch, she found both Andy and Maude still nestled like crescent moons, and a wide-eyed Tessie lying as part of that still-life, having draped the free arm of her twin around her. The gas had not had time to kill her, too.

No one had blamed Tessie; not by distraught questioning, not by implication, not by assignation of responsibility, and certainly not by withholding or in any way altering their affection for her. If anything, she was made the center of the family's shattered life, and the Sinking Creek community did not abandon her after the funeral either. Even now, Daylon said, Tessie is still regarded as a child of every family.

But from that afternoon, from the moment they pulled her whimpering from under Andy's arm, and after emerging from the weeks of catatonia that followed, Tessie never again slept inside the Hundley farmhouse. The men of Sinking Creek remodeled the kitchen, Daylon and Summerset redid every other room in the house, and when Tessie returned home from a rehab hospital, she seemed comfortable until night fell. She screamed until Summerset put a sleeping bag on the front porch swing for her to use, and he sat all night in a rocker beside her. By fall it was clear she was never again going to sleep inside that house, so they built a bedroom and bath in the barn.

In all other respects, she seemed to be healing. She has never stepped into Andy's bedroom again, but everyone understands that, Daylon maintained. She even went back to school. It wasn't long, however, before her teacher called Summerset and told him she thought Tessie might need some "professional help."

"You are a professional," Summerset told Mrs. Jackson, "help her."

"I don't mean help with her math or English, though she isn't really doing much. I just think there are other problems that need to be dealt with first." She chose her words carefully. She, too, loved and ached for the little girl. "She isn't progressing...socially, I guess I should say, as rapidly as her classmates."

Summerset acknowledged that he, too, had noticed this, but didn't she just need a bit more time?

Mrs. Jackson pushed no further, but soon Tessie was missing school and spending whole days in the woods. And soon after this, she ran away for the first time. She started school every fall for the next three years, always in the fifth grade, but by Thanksgiving of each year she was no longer going, and soon it was too embarrassing to enroll a fourteen year-old in a class full of ten year-olds. She never went back after some of the girls in her class refused to sit with her at lunch. Summerset did not press her. School officials looked the other way.

Daylon had concluded, as if the intervening years were a foregone conclusion, by simply stating, "And now Tessie is just what you see: a ten year-old girl in a twenty-eight year-old's body."

At length, Della twisted her body from Summerset's hold and, in a voice too conspicuously composed, said, "I better be putting these biscuits in. I've got to get to the plaza."

"No more for me, Del," said Summerset. "I'm going to take a quick ride on the four-wheeler. Tell everybody I'll be in around noon." He moved toward the back door, then turned and said to me, "We appreciate your offer of help, Mr. Trueman, but I'm not so sure it's a good idea just yet. I'm afraid we'd be sending a search party out after you tonight. These woods can turn you around sometimes." The door closed behind him, and through the kitchen window I saw his worn brown cap bobbing toward the barn.

"Don't put any more in on my account, babe," Daylon said. "I'll wrap a couple of these up and take them to the shop," he said, pointing at the plate on the table still heaped with biscuits.

"How 'bout you, Mr. Trueman? You bailing out on breakfast, too?" Though Della was asking about food, I felt the larger indictment.

Daylon caught it, too. "Sugar Bear, I said I'd look soon's I got home from work. Maybe Smoky'll let me leave a little early. Besides, I just don't think this is any different than any other time. What's got you so convinced of it, anyway?"

"Been out in the barn this morning?" Della said.

"No, I haven't. Why? She take anything from her room to make you think she's going to be gone longer'n usual?"

Their voices, though not raised in the kind of anger

Corinne and I might have displayed, or even the elevated tone of a heated business meeting, still crackled with a sustained and electric tension.

"That's just it. Nothing's missing. She didn't take anything extra," Della said as she stacked the raw biscuit disks on a plate and covered it in plastic wrap.

"Good, then. That probably means she's just gone for the day. She just got upset about seeing Andy's room."

I thought I shouldn't be there just then. "Andy's room" wouldn't have happened had I not fallen into it. I interrupted them. "Daylon, I think I can find my way up that path we took yesterday. I know it's not much, but I'll walk that."

It was as if I hadn't spoken.

Della reached into her pants packet and pulled out a scrap of paper, uncrinkled it and placed it on the table for Daylon to see. I could read it upside down, and I think she wanted me to.

*Pleas giv Flopsy to mr true-man to keep and ker for. She Loves him I thik and he will be gud to her to. Ther is food in my dror for her. She likes letus tell him. I wont be gone long.*

Daylon read carefully then pushed the paper to me. "Well, she says she won't be gone long. I say we take her at her word."

Della wiped the counter with a damp cloth. Her voice lost the hard edge from earlier and, though it wasn't the bright squeak I was accustomed to hearing from her, it was closer. "I don't know. I don't know. I just know she's never left a note before, even when she'd be gone three, four days. And she's never, ever gone off without taking whatever pet she had at the time. And Flopsy seemed to be her most favorite of all."

Daylon took that in, mulled it over. "Won't argue with that."

So now, it seemed, I had an indolent rabbit in my charge,

a half feral woman-child to find, her sister to placate, and no way to resolve the illogical guilt I felt about her disappearance. It appeared I had sins of different sorts in different sites to answer for. I'd tackle these first.

*******

"Trouble is," Daylon said to me, "no one was ever able to find Tessie when she first started doing this as a kid. I don't hold much hope for finding her now." He lowered his voice for me, "I still think she's just fine, wherever she is. Della's a worry-wart."

Della had finished cleaning up the breakfast dishes. She smacked her hands as if dusting them off. "You're probably right. We can't do no good moping around here. I'll go on to work and you go on to the shop. Best thing you can do, Mr. Trueman, might be to stick around the house in case she just shows up." She softened toward both her husband and me. "I'm too fat to go puffing through these hills, anyway," she laughed weakly.

Daylon stood and went to her. "Let me put some hug marks on you," he said, putting his arms around her, pinning her arms to her side. "Can't get 'em all the way around," he went on, and ducked his head as if to avoid a punch.

Della just laughed—a real laugh this time. "Maybe you're just too scrawny," she said, then wriggled free and squeezed him in return. "Now get to work so we can put even more food on this table. Tessie'll be hungry when she comes home."

A look passed between them that seemed more intimate than even their embrace had been. These people touch one another more than any family I had ever been around, I thought. And I thought, too, just briefly, that I wouldn't mind a hug.

I didn't stay at home as Della and Summerset had suggested. After Daylon and Della left for work, and I heard the whine of Summerset's ATV heading into the woods, I walked through the dusty chicken yard and into the cool, dark barn. There were maybe two dozen empty stalls lining either side of the huge space, and just to the right of the entrance was a stairway leading to what was once the hayloft, but which was now enclosed and had to be Tessie's room. No animals occupied the stalls since they were scattered throughout the farm's many hillside pastures, but I wondered if their smell invaded Tessie's room in the winter. Did the animals' moaning or nickering disturb her sleep, filter through her dreams, or perhaps comfort her and disperse her nightmares?

I intended to walk the trail Daylon and I had taken last night, despite their dire admonitions, as much for me as for any real help it might have been to the search. I was never one to sit idle, and since I had no job to go to and no project to complete, this was all I could do.

But first I had a rabbit to feed. This obligation gave me implied permission to enter Tessie's room, and I had been curious about it since I found out she didn't sleep in the house.

I climbed the stairway and opened the door to the room. The hayloft spanned the entire back half of the barn, had been framed, drywalled, and had had a floor and ceiling built. The effect was as if the hayloft were a shelf and a massive self-contained pod had been placed there. The room seemed utilitarian; comfortable without personality. I hadn't expected this. In fact, it was genderless, and I suspect this was the way Tessie, rather than her family, wanted it. To the right were a toilet, sink, and ponderous, claw-footed tub that I couldn't fathom how they had carried up here. Though Tessie wouldn't have needed privacy, I was still discomfited that the bathroom fixtures were open to the rest of the room. The bed, with its white wrought-iron frame, was covered in a white chenille spread that had been made-up neatly, and on the pillows rested a single stuffed animal, but it was so tattered and frayed I couldn't tell if it was a monkey or a bear. The dresser and chest-of-drawers were painted white, too, and nothing cluttered their surfaces. The floor was a bleached wood with an oval rug beside the bed where Tessie might step first thing in the morning.

There was a lot of white in this windowless room — the only real splash of color was a bright red heart appliquéd onto the middle of the bedspread — but the effect was neither blinding nor disconcerting. It just seemed clean, not antiseptically so, not sterile, just pure, I guess.

I heard a scrabbling sound to my far left that startled me momentarily, but before I located it, I realized it could only be Flopsy. The rabbit stirred in its cage and blinked noncommittally as I undid the latch. I had seen this creature in action before and was not worried that it would race from the cage when I opened its door and scurry behind or under furniture. I was certain that Flopsy possessed fewer rabbit characteristics than I did.

Though I was not an interloper, was, in fact, invited by implication, I didn't feel comfortable here, especially since I knew Tessie's tale. Back home in Cincy, our house lacked clutter, too, but that was a function of our maid service and the tendency — or perhaps, the need — to often open it for entertaining or the occasional photo shoot. My tastes did not necessarily gravitate toward *Architectural Digest*, nor did Corinne's, but it seemed our home leaned in that direction by some unseen necessity or momentum that I now couldn't explain.

Neither of us came from backgrounds that would suggest a proclivity toward any "style." Our house had clean, clear lines, but they were consciously chosen to be so, so I think that's why Tessie's simplicity disturbed me.

Corinne and I had chosen — well, I say chosen, but truly our style was selected by a team of outrageously exorbitant interior designers — severe simplicity because it was recherché. Tessie, I was sure, *chose* simplicity, too. But hers was a stripped down version of reality because it was all she could handle.

This room made her feel safe.

Because of that, I felt like a trespasser and wondered if her family members felt the same when they entered.

I picked up Flopsy, who offered no resistance, and left, softly closing the door behind me.

## CHAPTER 11

The problem wasn't finding the path, after all. Either enough of the weak mid-morning sun wove through the trees to illuminate the darker sections of the woods, or I was better at finding a path than I had given myself credit for. In fact, I even found the walking sticks that Daylon and I had used and discarded last night. No, the real conundrum was how to carry Flopsy because I had decided to take him on my hike. I knew I was not going to find Tessie. I had no doubt, after hearing the Hundleys talk about the vain efforts of experienced trackers to locate her, that she was probably aware of the whereabouts of every member of every search party, whether by intuition or concealment. She was far too adept in the forest to use an established trail if she didn't want to be found, but I thought that just maybe she would find me. My secret weapon was Flopsy.

But even before I thought of him as bait, I had already felt compelled to bring him along. I'm sure he would have been fine lolling about in his cage all day, noshing on the pellets Tessie left for him, but part of me wanted company for the trip. I had lived for weeks under the bridge with nothing for companionship but pamphlets, brochures, anger and fear, so I knew a bit about the difference between being alone and being lonely. I figured, without Tessie, Flopsy was the latter.

Carrying the little bag of sand, though, was awkward. He seemed boneless, almost liquid. So I fashioned a makeshift sling out of a t-shirt Daylon had loaned me, stuffed the little guy into it, and wore him across my stomach like a bota. Flopsy didn't protest but lay there passively, inert as dirt. Some company, I thought.

After an hour I reached the top of the hill and came out of the thicket into a clearing. Some rather impressive clouds, which mounted and tumbled over one another like the children of giants, now obscured the sun and in the near distance I heard the rumble of thunder. I sat Flopsy on the ground, turned my back to him, and walked a few paces away to take a leak. I realized it was irrational to be modest in front of a rabbit — a disinterested one at that — but I was.

I zipped up, then stretched. I had intended to sit awhile, but the freshening wind and those clouds alarmed me; and though I could see no lightning, the next grumble of thunder was much closer. Another followed it immediately, and within seconds gusts of wind bullied the big oaks that encircled the clearing. There was no way, I realized, that I would get back down the path, back up through the pasture, and down again to the farmhouse without getting drenched. Discomfort, even stinging rain, did not concern me. But the wind was so strong, I was afraid of being decapitated by some of the massive branches I heard snapping in the forest. Staying in the exposed clearing was not an option, either. By now lightning forked with disconcerting randomness overhead.

Speed and blind luck would be my allies, and I threw my lot in with the forest, which now swirled with flying debris. But before I had gotten too far into the woods, I realized the flapping cloth across my stomach was unoccupied. I had forgotten Flopsy. No real hurry, now, I thought, as the first nickel-sized raindrops hit the ground. I was going to be soaked anyway, and once the rain came, the wind might release its grip a bit, though for now gust after gust still trained from ridgetop to ridgetop.

I trudged back to get the rabbit, though I was pretty sure I'd find him nonplussed, perhaps bored. Indeed, he had scarcely moved from the spot where I had set him down. I leaned into another strong wind burst, the raindrops elongating and stinging like slivers of glass, then something dark flashed from behind my left shoulder and in front of my line of vision. Instinctively, I flinched and ducked, though the danger from the flying branch had already passed me.

But it wasn't a branch. It wasn't debris at all, and instead of harmlessly hitting the ground before me, it snatched Flopsy up in outspread talons and labored to regain the air, but couldn't.

Both the rabbit and the sharp-shinned hawk rolled on the ground, though the hawk did not loosen its hold, and the ensuing scramble had less to do with Flopsy's attempt to disengage himself than it did with the hawk's diminutive size. As I came nearer, the hawk flapped furiously, then stopped just as abruptly. I froze, too. I wasn't sure what to do. Reaching toward a bird of prey, no matter its size, seemed inherently dangerous; I didn't know if they were inclined to turn their attention from their intended meal to a potential attacker, but its shrill, angry cries kept me at bay. Its eyes were affixed on mine even as Flopsy's paws scrabbled fruitlessly for traction, and those eyes felt as savage, as ruthless, as admonitory as a nighttime siren. We were at an impasse.

When I didn't think the rain could fall any harder, it did. It fell intemperately, in sheets that nearly veiled the hawk and rabbit. I took a tentative step toward them and my footprint filled immediately with water. The splash of my step forward heightened the hawk's demeanor, or I think it did, though there was no discernible movement. Water had to be slashing its wide, black eyes, but they remained unblinking and wary. We stood this way for several minutes, and though the lightning seemed parked above me, strobing the hawk and helpless rabbit, I could not move.

We remained motionless, at least the sharp-shin and I did. Once or twice Flopsy experimented with movement, but the bird's grip was firm, and ultimately he seemed content with his plight. The rabbit did not seem to be in pain; I saw no blood. The hawk's talons were confined to Flopsy's loose-skinned nape, but I was sure that if I were to turn and slip back into the woods, Tessie's beloved pet would not last long. I envisioned the hawk's sharp beak first piercing and blinding its prey at its leisure, then pulling out the rabbit's entrails in long, warm strings.

For some reason, at just that moment, I thought of Darwin because both animals were innately aware that this scenario and their roles in it were to be expected. Neither appeared surprised to be in their respective situations. And I thought, too, that life, especially for man, the most complex of animals, would be much simpler if this sort of acceptance of condition could be adopted.

And then I thought: bullshit, I have to save that rabbit.

I took another step forward, and the hawk flapped with such fury that water sprayed in a halo around it. Another step elicited a cry so strident that I was forced to stop involuntarily. I took the sling from around my shoulder and wound it around my right arm for protection. I shielded my eyes with my left.

But I just couldn't summon the nerve to take the final step that would put me close enough to intervene. I just couldn't. I lowered my shielded arm.

The rain and wind eased, then stopped, though its dripping in the forest still sounded like a shower. The hawk ceased its cry, too, apparently satisfied with my distance; but its malevolent stare remained unbroken.

The rain's cessation did one other thing that I hadn't counted on—it allowed me to hear the low whimper from Flopsy, and I knew that what I had assumed to be passivity was truly paralyzing terror. Perhaps Tessie's love had somehow imbued this animal with enough sentience to be considered a soul-in-progress.

That sealed it. I again covered my face with my left arm and reached to grab Flopsy. My mistake, however, was wrapping my right hand and arm so tightly in Daylon's t-shirt that I had left no fingers free to grasp the rabbit. I made contact with Flopsy, but that didn't cause the hawk to release him. Instead, it redoubled its efforts to fly and with an explosion of wings got off the ground.

It was more a bound than flight, though, and the bird and its prey landed about ten feet away. I advanced less cautiously this time, and the hawk seemed to realize that I wasn't to be intimidated, so it wasted no time on active defense, choosing flight over fight.

This time it was successful, and I watched the bird lift off, stabilize, then fly toward the forest. "Get back here, you son-of-a-bitch," I screamed, then ran after it.

The effort of carrying cargo that outweighed it caused the hawk to land again, this time on a branch of the first oak tree it came to, some thirty feet away. I walked toward it deliberately, hoping that a more measured pace wouldn't startle it into flight again. It clearly was not going to loosen its grip on Flopsy. "I'll kill you, too, you bastard," I said in a low voice. "And I won't think twice about it."

By the time I reached the tree, my real dilemma became dishearteningly apparent. The first branch was twenty feet over my head. Climbing the thick trunk was not possible, and even if I could, the hawk would simply swoop away before I got to it. There was one hope, however. The bird was perched precariously on one talon while holding Flopsy with the other. It didn't look like such a secure grip after all.

But Flopsy was going to have to do something I'd never seen him do. Wriggle. Squirm. Move with some semblance of vigor. That was his only chance, but of course there was no way I could tell him that.

And so my duel with the young hawk continued, and the bird had every advantage. As if to taunt me by emphasizing my powerlessness, the sharp-shin no longer deigned to look at me. I wasn't a threat. Instead, it scanned both directions, appearing to decide between escape into the deeper forest or across the open space and out over the ridge top where updrafts from the valley below would make flight much easier. Once or twice it shifted as if to fly.

Hoping to delay its departure, to distract its attention, I started talking to it in more soothing tones. Oh, I still called it a vile sack of shit, all right, but I cooed rather than shouted the words. I thought of Tessie, how the first creature she would seek out on her return from her "sabbatical" from reality would be her precious Flopsy, and I knew I couldn't bear being the one who let her down. I have fired people, good people, from jobs they needed but just couldn't do well enough, and though I didn't relish doing so, I knew it was part of doing business in a cutthroat environment. And to their credit, they accepted their fate, just as I had assumed the hawk and Flopsy had understood their Darwinian roles. But I knew that Tessie neither deserved nor would understand such a blow as this.

I sat down on the soaked earth. The squishing noise I made caused the hawk to look down at me. Flopsy was as balanced on the limb as if he were some kind of mutant, fairy tale bird, but he still emitted a low, throaty sound.

"Okay, then," I said to the hawk, "what would you have me do? What will it take to get this deal done today?" There was, of course, no response from the hawk. "What can I trade you for that rabbit?" It was nonsense, I know, but I swear the hawk cocked its head to one side. I half expected it to croak "nevermore." And then, for the first time, I saw it blink — a long, slow blink — that seemed almost thoughtful.

Flopsy shifted an inch. The hawk stretched its wings out to rebalance them both, and maybe pinched the rabbit a bit harder because Flopsy didn't move again.

A slight breeze stirred the trees and shook water onto my upturned face. I squinted my eyes closed and placed my hands out on the ground behind me for equilibrium. My left hand slipped a bit in the mud, but my right hand rested on something sharp. It was the tip of a bone, and I pulled the yellowed thing from the mud and grass that had grown over most of its length. It was perhaps 18 inches long with one sharp end and one jagged, fractured end. I rubbed the mud from its surface. It was slightly curved, more like a boomerang than anything else, and I liked the way it fit my hand. I held it by the sharp tip and practiced a slow throwing motion in the opposite direction of the hawk.

But was this really the best plan? I was not an athlete, and, except for some rocks I threw into the creek under the bridge during hours of boredom, I hadn't really thrown anything *at* anything for many years. I wished for Corinne who not only *could* throw a ball, but had the confidence to take this one shot with so much at stake.

I pushed myself slowly to my feet, the hawk again watching me with interest, and bounced the bone in my hand to better gauge its heft. Negotiations had failed, and I would have only one chance.

Suddenly, the hawk looked over my head and past me, back across the clearing and toward the other side where earlier I had emerged from the wooded path. Its carriage straightened as if preparing to fly. I was afraid to turn to see what it was looking at, or for, because I was sure the bird would take off, and I'd not be able to see where it might land next.

But then I heard it, and without looking around I knew what it was. The Hundley's four-wheeler was spinning its way up the wet path and was about to burst into the clearing. I twisted my head around to spot it, then just as quickly twisted back. The bones in my neck popped with each twist, but I couldn't risk losing sight of the hawk and rabbit.

It was Summerset, and I couldn't have been more relieved. I was afraid that maybe Tessie had come home, found Flopsy and me missing, and set out to find us. I held up my hand toward the old man who realized I wanted quiet, that I was focused on something just on the fringe of the woods. He cut the ATV's engine and dismounted.

Each of his steps squished, and when he spoke, his voice was calm and just above a whisper. "You all right, son?" It was the same tone I had used since the hawk had landed in the tree.

Without turning to him, I pointed toward the branch, toward the alert hawk and the frightened rabbit.

"Appears Flopsy got himself in a pickle," he said.

"I set him down back there in the clearing, just for a second to...just for a second." I felt like I could look away for a moment now that someone was there to share the burden. I felt, too, that I needed to explain the unexplainable — how this was my fault, yes, but who in the world would think...? I needed some blame, but not all of it.

Summerset, however, wasn't going to give me any. In fact, there was a hint of a smile playing on his face, not a derisive smile, but it seemed both oddly placed and oddly timed. In the next moment, though, I understood.

"Sixty-eight years old and I never seen the like," he

whispered. "I seen them pick up field mice, moles, and snakes, but never something nigh as big as themselves. That's something, ain't it?"

I'm not sure whether that question was rhetorical or not, but I didn't feel like we had much time for this Discovery Channel moment. Summerset just didn't seem panicked. "What can we do? Anything?" I said.

"I know this is relative, but have you seen Flopsy move since the hawk's had him?"

"Yeah, some. He tried to get away while they were on the ground."

Summerset considered this. "That's a good sign." He took a cautious step closer to the tree and peered up at the pair. "It's a young hawk, probably just fledged, probably used to eating road kill. Might even be its first live hunt." He looked even more closely.

"So, Flopsy's safe?" I said, desperately needing relief.

"No, not really. Lotta times the hawk'll kill its prey with the initial impact. If not then, those sharp claws do the trick. But so far, looks like Flopsy's avoided both those fates. Right now, the best thing he can do is just what he's doing now."

I looked to see what old Hundley meant. As far as I could tell, Flopsy wasn't doing a damn thing. I said so.

"You ever been aggravated, Mr. Trueman?"

That one *had* to be rhetorical, so I didn't waste my breath.

He went on. "If Flopsy starts causing a ruckus, it's going to aggravate that hawk. For now, it's just trying to figure out what to do with him. It knows that Flopsy is food, but it doesn't know how to eat something that big, or that alive, just yet. It gets aggravated, it'll just kill him now — eat him later. You see, the bird is as confused as we are. Difference is, it's got more options."

I remembered the deer rib. "What about this?" I said and held it before him.

"Oh, he won't be interested in that. These birds prefer meat."

I didn't want him to think I was that simple. "No, I mean hit him with it."

"No offense, but you ever go around chucking deer bones at hawks before?" Nothing in his tone indicated derision, but I immediately felt like a Neanderthal, and that my plan was about as efficacious as a prayer to a mystical hawk god. Then, as if to console me, Summerset said, "I'm not saying it couldn't work. I'm just saying the odds are heaped against us. We're just going to get one chance. But I do have an idea." He put his hand on my shoulder. "I'm going back to the four-wheeler. You keep eyeballing that hawk. If it does take off before I'm back, try the bone. It'll be our only option then." He splashed back toward the ATV, stopped, and turned. "I don't know how this'll turn out, and I don't know what we'd tell Tessie if it goes south on us, Mr. Trueman, but it's not your fault. I'll tell her that much, at least."

The hawk let loose with a loud, raspy *keee-uck*, startling me into raising the bone as if to throw. I stood poised like an aboriginal hunter. I was still in that position when I heard Summerset slopping behind me.

"Let's try this," he said.

I lowered the bone and turned to see what "this" was. The old guy held a pistol.

"You're going to try to shoot it?" I'd seen enough hostage movies to know that it just didn't work in the real world. "What if you hit Flopsy?" His target simply wasn't that big, and the rabbit blocked most of its lower half.

"No sir, I won't kill a hawk, even now. No, this pistol's filled with snake-shot rounds, pellets like BB's. I use it to kill copperheads around the farm. Here's what I thought we'd try…" he said.

But I interrupted him. "*We* aren't trying anything. I've never shot a gun in my life. I already feel bad enough about this; it's my fault there's a rabbit in that tree. I'm not going to risk shooting him, too."

"Relax, Harry. I'm not asking you to kill anything. You don't strike me as the type to kill something you didn't have to. I'm not going to shoot either one of them either. Here's what I think will work," he said. "This snake-shot spreads out, sounds like a handful of rocks, especially to something with senses like that hawk there. I'm going to fire a round to the left of the hawk, then fast as I can to the right, then another just below it. I wouldn't be surprised if it could see some of the pellets as they fly by. Matter of fact, that's what I'm hoping. The bird will think it's going to have to fly up, and quick. And I hope it'll think more about escape than about dinner. It won't take off with that bothersome rabbit."

I agreed. I had to. I had nothing else to offer.

Summerset raised the pistol, sighted, then without firing, moved his hand quickly among the three positions he had planned. He seemed satisfied. "One other thing, Harry. You care to stand under the branch?"

I did as asked, but before I could ask why, the old man's pistol popped three times, and I looked skyward just in time to catch a surprised rabbit and a faceful of hawk shit.

# CHAPTER 12

I rode down the path on the back of the ATV, Flopsy secured in the soaked sling. The rabbit didn't seem fazed by either his brush with death or his experience with flight. If I expected relief and gratitude, I got neither.

"I'll tell Tessie we need to rename him Icarus," Summerset said as we jolted down a steep section of the trail. "Or maybe you ought to tell her when we get back."

I don't know which shocked me more — that Tessie had come home so soon, or that Summerset Hundley knew who Icarus was. Once we had negotiated that steep part, he turned around and grinned. "That's right, she's home already. I figured I'd find you on that path and that you'd want to know. Besides, she says she's got something for you."

"What is it?" I shouted over the ATV's whine.

"Don't know. Whatever it is, she's put it in your room, shut the door, and told us positively no entrance." He turned back to face the trail.

That sounded ominous. I didn't want a puppy, kitten, or any juvenile from any other species of the animal kingdom. I couldn't think of anything else that Tessie's "gift" could be.

The ATV crested the pasture hill from which we would descend to the farm. Summerset cut the engine.

"You ever drive one of these, Harry?" he said.

I told him I'd never even sat on one.

"Would you like to?" He was still facing forward, his

hands still on the throttle.

I hesitated.

"I think you'd like it," he said, and I knew then this was some kind of reward. "I just want to thank you, son, for what you've done for Tessie."

I'm not embarrassed accepting compliments; in fact, I've always viewed that ability as one of the finer social skills, but I didn't understand two things: I didn't know what I had done for Tessie, and I certainly couldn't fathom the depths of this man's gratitude.

"I don't know what you mean, Summerset," I said.

"I didn't for a minute think that Tessie was in danger this time, at least not like Della did, but I did think she'd be gone longer than customary." Summerset got off the ATV's seat and motioned for me to scoot up. "Last time she played the piano like that, she was gone about a week. It's usually just a couple of days. We can handle that; we've learned to. But this time I thought she seemed like she needed more room. Fact that she was just gone for a few hours tells me something. Something about you."

This was a compliment I had no desire to accept. When I did a good job, produced something of note, pioneered or piloted a worthy or innovative project, I accepted congratulations in the form of accolades or money. I'm not saying recognition was my impetus, just that it was anticipated. Summerset was lauding me for something for which I could see no tangible results and for which there was no clear, as I could tell, measure of success.

And so, since I didn't know what to say, I accepted his invitation to drive a four-wheeler, stalling it three or four times on the way down the hill.

Tessie met us at the back door, looking no worse for her night in the woods. Classical music issued from the countertop CD player — maybe Handel.

"I called Della like you asked, Daddy. Fussy, fussy, fussy, fuss-budget, she is," she sang.

"She just worries about you, girl. We all do."

Tessie took Flopsy from my sack and nuzzled her. "Looks like you had a grand time with Mr. Trueman here," she said to the rabbit whose expression committed him to nothing. Then, to me: "Was he any trouble? Did you find his food okay?"

I looked at Summerset who shook his head faintly. "No trouble, and, yes, I found the food just fine," I said.

She held the pet at arm's length as if inspecting him. I held my breath, and, I suspect, Summerset did, too. Satisfied, she pronounced, "Appears to me he really really really likes you. You want him to keep?"

We'd been through a harrowing hour, that rabbit and I, but I can't say I had bonded with him. His rescue had nothing to do with any fondness for him on my part. Quite simply, I had been given a task with an attached responsibility, and I needed to complete that task. I'd be better off if I thought of Tessie as a client and leave the caring to the capable hands of her family. Besides, I had no permanent home, no place to keep a pet. Summerset noted my hesitation and rescued me.

"Tess, I think Flopsy loves you much too much to leave you. What say you just allow Harry all the visitings he wants? That'd be best for all concerned." He scratched the rabbit's ears and leaned over as if to a held baby. "That okay with you, Flopsy?"

Tessie seemed content with this. I know I was. "Okey-doke. You can visit him any time you hanker. Just say the word. And if you want, maybe sometimes Flopsy could stay the night with you." She smiled and only the crinkles around her eyes betrayed her as a woman and not a child. "She's real good at keeping your feet warm."

The music from the CD player soared, and I realized I didn't know the piece. Tessie, holding her rabbit against her shoulder like an infant being burped, waltzed in time to its beat. Summerset and I flattened ourselves against the kitchen counter while she slid around the polished wooden floor, around the breakfast table, where hours earlier we had worried about her absence. There was grace in her movement. After her third or fourth circuit around the table, she pirouetted in place and stopped. "Would you like that? Flopsy spending the night with you?" she said.

I looked at the poor rabbit, wondering if the dance had made him dizzy. "Very much," I said.

Summerset interrupted, "I'm going out to the barn, Sis. Want me to put Flopsy up? Don't you have something you need to give Harry?"

She handed the dormant rabbit to her father and grabbed my hand. My instant reaction was to withdraw the hand because my palms perspired when I was uncomfortable. And I was uncomfortable. Ordinarily I prepared for a handshake by covertly wiping the hand dry on my pants—there's nothing more important in business than a solid handshake—then offering it confidently. Tessie had taken me by surprise, though, and I wondered if my sweaty palm repulsed her and if she judged me because of it. I felt my hand slip in hers, but she just grasped it tighter.

"Come with me," she said, leading me from the kitchen down the hallway. My wet shoes squeaked on the hardwood. I heard the back door close behind Summerset as we reached the stairway in the living room. Tessie still held my hand, and I thought her grip strengthened as we passed the baby grand piano looming like a disembodied face, the keys a gap-toothed grin.

I still had trouble thinking of the upstairs bedroom as mine rather than Tessie's, even though I knew that she had never slept in it; but she apparently had no such trouble. Although she had practically dragged me up the stairs, she stopped when we reached the threshold to the bedroom, despite having been in the room to place something in there while I had been up on the hill.

As soon as I opened the door, I knew immediately what it was. Tessie stood aside to let me go to it.

"I thought you might be tired of wearing Daylon's hand-me-downs," she said, then added with a laugh, "You're kinda little for 'em. No offense."

Henderson S. Turner's brown canvas duffel bag lay like a rotting carcass on the crisp white linens of the bed. I thought I was seeing a ghost. The duffel was weathered and filthy and smelled of the dust from under the bridge, and of something else: Having been away from the bridge for some time, I had forgotten the exhaust fume smell that mixed with the odor of the creek water and luxuriant foliage that bordered my "home." Those fumes had fostered a great many headaches, and I wondered if Daylon got them, too, from working every day in a garage.

I wasn't afraid to touch the bag; I was too disgusted. I had stolen it, and though I had told myself at the time that I would some day return it to its owner, as well as other things I had stolen from other cars in the plaza, I knew I would never do so. The duffel's real owner's clothes, toiletries, and other haphazard shards of his traveling life lay inside that bag. They had sustained me, but had he missed them? Was anything in there vital or sentimental to him? I had, after all, extracted the cash, electronics and prescriptions from his bag and left them in his car's back seat. I just needed clothes and toiletries, and surely he replaced those things easily enough.

But Henderson S. Turner's monogram on that toiletry bag had spawned Harry S. Trueman. I owed him for that, at least.

Tessie was as giddy as if she had uncovered a treasure chest. "I didn't look inside, no way, you don't have to worry about that, and I didn't tell Dad where I went to get it. I just thought if you had your stuff, you wouldn't have no excuse to leave." She lowered her eyes, and her cheeks blushed a shade just darker than her tangerine hair. "I know you ain't Harry Trueman. I know you're Duncan Post 'cause I heard you call yourself that. But I don't care and I won't tell. Long as you stay."

I sat on the edge of the bed while Tessie still stood in the doorway.

"You heard me wrong that day in the woods, Tessie," I said.

"Didn't."

"I don't mean you didn't hear *what* I said, just that you understood it wrong."

Tessie tilted her head.

I continued. "I was shouting happy birthday to a friend of mine who I wished I could be with just then. I wasn't telling myself happy birthday. That would be silly, wouldn't it?"

I wasn't prepared for the lies I was telling, hadn't rehearsed them. I was certain Tessie could somehow tell.

She waited for a beat after I finished, then straightened her head and smiled. "Harry Trueman, Duncan Post. I don't care. One of you is staying." She turned and I heard her thunder down the stairway.

Besides its grunge, there was another reason I didn't want to re-open the duffel bag. Though it now seemed like a delusion, I knew I had stuffed the bag with notes; some made on napkins, some in the margins of brochures and pamphlets, even some on paper towels and the plaza bathroom's institutional toilet paper squares. I hadn't been all that well back then.

But I knew I had to get into it, to get rid of any incriminating evidence, if nothing else. Tessie, to paraphrase Summerset's comment upon seeing Flopsy in the tree, had gotten me into a pickle.

I approached the duffel as I might a body bag, just as unsettled about what I would see. Grit stuck in the zipper teeth making it difficult to pull, but a final yank stretched it open like a maw, and I was hit with the smell of desiccated food and wadded clothes veined with perspiration stains. Interspersed among the mess were the scraps of paper that constituted the whole of my thinking during those days under the bridge. I was not nostalgic for them, did not want to spend time shuffling slowly through them as someone does when he runs across an attic box filled with old photos and ticket stubs.

I was, I realized, afraid of them. So much of those weeks remained vivid. So many sensory details attached themselves to me like scars or prison tattoos. But so much more seemed like watery, indistinct old 8 mm. movies, and I felt too removed to believe that I was in them — too afraid to rewind them. It confounded me to think I had so quickly sunk to such primitivism and had accepted it as a new reality.

But I was really no better off now. Physically I was, of course, but I was in even greater limbo than then because I was less a part of this world than I was under the bridge. I had nothing in common with these people. And yet, for all the times I had vowed to leave, why hadn't I? Why didn't I leave now, this minute?

I pulled the stinking clothes from the bag and piled them

on the floor to take downstairs to launder. Tessie's tragic story had kept me here, not because I could fix anything broken in her despite what Summerset had said, but because I saw some of myself in her. I had killed Richard Rice in a rage because I loved Corinne. Tessie had killed her twin and her mother through an impetuous accident of love, too. I was staying, I guess, to see if there was any hope for the girl. If there was any hope for me.

After I pulled the clothing from the bottom of the bag, took out the much needed toiletry bag, and picked out the hardened bread crusts and crumbs, only the hundreds of scraps of papers remained.

I was amused by some of them; appalled by others. There were the lists, of course; lists of things-to-do, both when I returned to my real world and lists of daily things-to-do under the bridge. The contrast was excruciating. One contained notes about important clients and deals to close, software to test and debug; the other was highlighted by such notable items as eating and teethbrushing. I had started a list of Corinne's favorite songs, but I could only think of three, and her favorite holidays, and her favorite flowers, birds and restaurants.

I am not an artist, but I found a napkin on which I had drawn her face. No one else would be able to tell it was her; it was only an angled view as if she were turning away from me — one eye, the outline of her nose, half her smile. But *I* knew.

I held the napkin up to the light coming through the window. The edges had curled and the ink had faded, but I decided to keep it. I pulled the wastebasket from beside the nightstand and emptied the handfuls of the other scraps into it. I didn't bother to read the rest.

Tessie was fixing a sandwich when I came downstairs with laundry bunched in my arms. I would do this obscene load myself because, until now, Della had always spirited away

my dirty clothes and placed clean ones of Daylon's on the foot
of my bed.

She looked up from her sandwich. "Them yours?" she
said, pointing with her chin.  But before I could answer, she
made a face and added, "Sheewww, course they are.  Daylon
works in a garage and he don't come home stinking like that.
Gonna have trouble getting the skunk out of those."

I agreed, of course, but for some reason her harshness
didn't offend, just surprised me.  It implied a comfort level, a
playfulness that she had never exposed to me.  I had seen her
tease Daylon, Della, and, to a lesser extent, her father, but she
had never broken politeness with me.

"Do you care if I use your washer," I said.

"It's not mine.  Belongs to everybody who lives under
this roof, so I suppose you can use it.  Want a pickle loaf sandwich while I got the fixings out?"

My hike after a minimal breakfast had raised a hunger.
"Please," I said and went into the laundry room just off the
kitchen.  The clothes made up a full load, and as I separated
each item, I wondered again about Henderson S. Turner's taste.
Where was he bound with such a collection of Bermuda shorts
and golf shirts, most in garish colors or outdated patterns?  Had
to be vacation, and I had spoiled it.  I resolved to dig out the
paper scrap with his address from the trash and repay him.
Somehow.

A plate with a pickle loaf sandwich and piled with potato chips sat on the table when I came back through the
kitchen.  Tessie sat across from my place, crunching a chip.
She had pulled my chair out as an invitation.  I wanted to take
the plate upstairs to eat in private, to mull over how the duffel's
return would affect my next move.  At least, I think that's why
I wanted to go upstairs.  But it may not have been that at all.
Had Daylon, Summerset, or Della asked me to sit, I would have

done so with little trepidation, but there was something about Tessie's uncomplicated approach that disquieted me. She could say or ask anything, and I might not be prepared to answer her.

I sat. We ate in silence for a few moments, and I looked all around the kitchen, feigning interest in everything and nothing, while pointedly not looking at Tessie. I could, however, feel her eyes on me.

"Whatcha hiding, Duncan Post Harry Trueman?" she said as if she were asking me if I liked the sandwich.

The bread balled up in my mouth. I could no more chew the huge lump of bread and pickle loaf than I could have swallowed clay. I held up a finger as if politeness required me to finish chewing before I answered.

Tessie didn't wait. "Did you steal something?" Her eyes widened; she set her sandwich down, leaned forward. "I stole a Snickers bar once from Ernie's Qwik Shop. Wasn't that long ago, neither. I thought I had money with me but I'd left it in my other jeans. I just really, really wanted a candy bar just then."

Apparently she interpreted my muteness as agreement. "You know what'll make you feel better, don't you?" she continued.

"What's that?"

"Do something good but don't tell nobody you done it. You tell somebody, it just makes it like you wanted the attention."

I thought this was a better option than admitting to my real crimes. "What if the person I stole from isn't around for me to do something nice for?"

"Oh, you don't have to do it for them, necessarily. Anyone who needs something will do."

"What did you do to make up for the Snickers bar?"

She looked at me as if I were crazy. "I brought you your stuff from under the bridge, silly."

There were times while I lived under the bridge that I thought I could hear the universe breathe. It sounded ludicrous to me now, but I think that just at this moment, I heard a hearty cosmic guffaw.

"Okay, then. Thanks for the advice. I'll give it a try."

"Know what else you could do?" she said. "You could do something nice for someone you don't like. That'd make it mean even more."

Tessie couldn't know that what I had done to Richard Rice couldn't be atoned for by buying someone a Snickers bar; and I wondered whether I would do something nice for him even if I could.

For some reason that thought made me feel the need to continue the conversation. It was like scratching poison ivy: simultaneously satisfying and provoking an irritation. "But what if I…what if I stole something really big? What if I stole something that can't be given back?"

Tessie crunched another potato chip; crumbs flew from her mouth. "What did you do — lose it?"

"I suppose you could say that."

Her chewing slowed as she considered this. "Well, you don't have to give it back. There wasn't no way I could give back that candy bar, you know. But the problem with doing something nice for someone else is a big one for you because me and Poppie and Della and Daylon is all you have right now, so we'd know if you did something nice for us, and that would take its goodness away."

This stumped her. In fact, her frustration seemed physical. She pushed her plate away from her, put her elbows on the table and hid her face in her hands. This odd meditation went on for a minute until she rubbed her face briskly, took her hands away, and said, "I know—maybe you could just give that person something you have that's equal as special as what you stole. Maybe there's no way else to do it."

I realized I had been anxious to hear her solution. I had. My itch was bleeding, but needed perversely to be scratched some more. "Tessie, what if my secret is worse than that? What if it wasn't stealing somebody's possessions? What if I hurt someone?"

I cannot describe the face she made. Computer face-morphing programs could not have captured the delicacy of her change of expression. I want to call it quizzical, as if she were trying to grasp my change of conversational direction, and maybe it *was* a look that implied a question, but it was more than that—there were simultaneous aspects of realization, of empathy, and perhaps a scrap of fear.

She stood, picked up her sandwich plate, and took it over to the kitchen counter. I had gone too far. Her freckled hand shook slightly. When she turned back to face me, that amalgamation of expressions was gone, replaced so quickly with a brightness that I wondered if it had been there at all. Or had I been using her face as a mirror?

"You committed one of the seven deafening sins," she said.

"Do you mean one of the seven *deadly* sins?"

"What're those? Della never told me about those; she just told me about the seven deafening ones. What ones do you know about?"

I laughed, but immediately tried to make it sound like a cough. I could have told her I knew them all, some more intimately than others. I could have told her about what Chaucer, Aquinas, Dante, and Lewis had to say about them, but I didn't. "Never mind. I guess I meant to say the seven deafening sins, too. I don't know what I was thinking, sorry.

Go on."

"Don't matter, yours are probably as good as mine. Anyways, I think it's time we went for a four-wheeler ride," she said.

I told her I had already been on one today, and it was quite enough.

"It's not a ride for fun, Duncan Harry; it's a ride I take when I get to feeling bad and don't feel like talking to nobody about why." She came around to me, took my hand for the second time that day and pulled me up. This time I didn't feel inclined to pull my hand away. "Might as well leave these dirty clothes on. It's going to be muddy."

## CHAPTER 13 — CORINNE

When Dexter Daugherty told Corinne he had a lead into Duncan's whereabouts, her first instinct was to dial Ariel's number immediately. But she didn't. Her fingers rested on the speed dial button, then tapped it too lightly to force it into action. She set the phone in her lap and replayed the investigator's words in her head.

"I'm not sure you've been completely honest with me, Mrs. Post, and that's your prerogative. Complete candor, however, would certainly make finding your husband—or what might have happened to your husband—that much easier."

Corinne didn't want to antagonize the investigator, but she was paying his bill, after all. Plus expenses. "Where is he?"

Daugherty's answer had surprised her. "I think it's interesting your first response wasn't *how is he* but *where*. The truth is I haven't found him, but I have found a place to focus my search," Daugherty said. "And it really wasn't that difficult."

Corinne, too, was surprised at her question. Perhaps she couldn't even consider any harm coming to Duncan because he had always seemed impervious to any real danger. He had always commanded situations, orchestrated them; he could never be the marionette, and so his physical safety had never been in question. In her hours of conversations with Ariel, Duncan's physical well-being was never deliberated. That Dexter Daugherty broached the subject alarmed her.

"How is he, then? And how could you know if you don't really know where he is?"

"Listen, Mrs. Post. I didn't call to engage in a semantic battle, and I didn't call to be intentionally obtuse. I've located his car, and I don't know why you didn't think to tell me something as basic as that he had taken it. That detail seems a pretty important one to leave out in all the times we talked," he said.

"I'm new at this missing husband game," Corinne said. "I'm sorry. Why didn't you ask? Seems like a pretty fundamental, first interview kind of question, doesn't it?" Now, she did not care if she irritated him.

"Touché," he said. "But to be frank, sometimes what clients don't tell me is every bit as revealing as what they do, Mrs. Post. And you didn't tell me very much at all."

Corinne tasted the ferrous tang of adrenaline she recalled when facing her elementary school principal. She wished Ariel were there.

Daugherty went on. "I don't, nor did I ever, seriously suspect foul play, at least not on your part. But for the life of me, I couldn't understand the why's of the whole story. Why did he leave? Why did you wait so long to search? Why me and not the police? But most important, why did you want to find him?" Daugherty paused so long that Corinne thought she had been put on hold. "But I've learned that the answers to those questions are crucial to my success or failure. When you wouldn't provide those answers, I realized you either didn't know them yourself or you were afraid of them."

Corinne hoped she wasn't going to cry. Suddenly, Daugherty's voice invited confession, but she would not do that. She had Ariel for that. "I'm sorry I've not been as open with you as I could have been," she said. And she stopped at that. "Please, Mr. Daugherty, where is Duncan?"

"Can I ask you for a few more days?" he said and his

voice softened. "It's my experience that telling you where I think he might be could cause you to get in the way. I promise I'll tell you the moment I spot him. Where he is, who he's with, what he's doing, how he looks. Everything. Can I trust you to be patient a little longer?"

Corinne promised. Ariel could have been right: maybe Duncan just needed this time to himself: and maybe the next move was by all rights his, not hers. Hiring a private investigator had been for her, she knew, not for Duncan.

"And can I ask you for one more thing?" he said.

She nodded.

"Will you tell me about Richard Rice now?"


When at length she roused herself, Corinne still did not hit Ariel's speed dial button. She called Richard Rice instead.

"Corinne!" he said as if they were long separated best friends. She despised Caller-ID—at least other people's having it. "Listen, I'm in an elevator in the left tit at P & G if I lose you; so if I do..."

"I'll call *you* back," she preempted. He claimed to be in one of the towers of the Proctor and Gamble Building, which to the prurient looked like women's breasts against the skyline. She knew, too, that this was his way of arrogating the conversation. If it got hot, he could just claim signal loss, snap his phone shut, and be more selective the next time it rang. She had seen him do it before. The conversation would take place at a time of his choosing, if it took place at all. In fact, she was a little surprised that he had even answered this time.

He ignored the frost in her tone. "What's up, girl? You doing okay? Any word about our Post-Man?"

Corinne could see him. If he really was in one of the Proctor and Gamble towers, and if he really was in an elevator, she knew that he was mugging for whatever strangers rode with him, winking maybe, rolling his eyes in mock annoyance, or miming "an old friend" if the fellow riders included attractive women. A cell phone was Richard's ultimate accessory, sleek and trendy, as much fashion as tool. He was who that kid waiter — what was his name? Brian? — would be in ten years.

Quit being smarmy, was what Ariel would say, and if Corinne did not necessarily see that as being stronger than she herself was, she knew it illustrated the fundamental difference between them. "Dexter Daugherty thinks he knows where Duncan is, Richard."

"Is he okay?"

Corinne was stung. The same Richard Rice who had ridden Duncan's business coattails to success, who (to her way of thinking) had contributed nothing of substance to showplace.com as the competition caught up with, then surpassed it, who had protected his own assets while Duncan insisted on risking everything, and who had betrayed — but Corinne would not stretch her indignation that far because the betrayal was hers more than his — his "best friend," had asked about Duncan's well-being as his first response.

"We don't know," she said and hoped the "we" indicated a sort of solidarity, a shared concern with others who cared about Duncan. And then to show that her anxiety was paramount among anyone who might care, she added, "I can only hope so."

"Where do you think he is?"

"Daugherty didn't tell me."

Richard snorted. "What kind of buffoon did you hire? He calls to tell you that he *might* know where Duncan is? Then he won't tell you where this hypothetical spotting took place? He can't even tell you that the Post-Man is okay? Let me call the guy, Corinne. I'll get some answers for you."

That was Richard. The Answer Man.

"No, don't call him. I didn't press him because what he said made sense. He'll know more in a couple of days he said, then I'll know."

"How could you not demand some answers?" Corinne heard a ding behind Richard's voice. He was in an elevator, at least. And then his voice lost its edge. "I have a stake in this, too, you know. He was my friend, my best friend, actually, for a long, long time. I don't suppose we'll be that again, but I'd feel a lot better about what I tried to do if I knew it didn't keep you two apart permanently. There really is something quaint about the two of you, in a post-modern, apocalyptic kind of way."

There. That was the part of Richard Rice that Corinne had flirted with—that part that took the blame despite the truth that she, too, had nearly stepped into the precipice. He did not include her in his guilt, though he could have.

Static scraped the line. "I think I'm about to lose you, babe. Call me tonight. We'll finish."

Corinne did not click off. She set the receiver in her lap until shrill beeping warned her the phone was off the hook. As if she didn't know. As if it mattered. She replaced the phone on its charger, but even before she could remove her hand, it rang.

She answered and heard birds in the background and maybe, yes, an airplane overhead, but the caller did not immediately speak. She looked at the phone's base—she had answered too fast for the identification to register.

Corinne took a chance. "Duncan?"

The caller sighed, then said, "You wish, Toots. No, it's just me again. Disappointed?"

Corinne wasn't sure. "Probably," she said, but she knew

the correct answer was that she was both disappointed and relieved. "Where are you?"

"Up on the roof of P & G. There's a fantastic garden up here, you know. You can see forever. All kinds of birds and flowers and shit, too. Nature everywhere. Duncan would hate it, but it's right up your alley."

"I thought you had a meeting."

"I'll be late. They'll wait for a good thing."

"What do you want, Richard? I told you I'd call you when I heard more from Daugherty."

He laughed. "I called to tell you what you wanted to know when you called me. You did call me a bit ago, remember?"

Though she knew it made no sense to do so, she nodded.

"And you may further remember, you never really told me anything of substance during said conversation," he said.

"I did. I told you that Daugherty —"

"That he *might* know where Duncan is, and that he *might* tell you something in a couple of days. Come on, Corinne, you knew nearly that much before you started tossing money at this guy. No, you called me for something else, so here it is: We don't and didn't love each other. We didn't even have a 'thing.' I wanted to get in your pants — I wanted that the first time Duncan introduced you to me. There's that whole Farmer's Daughter vibe you have. But it was no more than that for me."

"Good God, Richard, that's not what I —"

"Yes, it *is* what you wanted to ask. It is. You were just going to be more tactful."

"Maybe that's what I wanted, maybe not. But what I wanted to know even more was why you'd pursue your best friend's wife." Corinne hadn't known this was what she most wanted to know until she asked it.

Richard hesitated. In the phone's hissing background, Corinne heard a thrush. From her window she saw an ultra-marine September sky and knew that under other circum-stances she would declare this a perfect day. She imagined that Richard stood in an artificial Eden.

"You won't believe this, but I've asked myself the same question. The only answer I can come up with is that I knew it wouldn't happen. I knew one of us would stop if it every threatened to go beyond the emails, the party flirting, even the simulation game—damn, isn't that great software? Sell-ing like hotcakes in Europe." He laughed at his own aside. "Come on, Corinne. Outside of the virtual Richard screwing a virtual Corinne, we didn't even touch each other. Still, there was an electronic thrill, wasn't there?"

Corinne thought the phrase was apt—it was an elec-tronic thrill, invigorating and dangerous. "No," she said.

"Of course it was," Richard said as if Corinne hadn't spoken. "You know, I've had lots of women, but this was as much fun as any physical relationship I've ever had."

Corinne laughed in spite of herself. Richard Rice was infectious, and his self-absorption prevented him from saying the one thing that Corinne most feared: that she had not stopped the whole rolling ball when it began. Men like Rich-ard Rice couldn't be blamed, she thought, they'll do what they can, as long as they can. Richard had not held her to account, though she knew he had that right. She could not hate him without hating herself, and she could not hate herself and love Duncan. Why could she not see the world through Ariel's un-complicated granny glasses?

"You're smarter than I thought," she said.

"Maybe that's what happens when you get conked on the noggin with a computer monitor." It was his turn to laugh, and it was an authentic, not a rueful, laugh. "How long was I in the hospital, anyway, a week?"

This was another of his games, but she wouldn't play. "I don't know. I didn't visit," she said.

"Liar. Did Duncan?"

"No. He...was gone."

This seemed to surprise Richard. He said nothing. In the phone's background, she heard the shuffling of feet.

"What are you doing, Richard?" she said, then stood, went to her living room window, and looked out. A row of Japanese maples lined the long driveway, their rich burgundy leaves reeling in the breeze.

"Oh, I get it," he said. "It's like my asking what you're wearing, that kind of thing?"

She didn't think so, but she wasn't sure. "God. Do you always have to be so insanely sleazy? How you and Duncan could have ever been friends is incomprehensible. No, it's just that you say you're outside. I hear you walking along some path P & G has created on that rooftop. I imagine they've hired some landscaping firm to create the space based upon some psychological/marketing/public relations focus group analysis. It's supposed to somehow resemble a Zen garden, as if providing it to their clients and, at least ostensibly, to their employees, will provide them all with a sense of calm which will result in increased productivity — read, sales. I think they've done their homework. I think the research analysts have carefully selected just the right combination of plants, water features, even the shape of the path you're walking on right now, not out of some altruistic impulse to preserve an oasis of nature in the city, but because they have calculated this to be a good business move." Corinne realized she had begun talking faster, like her words flowed downhill. "There's a fountain up there somewhere, isn't there?"

Richard's footsteps had stopped. "Whoa, slow down there, Kreskin. What's wrong with all that, anyway? Does it matter why? It's pretty up here is all I know."

"The path curves, doesn't it? No straight lines?"

"So?"

"And the fountain I asked you about, is there one at the end of the path?"

"Where is this going, Corinne?"

With her finger on the window, Corinne traced the shaggy boundary of the furthest maple along the driveway. This soothed her. She leaned forward and blew breath from the back of her throat to fog the window, then traced the maple again. It dissipated quickly, but the oil from her skin left a delicate outline. "I don't know," she said.

"Yes, there's a fountain, but it's not working," he said. "Either that, or it's supposed to be a birdbath." She heard Richard splash his hand in the fountain's bowl.

Suddenly it seemed imperative that she picture the rooftop garden. "Are you near a tree?" she said.

"Yeah, they're all along the path. Not very big, though."

"Pick one of the leaves off." She waited. "What does it look like?"

"Oh, come on, Hiawatha, I don't know. Green. They're green leaves. Why?"

His voice didn't match his words; it smiled, they expressed exasperation. "I was right, wasn't I? This *is* some kind of Greenpeace phone sex game. Okay, I'll play along."

"I said, what's it look like? And I don't mean the color," she said.

"It looks like a hand."

Corinne held her right hand at arm's length. "You can do better than that. All leaves look something like a hand. Is it a hand with the fingers spread or closed together?" As she spoke, she stretched her own fingers apart, then closed them together, then apart again.

"Wait a second, let me get another one. The wind blew the first one away." She heard Richard rustle in another branch. "Closed."

She pictured a miniature Bradford; no, probably a gingko. She switched the phone from her left to her right hand and held the newly freed one before her, fingers closed like the gingko leaf. The diamond in her wedding ring caught sunlight from the window.

"You still there?" Richard said. "I said the leaf has its fingers closed. Now what?"

Corinne dropped her hand to her thigh with a slap. "What's going to happen when I find Duncan?" she said.

"Can't say. That's not really up to me. But I know one thing, Corinne. This is not entirely your or my fault. I'm not saying Dunc had this coming, but for a long time, I don't think he's had his priorities straight."

Corinne eased back to the sofa and sat on its wide arm. She realized this was the true reason she had called Richard Rice. In so many ways, he knew her husband better than she did. "How so?" she said.

"Maybe I'm not really the best person for this lecture because I'm the opposite side of his coin, but let me ask you this: when was the last time Duncan Post had some fun? I don't mean a golf game with some stiff suits, or one of those stupendously dull Broadway shows you two are forced to sit through at the Aronoff—I mean, how many times can you watch a grown man in a cat costume wail out 'Memories'— just so our company could be seen as 'supporters of the arts,' or just be seen, period? What I'm talking about is when is the last time the two of you lay naked in bed, letting chocolate syrup drip off your belly onto those expensive sheets of yours, and laughing, really laughing, at an old Peter Sellers movie? When's the last time you ate something that covered your whole plate, something with gravy, something that didn't look like art? Hell, Duncan and I lived for a whole month in college on Doritos and Spam because we were too busy and too broke working on the dream of showplace.com to even call for a pizza delivery. That was when work was fun, when it was a dream."

Corinne wanted, needed, to stop the assault. "Slow down a second, Nero; I believe you were fiddling while showplace.com burned. I don't think we avoided fun, I call it tending to responsibility."

"Think about it, Corinne. We live in a dotcom world. Nothing here is permanent; most of us are obsolete when we first feel complete. This was never going to be an Amazon.com or Ebay; couldn't be."

"It allows you to live pretty well, I'd say."

"That it does," he allowed. "But you've got to be willing to lose a million to make ten. In fact, you've got to figure that cycle will repeat itself many times. That's what Duncan didn't, and apparently doesn't, understand. He was trying to build not just something substantial and meaningful, but something immutable." Richard sighed, as if the analysis tired him. "I'll bet Duncan knew when he walked into the office that night that what he saw on our computer screen was simulated sex, that it wasn't and hadn't ever been real. He knew I'd been working on that software, and that it could make us other millions. That he saw it as a betrayal is understandable for someone who's always wanted to be traditional. But that wasn't what caused him to hit me with that monitor."

The memory, even now, caused Corinne to blush. "What else could it be?"

"The same thing that's bothered him since we were in college. Duncan could not control the whole animal. It had gotten too big. He's always lived in the future, thinking that if he couldn't see it clearly, he could at least predict it. What happened, or didn't happen, between you and me did not fit into his equation. He didn't foresee it." He paused. "Hey, can you hear that? Listen."

Corinne could tell Richard held the phone away from him. Water burbled.

"The fountain just came on. Must have been on a timer." He sounded giddy, released. "Damn, it *is* peaceful."

For moments, neither spoke while they listened to the water dance. "I'm going to have to get to that meeting, girl. Got to get started on the next million…or two. I think I want a fountain at home."

"Richard," Corinne said then stood. "I'm sorry Duncan hurt you."

"Oh, I've got a permanent lump on the back of my head that feels like a Volkswagen, but I'm still startlingly handsome." He laughed. "Tell you what: if you can get the info from that Daugherty ape, I'll go with you wherever you have to go to find our Post-Man. Besides, we'll have to throw him his birth-day bash — pardon the painful pun. We've missed each other's big 3-0 since he's been on hiatus."

"I might take you up on that," she said, and she knew she would.

"In fact, why don't you get that hippie chick friend of yours to go, too. She's hot in that leather-fringed, peasant-topped, Mother Earth kind of way," he said and flipped his phone off.

"Asshole," Corinne smiled into the phone's dead air, knowing that he was already on his way to the next meeting.

## CHAPTER 14

Apparently, old man Hundley had taken it easy on me during our ATV ride earlier that day. I know this by contrast because Tessie certainly did not. She tossed me an old volunteer fire department helmet of Daylon's, the red surface scratched and scuffed. I was afraid to ask if the damage had occurred when Daylon fought fires or during some horrific ATV accident.

"Where's yours?" I said after pulling the chinstrap tight.

"Can't hurt this old pumpkin," she said, tapping her knuckles against her temple. "Besides, I don't like to wear one on this ride. Like to see and smell everything. Don't tell Poppie?" And before I could insist that she wear mine, the familiar apian buzz of the vehicle's engine droned across the barnyard.

We sped off in a direction new to me; this time through the sweeping front yard, across the dirt road, and then down the steep slope that led to some shallow riffles of Sinking Creek. The ATV jounced and tilted, but Tessie's butt hovered just above the seat, her head still, her knees acting as shock absorbers responding to the rugged terrain. She looked like the slow-motion footage I'd seen of thoroughbred jockeys whose backs and heads seemed frozen parallel to the horse while everything below them churns violently.

I, on the other hand, held onto the metal cargo grid on the back of the four-wheeler with both hands, as my ass bounced off its wires. I felt like I was being paddled with a barbeque grill rack.

I knew it would do no good, but in a normal voice, which of course could not be heard, I told Tessie to slow down. I'm not sure I wanted her to hear. And just as I did, she let out a whoop, and we splashed across Sinking Creek, driving fans of water into the air, which drenched us before the ATV could climb the even steeper opposite bank.

Though shaggy from irregular use and overhung with whipping tree branches, the path was still distinct. Someone used it just enough to keep the forest from reclaiming it. I assumed that someone to be Tessie. The path paralleled the twisting creek, and I very quickly learned to pay as much attention to our course as if I were the driver because Tessie was just as likely to race through the dangling limbs or lashing grasses as she was to steer around them, even when she had that option. I ducked when she ducked, leaned when she leaned, to avoid whelps on my face or legs, or worse, a concussive blow from the forearm of an oak tree.

Tessie cheered with the speed, and I suspect if the ATV's whine weren't so loud, her joyous yelping would have echoed back from Sinking Creek's banks. In fact, once or twice I thought I was able to hear the echo. But it wasn't a traditional echo. Turns out, it was me.

Mud churned behind us, over us. It covered my face, got in my nose. At one point I held on with one hand and with the other grabbed a snapping coil of Tessie's tangerine hair and wiped some mud from my eyes. I felt like a reckless character in some violent video game, buffeted by forces both seen and unseen, not even in control of my own immediate safety. But I felt safe, nonetheless. Whereas Summerset had scaled and descended hills with caution, occasionally reaching one hand behind him to steady me, Tessie careened across the rough terrain, indeed *sought out* bumps or puddles, and all the furious while I felt safe.

The path crisscrossed the creek several times at shallow shoals. Each time, she accelerated to climb the opposite bank, and each time we flew over the blind lip and landed with a splat squarely onto the path's center. Cresting a particularly impressive bank, Tessie shouted for me to hold on as the ATV went airborne and, it seemed to me, nearly tipped backwards. She screamed something unintelligibly jubilant at the four-wheeler's apex, I grabbed for her waist, and only the sky loomed before us.

The back wheels landed first, then the front, and our speed never diminished. I felt a splatter of mud hit my teeth and realized this only happened because I had been grinning.

I've no idea how far we rode in terms of miles, or even how long the trip took. Time and distance in the woods are measured by alternate parameters. I learned this quickly in my stint under the bridge. I knew, for instance, that I could walk from there to the plaza in half an hour, but I knew that because I had a watch. Later, after I lost it, I measured that half hour by the landmarks I passed along my trail: the sycamore tree scorched and split by lightning, the kudzu patch that changed shape as the summer dragged along, and the narrow creek sandbar that displayed an assortment of animal footprints and sunning turtles who slipped like plates into the water as I approached.

I had cursed my watch's loss, and continued to look at my empty wrist long after its disappearance, but soon adjusted to this new way of marking…marking what? Time, distance? Somehow in the woods neither was clearly delineated, at least not to the same degree or with the same accuracy that I was accustomed to. I learned to judge some of this by the sun's movement, but here was something that baffled me — the moon rose and set at odd, and apparently random, times, sometimes before night fell. I don't think I had ever noticed that before, or if I had, it hadn't really registered.

So, Tessie and I could have ridden thirty minutes or ten miles. Or an hour or five miles. I don't know, but at length, we came to a wide clearing and the path's end, and Tessie cut the engine before we emerged from the woods. Exhaust curled up around us, and the buzzing in my ears continued even after I pulled the fire helmet from my head. I wondered if I looked like Daylon after a fire, with only his forehead clean where the helmet had protected it from the soot, and the whites of his eyes shining. Tessie dismounted with a feline leap, turned to me, and immediately lost her breath with laughter.

The sun had come out while we rode and gave the clearing a sharpness that seemed almost painful after the muted forest. Wisps of mist writhed from the drying grass, the only movement in what otherwise could have been a still-life since in the precise center of the open field stood a small, white clapboard church. I knew it was a church before I read the sign proclaiming it the Sinking Creek Baptist Church because the building was straight out of a Hollywood set designer's vision of a prototypical country chapel, scrubbed, sparkling, with a tower that held a brass bell whose patina revealed great age, and in the back field, a small, tree-spangled cemetery.

A gravel road curved in front of the church, and I knew we could have gotten here via that road rather than the circuitous path through the woods. I knew, too, that Tessie would never have done so. I waited for her laughter to slow. "Do you go to church here?" I said.

Tessie wiped the mud from her face. Then she licked her thumbs, scraped them across my cheekbones just below my eyes, and flicked the mud to the ground. No one, not even my mother, had ever performed such a toiletry on me as that.

She stood back to look at her handiwork. "There. Now you look like the opposite of a raccoon," she said and laughed again.

I resisted the urge to rub the area she had just wiped to remove any traces of saliva, but only because my hands were too muddy to do so.

I wondered why she didn't answer my innocuous question, so I asked again. "Is this where you go to church?"

By now she was walking across the field toward the church. I followed.

"Not really. Kind of, but not really. Used to, though. Everybody else does."

"You mean Della, Daylon, and your dad?"

"And everybody else in Sinking Creek. Well, everybody who goes to church," she said.

As Tessie neared the side of the church, she slowed and her posture took on the exaggerated stalking gait of a cartoon character sneaking up on something, back hunched, knees high.

"What are you doing?" I said.

"Shhh. I want to show you something," she whispered.

She tiptoed—I swear, tiptoed—to the building's side. Beneath the middle of the three windows there sat two stacked cinder blocks. Without them, neither of us could have easily looked inside. Tessie stepped up, held her hands over her eyes like a visor and peered through the dark window. She looked, it appeared, toward the back of the church, toward what I assumed to be the pulpit, and nowhere else. She didn't seem to be searching for anything, just staring laser-like at something in particular, and when at length she turned away from the window, she wore a smug look of vindication. She hopped from the blocks.

"Now you," she said.

Dutifully, I stepped onto the blocks. They wobbled

slightly, and I grabbed onto the wooden windowsill to steady myself. Once stable, I placed one hand over my eyes and pressed against the window as Tessie had. "What am I looking for?" I said after a moment because, as far as I could tell, there was nothing remarkable about the church. There were probably twenty rows of wooden pews on either side of a narrow aisle that led to an unadorned lectern carved with a simple cross. It wasn't as ornate as a meeting room in a Holiday Inn. In fact, it paled in comparison to the grand Lutheran Church where Corinne and I had married on what the lifestyle section of the *Cincinnati Enquirer* had called "a glorious May evening." She had searched for months for the proper venue. Yet, neither of us had set foot in that church since our last photo was taken at the bottom of the front stairs, smiling ridiculously widely, and stretching our arms illogically before our faces to guard us from the floating flower petals. Now that was a church.

"What am I looking for?" I said again. She still did not answer. I lowered my hand and turned to her.

She stood with her hand on a jutted hip. "Well, goofus, what do you see? Look again."

I peered back into the darkened sanctuary. "Pews, a podium, hymnals…" There were details that came to me now, but nothing special, "…a banner with some icons I don't recognize. Except for the fish; I know the fish has something to do with religion."

"Duncan Post," she huffed. "What's the most important thing you see in the whole room?"

I didn't see anything extraordinary, but I knew there must be a bible in there, and that must be what Tessie wanted me to answer. "A Bible?"

"Not that. Look up behind the pulpit. Up at the wall."

I did. Encased in the wall was a large stained-glass window. The figure was Jesus standing barefoot in a pastoral setting. His arms hung at his side, but the palms faced forward in invitation. His cream robe flowed to the ground, bunching on either side of his feet, and a scarlet outer shawl draped from his shoulders. This seemed pretty commonplace, I guessed. His expression, however, was unusual — enigmatic, rather than recognizably joyful. When I first glanced at it, it seemed almost sadly beatific, as if he were tolerating a mildly mischievous child not pictured in the scene. But the next time I looked at his face, the smile seemed more genuine, an untethered, if not happiness, then satisfaction. The smile, of course, had not really changed, but something did. Each time there were new nuances to the expression, and I found myself looking away from its face, then quickly back, and trying to define the altered aspect. This went on for at least a minute, and each time I thought I saw something new and justifiable in the figure's countenance. But I doubted that something this subtle could be what Tessie commanded me to see.

"The stained glass window? Is that what you brought me here to see?" I turned from the window, both to talk to her directly and to be able to turn back and look again at the stained glass Jesus to see if it wore another expression.

She smiled. "He's looking right at you, ain't he?"

"What do you mean?"

"He looks like he's looking right at you. In the eyes. You're standing out here, outside this church, peeking in the side window, and his eyes are looking right at you," she said.

I looked back. This time his was the smile of a complicit prankster. But she was right — the eyes did indeed look at me. I told her so.

"Good. Now come this way," she said, grabbing my hand and pulling me from the cinder block perch.

We ran — or rather she ran and I was dragged — around

to the small gravel parking lot in front of the church, then up the five concrete steps to the dual doors, each containing a small window. Tessie stationed herself in front of the left door and placed me in front of the right. Letting go of my hand, she put her face up to the window and motioned for me to do the same.

"Look there. Look at window Jesus," she said.

This time the face looked neutral. I couldn't sense either approval or approbation.

Tessie said, "He's looking right at us, don't you think?"

He was. But I expected this. I wanted to tell her that this was simply an illusion that many artists could create, nothing special about it. I'd seen the same effect created in works ranging from sculptures to holograms to mascots painted on gymnasium floors.

But before I could answer, she again grabbed my hand and pulled me down the steps toward the other side of the building. I knew what she was going to show me now. From our first perch I had seen that identical windows faced them, and that she wanted me to see that the stained glass figure could see us through those windows, too. Sure enough, when we got there, two stacked cinder blocks waited. And that, not the window's illusory guardianship, is what intrigued me.

"Get up there," she commanded, "and tell me he ain't looking at you there, too."

I climbed up. "That he is, Tess; that he is," I said after my cursory glance inside. Jesus' look was of benign sufferance, as if we shared the caretaker's role of this tortured soul.

Tessie's smile was triumphant. "Know what I bet?" she said.

"What's that?"

"Stay right here; don't move," she instructed, then took off running back around the front of the church. In seconds I saw her looking at me through the window on the opposite side of the building. She shouted, and I heard her clearly in the stillness.

"Look at window Jesus," she said and simultaneously pointed toward the stained glass window. Both of us placed our hands to our windows and squinted in. Jesus wore a patient smile. "Is he looking at you?" she yelled.

He was, of course. I told her so.

"Me, too. He's looking at both of us at the same time! I knew it!"

Her eyes remained riveted on the stained glass window. I did not look back up at it myself. I was afraid that, given the choice, the window Jesus might not be looking at me now.

We met back around on the front steps and sat down. Late summer cicadas filled the void of our silences with trills that rose to deafening screeches before subsiding, then starting again. I always thought I was uncomfortable with stillness, but I learned under the bridge that there is no real silence. There are just different things to hear.

"When did you put those cinder blocks under the windows, Tess? When you used to go here?"

"I didn't put them there."

"Who did?" And before I finished the question, I knew the answer.

"Don't know. Just one Sunday, they was there."

"So, it happened before you stopped coming here," I said.

"Oh, I never stopped coming here. I never told you that. I just told you I didn't go to church." Tessie's tone was a lecture. She made me feel as if I couldn't grasp even the simplest of concepts, and that it was requiring great patience for her to tolerate that. "I still come here every Sunday, rain or shine, snow or sleet. Hail, too, I guess. I just don't come till everybody's inside, and I stay out here."

"You *watch* church?"

"From right here on these blocks," she said as if stating the obvious.

"So, someone from the church probably put those blocks there so you could see in?" I assumed it to be Summerset or Daylon.

"Nobody knows I'm here, so I don't figure nobody bothered to put them here. Least I didn't want anybody to," she said. She picked a pebble from the step and tossed it into the gravel lot. "It's plain as can be, Duncan Post, who put those blocks there."

Please, no, I thought. Please don't let her say what I know she is going to say. Then, she did.

"Window Jesus saw me outside. He always saw me when I was inside, but it surprised me first time I was outside and saw him looking. He set the blocks there so I wouldn't have to stand on tiptoes and stiff my neck."

Tessie had brought me here to her "special place" after our conversation about the seven deafening sins and how to be absolved for them, and though I didn't fully grasp why she thought seeing window Jesus could do that, I respected her sincere but transparent attempt. I thanked her.

She considered my thanks and accepted it as forthright. It was, I suppose, as genuine as I was capable of.

"You like it here?" she said.

"It's nice. Peaceful. Is this where you come when you leave home for awhile?" I wanted to tread carefully, but I thought it might be nice to report this to Summerset et al, to relieve them of that anxiety they felt at her disappearances. It might be my way of thanking them for, well, for a lot of things.

"Goodness, no. I come here when I need to think about stuff. Stuff like what you're thinking about." She lowered her voice and leaned over to me. "Stuff like one of those sins. Window Jesus lets me know it's okay I make mistakes."

"How so?

"Smiles. He smiles at me even when I've been not-so-good. He always gives me exactly the same smile. So he knows if I feel bad about what I done, he forgives me. Did he smile at you when you was looking?"

Her wide, pretty face seemed open to either answer I might give, so I opted for honesty. "He did."

She leaned back. "Of course. So now you feel better about what you might have done to somebody?"

This time I chose dishonesty. "That I do, Tessie. That I do."

"See?"

"But this isn't where you come those other times?" I pressed.

"I said no," and there was a firmness to her voice like a palm held before her face. I let it drop.

Then I had an idea, and it was both for Tessie's benefit and for my own curiosity. "Let's walk around back and see if window Jesus can see out of the back of his eyes, too."

If I thought she'd jump at this variation on the game she started, I was very wrong. Tessie's expressive face grew immediately blank. "He can," she said tonelessly.

"Well, let's go see," I said and stood, offering my hand to pull her up.

She looked at my hand as if it had crap on it. "I said, I know he can. Now, you can go look if you don't believe me, but I'm staying right here."

I didn't insist because I knew that, yet again, I had trespassed on some hidden patch of painful ground in Tessie's past.

She put her elbows on the step behind her. "You go on,

though. I'm just going to sit for a spell in the sun," she said, then closed her eyes and raised her face expectantly toward the sky, accepting the warmth as a sunflower might.

And so I did; I did walk around the shady side of the church through the still damp grass, and before I got there I knew two things: I knew that window Jesus would appear to be looking at me, and I knew what that tiny church cemetery in the back held.

When I emerged from the shade into the sunlight of the field behind the church, I didn't bother to look at the stained glass window. Instead, I walked the twenty yards back to the graves. Light winds sighed through the tall cedars, whose deep smell brushed over me like a cobweb.

Neither the monuments themselves nor their layout was orderly. The cemetery lacked the crisp geometry and uniformity of, say, a military burial ground, or even, for that matter, some municipal graveyard, pre-plotted by companies for whom death was big business. No, this seemed as though each death took the church's congregation by surprise, and that they gathered, took stock of available space, either beside a cedar or in the sun, then dug a hole. Some stones dripped with sap, looked stained and worn. Others stayed polished and clean. They ranged from ornately carved affairs with lines of Bible verses, to simple sandstone scraped only with names and dates of birth and death.

I walked slowly through them. A couple of times I thought of turning back because I didn't know if I really wanted to see the Hundley's names. Some of the dates startled me with their brevity, and I found myself mentally subtracting the birth from the death dates and dreading those I found whose lives were shorter than mine. There were a disconcerting number of those.

The shade of the cedar trees and the power of their perfume began to close in on me, and I headed for the sun. I found them there. Summerset had chosen the perfect site, part of the day in the shade, part in the light, and though it was, of course, illogical, I knew he had done so for their perceived comfort. Or for his.

There were others named Hundley nearby, the birth dates indicating that some were ancestors and others contemporaries of Summerset's, possibly cousins or even brothers, and though the two stones on the margin of the Hundley's — those that bore Maude's and Andy's names and the simple inscription "Not My Will But Thine" — were similar in style and size, they stood out to me immediately.

Andy's grave lay just to the left of his mother's, and their headstones were identical except in size, Maude's being just taller, as if she still watched over her son. I had the strange notion that she lay on her side, as she had at their death, and reached to encircle the boy again. One day, I was sure, Summerset would flank him, and that room for one more would be left in between.

I don't know why I had needed to find them; I don't know why I dreaded seeing them. And most of all, I don't know why, when at last I knelt before them, tracing the grooves of their names with the fingers of my right hand, first Maude's and then Andy's, dampness soaking through the knees of my pants, why tears chased themselves down my face.


The clearing's stillness was broken by Tessie's shout: "If you're going with me, Harry Trueman, you better get out here," followed immediately by the whirring, then catching, of the ATV's ignition. From the edge of the woods where we had left the vehicle, she stood up on the four-wheeler's pegs, raised a hand and waved as if she were riding a rodeo bull. I waved back, struggled up on creaky knees and headed toward her. But before I left the back of the church, I looked once more toward window Jesus. The sun glinted too brilliantly off the window, however, to see if he was looking back.

## CHAPTER 15 – DEXTER/CORINNE

Dexter Daugherty pushed the blue plastic tray to the far edge of the table, disgusted with another failed resolution to eat better and, if not lose weight, at least feel healthier. The tray held two crumpled taco wrappers and a paper plate with only the smears of refried beans and the vivid, artificially cheerful yellow of nacho cheese sauce. It mocked him now that he was full. From a briefcase parked beside his feet, he extracted several pictures of Duncan Post and spread them on the cleared section of the table. The pictures ranged from grainy newspaper photos to candid snapshots of Duncan at play, to more formally posed glossies, all provided by Corinne early in Dexter's search for her husband.

But "search" was not a particularly apt term for what Dexter had done, he mused, because once he had conducted some background research into the Posts, it only took two phone calls for him to find Duncan's approximate location. And he had to admit this was less the result of stellar detective work and more the fruits of cultivating relationships within the Ohio State Police Department. That and blind luck, of course.

But in the intervening weeks, he had not revealed her husband's whereabouts to Corinne Post, and for the life of him, he could not say why. Though they were not protected by the same confidentiality privilege enjoyed by patients and doctors, much less priests and confessors, Dexter had always taken that as an implicit agreement with his clients. Corinne had selected him, she said at their first meeting, precisely because of his reputation for discretion. And yet, he had taken this confidentiality to the opposite extreme. Not only had he kept his investigation private so far, he had even withheld the single, simple result for which she had hired him.

Dexter decided that his reason for doing so was justifiable. He wasn't going to charge her for any of his time since he had verified where Duncan was. He was jaded, and wasn't that understandable after a twenty year career of digging through both the figurative and literal trash of human existence? His instinct told him this case offered something else — a glimpse into Corinne Post's attempt at redemption. It hadn't begun that way, of course. It seemed in the beginning to be another in the long tradition of cheating spouses (either one was the potential culprit here — he couldn't decide) who hid their indiscretions or their money or their real motivations behind façades of caring or "damaged" reputations. It was all so much bullshit, yet disgusting as these cases were, they afforded some private investigators very comfortable après-work lifestyles.

But once Dexter saw that there had been no foul play, nothing overtly criminal in this case, he had become intrigued by Corinne's seemingly selfless desire to find her husband. And what husband risks losing such beauty, such prestige, and such wealth to hole up in some "holler" in rural Virginia in the home of a man he doesn't know and shares nothing with? Okay, he was hurt by something that transpired between his wife and this Rice cat, but if she was to be believed — and Dexter did — this "virtual indiscretion" was less than nothing. Rich guys lived in more complex and amoral worlds than this.

Yet Daugherty liked the idea. He liked what he had come to know about both of these people. He would leave them to one another soon, but first he wanted to meet this Summerset Hundley who seemed to be protecting Post as tenaciously as Corinne did.

After he took Corinne's case, Dexter's first call had been to a friend in the Ohio State Police office. A quick computer check discovered that the Porsche registered to Duncan Post had been towed from the shoulder of Interstate 81 to the travel plaza just south, then from there impounded at a garage in a little town called Sinking Creek after an employee reported that no one claimed it from the plaza. That employee, Dexter learned, was Summerset Hundley. Apparently, only a single, unanswered phone call to the Post home was made. The Virginia State Police pursued it no further after impoundment.

Dexter's second call, then, had been to Hundley at the travel plaza. Yes, he was familiar with the car — it had simply run out of gas. No, he was not aware of any driver. Yes, he thought it odd that no one had claimed such a nice car. No, he hadn't heard of anyone named Duncan Post. And yes, he would keep his eyes open for anything unusual.

And then Summerset Hundley had asked Dexter a question that told the investigator exactly what he wanted to know: "Has this Mr. Post done something real bad?"

Yet it still wasn't this phrasing that sealed the deal for him. When Daugherty answered in the negative, Hundley's response was a relieved, "Well, that's good," and that relief was what he was trained to hear. It was that relief that told him that Post was in no danger, hadn't been kidnapped, killed, or coerced, and that the dotcom wunderkind was doing no harm to anyone else, either.

Duncan Post had quite simply run away from home.

\*\*\*\*\*\*\*\*\*\*\*\*\*\*\*\*\*\*\*\*\*\*\*\*\*\*\*\*\*\*\*\*\*\*\*\*\*\*\*\*\*\*

"Oh, yes, ma'am, I'm going with you," Ariel told Corinne.

"That's not necessary. I just called to tell you the news."

"You're letting Richard Rice go with you, but I'm not invited?" Ariel's playful indignance indicated she knew she would, in fact, be part of the trip to wherever.

A couple of mild, disingenuous protests later, Corinne admitted, "Well, if you think you can get away, maybe it would be good to have you along."

"Rinnie, honey, you *have* to take me along. Someone needs to occasionally smack the shit out of Richard Rice, and probably smack you, too, truth be told," she said, then dropped the playful tone and continued. "And I don't know if you've thought much about this, honey, but are you really ready for what you might find? No...for *who* you might find?"

Corinne was not. She had thought about this, had realized this was why she wanted both Richard and Ariel with her when she saw Duncan for the first time after so many months. "Yes," she said. "I'm ready for whatever."

"That's not true, but we'll go with that for now," Ariel said and let out something that sounded like a whoop. "A road trip. I can't wait, and I don't even know where we're going."

Corinne hung up. Daugherty would call soon—in the next few days he had said—and Corinne thought how true it was that she really did not know where she was going.
*******************************

Dexter put two pictures—one candid shot of Duncan awkwardly petting a horse, and a posed shot of Duncan and Corinne on the beach during their honeymoon—in his shirt pocket. These he would show Summerset in a few moments. He put the remaining photos back into his briefcase, snapped it shut, and leaned back in his chair.

He would walk back through the broad opening of the plaza's Taco Bell and introduce himself to Summerset Hundley, but the investigator in him wanted to observe the man unnoticed for a bit longer. An hour ago, when he had first arrived after the drive from the Bristol airport, he thought he'd march into the plaza, find Hundley, and sit for a while, eliciting from, and sharing information with, the old man. But once he got out of the rental car and stretched his stiff legs and back, something in the smells around him made him delay that plan.

Though this was a good deal south of Cincinnati, it was cooler here, and the leaves had already begun to turn. Back home they just looked tired. Must be the altitude, he thought. He looked across the expanse of blacktop toward the high hills. It is…pretty, he decided, and laughed because *pretty* was the only word he could come up with.

The parking lot smelled like French fries and diesel exhaust, but behind those smells he got a whiff of something else: an earthy smell of downed leaves and damp ground that recalled for him those hours spent playing football for fun as a kid, before it became something more as a high school, then a college, athlete. Though there would never be a man's cologne named after it, there should be. It was a good smell, and he wondered if there was something in the smells that kept Duncan here.

The main room inside the entrance that served as the plaza's hub buzzed with people, travelers out for an early fall weekend, but Dexter had picked out Hundley immediately. He wore an unbuttoned maroon vest over a crisp white shirt and leaned over the glass-topped desk pointing out something on a map to a middle-aged couple. He spoke animatedly, and the couple smiled occasionally and nodded. They thanked him with a handshake, and Hundley put his left hand on top of the clasp, too.  The man must love his job, Dexter thought, because he probably gives those very same directions to so many other drivers.

The first restaurant to the left was the Taco Bell he rested in now, and where Dexter decided to forego the initiation of his new diet until tomorrow.  He wasn't here to spy on the man, nor did he think that was necessary.  He fully intended to disclose his identity to Hundley and arrange a meeting with Duncan Post.

After Dexter's initial phone conversation with Summerset, they had spoken five or six more times.  There was confusion—at least on Hundley's part—about the name of the man that Dexter sought.

"I'm sorry, sir," Hundley had drawled, "I can't say I know anybody by that name."

Dexter explained as patiently as possible that Duncan might not be using his real name, but after he assured him that Duncan was neither in trouble nor dangerous, Summerset couldn't accept that someone with nothing to hide would willfully take a different name.  Once the old man acknowledged the resemblance of someone he met at the plaza to the man Dexter described, the investigator knew he had found Duncan Post.  He knew, too, that to go any further, he might have to earn the trust of the man who seemed to be taking on the role of Duncan's protector.

Summerset was not necessarily expecting him, but their last conversation had ended with his telling Dexter he would cooperate in any way he could.

From his vantage point inside the restaurant, Dexter watched Summerset passing out maps, pointing toward one of the several fast food joints, gift shops, and restrooms in the plaza, and all the while, even in the brief interludes between dispensing advice and information, he smiled. He made eye contact with every person who walked through the plaza's automatic doors. He had done so with Dexter, too, when he came in earlier, but Dexter simply looked through him and away, appearing preoccupied, as if he already knew exactly where he was going. It was an old trick he used to distance himself from the action until he could get his bearings, assess the situation, and formulate his course of action. Watch others, while not drawing attention to himself.

There was the briefest moment, though, when Dexter wondered if the old man might have known who he was. Could there have been a spark of recognition, or curiosity, or suspicion in Summerset's steady smile and slight nod? But that, of course, was paranoid, and paranoia was a luxury that people in his business could not allow themselves. Besides, this visit was totally unannounced, in fact, was as spontaneous as Dexter could be.

Dexter looked around at the scores of other travelers and their garb. It was—what would he call it?—eclectic. People dressed in sweatsuits, people dressed in business suits, and everything in between. His khaki corduroys and dark brown shirt were as good as camouflage. He was safe. He'd be revealed when he chose.

Dexter crossed the broad atrium and entered the gift shop across from the Taco Bell. He knew as he walked past the information kiosk that Summerset would glance briefly at him, would follow him with his eyes for a step or two in case Dexter needed help, because in this past hour he had watched him do so countless times. But the investigator's walk had been forceful, purposeful, and he hadn't made eye contact.

The gift shop afforded him some additional time and a different angle from which to observe Summerset. Like a poker player, he was looking for a tell, some giveaway into the man's true feelings as he dealt with the occasional asshole. Dexter figured he would maintain professional decorum, but there'd be something—a flattening of the smile, a nanosecond's paralysis of the solicitous expression—that would betray some lack of patience or tolerance.

He needed this. He wouldn't see it as a character flaw, just a sign of humanity, and that would, to Dexter's way of thinking, be a comfort.

He picked up a few knickknacks, thumbed through some magazines, and unfolded and held up some sweatshirts with inane slogans, all the while watching Hundley.

Nothing, though. No change of demeanor. The man seemed genuinely eager to help both those who needed it and those who demanded it. Though this contradicted what he knew of human nature, he chalked it up as the exception that proved the rule. Perhaps it was possible that the Summerset Hundley with whom he had spoken on the phone was real, and that he wasn't sheltering Duncan Post for any reason other than altruism. Daugherty had uncovered no previous ties between them, nothing to suggest that Post had sought the man for refuge or solace. It was what it seemed: a serendipitous meeting between a man who needed help and this man who needed to give it.

Dexter pulled the pictures of Duncan from his shirt pocket and scrutinized them again. Maybe Duncan was somewhere in the plaza even now. Dexter tried to envision his subject with facial hair, different haircuts, with more weight, with less; he opened his mind to the variety of possibilities that his job often demanded.

"That's probably a bit small for you," a voice behind his left shoulder said. "'Less it's not for you."

Though he was startled, he didn't flinch; however, he

was a shade disappointed in himself. People simply didn't catch him off guard.

He turned to see a squat, wide-faced woman with an impressive pile of brown hair twirled tightly atop her head. The hair is what Dexter looked at. "Beg pardon?" he said.

She pointed at the sweatshirt he had draped over his left forearm when he had pulled the pictures out for study. "That sweatshirt is a small; the larges is over on this table, but they run kind of small, too, so maybe you need a Extra-Large, in which case, they're all over on this table, but by this time of day and with this big a crowd, they're liable to be anywhichwhere. I have a devil of a time keeping everything tidied up while still manning—or maybe I should say womanning—the register, answering the phone, signing for deliveries, and just generally swabbing the decks." She laughed at her own cleverness.

Dexter marveled at the woman's torrent of words. He laid the picture on the table to free his hand to refold the sweatshirt.

She went on. "But excuse me for being a Little Miss Buttinski. You probably wasn't even buying it for you. I don't know why I didn't think of that. It's probably a souvenir for somebody. Gosh, I'm the dullest knife in the drawer." She reached toward the photos that Dexter had placed on the glass display case. "Maybe I can guesstimate the size if I see a picture of the precipitant."

Quickly, he put his hand on the pictures. "No, that's all right. I was just looking, just killing time. I'll probably just get a magazine and get back on the road," he said.

But it was too late.

The woman reacted as if it were Christmas. "Hey, that's Mr. Harry Trueman," she squealed and reached again for the pictures.

Dexter had known that Post must have been using an alias, especially once Summerset Hundley had told him he didn't know anyone by that name; but Harry Truman? That would hardly have been the tactic of someone trying to avoid discovery. Certainly, it would have spawned more questions than it would have quelled. And why would a gift shop girl recognize his subject by both face and, well, "name"?

"You know him?" Dexter said and held the photos toward her. This time she did not touch them. Instead, she held her arms behind her back and leaned toward them, as if examining a corpse. Clearly, she did know Duncan Post, but as she continued to inspect the pictures, Dexter saw something in her face begin to close down, like shutters being drawn and locks snapping shut. She looked up from the pictures, but not toward Dexter. She seemed to scan through the gift shop's opening toward the atrium, toward, Dexter was sure, Summerset Hundley. The investigator looked in the same direction. Hundley was kneeling in front of a brochure rack, selecting some of the literature and handing it over his shoulder to a woman holding a baby behind him. His back was to the gift shop girl.

Apparently, she wasn't waiting for any communication from Hundley, but it seemed that she drew fortification by simply looking at him, because when Dexter looked back at her, she met his eyes with a boldness that shook him. Her smile did not include her eyes.

"No, sir, I was mistaken. I hadn't got a real good look at first, but now I can see I was wrong." She unfolded, then refolded the same sweatshirt. "He just looks like somebody I went to high school with. Magazines is over there," she said, pointing toward the rack with her chin. "Let me know if I can help you find anything." She walked toward of couple of teen-aged girls picking up lip-gloss and charm bracelets. "Help you, ladies?" Dexter heard her say.

Dexter would not bother her. Grilling her would not elicit any more information, and now that he had been discovered, his time was brief. He picked up a pack of gum, handed the woman—whose nametag read "Della"—a dollar, and left without waiting for his change. He angled his body away from Summerset as he walked through the automatic doors into crystalline October sunshine.

He would not talk to Summerset Hundley either; would not arrange a meeting with Duncan Post. He had nearly overstepped his purview and was mildly disappointed in his lack of discipline. But, dammit, he wanted one happy ending, one case whose complexity wasn't the result of malevolence but of genuine human emotion. No, he would close the book on Hundley and he would snoop no deeper in this plaza.

This case may or may not end happily-ever-after, but that was neither in his hands nor of his concern. From what little he really knew of the Posts, of Summerset Hundley, of their true motives, things could still go right for these people.

Or things could go wrong. It was best not to give a rat's ass.

His rental car, a silver Ford Taurus, too small, really, for his hulking frame, wasn't far from the plaza's entrance, but Dexter did not walk straight to it. Instead, he ambled toward the parking lot's fringes and looked into the deep woods that encircled him. He did love this smell, even found himself nostalgic for the feel of the dirt from the football fields of his youth, dirt that clung to his face mask, dirt that tangled in his hair, even clogged his ears, and that he would watch dissolve into mud and swirl down the drain of the steamy locker room showers after practice. Though he thought every day about football, had incorporated many of its lessons into his life's philosophy, he had not thought about the dirt in years. In his business, he thought when at length he shuffled back to his car, "dirt" meant a whole other ball game.

He could bill Corinne Post for this trip, but he knew he wouldn't. He'd simply drive back to the Bristol airport and fly back to Cincinnati. Drawing a deep breath, then another, he flipped open his cell and dialed her number.

Corinne had no idea what to pack, or how much. She opened the door to Duncan's study, the first time she had done so since the night he left, and unbuttoned her cardigan. Though every room in the house was the same temperature, somehow this one felt warmer. She had not avoided this room, not in the way that someone makes a missing person's room into a shrine out of respect or grief, she had just not experienced any occasion to enter it. Now, however, she needed to use his computer to find out the weather in some place called Sinking Creek, Virginia.

Corinne had never really liked Duncan's study. It just didn't "say" Duncan to her. It seemed pretentious. He could be superficial, and she could see how others might have the wrong impression about him, but this was because he was fascinated by so many things, wanted to know *something* about *everything*. In some people this might have been trivial knowledge gathered solely to show off, but she had never felt this was Duncan's purpose. His was genuine curiosity; but aside from computer work, nothing could interest him for long.

Duncan had defended his study during its construction and maintained that the almost black mahogany of the woodwork, and of the ponderous desk and bookcases felt "traditional." It was a heavy Georgian, something from an English cozy, at odds with the ultra-contemporary look of the rest of the house. Ariel once confided to Corinne that this was the room where Colonel Mustard killed Mrs. Peacock with a candlestick.

"And since when would I characterize you as 'traditional?'" Corinne said.

"Okay, then, maybe traditional is not the right word. Maybe it's just solid…stable," he searched. It wasn't a fight, but it could turn into one.

"Look at this," Corinne said, pointing at the rich red brocaded fabric of the overstuffed sofa and chairs. Then she reached for a drawer pull shaped like a lion's head on the massive desk and gave it a yank. She closed it and laughed at the effort it took. "All you need now is the head of a water buffalo or something staring at us from over your fireplace."

She had begun the conversation good-naturedly and wanted Duncan to laugh with her. He didn't.

She sank into the couch, dwarfed by its scale like Fay Wray in the hand of Kong, she thought, and patted the seat beside her. She didn't know she could hurt his feelings; in fact, she wasn't even sure that's what had just happened, but he didn't come.

His back still to her, he stood by the desk. "I guess my computers don't really match the décor, do they?" he said. Corinne recognized his tone as both petulant and mollifying. She didn't know what to do with either. Again she stroked the sofa. "Duncan."

He turned. He was smiling. "I guess I wanted something with some weight. All that damn Bauhaus furniture looks like it might float away if no one's sitting on it. Looks like bird skeletons and kindling."

Corinne was glad to see the smile. "I think you're probably right to leave the computers in here," she said, and since he was coming no closer to the sofa, she stood and went to him. They did not touch; instead, she ran her hand along the keyboard of one of the three computers on the desk. "Maybe old King George the whatever never had one, but at least there are plenty of ways to hide the cords in here. Try doing that in any other room." It was a small compromise, this tacit conciliation, but it felt like an embrace.

And Corinne had to admit that Duncan did love his study. Whenever she wasn't quite sure where in the house he was, she would find him here, sometimes working at the bank of computers, sometimes just standing in front of the unlit fireplace. The room's scale dwarfed him, too, but he told her once that he occasionally liked to feel "insignificant."

"Welcome to my world," she had said.

And now upon entering the study, she again felt that same sense of inconsequence. She dropped her sweater on the sofa, sat in Duncan's desk chair, turned on one of the computers, and waited for it to whir and beep into life.

A couple of mouse clicks told her that the closest airport to Sinking Creek was a two hours' flight from Cincy. If she left tomorrow morning she could be there before noon, but Dexter Daugherty told her that she needed to go first to the Sinking Creek Travel Plaza on Interstate 81. He hadn't been cryptic, necessarily, but she wouldn't describe his demeanor as particularly forthcoming, claiming that he hadn't been in touch with Duncan. But she hadn't hired him to do that, just to find him, he said.

"I've found out where he is," he told her, "but I didn't make contact with him. He's safe, though."

"How do you know that if you didn't see or talk to him?"

There had been a pause before he answered. It sounded as if Dexter Daugherty were drawing a deep breath. Corinne heard traffic in the background. He let out the breath. "I know. That's all I can say. I'm closing the case when we hang up, Mrs. Post. I just wanted to say thank you for letting me handle it."

"Will he be at that travel plaza? Will he even still be in this — what is it, Stinking Creek — when I get there?" She tried not to sound frantic.

"Sinking Creek," he corrected. "I don't have any authority to incarcerate or even detain anybody, and I can't make an ironclad guarantee that he'll be there. But..." he paused again, "he'd be a fool not to be," he said softly. "And one other thing."

She held her pen poised over her notepad, certain there must be further instructions about the particulars of Duncan's location. "I'm ready."

"Be careful."

This had stunned Corinne. No reply came to her; nothing that could make sense, anyway, and so her response, the only nicety she was conditioned to say, surprised even herself. "Thank you," she said. Though after she hung up, her mind crackled with the dozens of other questions or responses she wished she had said.

On the computer, she clicked out of the travel program without purchasing the airline tickets for Richard, Ariel, and herself, and leaned back in the chair. Behind the computer desktop's program icons, the screen's background was a nature scene — some generic snow-capped mountains in the distance, a broad, shallow trout stream tumbling over rocks in the foreground. She hadn't really paid much attention before. She would have thought he'd have chosen something from the world of space or something that felt technological or industrial, something with soaring lines or pipes or connections, for his computer's wallpaper. It must have been the default setting, she concluded, and Duncan had just been too preoccupied to fool with it.

This time tomorrow, she could very well be talking in

person to her husband. This time tomorrow. She had so much to say, she thought, but when she tried to imagine the conversation, at least how it might open, she couldn't. She was taking Ariel and Richard as buffers, she knew, and toyed with the idea of simply leaving tonight without telling them. Taking Richard was a risk anyway, and though Ariel had always amused Duncan, he didn't find her intellectually challenging. He tolerated her because she was important to Corinne.

No, there was no real need to show up *en masse* for this meeting, but Corinne also knew this from their months of separation: she was a coward. And apparently Duncan was too. If he could run away from this "situation," then she was entitled to amass her courage in whatever form it needed to take.

And there was the matter of Daugherty's inscrutable *be careful*—his last words to her—to consider. At face value she took it as a wish for a traveling mercy. But it could have been a warning. Or a censure.

## CHAPTER 16

Several times in the past few months, Daylon had mentioned that Summerset had a business proposition for me. I couldn't imagine what it could be, especially after my performance handing out coffee at the rest area during the July 4th weekend. I was, however, intrigued, though I had never, and didn't now, have any intention of staying here. That these were decent people I had no doubt. They just weren't mine.

Still, if I could do the old guy a favor, I'd try, so when Daylon came home from the garage one day, I met him on the front porch and asked him about Summerset's proposal.

"He still hasn't mentioned it to you?" Daylon said, wiping his hands on the front of his jeans and sitting down on the wicker swing. "Maybe he figures you won't be interested."

"I'm not. Not really." I sat on the top step, half-turned to face him.

Daylon pushed the porch floor gently with the toe of his work boots to set the swing squeaking into motion. "I went to him with that idea you had about, what was it, an industry park?"

"What did he say?"

"Nothing. Summerset don't out and out put anybody or anything down. He figures everbody's got the rights to their opinions, but I could tell he didn't like it."

The front door opened, and Della came out with two glasses of iced tea. I hadn't gotten used to this sugary drink that all the Hundleys consumed with gusto. I liked mine with a bit of sugar substitute, so this was cloying and thick. Daylon thanked his "baby girl" and gulped the whole glass in one long pull.

"Want another?" she said, reaching for his empty.

"He can have this one. I haven't taken a drink yet," I said and handed him my glass.

Della bumped her butt against Daylon's shoulder. "Scooch over. There's no man talk this woman can't hear," she said. The swing sagged. Della put a meaty hand on her husband's knee. Her lap would have held him comfortably, but he exuded a lean, fit strength that made that dwarfing irrelevant. They had always seemed an odd couple to me, this pair of physically mismatched socks, but they could be worn with the same outfit.

"I was just about to tell Harry about your Dad's business idea. Should I, or should I wait for him?"

"Don't matter. That's not the point, anyway. Point is, do we want to stay on this farm, Daylon? Daddy's idea'll work with or without Mr. Trueman, here—no offense, Harry. So we have to be ready for the windbreak when it comes."

"What do you want to do?" Daylon asked.

Della stood up and walked down the porch a few feet. She put her hands on the banister and looked down across the gentle slope of the front yard to the tree-lined banks of Sinking Creek and into the fields, then hills, beyond. A soft evening haze had begun to settle.

I couldn't imagine Della leaving this place. It had a charm, granted, but that wasn't it. Cincinnati was too small for me, I had often thought, but it was far too big for people like Della and Daylon. I wanted to say that. But the longer Della stood there, looking at everything and nothing at once, and the longer the silence continued, broken only by the creaking rhythm of Daylon's slow swinging, the more I felt like an intruder. My voice would have been as discordant as a car crash, and about as welcome.

For his part, Daylon didn't act impatient with Della's hesitance to answer. He just swung and sipped occasionally from the glass I'd given him. He, too, looked out across the valley. And then I did.

I wasn't used to being put on hold. Business deals were made or delayed, but an answer of some sort was given promptly. This, however, didn't feel like any of those moments. Somehow, it felt like it held much more import.

Finally, Della turned and faced her husband. "Where would we go?"

"Anywhere you'd want to."

"And Tessie? What would we do with her?" Della asked.

"Tessie will always be with us, Del, wherever we go," he said. "We've talked about that part a million times."

"I just wanted to hear you say that again." She brightened, became playful. "Can you see Tessie traipsing down the Chomps Elleezie? Or me, for that matter? Wearing a fancy hat, sticking our noses in the air, and saying things like *it's such a fine day, don't you agree?* or *shall we get a glass of wine and look at the Mona Lisa some more?*"

She stood, crooked her elbow out, and minced a few steps in place as though she and Tessie were walking arm in arm.

"Hell, I don't know how to work on French cars and mopeds," Daylon laughed. "Del, I don't think we're talking about that kind of money, though."

"I know, I know," she said and sat again with her husband. Their swinging began once more, the chains creaking a louder complaint with Della in the seat.

"We could move into Bristol; plenty of stuff to do there," Daylon offered. "Or Knoxville, or Roanoke, or California."

The vision of such unlimited potential seemed to daze them because they simultaneously stopped pushing their toes against the porch floor to power the swing. I was grateful for the squeak's absence at first, but then there was nothing to fill this potent void.

The first lightning bug of the evening, and one of the last of the season, flashed weakly in front of me. I cupped my hand and scooped the bug into it. As a kid, I remember swatting them with a wiffle ball bat in my back yard and watching their fluorescence fade. I couldn't imagine doing that to these miracles now. This one crawled to the lip of my palm and took off again.

My movement seemed to pull both of them back from the Eiffel Tower, or whatever icon of the exotic they dreamt of, because they turned their attention to me as if I were new to the conversation.

Della spoke first. "You've probably been all over, Harry. If you was to come into a pile of money, where would you go to settle?"

I rested my back against the porch rail post and brought my feet up from the first step onto the porch itself. Once, I might have said New York or Silicon Valley, someplace near the epicenter of finance or technology, but now—inspired by Della's tourist version of Paris—strolling along the Seine, with cherry blossoms fluttering, holding Corinne's hand, was a tempting, impossible fantasy. We could have gone anywhere at one time. Now, *we* could go nowhere. Hell, now I'd take Cincinnati in a dreary, steady, cold March rain.

"Never really thought about it," I said.

"Well, that's the point," Della said. "Now you can. If Dad's plan is right, we'll all have enough money to go where we need to go."

"What do you mean *need*?"

Daylon put his arm on the back of the swing and scratched his wife's shoulder while she went on. "Oh, I'm just yapping. I don't even know what I meant by that," she said. "Me and Daylon have never been more than 100 miles from Sinking Creek, and when we were, we couldn't wait to get back. I guess I wonder if we need to keep up this big ol' farm, if something ever happens to Daddy."

Daylon picked up his wife's thread. "It's not so much where in the world we might go, it's where in Sinking Creek we might go."

That made sense to me. These people would get chewed up in Mayberry. I sure couldn't see them in Atlanta. And for Tessie, any city would be a prison.

"Do you *want* to live on this farm, or are you considering it out of an obligation to Summerset?" I said, though I thought there might not be much of a difference.

"Mom and Daddy were married on this porch," Della said and pointed to the space in front of the big picture window, as if the bride and groom stood there now. "And twenty-odd years later this porch was jam-packed with folks taking a smoke or a spit between goings-in to see Mama and Andy in their caskets." Her husband's scratching of her shoulder turned into stroking. "You think I want to leave this farm? Some of our people was buried on these hilltops before the Baptist Church was built. Me and Daddy go clean the stones on Decoration Day, and Daylon clears the weeds. No sir, we don't want to leave, but I see what it's doing to Daddy, trying to keep this place up, and I can't allow it to break Daylon down."

Her voice held the hard edge of finality, and I got a glimpse of what Della Hundley Monroe would be when she was old — a powerful force, whose strength wouldn't be apparent until it was needed. I thought of my mother, whom I rarely called and who I wouldn't have ever described as noble, sitting in our backyard during a summer cookout many years ago. She nursed a Vodka Collins while my Dad grilled steaks for some of the neighborhood families. There were no kids my age there so I sat on the end of her webbed lawn chair, her sandaled feet hugging my skinny butt. The men stood by the grill, holding cold bottles of beer and laughing at Dad's bawdy, whispered jokes, and the wives sat in a semicircle around Mom in matching chairs. They had long tanned legs, and crossed and uncrossed them languorously like vines. Ice melted in their glasses. Their kids, all older than me, played volleyball over a net that Dad and I had set up that morning.

I could have played. The most athletic of the boys had said he'd take the "squirt" on his team, but I, flustered, said I had to help Mom. No one pressed me, and though Dad occasionally looked over and asked me why I wasn't over there "mixing it up" with the other kids, he didn't wait for my answer before turning back to the pride of lions gathered around the searing meat.

I don't remember what the women talked about. I'm sure it was their children or Reagan or who shot J.R., but I do remember this: one of the women, a pretty blonde in red shorts and a white halter top with a Christie Brinkley hair-do, asked me what I wanted to be when I grew up. It happened that, just at that moment, a lull took place in the men's conversation, too, so they had turned toward us.

I don't know, I told her — told everybody, I guess — an engineer, maybe. She laughed — isn't that cute, she said, doesn't every boy want to drive a train at some time; what is it about trains? Before I could tell her I didn't want to be *that* kind of engineer, she had already turned to the woman beside her and started another pointless conversation. I burned to tell this pretty woman that I would some day make enough money to buy this entire neighborhood, that she would some day read about me and ask her fading husband "isn't that the scrawny Post boy who grew up next door to us?" I fidgeted on the end of the chair, my butt cheeks nearly slipping between the woven straps. I looked around helplessly toward Mom, hoping she would intercede, stop Christie Brinkley's conversation and announce that "no, my son is *not* going to work on a train. He is not going to be an insurance adjuster like his father. He is going to change the world." I wanted Mom to do that. Or so I thought at first.

But that would have required everyone to stop what they were doing, look at me, and make some appropriately admiring remark. And that I did not want. Not now.

Mom saw all that in my look, and so as the conversation bubbled all around us — the men at the fire, the women on the patio, the older kids screaming at play — she simply scrunched my butt with her feet like a hug. She squeezed and smiled, and I knew that whether I got to tell them what I was going to be or not did not matter.

"Oh, baby, I've got the strength of ten men," Daylon said, and simulated a body builder's pose. "This farm won't whup me. If you want to live here, we live here. Simple as that."

They had had this conversation many times before, I was sure. I was equally certain it had taken a similar route, but with one important difference: apparently something had happened since Daylon and I had spoken weeks before about potential ways to turn the farm into a money-maker, something that provided them with the kinds of options that only financial security could offer. They were faced with the most frightening of prospects — some of their wilder dreams might come true.

"What would you do if you went somewhere else?" I interrupted.

Neither spoke, and the creaking swing began again.

Finally, Daylon turned to his wife, then back to me. "You're going to think this is pretty silly, Harry, especially since you're not from here. But the only thing I ever wanted, the only thing I was ever any good at, is opening my own garage. I like engines; I like taking something that don't work, or don't work right, and making it good as new." Beside him Della smiled. "There's just something about figuring out a problem by listening for a certain sound, looking for a certain movement, sniffing for a particular smell, or just plain thinking with your gut, that makes me feel like the end of the day's better'n the beginning."

I didn't immediately answer because for the first time I would have to admit that ambition was relative and personal, and I would not have thought that a few months ago. "That's a lot of headache, owning your own business," I said.

That was my clichéd response, but I swear they stopped swinging and considered what I'd said as if it were oracular wisdom.

"It would, true. But there's plenty of good mechanics I know, and mostly, I'd have Della to help out, run the office."

"That's her dream? To work in the office of your garage?" I tried hard to keep any trace of incredulity from surfacing.

"You was married, you told me once," said Daylon, as if that was all I needed to hear.

It was not a question, but if it were, how would I have answered it? Would I have addressed the *once*? Would I have clarified his assumption—told him I was, indeed, married, even now? Hell, in the eyes of the law, was I still married, or had Corinne done something to distance herself legally from a murderer at worst, a deserter at best? "That's right," I said.

"Did you work together?"

"Not in the way you mean. Well, okay, not at all," I said, and thought of all the times Richard had insisted we include Corinne in some public aspect of the business. I thought of Corinne's repulsion at being included simply to provide "eye candy." At the time, I hadn't seen Richard's motivation as prurient, and I hadn't thought that Corinne's rebuff was the result of her desire to be more fully involved.

"What did she do for a living, your wife?" Della said, and before I would have had time to answer, she added, "I'm sorry, that's rude to ask before I even know her name. What is her name? Oh, goodness, that's rude, too, because I'm assumpting that she's not…oh, I'm so sorry, Harry. Is your wife…," she stumbled, then, "have you lost your wife?"

I was so glad the wheel stopped spinning on that question because that one I could answer. "Yes, I've lost her."

Their predictable apologies followed, buttressed by a reverent quiet.

After a few moments, during which I contemplated straightening out the equivocation, Daylon said, "Then you see why me'n Del have always wanted to work together." With that my window to straighten out their misperception closed.

I nodded.

"And can you imagine the lunches she'd bring us every day?" he said and poked his index finger into her soft belly.

Their laughter was a candle on the now-dark porch.


Minutes later, Summerset's truck turned from the paved road up the gravel driveway and around the house to the barn. I heard both truck doors close; he and Tessie had gone to a neighbor's to pick up some quilts to be put in the travel plaza's gift shop.

"Decision's made," Daylon said. "We'll let your dad tell Harry about his idea."

Della stood and opened the front door. "Oooh, this *is* exciting. Hope they ain't hungry. I'm going to turn the stove down on supper. It'll wait," she said, the screen door smacking behind her.

"If Del's willing to hold supper, this will be big news," Daylon said. He extended a hand to pull me up, and we followed his wife down the hallway to the kitchen. Summerset and Tessie were coming through the back door.

Tessie went straight to the stove, lifted pot lids and sniffed the wafting steam.

"Stay out of them pots, Tessie Hundley. Dinner's postponed for a spell," Della said.

Summerset sat on a kitchen chair grunting slightly as he pulled off a tan boot. At the mention of a delayed dinner, he looked up. Della was ready.

"Daylon thinks it's time you let Harry in on the business plan," she said.

"Oh, Daylon does, does Daylon?" Summerset, still working on his other boot, winked at his son-in-law. "And why does Daylon think this is the right time? What if I told you that Tessie and me think it's time to eat?"

From near the stove, Tessie said, "Ain't nobody else hungry?"

I couldn't let this go on. "Actually, Summerset, I've been meaning to ask you about it for some time. Daylon mentioned it weeks ago, but you yourself hinted something about it once before, back when I wasn't really...back when I got sick."

"We thought we'd wait till you got home. See what you wanted to do," Daylon said.

Summerset straightened his back and stood. "Come with me, anybody who wants to be in on this. It's back in my room."

In single file, led by the old farmer, we marched down the hallway to the closed door of Summerset's bedroom — all of us except Tessie, that is, who, as soon as we were gone, could be heard in the silverware drawer.

I had never seen inside Summerset's room. The door was always closed, and Tessie's abbreviated tour of the house had consisted of showing me only the open rooms and simply pointing at closed doors and announcing their functions. After I had fallen into Andy's room, I confined my travels to those rooms whose open doors felt like invitations. I had no wish to encroach, and, to be frank, I had been indifferent about their lives.

But now I found myself curious about Summerset's room. He opened the door, switched the light on, and stepped aside for the rest of us to enter. Back in the kitchen, Tessie dropped a pot lid. The sound caused Della to mutter, "I told her not to mess with dinner, yet," and stomp down the hallway toward her, but that clanging is not what startled me. What nearly caused me to put my hand to my mouth in melodramatic shock sat over on a corner desk, flanked by pictures of the Hundleys I knew and those I knew in story.

It was a computer.

And it was on. The screensaver scrolled "Virginia Department of Transportation" endlessly across the monitor. I guess my surprise was evident because Summerset walked over to it instead of toward whatever else we had been brought in the room to see. "You know anything about computers, Harry?"

Was this a trick question? I thought I knew enough about these people to realize it wasn't some sort of trap, but I also knew enough about the information age to put my guard back up. "A little," I said. "Why?"

To enhance my insouciance, I feigned interest in the rest of Summerset's room. The bed was made, and two things struck me about that: first, that Summerset must have made it because I never knew Della to walk into the room; and second, that this was an awfully small bed for Summerset to have shared with his wife. Seemed cramped. Corinne and I slept in a huge, custom number that we joked about having two zip codes. "Beautiful quilt," I said before he could answer my "why."

He had sat down at the desk chair in front of the computer and moved the mouse, dissolving the screensaver.

"It is, isn't it?" he said. "Maudie sewed it."

I touched it. Though my remark had been polite, the quilt was truly pretty, the handiwork intricate. I looked more closely.

"Hers was good, but you should see some of the others in Sinking Creek. It's like a competition. Every woman around here tries to outquilt the others. You can bet you're going to get two or three handmade quilts every Christmas." He turned in his chair to face me. "Want one? I got a closet-full."

Before I could protest, Della, having returned from the kitchen, stood behind me and said, "I'll let you pick one out later, Harry. We want to keep those Mommy made, but there are plenty of others. Even have one that me and Tessie tried our hands at."

Now I get an offer, I thought. There were some cold nights under that bridge when I would have given big money for something other than my flimsy Wal-Mart blankets. "Thanks, but I really couldn't. I'm sure they're much too..." I wanted to say *expensive*, but corrected myself. "I'm sure they're worth too much to be giving away."

"You'll take one," Daylon whispered, "or they'll never leave you alone."

It was hypocritical, perhaps; after all, I'd accepted their food, their lodging, their unrequested care and comfort, but I simply didn't want anything tangible from this stay. I hadn't wanted, didn't need, Tessie's dolorous rabbit, and I had no use now for a quilt. But before I could object again, Summerset tapped some more on the computer keyboard, then called to me.

"Come here, if you don't care, Harry. This is what I wanted to talk to you about. This is my business proposition."

I was dying to sit down at that computer, to slip back into the ones and zeroes, to see how far the world had spun since I had left it. My finger twitched involuntarily, eager to click the mouse. What emails needed my attention? From that screen I could see what the world knew about me, and what it didn't. I could maybe figure out where Corinne was and what she was up to. But then I was sickened by the thought that I would read about Richard Rice, too. The story would have been too sensational not to have been reported. Back in the summer I had tried to find those things out by filching newspapers left in the travel plaza's restrooms, and restaurants, but the news was apparently too local to be picked up in any papers outside the Cincinnati region. That had been a blessing for my anonymity both under the bridge and in Sinking Creek, but a part of me had been insulted. I thought I was bigger news.

"I didn't know you had a computer," I said as I approached and hovered over Summerset's shoulder.

"State give it to me," he said dismissively. "Said I needed it for the plaza's inventory, scheduling, and so forth and so on. I can use it, but I'm no whiz. I can see where it might be kind of fun, though. Tessie'll get on it some and fool around. But Della? Avoids it like bad road."

I started to say that if she and Daylon opened a garage, her "helping out in the office" would necessarily involve computer use in the brave new world of business, but I bit my lip. "Tessie likes it, though?" I said.

"Loves it. I got her some school programs—simple math, reading, and such. Since you been here, she plays on it. Tells me she's moved up to 6^th grade work. I don't know, Harry. Maybe there's hope." That word was some kind of cue because Summerset seemed to forget the computer and his reason for calling me into the room. Daylon and Della had sat down on his bed. I think they sensed what was coming, and its rawness wearied them.

It frightened me.

I was about to say the right thing, that there was always hope, you should never give up, I'm sure there's someone who could help her, she's a wonderful girl as she is. But it occurred to me I didn't really know what his version of hope might be. I readied the appropriate cliché, even if I didn't believe it, but Summerset spoke before I could.

"There was a time when I couldn't even look at her, I'm ashamed to say. I know Daylon told you our story, and it's okay he did. What Tessie done was an accident. I know that now and I knew it then, so I'm embarrassed about how I felt for the longest time."

Behind me, Daylon and Della stirred. I couldn't imagine how difficult this was for them to hear, especially Della. "I didn't raise my voice around her," he continued, "didn't heap any blame on her, didn't ever ask her how or why what happened happened. But I wanted to, and that wanting scraped my insides."

Summerset was looking beside, rather than directly at,

me. Pain at the memory altered his face almost imperceptibly, though I thought he looked radically changed — indistinct, as though someone had sat a condensing glass on a watercolor painting. I wanted to stop him before all the colors coalesced into black.

But he went on. "And I'm most ashamed of this: when she went through that spell where she went into her dark place, and the doctors told me the best place for her was in their hospital, I was…I was glad to see her go for awhile. I needed her gone because having her here made my grieving too hard."

Della stood, walked over to him, and smoothed the silver hair on his temples. I wanted no part of this confession and couldn't fathom why he had just handed me this weight that didn't belong to me, even peripherally.

"I think you've probably been a pretty fine father," I said. "I'm sure raising Tessie under those circumstances took a ton of patience."

He smiled then, and it was good to see. I felt he was reeling back the burden. It was neither a test nor a lure, and in fact, I'm sure it wasn't premeditated. We had both been withholding secrets since we'd met. His just broke loose first. I understood.

"Well, it does take patience," he allowed, "but no more than this little girl and her worthless husband do," he said, grabbing Della's hand. "But, come here. Here's what I brought you in to show." He turned back to the computer.

I leaned over his shoulder to see the screen, bumping into Della's beehive. Daylon sidled up beside me.

Summerset said, "Feel free to help me out if you see me doing something wrong here." He opened an email program then highlighted a message. "They give me an email account and taught me how to use it, but I don't have anybody to send anything to, just reports to the state."

The monitor whitewashed our faces in the bedroom's dim light, and I felt drawn into that computer, comfortable inside its hard plastic skin.

He clicked on the highlighted message until it filled the screen. "Just when I think things is tough, I get a message like this, Harry, and I thought of you. How this person found me and how the poor guy knew I'd be willing to help is beyond me, but good fortune has been thrown in our laps, and I want you in on it. Bible tells us we might entertain angels unaware. Maybe your luck's about to change, too."

Summerset sat back and folded his arms. Clearly, Della and Daylon had seen this because they watched my reaction instead of reading the screen.

I knew what it was before I finished the first line, but I read on anyway. Its subject line, though only marginally different than the dozens of nearly identical messages I'd deleted from my own computer, read: "Please help the poor boy."

Dear Sir,

Perhaps you to heard of County of Sudan of the continent of Africa. On the further, you too may know of the many of genocide in my homeland and it is because of this I do make to entreaty you. I got your name and contact from among other names due to it is esteeming nature and the recommendations given to me as a reputable and trustworthy person that I can do business with as per the recommendation. I must not hesitate to confined in you for this simple and sincere boy.

My father was a very wealthy cocoa merchant in Khartoum the Economic

Capital of Sudan. My father was poisoned to the death by his business associates on one of their outings on a business trip. My mother died when I was a baby and sense then my father had took me so special. Before the death of my father on November, 2001 in a private hospital here in Khartoum, he secretly called me to his bedside and told me that he has the sum of US $12.5M left in fixed/suspense account in one of his Prime banks here in Khartoum, that he used my name as his only son for the next of kin in the depositing the fund. He also explained to me that it was because of his wealth that he was poisoned by his business associates.

That I should seek for a foreign partner in a country of my choose where I will transfer this money and use it for investment in a viable venture. Sir, I am honoroubly seeking your assistance in the following ways: 1) To provide a Bank account into which this money would be transferred 2) To make arrangement for me to come over to your country for investment and to secure Residence permit in your country. Moreover, sir, I am willing to offer you 30% of the total Sum as compensation for your effort input after the successful transfer this fund into you nominated account overseas. Further more, you indicate you option towards assisting me as I believe this transaction

could be concluded within fourteen (14)
working days.  Please signify your interest in helping this poor boy.

Anticipating to hear from you soon.
Thanks and God's heaping blessings you
Best regards,
Vy'euo Nebe Nkuped


I wanted to never finish reading this because I knew I'd
have to look away from the screen and into their grins.  Then
time would continue, and the next few minutes would not be
pleasant.

"Tragic story for this poor Mr. Nkuped, isn't it?" Della
said when the silence grew too heavy.  "But maybe we can
help him and ourselves, too.  That wouldn't be wrong, would
it?"

"Harry, how can we use this internet to check up on
him, make sure he's not been captured?" said Summerset.

I picked up a pen from the cup beside the computer
and pulled a piece of paper from the printer.  I wrote *Vy'euo
Nebe Nkuped*.  Beneath it, I unscrambled the name:  YOU'VE
BEEN PUNKED.

## CHAPTER 17

I would have felt like a post-party piñata. I wouldn't have been that naive, of course, but if I had permitted myself their kind of disingenuous faith in the inherent goodness of mankind, I would have deserved the pummeling they just took. And yet, I didn't see a shoulder slump or hear a sigh. There was no railing against the perpetrator of what I explained to them was known as a phishing scam.

Instead of their curses, all I heard was Daylon remark that he guessed it was a fact that if it sounded too good to be true, well…

And Della said nothing about the loss of Paris or of her dream of working in Daylon's garage, saying instead that she was sorry for the two men in her life and for Tessie, but she now had to get in there and finish fixing supper because…

And Summerset. Summerset, who, childishly or not, had probably staked more on this dream than anyone else, simply because he knew there was less time for him to see a dream fulfilled than for the others, showed no anger, no frustration, no incredulity. Remarkably, he admired the scammer's ingenuity.

"I sure owe you for this, Harry," he said. "I was going to give the guy my bank account number. But you got to admit, he is pretty clever."

"They trick a few," I admitted, though I couldn't tell him it was not a sophisticated scam without embarrassing him.

I didn't think it really required much savvy to see through this. "You just have to be careful when you're doing business on the internet, that's all. Don't give up on the computer, Summerset. You don't want to throw out the baby with the bath water."

He grinned at my use of a colloquialism I had heard somewhere in that house.

"We're teaching you some things, too, I reckon."

"I can see why that story would appeal to you. Don't beat yourself up," I said.

"I allow I let it cloud me when he told me about losing his mom and dad," he said, shaking his head. "And I suppose I was a touch flattered by being picked. Like I was somebody he could trust."

"If it makes you feel any better, there's nobody I'd trust more," I said, and in that moment I knew that was as true a statement as I had ever made.

"That's nice. You got $12 million dollars you want me to invest for you?" He laughed, and behind me Daylon did, too.

"I wish."


After dinner I asked Summerset if I could use his computer. "Have at it," he told me. "Just don't take any wooden nickels. Like I almost did."

Tessie spoke up, "Want me to show you how to use it? You could watch me do my homework."

Della turned from the sink to see my response. I hesitated. I desperately wanted—though it felt like a need—to use the machine. I had so much to do that required privacy: check email, research some archived issues of the Cincinnati papers, but mostly I wanted to check Corinne's email. I could access it on the web, but I wondered if she might have established some other accounts of which I was unaware. That seemed possible, even likely, given the other hidden life she had lived.

Summerset spoke before I did, however. "Why don't we let Harry use it for a spell in private, Sis? You can work on your studies after that."

"I'd love to see what you're working on. After while," I said.

This placated her. "I'll go get Flopsy and we'll be back in…" she looked up at the kitchen clock over the stove and moved her lips in calculation, "…in one hour and one-fourth hours." With that she went through the back door and toward her white bedroom in the barn.

"She's been working on fractions," Summerset clarified. "Truth is she'll probably be back in an hour, if not sooner."

So, I had an hour. The mouse felt like a packet of gold in my palm, and the computer, much to my surprise, was an up-to-date machine with more than adequate computing power and memory. It wasn't the state-of-the-art equipment my former work demanded, but the Virginia Department of Transportation had not scrimped on Summerset's workstation, either.

I opened the browser and typed in the web address for showplace.com. The computer screen showed an error message indicating the site was no longer active. I had expected this but was still stung by the finality of seeing its absence from the cyber constellation. It was a kind of grief, I realized, and shared some of the same emotions as any loss. I had, after all, given birth to something that had a useful, productive life that impacted a great many people in a positive way. That's not an insignificant achievement, and the site's birth and growth were almost wholly my doing. That's not entirely true, I admit;

Richard's very public face and persona were instrumental in the buzz that made us recognizable, but personal charm can only account for so much in the world of technology. Constant innovation is its lifeblood, and I kept it pumping.

The cessation of that heartbeat, then, was a kind of death to me, and I would not apologize for feeling so. I watched the cursor turn into an hourglass on the error page, filling and emptying, searching for an active link. That its filling and emptying didn't slow, then stop, reminded me of everything I knew for certain about that world: it stopped for no one, for nothing; took no note of the passing of any of its inhabitants. Like a tree, the loss of a branch merely initiated the growth of a new one.

And since the cursor obviously wasn't going to join me in my moment of grief, I had to let its insistent pulse drive me forward. Showplace.com being gone, I went next to a webmail site to access my email. As I figured, my inbox was full, and scrolling down the subject line list let me see the full range of communications I had severed: "urgent: questions about contract," "re: July 6th meeting/where are you?" "Get back to me pronto. Rice won't do." I had let a great many people down, it appeared, but I wouldn't call them disappointed. After a while, the emails were less passionate and more business-like. They'd simply taken their business elsewhere.

It struck me that no one was really interested in my well-being. There was nothing personal in those messages. But of course if there had been, I might have been surprised at the time, perhaps even put off by the familiarity. By the time I got to the list's end, the dates were more sporadic. In early June there were dozens per day, by late September there were days that passed with no messages. And then the final message appeared on the screen. I looked at the desk calendar beside the computer. That final message had been sent today. The address belonged to Corinne.

My breath caught, and I took my hand from the mouse as if it had begun glowing with heat. I leaned forward in disbelief. It was, indeed, her address. There was nothing in the subject line. All I had to do was click on it, and I would be as close to her as I had been since I left her tending to Richard Rice on the floor of our offices nearly five months ago.

Had I missed other messages from Corinne as I scrolled the long list? I could touch the mouse long enough to check that, couldn't I? I didn't have to click on that message just yet. My hand, however, shook as I placed it again on the mouse, and I had real trouble scrolling back up to the top of the message list. I'd look at each one again and then delete them all; they disappeared upward until only Corinne's remained. The cursor hovered over it, and still I could not click it.

But then I did. I hadn't realized I'd been putting enough pressure on the mouse button to engage it, but I had. The tiny click sounded like a gun's firing. I released it again and sat back in the wooden chair. Instantly the screen changed. The message area was stark, only a single sentence stood there like a line of overwhelmed soldiers. "Are you there? Corinne" it said.

"Who's that from?" a voice behind me said, sending adrenalin into my mouth and causing my heart to thump noticeably. My hand recoiled from the mouse autonomously, as if I'd been caught stealing money from my father's sock drawer.

She had Flopsy looped around her neck like a muffler. He shifted slightly to maintain balance as she leaned forward toward the computer screen. After his escapade with the sharp-shinned hawk, this height was nothing for him. Tessie squinted at the words. Flopsy looked at me, just inches from my face, and I swear I think a look of gratitude came from him, or if not, perhaps it was a look of camaraderie, as if we shared something like vigilance for her. I decided I was going crazy to think so, and just as I thought this, Flopsy looked away.

With a quick click I could remove the message from the screen, but that would appear suspicious, and the truth was I did feel guilty. So, I let Tessie look. She mouthed the words to herself. Of course, they weren't troublesome, even for Tessie's truncated education.

She looked up. "Who's Corn?" she said.

I corrected her pronunciation.

She repeated the name slowly, trying it out two-three times as if the language were foreign. "Okay, who's Cor-Inn," she said finally, stressing both syllables equally.

I've never been in war, but this felt like a minefield. And since I didn't know which direction might explode me, I chose not to go straight ahead. "A friend of mine," I lied.

"Is she worried about you?"

"I don't know. No. Maybe."

This seemed to satisfy her. "She shouldn't be. There's no reason to be, tell her. We're taking care of you," she said.

At that, she placed Flopsy in my lap. The rabbit circled once like a dog and lay down.

I clicked the message off. Didn't delete it, just clicked it off.

"Aren't you going to answer it?" Tessie said. I was surprised but assumed she had seen Summerset correspond electronically. I stood up, held Flopsy in my cradled arm as Tessie had taught me, and motioned for her to sit down.

"You'd better get to work. What is it tonight? Math? Reading?"

Tessie looked at the screen, placed her hand on the mouse, began clicking; then, still facing the computer, she smiled. "I know why you ain't answering," she said.

"Why's that?"

*"You're* worried about *her."*

With my free hand, I ruffled the back of her tangerine hair. "Think you're pretty smart, don't you, Tessie Hundley? Now, get busy on some of this work, and let me see what you can do."

But treating her as an obedient pup or a favored sibling was, I knew immediately, precisely the wrong thing to do. She was not pacified. In fact, she became progressively more fidgety. She did open up an elementary math program, but began clicking on some arithmetic problems without bothering to compute the answer. The pace of her clicking sped up, reminding me of her Chopsticks episode, and I thought I should probably leave the room in case my presence was making her nervous.

I placed Flopsy back in her lap and turned to leave, but before I got out of the room, the old hardwood floors creaking beneath each step, Tessie stopped me with a question. "I said, you're worried about her, aren't you?"

I couldn't see her face now, but a peripatetic energy emanated from her. I've always been proud of my ability to read people; however, my experience had been relegated to people much like myself. Verbal sparring, subtle probing for information, nearly senatorial pleasantries were de rigueur. Sinking Creek's verbal cues were both more blunt and yet more nuanced than I could handle. I felt that whatever I said next would determine a great deal. My problem was I didn't know what was being determined.

And then, it struck me. "You remember when we talked about those seven deafening sins, and you told me about stealing the Snickers and I told you about doing something to somebody I couldn't take back? Remember that?"

"Oh, I get it," she said, and when she shifted to face me, she wore a look of concern. "She's who you did the sin to, isn't she?"

"She is. She is."

"Then you really ought to answer her. Even if your answer don't smooth her, it'll do *you* wonders. Be a step in the right direction, at least."

She was right, in a strange way, and I told her so.

She added, "Time don't run out on your chance to do something nice to make up for it."

"I hope you're right, Tessie," I said.

"Course I am."

I was just about to make her return to her math problems, to redo them with some semblance of effort, when Della screamed from the kitchen.

At first I thought she was calling Daylon for dinner, but Tessie must have recognized an urgency in the tone because she sprang from her chair, tossed Flopsy on Summerset's bed, and grabbed my arm as she passed, spinning me toward and into the door frame. She was down the hallway before I could gather my senses enough to follow. I heard her bound into the kitchen, and simultaneously I heard the clomping of Daylon's heavier steps coming down from the second floor. He and I converged in the kitchen from opposite doorways to find both women kneeling over Summerset, who was slumped awkwardly on the floor.

Della had her hands on his face, pulling up his eyelids then placing her fingers on his wrist. Her face was tight, concentrated. Though she had screamed for Daylon, his presence did not seem necessary to her action. Tessie, though, sat back on her haunches and stared at her limp father. I can't say her face was blank, nor would I call her look concerned. She was puzzled and helpless, and those looks combined into a terrible, emotionless void.

"Call Doc Baker. Now!" Della said without looking up

from her father. She straightened Summerset out into a more comfortable supine position.

Daylon immediately went to the wall phone by the kitchen's back door and dialed.

She couldn't have been thinking clearly, though her actions seemed nimble and purposeful. Dr. Baker, it had been explained to me, was a veterinarian. Surely she meant for Daylon to call someone else. I spoke up. "Dial 9-1-1."

Without looking toward me, Daylon said, "We don't have that in Sinking Creek. Not yet, anyway."

"Well, then, call a real doctor, Daylon. Don't waste time calling a vet."

But Daylon was already talking to someone.

I couldn't think. I was helpless, didn't know first aid, had no knowledge of the area, knew nothing about local doctors; in fact, I didn't even know if there was a hospital nearby.

Tessie started to rock slowly on her haunches, apparently as paralyzed by her powerlessness as I was. She didn't reach toward her father, nor did she take her eyes from him.

Just beneath Daylon's frenetic conversation with Dr. Baker, I thought I heard a moan come from Summerset. It was followed by his eyelids fluttering, then opening. Della told Tessie to get a wet washcloth. Tessie's rocking stopped, but she still sat on the floor.

Della raised her voice, though its cadence was controlled, "Tessie, I said to get a washcloth from the drawer, wet it with cold tap water, and bring it to me."

Daylon was off the phone by now and rummaged through a drawer for the washcloth. Tessie, however, stood quickly and stepped in front of him. "Go on, I'll get it," she said.

"Doc Baker'll be right here, Del. He said not to move…" Before Daylon could finish his sentence, Summerset raised his

PAUL MARTIN

head weakly and tried to push himself up on shaky elbows.

"I'm okay," he said. "Don't you get Doc Baker over here this late for nothing."

Della supported his head with her left hand while gently pushing on his chest with her right. "You just lay right back down on the floor," she said, placing Tessie's damp cloth on his forehead. He didn't resist. "Doc Baker's used to delivering calves and colts at all hours. I don't think he'll mind this house call." Her tone was soft, delicate almost, but I saw hardness in her eyes — and fear.

Daylon knelt beside them with a rolled towel to put under Summerset's head, while Tessie stood over them, forming a surreal manger scene.

Summerset's breathing was deeper now and more regular. He chose not to fight and closed his eyes to succumb to whatever discomfort put him on the floor in the first place. "I'm sorry," he said to Della, or maybe to everyone. "I just had a little dizzy spell. It's all over now." But he seemed satisfied to stay on the floor.

My father had a heart attack when I was in college. I wasn't there when it happened, but what struck me when I got to the hospital the next day was the color — or should I say the *lack* of color — of his skin. It seemed translucent, the blue and purple veins as distinct as ink on paper. He was sitting up when I got to his room, chatting with the nurses and charming the orderlies. He'd go home tomorrow, he told me, though the nurse by the bed laughed and said it might be a day or two longer than that. It was two weeks, and though everyone in the hospital predicted a speedy convalescence — after all, they'd never had a patient with such an outgoing, positive attitude — he was never the same. He drew the blinds at home, turned on the TV, and as far as I know, has never wanted to do anything since. Mom once said she missed the sex, but that was all. And his malleability made that trade almost even.

Summerset's skin was devoid of color as my father's had been, and I had visions of this Dr. Baker showing up in a horse-drawn carriage, hoof clops announcing his too-late arrival, but I heard his big SUV crunch into the driveway within a few minutes, and by the time he opened the back door without first knocking, Summerset's pallor was not so severe. His eyes were open and alert, and Della had allowed him to sit in a kitchen chair with a glass of water.

The veterinarian looked to be about Summerset's age, thinly built with long arms and skinny, heavily veined hands that extruded from his too-short sweater sleeves like a magician's bouquet. He was more brittle than his contemporary.

"I'm sorry they drug you away from your supper, Randall. There's nothing wrong with this old man that a good sit-down won't fix. I just got a little dizzy is all," Summerset explained.

Dr. Baker set a valise on the kitchen table and looked into his friend's eyes. He removed a stethoscope from the valise, draped it around his ears, blew on its disk, and placed it on Summerset's chest. "We could all use a sit-down, Summer, but ain't all of us falling on the floor. Let me just look you over. It's no trouble, me and Greta were already done eating," he said as if the conversation were perfectly normal. I thought, however, that his face seemed more serious than his words. He listened to a few places on Summerset's chest, then his back.

I wanted to shout to someone, anyone, that, *hey, this is a vet. Got it — a vet? You're entrusting your father's life to a guy who probably stuck his hand up a cow's ass today. You sure this is your preferred health care provider?* Yes, that's what first came to me, but as I bit my tongue and watched him simultaneously calm, assess, and evaluate Summerset, and I saw the comfort he brought to Della, Daylon, and even to Tessie, who had gone into her father's bedroom to retrieve her pet rabbit and now stood stroking him contentedly, I forgot my objections. Dr. Baker did not cure anything or even avert a potential crisis, but I somehow felt he would navigate this family through this evening and offer them a course of appropriate action.

And that's what he did. "You're probably fit as a fiddle, my friend, but why don't you let Daylon here take you into the hospital in Bristol? I know a fella there I can call, and you can spend the night. Let them watch over you till tomorrow and we can get a cardiologist in to check your ticker first thing in the morning?"

Summerset considered this. "You think I ought to?"

"Couldn't hurt."

"I don't know," he said, and took a drink from his water glass. "Seems like a lot of bother for nothing."

Dr. Baker removed a blood pressure cuff from his bag and wrapped it around Summerset's bicep. "Do what you want, old man. I'm just telling you, it couldn't hurt to have that old pump looked at."

Their banter continued, as did the vet's appraisal of Summerset's condition. At length he said, "Everything sounds okay in there. Regular and strong enough. But like I said, another opinion wouldn't be a bad thing. Especially if it comes from someone whose patients have a first *and* a last name."

Summerset stood. He was a bit wobbly, but he stood. "Thanks to you, Randall, and again I'm sorry these young'uns panicked and drug you out tonight. I'll think about your counsel." With that he extended a hand toward his friend.

Their handshake was warm, intimate in some ways as a kiss. There was genuine affection in both faces as the doctor stood and locked eyes with Summerset.

"You're not going to Bristol tonight, are you?" Dr. Baker

said.

"No."

"I didn't expect so." Dr. Baker collected his blood pressure cuff, his stethoscope, some other tools that I'm not sure were meant for human use, and fastened the clasp on his valise. Then, he turned to me. "Well, Mr. Trueman, you look a far sight better than last time I saw you."

I reached to shake his hand. "I suppose I do, though I don't recall much about our meeting. I guess I owe you some thanks, too."

"Oh, my thanks is that you've followed my orders better than some of my patients whose names I won't mention," he said, peering pointedly over his glasses at Summerset. "You looked pretty tuckered back in July, but you've got some meat on your bones now. Della's cooking'll do that. You going to stay in Sinking Creek?"

I knew he was making small talk, but I had no idea how to answer this tactfully. "Not much longer. I'm afraid my vacation's about over. I've taken too much of the Hundley's hospitality as it is," I said.

He nodded. "You don't know them very well. They've got plenty hospitality left, I'm sure." He picked up his valise and addressed Della as if her father weren't standing beside them. "Give your mule of a father an aspirin and keep a close eye on him this evening. See if you can get his stubborn behind into Bristol this week to see a real doctor. Call me tonight if you need anything, and I'll call you tomorrow with a name and a phone number."

He looked once more at Summerset, shook his head and walked toward the back door. Summerset placed his hand on the veterinarian's shoulder. "I'll walk you out, Randall," he said.

## CHAPTER 18 — CORINNE

Ultimately Corinne chose not to buy three airline tickets, deciding instead to drive the Land Rover. Though the only time that vehicle's tires had seen "rough" terrain was when she accidentally backed it off the concrete driveway pad and into the lawn, she reasoned that Virginia had mountains, and, well, you just never knew.

She knew, too, that that was not the real reason behind her decision. Her own car gave her a small sense of control, and this comforted her. And yet, she thought as she tossed clothes of varying degrees of both warmth and allure into a cavernous suitcase, that wasn't quite it either. The drive would take, if her mapping skills were correct, probably ten hours, eight more than it would take a flight and short rental car hop to get her to Shrinking, Stinking, or Sinking Creek—she could never remember which. Those additional hours would afford her time for courage building, and with Ariel and Richard in the car with her, a chance for her to solidify her thoughts.

She tugged at her bag's zipper, pushed on the load that continued bubbling from it then finished zipping. Beside her hand, a water drop fell, and she realized with no small amount of alarm that she was crying. If she had not figured out her feelings by now, would even those extra eight hours help?

Predictably, Ariel had been delighted with the idea of going by car rather than plane. She had always regretted that she was too young to remember much about the cross-country odysseys she had taken in her parents' VW Microbus to various music festivals and counter-culture gatherings. It was her turn now, she had said, and if she could get Thyme's ass away from the TV long enough, she wished he would go. "Maybe I'll meet a real mountain man down there," she'd said. "Someone who shares more of my karma than just a Simon and Garfunkel name, long hair, and a belief in the transience of marriage, which, if he doesn't shape up, will be even shorter than he thinks."

Just as predictably, Richard balked at any method of travel other than flying. "Two things;" he'd said. "First, time is more than just money. Time is… well, time — the only commodity that absolutely cannot be replaced. And second…the extra hours will simply give you two more time to fight over me."

If either of Corinne's co-travelers were anxious about their meeting with Duncan, neither showed it. That, perhaps as much as anything, was why she wanted them to go. And why she dreaded it.


Once they had crossed the Newport Bridge into Kentucky, and the traffic thinned, the reality of this trip sank in and Corinne grew agitated. She missed turns, worried aloud about needing gas, or food, or a soda, or having forgotten something important. She patted her jeans pocket to reassure herself that the slip of paper with the contact's name Dexter Daugherty had given her was, in fact, real and present.

The scenery changed from lightly industrial to thinly residential and finally to thickly wooded once they found themselves on the Mountain State Parkway. Ariel could not get over its beauty, at one point lowering her window and drawing deep breaths of the dense pine forest lining the roadway.

From the backseat, Richard complained, "Come on, girl, get that window up. I'm sure I'm allergic to some of that shit."

Ariel did not respond. Instead she turned to Corinne as if they were the only two in the car. "Is that the same person who yelled *shotgun* and tried to jump in the front seat like he was a sophomore in high school? I'd turn around and tell him to shut up, but I don't want to look at something regrettable and miss something unforgettable." Still looking out her window, she held up her middle finger in Richard's direction.

Corinne laughed. Richard, too.

The repartee continued as the miles clicked by, but Corinne was less compelled to contribute to it, until, finally, she felt alienated from it entirely. It became white noise and she listened to her best friend and — she didn't quite know what to call him, so she settled on — *her husband's former business partner* as she might a radio drama.

"This is your fault, you know," Ariel said. "I hope the first thing Duncan does is kick your ass. Then says hello. And then maybe kicks your ass again."

"I hope so, too. Can you love a man who can't fight?"

"I couldn't love you if you were heavyweight champion of the world. No woman could."

"Ouch," he said, glancing at the back of Corinne's head. "I deserve some of that. But let's be honest here, I'm not the only blameworthy actor in this tragedy."

Ariel laughed. "You used the word 'honesty.' That's rich. But, if you're suggesting that Corinne —"

"Oh, I didn't say Corinne, though she's not some cement saint deep in a grotto surrounded by candles — sorry, Corinne, honey, but you know it's true — and worshipped by legions of miracle seeking sycophants. Nope, not at all was I referring to our mutual muse."

"Duncan?"

"The very.  Listen, I don't want to suggest that the Post-Man deserved to have his wife flirt with his best friend—and make no mistake, flirting is ALL that happened, much to both my amazement and chagrin—but, as I told our darling driver in an earlier conversation, they lived in that house like barely friendly step-siblings waiting for either one to take an interest in the other.  They both had more in common with me than they did each other."

"So as you see it, you did them a favor?" Ariel sounded like a prosecutor.

"I did."

"Ass."

"I'm hurt."

"Pompous ass."

"Look.  You and I are cramped up in this tin can, travel-ing these serpentine roads into Mud Suck, Egypt, just to wit-ness the cinematic reunion of two star-crossed, mismatched lovers who wouldn't have met if your tour company hadn't underbooked a football weekend.  Now, that was a mistake straight from Business 101.  Don't tell me it's not practically Shakespearean.  Had the virtual Richard Rice not shagged the virtual Corinne Post, the real Corinne Post would never have known she really loved the real Duncan Post—whoever that turns out to be."

Ariel gave this some thought.  "Let's just say I buy that convoluted, perverse piece of logic; what explains your deci-sion to come on this trip?  What are you getting out of this?"

Perhaps Richard had rehearsed this, perhaps not, but Corinne knew his answer was true.  "Pure altruism.  That and—I know you're not going to believe this—I want to apologize in person.  I want to be the second person, after our contrite heroine here, to speak to him."

"You're right; I don't believe you.  This has something

to do with business, doesn't it?" Ariel said.

"Oh, I'm always looking for new business ventures, and, assuming the Post-man doesn't conk me on the head again, there are plenty of opportunities I'll make him aware of. After, that is, we have our tear-filled, heartfelt reunion." He leaned forward and tapped the back of her shoulder. "And you? While we're in the interrogation mode, I'm not sure why you're here."

"Because Rinnie asked me to come."

Corinne pushed the car radio's scan button, but the only stations that rural Kentucky seemed to offer didn't satisfy her. She switched it off. Richard stretched out across the length of the back seat. Ariel hummed a nameless tune. The last sentence still ricocheted inside the car.

"Ask her. Ask her why she wanted me to come, and, while you're at it, why she's allowing you to tag along, too."

"Easy, muchacha, we're on the same side here. We both want these two lovebirds to nest together again; our reasons are just different. Mine is to assuage the guilty conscience that prevents my sleeping soundly." Here, Ariel burst into laughter. "But you, my lovely, don't really believe in love."

"Then maybe you've hit on — and I hope you'll pardon that unfortunate turn of phrase — the reason both of us are really here," she said.

"Which is?"

"Balance. Moderation. A point/counterpoint approach to her situation."

"I don't believe in balance," Richard said. "The quest for balance is inherently unbalanced. I believe even less in moderation."

"Go figure. Look where that philosophy has gotten you."

Richard wadded his sweater to use as a pillow. "Never

mind me. This is about your friend Corinne and my friend Duncan or vice versa, I suppose, and their need to work some things out. I see us as therapists of a sort."

Corinne thought that just then a therapist would be handy for all of them.

" Freud must be spinning in his grave," said Ariel.

Richard squirmed, trying to get comfortable in the too small back seat. "Then he has more room than I do." He finally situated himself. "He was an atheist, you know."

"Freud? I thought he was a Jew."

"Strictly a business decision; at least after he decided that all religion was illusory," Richard explained. "But his Jewishness gave him a built-in audience, not to mention a readership. There's a lesson there."

"Are you an atheist? You strike me as one."

"Me? No way. I don't even believe in Freud. And I've no patience with agnostics who are too cowardly to even take a stand to not believe. Let's take an unscientific poll. Raise your hand if you believe in God." Richard raised his hand and waited. Ariel shrugged her shoulders. Corrine raised hers robotically. "There. It's decided, then. For me and Corinne, at least, this trip is officially a pilgrimage. We're going to worship at the altar of love. Freud be damned. Which, of course, he is. And this leads me back to an unanswered question: why are you here, my counter-culture queen?"

Ariel enjoyed the sparring. "Because, despite what you said earlier, if nothing else, I do, in fact, believe in love. I just don't believe it lasts forever. At least not in my experience. But I do think Rinnie might have that capacity, and that hope is why I'm here."

" As a witness or as a consultant? Or, more pathetically, as a potential convert?"

Corinne swerved to miss a dead skunk in the middle of

the road. Ariel sang the first line of Louden Wainwright's song "Dead Skunk in the Middle of the Road." Within moments the car's air filled with the smell. They crinkled their noses almost simultaneously.

"Does it matter?" Ariel said.

"Sure, it does. If you're here simply to provide comfort or a sense of moral certitude, you're here for the wrong reasons. And Corinne is wrong to use you that way." At this, Ariel finally turned in her seat to face Richard then looked over at Corinne who still stared at the road ahead, though her apparent obliviousness was thinly disguised. "Because you can't offer the former and don't really feel the latter."

"And you, oh sage?"

"I told you why I'm here," Richard said. "I'm here to apologize, not ask for forgiveness for being flawed. What Duncan does with that apology is strictly up to him. What I'd like to see is his and Corinne's reconciliation. That is how I would know that he forgave me, but short of that, I'll never really know, and in the end, that can't matter. This trip, for me, is about me; does that surprise you?"

"Not at all. It simply reinforces what I've always warned people about you."

The conversation lost steam. Richard achieved a level of contorted comfort stretched across the back seat. He closed his eyes, plumped his sweater, and seemed to drift into a light sleep. Ariel occasionally turned to look at him. After some time she took her sweater from the seat beside her and draped it over him.

"Thanks, babe," he said, startling her. "Want to slip back here and snuggle to keep me warm?"

She yanked her sweater off him. "You're despicable."

"In a cuddly way? Listen, if you believe in love, transient or otherwise, I contend you believe in God."

"Well, that's simplistic. The universe is a bit more complex than that, don't you think?"

Richard sat up. "That's true, but our part in it isn't. You love all things natural, right? Brown rice, unbleached cotton, organic vegetables, free-range chickens, trees, clouds, bunnies?"

"Your point?"

"And that stuff was around before unbridled technology and industry — the kind that made me rich — and now it's considered a significant advancement if we return to those things. That which was common is now trendy. I see that as an example of man getting in his own way, and now trying to get back out."

"What's all that have to do with religion?" Ariel said.

"With religion, nothing. With believing in God, though, everything. You can call it *nature* if you want to. I just need a more formal name for it. So, let's call it nature, and then let's agree that even Darwin says that nature's most primal instinct is to reproduce itself. That implies a sentience on the cellular level of the need for another cell of a similar sort, and that sentience is what I can only call love. This Land Rover we're riding in, then, is nothing more than a giant cell rushing to mate with another cell."

"Jesus," Ariel sighed. "Of course, you'd reduce everything, even love, to sex."

Richard smiled. "Not sex; get your mind out of the gutter — that's my province. I'm saying, if you'll allow me to get poetic for a moment, that this is life's longing for itself. Corinne's trying to reconnect with Duncan because they screwed up the first time. They had something; they just didn't know what it was. Post-man and I had something, too — call it friendship — and thus I travel to find it again.

"For you, my sweet, this journey is just as important. I

just don't think you'll know why you're on it until you find
out who you really are. Or maybe those goals are one and the
same."

At last, Ariel felt she was on solid ground. "My goals
are Corinne's goals, and that, my sweet, is a concept you'll
never understand. Maybe I never stopped to think about my
reasons for tagging along, as you put it, because my why is
not relevant. Rinnie needs me—I'm here. And as for your
mostly nonsensical diatribe about God, nature, and love, you'll
be surprised to know I think there's a kernel of truth hidden in
the bullshit. It's a shame the message is lost because the mes-
senger is unreliable.

"For Rinnie's sake, though, I'll concede your premise. I
do believe in nature, and if you want to call that love, and call
love God, then I won't argue the semantics. My grandfather
liked to say that even a blind pig occasionally finds an acorn.
If this is your brand of optimism, I approve. I'm all for more
optimism in this world."

"Compliment accepted," he said.

Corinne swerved again, but, looking back, neither Richard nor Ariel saw what she had steered to avoid. The Land
Rover's engine purred efficiently, then its pitch changed as they
ascended a steep hill. The road was laid in an impressive cut-
through of a mountain which revealed strata of varying colors
and textures. At the cut-through's apex a sign announced,
"Welcome to Virginia."

Corinne startled everyone by speaking for the first time
in an hour. "I'm getting a little tired. Anyone else want to
drive a while?"

Corinne was tired, but she knew her weariness to be
less physical than emotional. Stripping veneer was hard work,
and when combined with long distance driving, was down-

right cumbrous. Ariel, Corinne knew in her core, was not some hippie dilettante, and the more Richard tried to categorize, and thus marginalize, her, the more Ariel revealed her depth. That Ariel would value her friendship with her made Corinne appreciate her own worth the more.

This she already knew about Ariel, but Richard posed the real conundrum. He was easier to accept when she viewed him as nothing more than a diversion, but now she was forced to reevaluate him, to ascribe depth to him.

Ariel had taken over the driving with Richard moving to the front passenger seat to act, as he said, as her co-pilot. He covered his eyes in mock fear and occasionally turned to Corinne, now lying across the back seat as Richard had done, and saying, "Ladies and gentlemen, please assume the crash position."

Ariel did drive fast, but she clearly enjoyed his artificial fright. Once the two occupied parallel seats, their conversation lacked contention, relying instead upon good-natured barbs for momentum.

To Corinne it was amusing in its way but not the reason she had orchestrated the new seating arrangement. She hadn't enjoyed being the topic of their prior conversation, but she realized its usefulness and why she hadn't played a role in it. She was emotionally paralyzed. It wasn't fear, necessarily, though there was some of that in it—how could there not be? She let them express for her those feelings she would not confront herself. Duncan's first words to her—not hers to him— would steer the course of the rest of her life, she knew. She had not been particularly successful at captaining her own ship. That struggle to do so had contributed to…to what? Not hers and Duncan's "undoing"—that was too strong—but maybe the discomfort she felt in her own skin.

She was not Ariel. She was not Richard. She was not

even Duncan, but he of all people would be the person she could most entrust herself to. Ariel, Richard, and Duncan were leaders. Her whole life, teachers and counselors of one sort or another had spouted the platitude that she was a captain of her own fate, that she could be whatever she wanted to be.

In the back seat, Corinne curled and turned over to face her own seatback. What was wrong with not wanting to lead, with not wanting — with all her being — with *not* wanting to do anything but allow someone or something she trusted to show her the world? If there were leaders, there had to be followers, too.

In the front seat, Ariel and Richard, a tour guide and a risk-taker, challenged each other, forced clarifications, stretched their own beliefs. And Corinne envied their certainties but more admired their admissions of some uncertainties. And then she settled into a comfort of her own making because she herself knew one certain thing: that not every question had an answer.

Soon, the road's rhythm and the even sounds of her fellow passenger's voices lulled her to sleep.

## CHAPTER 19

Upstairs in my bedroom that night I felt my isolation from the rest of the house more acutely than I had since I'd been there. Daylon and Della's room was downstairs, and, of course, Tessie slept in her colorless room in the barn. The house's top floor was mine. Ordinarily, I could hear some noises from downstairs: a flushing toilet, somebody padding to the kitchen for a drink, the murmur of late-night television. I liked silence, but I had grown accustomed to the integral sounds of this house's interior life, a life lived with an easy but purposeful pace.

Yet tonight I heard none of these signals of the routine. I felt as though my room had been insulated while I was un-aware. Perhaps, I have to admit, this was because I was listen-ing with intent for sounds from downstairs. And I'm equally sure the stillness that marched throughout the house was a sentinel's quiet. Della and Daylon were certainly lying mo-tionless in their bed, their door opened just a crack, listening for any reassuring rustle from their father's room.

Summerset had rejected Della's mild insistence that he follow Dr. Baker's advice and spend the night in a Bristol hos-pital. Daylon took his wife's cue and offered to drive him there, and both affirmed their willingness to stay with him.

And I spoke up, too, countering his objections to their missing work the next day with my offer to go with him in-stead and stay there as long as needed.

He had dismissed their proposals with kindness, if not grace, but he seemed genuinely touched by mine. "Thank you, no, son," he said. "but I've been enough trouble to everybody this evening, and I think a good night's sleep is all we need."

And so, no one slept. I knew that I'd be unable to hear anything from Summerset's room to comfort me, no snoring — I didn't even know if he did so — no rustling, no sighs; so I listened instead for movement from Daylon and Della's room and hoped not to hear running steps.

I don't know anything about prayer except that Dad called it voodoo. Mom prayed before Thanksgiving and Christmas dinners. I didn't lie there sleepless and pray for Summerset because I didn't know how and didn't know what good it would do, anyway. What I did do, though, was try to imagine Tessie's window Jesus, and if I were standing right now in the open field between the back of that church and its little cemetery, what kind of look he would be giving me.

Sometime during the middle of that sleepless night, I did hear a sound. The back door, never locked, creaked open. I knew it was Tessie slipping in. She sometimes did so to fix a sandwich or eat a piece of leftover pie, and sometimes I'd hear Della get up to join her, the women's unintelligible conversation filtering up from the kitchen table to lie just below my consciousness and, like the pillow beneath my head, soften me back to sleep. This night, however, I did not hear the refrigerator door open or close, or the silverware drawer slide out, or the bread wrapper crinkling. In time I simply forgot about Tessie's coming inside, and, though I was not asleep, I wasn't quite awake either.

That's why the low music didn't register at first. Irrational as it may seem, piano music played for several minutes before I realized it was coming from the baby grand in the living room and was not, in fact, part of the complicated fabric of a dream.

Tessie played beautifully. Daylon had told me that she possessed an unusual, nearly prodigal, talent as a child before her family's tragedy, but until now I had only heard her un-hinged rendition of Chopsticks, or so I thought at first. It now occurred to me that, while immobilized upstairs during my convalescence, I had often heard classical music that I assumed to be coming from a stereo. And I'm sure some of it was re-corded because there were instruments besides piano in pieces I had recognized. But others, the solo piano pieces…well, I now thought Tessie had been their source.

The music this night was clearly used as balm to the player. I looked at the wind-up clock on my nightstand. The fluorescent hands glowed a ghostly 3:30, and I expected at any moment to hear Della stomp into the living room to stop her sister's playing. But the music continued. There could be no question that everyone else in the house listened to her im-promptu concert because it grew louder by almost unnotice-able degrees until I'm sure it could be heard even outside. Tessie controlled the volume that ranged from the soft to the soaring. And still no one, as far as I could tell, got up to silence her.

I dressed and went downstairs to the living room flooded with light. At first I tiptoed, uncertain whether my appearance would unsettle the fragile pianist, then decided to simply walk into the room as I normally would.

Tessie was not oblivious to her surroundings as she had been the last time I saw her before this piano. This concert seemed controlled, almost rehearsed. To my admittedly un-trained ear, the performance was flawless.

She heard me enter the room from the stairway, looked up quickly and nodded. Her fingers, however, never stopped. She played with her whole body as if each note required a unique posture. Her long hair acted as a metronome; her fingers stretched and blurred across the keys. And through it all, her facial expression changed like a cloud formation: shifting, reforming, lengthening then contracting, eyes closing then opening suddenly as though some of the chords especially pleased her. Her lips whitened when she pursed them; reddened when she bit them. There was a joy in her effort that came through in both her physical attitude and in the piano's bright, clear notes.

I sat in one of the uncomfortable high-backed chairs. If Della hadn't come by now, I assumed she wouldn't. I guessed this had happened before. Within minutes—maybe five, maybe thirty, I don't really know—I lost myself within the music's spirals. Tessie transitioned seamlessly between compositions, and, oh, those compositions. I had heard pianists with talent—professional, elite musicians—but Tessie's passionate playing rivaled theirs. The pieces ranged from complex songs full of halting, haunting, disturbing rhythms to the pastoral, serene, and lyrical melodies that I associated with movie scores. There were no apparent thematic connections within her playlist that I could discern, yet the bridges between them were not abrupt either. They flowed organically from piece to piece, style to style, chosen seemingly not at random but by some larger, invisible design.

At some point I saw Summerset standing in the living room's entryway. I had been so entranced I hadn't seen him appear, and, of course, hadn't heard him, so I didn't know how long he had been there. I looked to see if he was annoyed at the late night disturbance, especially on a night in which he could really use the rest, or if he were taken by some other emotion I might have expected—concern, for instance. Perhaps he anticipated the frenzied Tessie. But he was neither perturbed nor anxious.

His eyes were closed and his chin raised as if he smelled something that evoked a long ago and pleasant memory. I was struck that I ascribed to Tessie's playing the ability to engage a sense other than hearing, but I knew it to be true. There were not just sounds in her music, but smells and textures, visions for Summerset that I knew were different than the ones I so vividly conjured. I even thought in passing that if I were to stick out my tongue, a note or two might dissolve there like a snowflake.

Summerset's color was better, though the dark wedges under his eyes looked like slices of a storm. He didn't look ill, but he didn't look altogether well, either. Tired, I guess. Probably sleep would have best served him, but there was something about the way he stood there absorbing sound, like an anemone sucking and filtering nourishment from the surrounding sea, that made me think of Tessie's music as medicine.

He opened his eyes, met mine, and smiled an easy, faint smile. He walked softly into the room like a kid approaching the tree on Christmas morning and sat in the other high-backed chair next to mine. Immediately he leaned his head into the chair back and closed his eyes again. His head bobbed and swayed in time to the music. He wore a yellowed tank-top undershirt with frayed straps and blue and white striped seersucker boxer shorts, and didn't seem at all self-conscious about appearing before a near stranger in such sleepwear. Within moments, I paid little attention to that, too. But what I did notice was that he didn't exude the same sense of strength as he did in his bibbed overalls and flannel shirts or even in the khaki pants, white shirt, and Virginia Department of Transportation vest that constituted his travel plaza uniform. He looked as assailable as an unshelled turtle.

Oh, certainly, his forearms were muscled and the veins of his hands pulsed, but his rounded shoulders were covered in skin that looked like Della's uncooked biscuit dough; and his legs, with their sparse hair and thin calves didn't measure up to the block of a man who stolidly carried two five gallon buckets of feed or water through the barn. I now thought of his slow, measured steps as less the expression of an inexorable force as the indication of the inevitable diminishing of vigor. The loss this family would feel, indeed, that all of the community of Sinking Creek, of Virginia, USA, North America, earth would feel would be greater than the extinguishing of the blip on the radar screen that showplace.com had been.

Tessie played on, at one point looking toward me again and seeing for the first time her father in attendance. To me she smiled; to her father she beamed.

Soon—and like Summerset's entrance, I didn't notice them immediately—Della and Daylon joined us. Daylon stayed in the doorway wearing, incredibly and comically, a sleeping ensemble similar to Summerset's except for his boxers which were white with red hearts and, get this, his baseball cap, as if that were all he needed to turn this outfit from pajamas into something that might be worn outside. Della wore a blue duster that not even my grandmother would have worn, and, for the first time since I'd been in Sinking Creek, her hair flowed down rather than lay heaped on her head. It was as long as Tessie's, and, though its color was not as remarkable as her sister's, it shone like singed cinnamon. She looked ten years younger.

I stood and motioned for her to take my chair beside her father's, then I moved to the fireplace. And there we were, Daylon in the doorway, Della and Summerset seated with joined hands, and I beneath their family portrait, when the sun rose that morning.

Della fixed breakfast after Tessie's recital, which ended as arbitrarily as it had begun. She simply got up from the piano and, amid applause, which she acknowledged with only a shy smile, announced that she wasn't hungry and that she thought she'd go get some sleep now.

Summerset looked stronger, though he had to be at least as tired and sleepy as the rest of us were.

"Gonna make for a long day," Daylon said, shoving a strip of bacon into his mouth, "but it sure was worth it to hear Tess on that piano again. Ain't lost a thing, has she?"

"Some gifts are too precious to lose. Even Tessie knows that," said Summerset. "I think I always knew she'd play like that again."

Then I knew with certainty that what I'd heard while confined upstairs had to have been her, and I started to speak up, to tell them she had stayed in practice. If it had been me, I'd have wanted to know.

But before I could say anything, Della placed a bowl of oatmeal before her father. "No bacon for you, Daddy. No eggs, neither. If you won't go to Bristol, we're going to try this approach for keeping you on this earth."

Summerset did not protest, instead dipping into the bowl of glutinous gruel with a feigned heartiness. "Takes more than a dizzy spell to get rid of me, don't worry. But if it'll make you fell better, I'll eat this horse feed."

"And you know what I think?" Della continued. "I think last night is Tessie's medicine for you. Bless her soul, Daddy, that's all she can do."

It was her medicine, I saw. Della was right, and I thought, too, that back in the summer, it had been medicine for me, as well, and I had no right to tell them I had heard her play since they last had. They deserved to think this was their miracle.

Breakfast finished, Daylon stood, placed his dishes on the counter and filled a thermos with coffee. "I'll be needing this joe and more," he said then chuckled. "Maybe I'll roll my crawler underneath an engine block and pretend to work. I bet I can grab a half hour nap before Smoky catches on."

Della took Summerset's bowl and spoon away before he could get up to clear them himself. "Daddy, would you think about calling Ramsey or somebody to take your place today? You could use the sleep. I'll keep an eye peeled from the gift shop—make sure things is copacabanic. Won't be a big travel day. We can handle it."

"What's that job entail, Summerset?" I interrupted. "I don't mean all your managerial duties—the scheduling, inventory, whatever else—but the 9 to 5 responsibilities? You're just answering questions about routes or hotels or local attractions, right?"

"Well, I admit it's not brain surgery, if that's what you're asking," he said.

"I'm just saying, why don't you let me take your place today? I can handle the simple questions, or use your kiosk computer to answer the tougher ones. And for the toughest problems, I'll just plead ignorance, tell them to take pity on a first-day employee, then send them to Della in the gift shop. I can solve problems."

From beside the kitchen sink, Della grinned when I held her up as my ultimate resource. Summerset, too, seemed appreciative. He leaned back in his chair and tapped his forefinger on the lip of his coffee cup. "I *am* bushed," he said, but added quickly, "but I rejoiced to hear Tessie on that baby grand. Maudie'd be proud, too."

"What do you say? No need to pay me, just get me one of those spiffy vests and white shirts, maybe a pair of Daylon's dress pants, and I'll man your post." I found myself genuinely interested in doing this. If, in fact, the authorities wanted me for killing Richard Rice, this would be as good a way to get caught as any. But that's not why I wanted to do this. Sure, I believed I needed to pay for that; but to tell the truth, there was an attractive logic in Tessie's advice to do something nice for someone else as atonement. It would be delusional to think that an eight-hour's stint in the information booth of an interstate travel plaza was proper penance for murder, however, and I was not delusional. I was a coward.

If I were captured, I'd surrender. If not, well then, that's what was meant to happen. I would not turn myself in, as I once thought I might. But I would not actively run away, either. This, then, would be my Little Big Horn.

And maybe I could stockpile a few good deeds in the interim so when the Hundleys learned the monstrous truth about me, they might have something with which to balance their revulsion.

And yet, there was more to my desire to work than even this. Since May, I had been in a self-imposed quarantine. I lived under a bridge, for God's sakes. That fact was nearly incomprehensible to me now. And for the last several weeks I had convalesced in the house of a family I did not know, and whose lifestyle was as foreign to me as if it were not only from another place but also another time. I needed to talk to other people, even if the "conversations" consisted of superficial questions about superficial matters, to provide contrast. I needed to escape the isolation to see how much I had changed. And in what ways.

"Far as I know, there's no one coming from the state today. No meetings of any kind. Della can sign for deliveries. Harry, I think I'll take you up on that offer. A good long nap just might do this old man some good," said Summerset.

Della took off her apron and folded her dishtowel. "I'd

better get ready. You can ride to work with me, Harry," she said, disappearing down the hall.

Daylon left, too, promising to come back in a flash with a pair of dress pants he had outgrown. They'd fit me, though, he said. And so I would be going to work, neither dressed in the jeans and sweatshirt as I might when I was part of a room full of geeks tossing nerf balls between writing and debugging software, nor in a tailored suit for a meeting with a potential investor or venture capitalist, but in a borrowed state-issued vest and a pair of hand-me-down khaki pants.

As I dressed, I thought my ignominy was total, but after I emerged from my bedroom in that outfit, and the Hundleys pronounced me "as handsome as a show dog," I felt the compliment's sincerity.

The ride from the Hundley's to the plaza revealed how truly labyrinthine Sinking Creek was. I hadn't been conscious when I was transported here, hadn't traveled anywhere by road since then. The only trips I had taken were by four-wheeler or on foot into the woods of the Hundley property; the only destination had been through those same woods to the tiny church as Tessie's one-man tour group.

The dirt road in front of their house followed the twists of the creek itself. We rode behind Daylon's old truck until this road intersected a minimally larger paved road, where Daylon turned right with a honk and a wave while we turned left.

"Smoky's Garage is that way, in downtown Sinking Creek," Della explained with no trace of irony. "We go left toward the highway."

The sky was aquamarine, the trees by now wore their October colors; and, since the road wouldn't allow me any clear, straight sight lines, those colors are what I concentrated on.

The land around Cincinnati proper was a broad flood plain, in no way as perspective-destroying as Kansas or Missouri, but spacious enough. These Virginia mountains, which had induced claustrophobia months ago, now hovered over and around us like a hug. As nurturing an image as that seemed, however, I knew in my deepest places that this hug was not for me, and that in time I would try to wriggle from its grasp as a child might escape his mother's arms, though he loved the touch.

"Nervous?" Della said as the truck jounced over the asphalt patches that dotted the old pavement.

I wondered briefly if she had mined my thoughts. "About what?"

"First day at work, course."

I knew what she wanted to hear, and, in fact, maybe I was. "A little," I said.

"Well, don't forget: anything you can't answer, don't make something up. You could get somebody lost, or worse. Just throw me a signal and I'll come running. Don't be embarrassed if there's something you don't know. No shame in not knowing, Daddy always says." With that she was off and running. Della's speech always verged on rambling, but when she was on solid ground, she could really pick up speed.

I had no intentions of purposely misleading a confused traveler. I just wanted to get through this day. Just wanted to help Summerset out a bit. Just wanted to walk out of the travel plaza at 5 p.m., take off this floppy vest and get back home to the computer. I certainly didn't foresee any problems. How hard could this job be?


Turns out, the job wasn't hard, at least in a physical sense. Once, when I was a kid, I was standing on the curb in front of our house putting some letters in the mailbox for Mom, and some guy in a delivery truck slowed down, lowered his window, and asked for directions to somewhere — a local hardware or grocery store, something — and I recognized the place. The problem was, as I tried to tell him how to get from here to there, using landmarks and hand gestures, and starting and restarting him from a variety of orientations, I realized he very quickly tuned me out, politely waited for me to finish, and finally drove off, only to stop at the end of my block and ask some adult bike rider for the same directions.

That episode didn't shake my confidence in my ability to give directions; it just made me less willing to do so. In fact, nearly every time I was asked by other strangers for directions, I either peremptorily told them I didn't know their destination, or I intentionally gave them spurious directions. It wasn't a prank that gave me satisfaction or amusement; it was that I wanted to be appreciated for my effort, for my expertise.

No, this job wasn't demanding or tiring, but what I soon found was that it required a sense of responsibility I found wearing. Years before, that delivery truck driver was going to find his destination one way or another, and soon. He could have gotten out of my sight before he stopped again, but the completion of his task was more important to him than my childish sense of inadequacy. Here at the plaza, I was determined to tell these people how to get where they were going as expeditiously as possible.

They seemed genuinely grateful when I highlighted their maps or recommended a route, and the many, many questions I had to refer to Della didn't appear to lessen their confidence in me or my efforts on their behalves.

One guy tried to tip me a dollar, and when I didn't accept it, he put it in a March of Dimes jar on the kiosk's counter.

There were rude people, too; people for whom no level

of detail could be clear enough, and part of me—a very large part—wanted to ask them if they needed somebody to actually drive them there.  And when that part of me roiled just below the surface like a bass about to burst the water's skin to inhale a tasty bug, I thought of the first time I saw Summerset in action, patiently dealing with two college guys who taunted him in French for their own amusement.  Now, I think he had to have known what was happening, despite his unfamiliarity with the language.  He understood people, and something about those kids would have told him of their insincerity, and yet he talked to them with a yeoman's earnestness that gave him nobility I had not then recognized.

The morning sped by.  I was not particularly busy and my greatest discomfort came from smiling and nodding at every visitor who looked my way.  "Make it seem like you're asking them if they need help without asking them out loud," Della had told me as we got out of the car that morning.  "Daddy always says they shouldn't be a-scared to ask him for help; they should just feel like they can ask him anything."

And so I did.  Smiles do not come naturally for me.  I prefer a measure of formality, but I did notice that most of my smiles were returned, even by travelers who decidedly did not need assistance, who might simply have stopped for fast food, or a bathroom visit, or to just stretch their road-cramped legs.  Still others appeared disquieted by a smile, glancing quickly behind them as if to see whom I might really have been looking at because we certainly didn't know each other.

I understood those people, and made sure I didn't disturb them again.

So, it became a kind of game to me, and to entertain myself, I kept a count of every ten people who walked in: how many of them smiled back at me versus how many of them looked through or away from me.

Della and I ate lunch together, replaced at our respective posts by people I vaguely recalled from my days of haunting the plaza as a shadow who needed food. I wondered if they had seen me as I had watched them; indeed, as I had watched everyone who worked there.

She asked the obligatory questions about my first hours, imbuing my "job" with an importance I might have equated with a Cabinet post. "Now, do you think everybody who needed help got it?" she asked.

I bit into a double-cheeseburger, then dabbed the ketchup off the side of my mouth with a yellow napkin. "I suppose. But, how would I really know?"

"Oh, we'd find out alright. They'll fill out a comment card either here or at some other rest area down the road. We always get real high marks for friendliness and courtesyness. It's our trademark."

"And do you get a bonus, then?"

She looked at me as she might a first-grader. "Why, no, silly. They can't go around giving bonuses for being friendly. It's what you're supposed to do. "

I nodded, properly chastised.

She went on. "But we do get a certificate. We keep them framed on the wall in the business offices, and we're real proud. If we don't get one at the end of the quarter, Daddy'll have a meeting and show everybody a blank spot on the wall. *Should have been filled up,* he'll say, and that's all he needs to say, too. Everybody is kind of hang-dog for a couple of days, you can tell. I'll show them to you after we get off this evening."

*Oh, boy,* I thought. "Can't wait," I said.

She either didn't catch the sarcasm, or it was weaker than I was used to displaying. Or maybe I hadn't meant it to be sarcastic.

I wiped my hands and stood, pointing to a wall clock.

"Looks like it's back to work, Della. Got to keep the traveling public safe, happy, and well-informed."

Della grabbed my sleeve. "Sit just a minute more, Harry," she said, and her suddenly wide eyes told me this was important; this was the real lunch conversation she wanted to have. "Do you think Daddy's going to be okay?"

I admit that worry had floated in the back of my mind all morning, too. Gone now was the Della who had handled last night's episode with such calm. Sitting before me was a daughter afraid of being lost, yet used to so much loss.

"He's going to be fine," I said.

"How do you know?"

I didn't know, of course. I had just said what anybody would have said. And I realized that wasn't good enough, either for Della or for me. "Okay, I don't really know. What I do know, though, is that Summerset Hundley is not checking out any time soon. He's strong in lots of ways, Della. Maybe not strong enough to keep doing everything he's used to doing, but strong enough to keep on living. I get the sense that Dr. Baker isn't all that worried, either. That maybe your dad was just exhausted and what happened wasn't a heart attack. I can't for one minute think that the doc would have left last night if he thought otherwise."

This seemed to square with Della's thinking. She let go of my sleeve. "Daddy needs more help around the farm, doesn't he?" she said, and I could see her forming a plan of attack.

"It's not just the farm," I said. "In fact, I think the work there is what gives him peace. Della, it's the worry that exhausts him."

"About what?"

"About the farm, for sure. But about Tessie, too, and about you and Daylon and your futures, about this silly travel plaza, about Sinking Creek. Your dad needs to let go of some of his worries. He can't take care of everybody," I said. "He's got to trust the idea that some things and all people ultimately have to take care of themselves." That was all the wisdom I could muster.

"Is he going to die?" I hadn't realized that Della was such a bottom-line kind of woman.

How could I answer that? "No," I said. "Not any time soon."

Della knew how ridiculous, how specious, my guarantee was. And so did I. I had made ironclad business guarantees regarding my products and my word, and I had made good on all of them. Maybe I hadn't been so reliable about all my wedding vows, but there were mitigating circumstances, I believed. But this guarantee of Summerset's continued health did not feel fake as I made it.

Della finally stood, too, and placed her lunch trash on her tray. "Sorry, Harry, to put you on the spot. I know even God his own self won't make that promise to me. It's just nice to hear somebody with no stock in the matter, one way or the other, say what I want to hear."

She picked up her tray, took it to a trash bin, and was out the door and gone. Her step seemed lighter.

Mine should have been lighter, too, but it wasn't. Of course, Della was right to say that I had no real stock in the "matter" of Summerset Hundley. I could be gone tomorrow. Should be, in truth. But there were plenty of yesterdays when I should have been gone, and for one reason or another, I had stayed. I had done so at first because I was hiding, then I was sick, then intrigued by Tessie's story, and finally — well, I don't know. Inertia, maybe? No, that lie was…no, how would Daylon say it? *That dog wouldn't hunt.* I hadn't really understood that catch-all colloquialism, and I'm not even sure it fit now. But, it felt like it did.

Della was wrong. I didn't know what my stake was, but I sure felt I had one.

My work and my life had always been seamless. I never consciously thought about how much I enjoyed going to, being at, or thinking about work because it wasn't about my occupying a physical space. It wasn't about being in a particular place at a particular time because wherever I was and whatever else I might have been doing, I was working. Even during those stretched hours under the bridge I was working. It was, I saw now, futile and crazed, but it was a form of work. I just could not show anyone what I had done.

That work was remarkably similar to what I did this day at the travel plaza. Neither produced anything tangible, yet each was eminently useful. People used my software and its applications. It enhanced their lives by streamlining them, releasing time to be used for other things. Here, people used my information or route tips for much the same reason. I steered them more efficiently toward their intended destinations, or gave them options to make their journey more pleasurable.

I lived for the challenge of technology, and I could see how Summerset would enjoy the travel plaza work; but there was another side to him that was left unsatisfied by it. At the end of every day, he needed to hold something solid to let him know he had passed that way. He needed something that gravity could grasp, and that he could say he produced. The farm did that for him. He built fences, held newborn calves, repaired broken tractors, painted barns. Though I had only watched as he did those things, I understood his need for them.

Were we really so different?

I never looked up at the clock that afternoon, even when a lull in traffic afforded me time to wander over to the gift shop and browse the magazines. I could have surfed the Internet from the workstation's computer, but I didn't know if the Department of Transportation monitored its use by keystroke software to maximize productivity. It seemed a longshot, but I didn't want to get Summerset in trouble. Besides, I just didn't really feel like it then. Della stood behind her counter filling out paperwork. I looked back at my deserted kiosk and realized I had straightened the brochures on the desktop and arranged them in order from large to small. I could tell I had been there.

I thought I might even suggest to Summerset that I take another shift tomorrow to allow him one more day's rest.

My moment of indolence was short-lived, however, because the front doors swooshed open and a legion of senior citizens trooped in from a tour bus, stretching their backs and legs, and congregating in the atrium before dispersing to the restrooms, restaurants, and gift shops. Though they would probably have no travel questions, their every need anticipated and fulfilled by a guide like Corinne had been, an empty welcome desk would not reflect well on the plaza, so I left the magazines to man my post and put my gleaming, albeit artificial, smile back on display.

It must a been a pair or more of buses because within minutes the broad entryway teemed with shuffling daytrippers clogging the ingress and egress to the plaza's arteries that branched from my desk area. I felt like the eye of a very slow hurricane. Silver, blue, and mauve-haired women clutched their purses and pointed at nothing. Their bald or balding men walked a step behind them. The women chattered and laughed. The men simply looked bewildered, knowing their prostates demanded attention but uncertain about a bathroom's location. There was plenty of motion but no real progress, and so the whole scene was like a swarm of bees that couldn't decide upon a flower.

They all looked alike after a few minutes. Some of the men wandered to the kiosk, picked up a brochure or two, caught my eye and wanted to say *cold enough for ya?* or *hot enough for ya?* but it was neither, and so they just smiled awkwardly, pretended to be fascinated by their brochures, and dove back into the swarm. How did they find their queens, I wondered, then decided that they were probably interchangeable until they'd get back on the buses and return to their assigned seats. I suspect there was a comfort in that. But for now, they milled.

I liked being *in* the maelstrom without being *of* it. I wouldn't want to actually ever be on a tour such as this, couldn't envision myself as an old man stepping off one of those mammoth air-conditioned, tinted-windowed beasts, and blinking in the blinding sunshine of a travel plaza's parking lot, only to be herded in and out, on our way to see the world's largest ball of twine or a display of 19th century thimbles. But, I have to admit, I could see why Corinne was attracted to the job of leading such a group. These people all, to varying degrees, wore smiles. Their backs ached, their joints creaked, their food was foreign, their routines disrupted, yet they smiled. I felt, as I stood motionless in the midst of their vortex, as if I were surrounded by a moving, circular grin.

It became a bit disorienting, and for a second, I thought I might be spinning into the kind of unconsciousness that had overtaken me back on July 4th. I wasn't feverous with illness, however, nor weak with hunger or fatigue. I think maybe I just wasn't used to seeing that many people in one place enjoying themselves unrestrainedly. I leaned forward on my stool and placed my elbows on the desk, chin on my hands, and their chattering joy no longer dizzied me.

But moments later, the whole scene got to me again. It must have. Because at the outer edge of their ring, I caught a quick glimpse of a face that could not have been there. It seemed to surface from a great depth, get caught in the current of travelers, and then I lost it.

It could not have been, but in that brief instant I thought I had seen the face of Corinne.

I stood quickly to look over the heads of the stooped travelers, but she was not there. And, of course, she had not been. Still, I couldn't shake the thought that I had seen her. This could only mean that I was losing my grip on reality. I blinked exaggeratedly as if that would clear my mind as well as my eyes, but I couldn't help myself — I kept looking.

Off to my left, heading down a hallway that led to a Burger King, restrooms, a cafeteria, was the back of the head that could have been Corinne: blonde hair bouncing off her neck, a regal posture and gait that stood out from the crowd of old men and women whose heights were the same as hers but who seemed smaller. I focused on the back of this head as it wove its way through the throng until I lost it in the distance.

I hadn't breathed since I first saw that woman. I didn't realize this until I could no longer see her. I also didn't realize I had been standing on my tiptoes, fingertips on the desktop and neck stretched like it was made of elastic.

"You look like you've just seen a ghost, Mr....Mr. Trueman," a voice grated beneath me. One of the tour bus women stood there, her soft uplifted face belying the gravelly smoker's voice that came from it. She looked from my nametag to my face and back. "He was my husband's favorite president. I didn't think much of him, but my husband thought he hung the moon. He's dead now, of course."

"Yes, I know," I said, returning my heels to the ground, relaxing my shaking calf muscles.

"You knew my Gerald?" She looked incredulous.

"No, I meant President Truman. I assumed that's who you meant." I continued looking over her head as inconspicuously as possible to catch another glimpse of the woman who resembled Corinne. I knew it couldn't be her, but it would feel good to see something that looked like her. There was another exit out that back hallway she had entered, but I was counting on her coming back this way.

"He'd have liked you, Gerald would, if only because of your name," she droned. "You named after him?"

"Sort of," I said, then knew I'd have to spend some time explaining that, so I added the rest of the lie. "Yes, actually I am. Can I help you with anything ma'am?" I needed to get back to my search.

"No, not really. I just saw you looking at the crowd real hard and wondered if you were looking for anybody in particular. I know most everybody on the trip, so maybe I could help you."

It was worth a shot. "What's your guide's name?"

"Which one? There's two, one on each bus." She seemed pleased to be able to offer information. But I wasn't sure I wanted to hear her answer.

"Both. Let's go with both."

"Well, on my bus it's Beth. She's nice enough, but she's slow. Maybe she thinks that because we're old, she needs to walk slow and talk slow. Anyway, I'd like her to move a bit faster. We're not getting any younger, I'd like to tell her. What she doesn't seem to realize is…"

"And the other one, what's her name?"

She didn't appreciate my interrupting her. "Well," she huffed. "Her name is something strange. Sounds like a black person's name. Lakita or LaShanda, or something like that. But she's not a black person, she's as..."

And she went on, but I had already tuned her out. If the girl I had seen was a tour guide, she certainly wasn't Corinne. Apparently she was just another traveler. When, or if, she came back through the atrium, I no longer needed to see her. I didn't have room for the disappointment.

Gerald's wife continued yapping, and I wanted to pay attention, I really did, I sincerely wanted to appease her loneliness, but I had just been delivered a shock. True, it was a shock administered by my own imagination, but I was completely unprepared for the sheer force of the feelings my "non-encounter" with Corinne engendered. I felt as if my bone marrow had been removed, and my tongue had been botoxed. I looked at Gerald's wife, whose mouth still moved, though I wasn't hearing any words, and smiled. Not at anything she said, but at my own thought that if these last five minutes had taught me anything, it was that if I were to ever see Corinne again, I would be rendered speechless and immobile—a far cry from the glib pursuer I had been when we first met four years ago this very month.

Gerald's wife's words came to me then, as if the volume of a television had been gradually increased.

"What's that?" I said, turning my full attention toward her for the first time.

"I said, I think I'll go outside for a smoke before we reload the buses. Just wanted to thank you for the talk."

"Oh, sure. Sorry I couldn't have been more help with something," I said, and I was genuinely sorry that I hadn't helped her at all, though I'm not sure she had really asked for any.

"That's okay. I wish I could have helped you," she said, then turned and disappeared into the stream of people who seemed to be heading outside by some unheard accord.

I tried to watch her as she left, but there were so many similar shades of silver-blue hair that it was like trying to identify a single fish in a hatchery.

But then the blonde I had glimpsed before joined their current from the side and was swept along with them toward the front entrance. She had come from the long hallway that held restrooms and the Burger King, and I cursed myself for no longer watching for her return. I saw her first in profile, and then just before her full face turned toward me, an elderly man stepped in front of her. In the space of my next breath, they were both out the door.

## CHAPTER 20 — CORINNE

When Corinne returned to the Land Rover, she was met by two upturned faces that reminded her of expectant children.

"I couldn't have found Shaquille O'Neal in there," she said pointing toward the mass exodus of elderly tourists melting out of the travel plaza.

Richard turned to Ariel. "I told you one of us should have gone in with her."

She ignored him, speaking instead to Corinne. "Well, looks like they're loading up. Let's wait a couple of minutes for it to clear, then go find this Hundley guy and get on with this."

Corinne said nothing, just closed her car door and rested both hands on the top of the steering wheel. She stared ahead.

Ariel placed a hand on Corinne's shoulder and squeezed.

From the back seat, Richard spoke up. "Post-Man ever try to kill you?" She didn't answer. Ariel faced him, her eyebrows raised in question. "Well, he did me. But I'm here to see him anyway. Hell, maybe his first reaction will be to try to kill me again. I don't know. Point is, Corinne, it's too late to be a chicken shit. You're here; we're here. Everybody's taken time off work and come a long way to make this happen. I don't know how it will turn out, but that's in Duncan's hands anyway. Let's just go ask this Hundley where our boy is, and go get him."

He looked from the back of Corinne's head to Ariel's face, which, to his surprise, did not look back at him with disapproval.

"Asshole's right, Rinnie," she said. "I'll do it for you if you want. I'll find out what I can and we'll go from there. What do you say?"

But Corinne did not answer.

"Let me do it," Richard said, opening his door. "Who is it I'm asking for?"

"Let's do this, instead," Corinne spoke up just before Richard climbed out. "Let's get into this little Sinking Creek place, get a hotel and come back first thing in the morning. That sound okay with you guys?" It was clear that this was not a request. This was non-negotiable, even Richard got that.

In answer, Ariel spread the map out on the seat between them and with an index finger slowly traced from where they sat on Interstate 81 across the half-inch to Sinking Creek proper.

Richard huffed. "Okay, hot stuff, I'll waste another day here, but no more. I've got an empire to rebuild, and I'm pretty sure I can't do it from this burg. I don't figure there are any wireless hot spots."

"He may be right about this place," Ariel said. "Sinking Creek doesn't seem to be much more than a gnat's butt on the map. I don't know that there'll be a hotel there."

"Probably not one I'm going to bed down in," said Richard.

Corinne started the Land Rover. "Well, then, we'll just rough it," she laughed. "We'll sleep under the stars if we can't find a place. Surely, people have slept in worse."

Within minutes they were convinced that the perplexing network of poorly signed roads, ranging, as Richard said, from narrow to threadlike, had swallowed them into a Twilight Zone from which they would never emerge. Corinne and Ariel wore smiles, remarking often about the beauty of the hills; Richard complained that he was getting queasy.

Just as they were about to pull over to reevaluate their map, they rounded a bend and saw a simple green sign with white letters declaring "Sinking Creek, Unincorporated".

Before them the road revealed a cluster of buildings lining both sides: a combination video rental and grocery store; a café with yellowed lace curtains scalloping the window; a volunteer fire station with two men sitting in front, their metal chairs tipped onto their back legs, the men's heads resting uncomfortably against the red brick wall. One of them smoked; the other raised a hand at Corinne's car as it passed. Ariel raised hers in response. There was an old five-and-dime that looked closed, its windows covered with a thin layer of whitewash. Beside it was a small building whose newness made it look orphaned; its clean green awning proclaimed it a lawyer's office. A weedy vacant lot separated it from the last structure on the block—a big, dirty-white concrete block building surrounded by cars that varied from obviously new to obviously disabled. Above its front door, an oval sign read, despite peeling paint, *Smoky's Auto Repair and Towing*.

Smoky's appeared to be the only thriving business in sight. Grease monkeys rolled tires across the broken concrete lot. Some lifted up cars with rolling hydraulic jacks. The high hammering whine of air wrenches startled Corinne as she drove slowly down Sinking Creek's main street, its only street really, her head swiveling from side to side.

"God, I expect any minute to be pulled over by Barney Fife," Richard said. "How could anybody live here?"

His question hung there. Corinne crept on. No one in the garage's lot looked up at their car as it passed. The next block held some well-kept two and three story homes. Massive oak trees dominated their yards. After a couple more blocks, the road turned another bend and they found themselves on an open road again, a faceless forest with a crease in the middle.

"That's it?" Richard said. "That was Sinking Creek? Now I know what people mean when they say they come from a place so small you'll miss it if you blink."

"I thought it was charming," Ariel said.

"I wish I had blinked."

Corinne whipped off the road onto the shoulder. "I'm going back."

"What on earth for?" Richard demanded. "There's obviously no motel. Let's just get back to interstate and head down to Bristol for the night."

"Humor me," she answered.

"Am I missing something?" Richard pulled himself forward and rested his arms on the seat back in front of him. "Do you think that one block we saw represents just the tip of the iceberg for metropolitan Sinking Creek; that there are blocks and blocks of bustling commercial district just behind it?" Ariel shot him a dagger-sharp look. Corinne ignored him, intent on the snaking road before her. "Listen, ladies, here's a rule-of-thumb: any burg that has a store that will simultaneously sell you pimento cheese spread and a worn out VHS copy of *Pretty Woman* is not just a cultural wasteland, it's uninhabitable, period. Let my voice of reason prevail. Let's find a decent bed in Bristol — if there's one even there, which I'm not so sure about — have some greasy barbecued ribs for dinner, then rescue the Post-Man first thing in the morning. It'll be like an intervention. I'm sure he's longing to breathe some humid Ohio River air by now."

By this time, the Land Rover had negotiated the S-curve

that opened into the tree-lined blocks of Sinking Creek.

"Love it," sighed Ariel, rolling down her window. "I wonder if I could get Thyme to move here."

"You're shitting me," Richard said, scooting back into his seat.

Corinne slowed the car and flicked on her left blinker to indicate she would turn into the crowded lot of Smoky's Garage. There were no cars either behind or approaching her, but she paused before completing the turn. The blinker's rhythm sounded like a single soldier marching.

Richard laughed. "Can't do it, can you? Good girl. Now, before someone notices us, press down on the gas pedal and let's get the hell out of Hooterville before I start hearing 'Dueling Banjos' and get asked to do a pig imitation."

If the girls caught the allusion, neither showed it. But Corinne clearly took his remarks as a challenge. She turned into the garage's lot and parked between a late model Honda and a behemoth pick-up that bore little resemblance to its show-room appearance. Ariel let out a low whistle. "I'd need an extension ladder to get into that," she said.

"And a psychiatric examination," Richard added.

"I don't know," she said. "I think it oozes sex appeal."

Richard snorted.

And then they simply sat there. No one moved because no one knew what their next move should be.

At length Richard said, "Ladies, I don't think garages offer curb service. Somebody's going to have to get out and talk to somebody else. That's how conversation works. Even here, I'll wager. Want me to?"

Corinne and Ariel debarked simultaneously. The men in the lot, both those whose blue shirts with sewn-on ovals identified them as employees, and the customers, also all men, whose ease on the lot indicated that Smoky's was as much gathering place as business, stopped their hammering, pumping, prying, even their talking, to watch, without seeming to do so, the long-legged strides of two beautiful women who walked across their lot searching for someone, anyone, who looked like he could provide some information.

No one said a word, and after that hiccup in time, they continued what they had been doing, or pretended to. From his vantage point inside the Land Rover, Richard thought the whole scene resembled a mime's performance. Mechanics ostensibly went back to their work, and the knots of customers returned their focus to explaining their cars' idiosyncrasies to other employees or to each other. But all of this was done with a minimum of sound. No power tools shrieked, no mallets pounded, nobody yelled across the lot for assistance. And though no one stared at the two fawns stepping tentatively in their midst, no one looked away for long, either.

Then, just before they reached the glass door to the garage's office, it opened from inside, and out came Smoky, as announced by his oval. He wore the same outfit as his employees: grease-stained jeans and a blue denim workshirt. His oval, however, was larger, his name in block, rather than script, letters — and all capitals. He tossed a cigarette butt on the cracked concrete, and twisted it out with a work boot. He extended a thick, grimy hand toward Ariel. "Help you, ladies?"

Ariel stepped forward, grasped his hand, then released it and stepped aside so Corinne could do the same.

"We're a little lost," Ariel said.

Smoky let out a gruff laugh. "I reckon. But if it ain't car trouble, I'm not sure I'll be able to help." The relative quiet on his lot got his attention. "'Scuse me a second, ladies. Seems my workers just developed a bad case of the stand-arounds." He cleared his throat and raised his voice to announcement level. "Everyone, this here's…" he looked expectantly at Ariel.

She grinned broadly, aware of and welcoming the attention. "Ariel," she said, drawing her name out to more syllables than it warranted and placing an emphasis on the last one. Neither Richard nor Corinne had ever pronounced it that way. Inside the car, Richard laughed. She then put a hand on Corinne's elbow. "And this is Corinne." Richard thought he detected the slightest Southern lilt in a voice he knew as Midwestern and brassy.

"...Arianne and Corelle," Smoky continued in stentorian tones. "They're not from here. They don't need automotive assistance. They've stopped for directions." His employees continued their feigned tasks. "So, GET YOUR ASSES BACK TO WHAT I PAY YOU TO DO!"

Air wrenches whined again immediately. He turned back to the women, their conversation now safe inside the protective din of the garage's noise.

Smoky pulled a pack of cigarettes from his shirt pocket, shook one out, tore off the filter, and put it in his mouth. He held the pack toward the women, alternately directing it to Ariel then Corinne.

Both shook their heads.

"So now, ladies, where you trying to get to?" he said, lighting the cigarette.

Meanwhile, Richard decided to get out of the car and stretch his legs by wandering around the lot. He was certain that Smoky would have to tell them that Sinking Creek did not offer any overnight accommodations and they would — as Richard had predicted and would be only too happy to remind them — have to return to interstate and drive south to Bristol for the night. He could taste the barbecued ribs now.

He scuffed aimlessly through the pebbles dotting the lot, careful not to kick any of the loose rocks into the shiny pick-ups that seemed to dominate the garage's business. Two men stood beside a tower of enormous tires each of which seemed to be too tall and too thick to be attached to anything but massive land-moving equipment. The sign beside them shouted *Sell On Mudders!* The men looked up as he passed and nodded. Richard nodded back, then looked away quickly before they would have time to begin some inane conversation. There was too much activity, too many clusters of people on the lot to safely pause anywhere without being expected to make small talk. Richard was good at small talk, but he surely couldn't do so when the topic might be fuel injectors or compression ratios or the relative merits of various tread patterns, so he wandered around to the side of the garage and then behind it.

It was cool back here and quiet by comparison. There was another block of houses on the other side of a graveled alley, and maybe one more beyond that, so Sinking Creek was bigger than Richard had at first thought. But only minimally so because in the near distance Richard saw the hills that formed the backyards of that last row of houses. Having no real experience with either, he wondered if they were considered hills or mountains, and what altitude requirements were necessary to make the distinction. More than the elevation, however, Richard noted that the hillside blazed with autumn, as if fire were spilling into Sinking Creek from the surrounding heights.

All that looking up made him a bit dizzy, especially after being so long sedentary. He leaned against a car parked adjacent to the back of the garage to steady himself. The car, most of which was covered by an ill-fitting beige canvas tarpaulin, had been there for some time, as evidenced by the thick layer of dust. Richard straightened immediately and slapped his hands, then his seat, to remove it.

Then the sliver of the car that showed below the tarp

caught his eye. Though dulled by the film of gray dust, it was candy apple red and the spoked wheels were both sporty and — Richard knew, though he knew little else about cars — very, very expensive. He had to see it, had to see what must be Smoky's lifelong, indulgent dream. The garage owner surely bought it wrecked and was using his garage's manpower to restore it. Whatever, Richard loved sports cars.

He tugged at the canvas covering the hood and peeled it carefully. He half-expected a gasp from a non-existent audience. Instead, the gasp came from his own throat. He dropped the tarp and stepped back.

He looked around guiltily, then walked to the car's rear, already certain about what he'd find there. And there it was: an Ohio license plate that read DOTCOM. Duncan's vanity plate. Richard felt an archaeological thrill. He didn't bother replacing the tarp; in fact, he would need to bring the girls around here to prove that Duncan was here, or at least had been.

But then a question stabbed him. Why was his friend's Porsche here and not with him? And it seemed as though it had been here for a while. The private investigator had not told Corinne that any harm had come to Duncan. Or had he, and Corinne had simply not told Richard? She had acted strangely the entire trip. Richard did not entertain this thought for long, however, preferring instead to bathe in the excitement of discovery. Before he went around to tell Corinne, he looked in the driver's side window.

Everything looked fine. There was a half empty bottled water in a cup holder and a fast food hamburger wrapper (that Richard doubted his friend had eaten) crumpled in the passenger seat, but otherwise the car seemed as pristine as the last time he had ridden in it with his partner.

Richard was aghast, and now wondered if the car had

been stolen. That would explain the covering, the obscure parking place behind the garage. Duncan Post had met with foul play and his car had ended up here.

But just as this and a dozen peripheral and equally sinister scenarios began to spiral from his imagination, he heard footsteps crunching from around the side of the building. He quickly picked up the tarp and tried to replace it on the car by flicking it in the air. It was too heavy, however, and Richard barely got it on the hood, looking like a failed parachute, before Smoky turned the corner followed by Corinne, Ariel, and a raw-boned, blonde employee.

"There you are," Ariel said. "It's like chasing some kid around the mall."

Richard walked to meet them, hoping to short-circuit their notice of his snooping. "Stretching my legs," he explained. "I was just on my way back around." He hoped his voice dispensed conviction.

"Let's get a move on, then. This gentleman…" Ariel turned to the tall, grimy employee, tilted her head, flashed all of her perfect teeth, and scrutinized his name oval as if it were a favorite poem. He blushed, his cheeks brightening first, followed by a wave of red that radiated outward to encompass his entire face, neck, and ears. He discovered his feet. Smoky shook his head and reached in his shirt pocket for another cigarette. "…Daylon here is going to give us some help."

Richard's charge toward them did indeed parry their thrust. He shepherded the group back around toward the front of the garage, though Smoky looked back at the Porsche. "Ya'll go on," he said. "I'm just going to straighten up this car cover. Wind must've blown it." He shot Richard an annoyed look, and it was this look, this annoyance rather than guilt, that told Richard that Duncan clearly was not rotting in the car's trunk.

The girls had safely rounded the corner. "Really nice

car," Richard said to Smoky as an apology.

After thanking the garage owner, the three — what could they call themselves, tourists? — climbed back into the Land Rover. The smudged employee, Daylon, followed Corinne to her door and closed it behind her. Her window slid down.

"So, you're off at five? We really don't want to put you to any trouble," Corinne said.

"Oh, it's no trouble, ma'am," Daylon said. The word *ma'am* startled Richard, coming as it did from someone who had to be very near their age. "Come back at five; meanwhile, I'll make a phone call to my father-in-law. There's no sense in you all going all the way back to Bristol for the night. If he's expecting you, you can just follow me out to the house after I get off work. I'll get ahold of Della, too," he said, grinned, and leaned toward the open window to catch Richard's eye. "Might be some dinner in it for you, too. If you're hungry."

Richard nodded, feigning appreciation of the "guy" gesture.

Ariel spoke up, her voice an octave too high, "I could eat you up. You're a gem."

Daylon blushed again. "'Preciate that, ma'am. But remember: the name's Daylon." He rubbed his oval.

Richard cringed. It had to be a joke. Had to be. He waited for a telltale smile to betray Daylon's face. It didn't come.

## CHAPTER 21

Della thought my silence on the ride home was the result of exhaustion.

"Harder work than you thought, isn't it?"

The job had required minimal physical activity and nothing beyond rote thought, but I *was* tired. I'd let her think it was demanding, though. She seemed to need, would appreciate, that. "Yeah, I'm bushed," I said, watching the road more intently than I had this morning, trying to memorize its turns.

But the real reason for my fatigue, though I couldn't tell Della, was so complex I was still trying to work it out. I had seen a woman whose resemblance to Corinne had unsettled me to an alarming degree. My final hour at the plaza's information kiosk after that woman had walked out had been filled with conflict. All along, I had known that I would eventually see Corinne again, and though I did not know the full circumstances under which I would do so — would I be under arrest; would I surreptitiously, romantically, steal into Cincinnati for a nighttime, one-time, reunion, only to part again for a life on the run; would I stay away so long that I wouldn't see her until I braved an anonymous, disguised foray into the city and see her, now a handsome middle-aged woman on the arm of another, even more successful, businessman, perhaps one I would have had dealings with? — I was bone-certain I would see her again.

And yet this briefest of encounters with her

doppelganger had unnerved me because I couldn't identify my feelings. They weren't comprised of overwhelming joy, guilt, relief, or a recognizable combination of those ingredients. At least I didn't think so. I think I was agitated because I had expected a flood that hadn't come. The only emotion that would have surprised me was, well, none.

Meanwhile in the seat beside me, Della Hundley Monroe droned on about what she needed to do to get supper on the table, fretting that that "scatterbrained Tessie" probably forgot to get the pork chops out of the deep freeze and lay them out. I rarely understood her fully — her idioms, cadence, and generally jumbled syntax baffled and ultimately frustrated me — but I suddenly thought that her last sentence was funny precisely because I did understand it. I had never in my life heard of an appliance called a deep freeze. But I knew she referred to the upright freezer in the Hundley basement. "Laying out" the pork chops, as violent and filled with mortality as that image sounded, meant only that Tessie was to defrost them in time for dinner. Though I couldn't imagine any chef in any self-respecting restaurant "laying out" pork chops, I had eaten Della's before. And I had learned they were damned good. I had learned other things from the Hundleys, too: not to cut off my nose to spite my face; that a good belch to Daylon was followed by not only an *excuse me,*" but that it *felt better out than in,* that pickle loaf had to be eaten with mayonnaise unless it was fried, in which case you could use mustard; that the weather could either be colder than a witch's tit or hotter than bull balls; that one should never weed-eat the hog lot with one's mouth open; that a pint's a pound the world around; and that I could drink wine, even good wine, from a jar that once held something else.

My silent review of these lessons made me chuckle, apparently aloud.

" 'S'not funny," Della was saying, when I realized she was responding to me. "You think I want to come home from being on my flat feet all day and figure out what to fix for three total strangers that Daylon's dragging home?"

"You and Daylon are having company?"

"He called from work. Said there were some people who came into Smoky's and needed to talk to Daddy, and they were going to follow him to the house after he got off. I'll swan, between Tessie hauling home broke-winged birds and every stray dog, cat, mole, or turtle up and down Sinking Creek, and Daylon feeling sorry for some poor soul from Smoky's whose wife booted him out because he'd rather shoot pool and drink Rolling Rock than take her to the movies, me and Daddy don't get no peace."

I thought I ought to apologize for being "hauled" home: another broke-winged bird.

"Before you say it, Harry, I'm not talking about you," she anticipated. "Daddy brings somebody home, it's for a reason. He don't need to explain nothing to me. It was plain first time I saw you at the plaza you needed help." I wondered when the first time she saw me had been. I had been, I thought, invisible until I served coffee. "But Daddy finds ways to help a lot of people without bringing them home. He took a shine to you, that's clear, and I wasn't sure for the longest time why that was."

Della navigated these serpentine roads adroitly, her meaty hand on the top of the steering wheel belying the subtlety of her turns. The podium was hers; nothing I would say, no question I would ask, would get to the heart of her monologue sooner that she was going to get there anyway. The car's rhythm marched not only to her speech's speed but also to its chronology of revelation.

"I'm not sure Daddy his own self could have told you

why he brought you home instead of calling an ambulance after you collapsed on July 4th. Least, not at the time. At first I was aggravated. Seemed like he was just bringing home a pet for Tessie. And fact is, she's been changed in lots of ways since you got here. Daylon likes you, too, but I'm sure you've cogitated that for yourself." She paused.

We were getting near the Hundley house, and at first I thought she wanted to deliver her final point as we pulled into the driveway so there would be little time for awkwardness, but I realized I had never known Della to be awkward. The discomfort would be mine.

"Harry, I think he's so protective of you because he thinks you are who Andy might have been if he'd got to grow up," she finished, and saying that took something out of her.

The thought had crossed my mind before, too. I had never dismissed nor pursued it, though, because it simply wasn't relevant. If I had fulfilled a need for the old guy, well, he had certainly deserved anything I could do for him. Allowing his projection onto me had done no harm.

"Are you okay with that?" I said. "Do you think so, too? That your brother was like me?"

"Can't really say. He was ten when he died, and twenty years is a lot of growing."

I nodded. We pulled off the pavement onto the graveled Hundley driveway. "You're right. It's hard to know who or what Andy might have become. Even where he might have ended up," I said.

She put the car in park and pulled her jangling key chain from the ignition. "It's not that so much. I think knowing what I know about Dad and about Sinking Creek, I think I know who Andy would be right now."

"Then what do you mean?"

She stood outside the car now, her door still open; I

hadn't yet moved. She leaned down to look at me across the front seat. "I mean, and don't take this the wrong way, that I still don't know who *you* are."

Back in my room, still stung by Della's unflinching honesty, I changed from Summerset's travel plaza vest and Daylon's khaki pants into some of Henderson S. Turner's ill-fitting cargo shorts and another of his floral tropical shirts and went down to the kitchen. Della stood at the counter, her back to me, and though she moved only a few paces from left to right, her whole body seemed like a perpetual motion machine, her arms those of a multi-limbed Hindu god that worked independently of one another, chopping, sorting, rinsing.

On the table, propped against the rooster and hen shaped salt and pepper shakers leaned a note from Summerset:

"Feeling lots better everbody quit worring. Me and Tessie are up at the barn. Expecting some folks around suppertime so fix extra. PS: Tessie says tell you Flopsy is with us, case your worried about him too. Dad."

I thought about taking the long walk up to the barn to see if I could lend a hand there, as I had sometimes done, but I had never helped Della in the kitchen. I had offered on occasion, out of obligatory compunction, knowing fully that she would refuse with the admonition that "this is woman's work." I guess as a kid I might have thought this, but the "woman's work" here seemed much more elaborate, ritualistic, even mysterious.

I decided, then, that I would engage in some "woman's work," and when her back was turned I simply opened the deep cabinet drawer beside the sink where she kept aprons. I pulled the top one out, shook it from its folds and put it around my neck before she could protest.

She didn't. She couldn't.

By the time I had tied its strings around my back, Della was shaking with laughter. I suspect, though I had never seen her cry, that she did so easily because within seconds tears coursed down her cheeks one after another in such regular and prolific intervals, I thought of a pulse. They dripped, dripped, dripped from her chin. She could not talk, so she just pointed at the apron's front, tried to speak, then convulsed again into nearly asthmatic wheezing.

I had wanted her to smile, to soften, this one Hundley whose wariness toward me I couldn't penetrate. Without trying, I had made an impression, I think I can say a positive one, on every other family member. Summerset had taken to me immediately, though I had resisted mightily. Perhaps I was a surrogate for him. I'm no psychologist; I can't make that assessment. But he had Daylon, who was son-in-law, helping hand, and stalwart friend. He was surrogate enough, surely, so I wasn't convinced that Della's theory was right.

For his part, Daylon had accepted me without reservation, in the manner of a child. He had never accorded to me any mystery or sinister machinations. My appearance in his life was fact, without need for explanation or apology. I knew of none of my peers who expected so little of me in return for their friendship. I found myself looking inordinately forward to our after-dinner walks in the hills.

And Tessie. I realized I had spent much of the thought I devoted to her in pity, a wasteful capital. She was pathetic in so many ways. I didn't see her story as inspirational because I was certain it would not have a happy ending. Yet that didn't make her tragic either. Invisible was more like it, or at least that would have made me more comfortable. Tessie, though, would not let herself go unnoticed even as she refused to cry for attention. How many Tessies did I pass every day in Cincinnati without seeing them? How much of Tessie was there in every person I knew? Including me?

Tessie was not crazy. Tessie was not even disturbed, and I don't care how many psychological tests would have proven me wrong. She simply chose unusual defense mechanisms to combat everything from the small, sharp nicks to the whistling body blows that life delivers to us all. Or, more accurately, these mechanisms chose her.

I counted it as one of the greatest compliments of my life that Tessie offered me the last slice of pickle loaf in the package, once I learned from Daylon that simply didn't happen to just anybody.

I was leaving soon; I knew that for sure now. And whether Tessie's feelings toward me emulated those she might have had for a sibling, or whether, to use Daylon's terminology, she had a "crush" on me didn't matter. I knew my departure would be difficult for her. The only good thing I can say is that, given what I now knew about myself, this leaving would be difficult for me as well.

Tessie had endured. Tessie would endure.

But this brought me to Della. I had been guilty of underestimating her. She was flighty and undereducated, at least traditionally so, to be sure. But to this family she was protector, organizer, glue, advocate, worrier, warrior, and nurturer. If Summerset was the family's bedrock, Daylon its resilient backbone, Tessie its mystical visionary, then Della was its guardian goddess. No one, not even Summerset, embodied the Hundley's past, present, and future as Della did.

That is why I had not had the impact on her that I had on the others. She was too big. She held too much. She could foresee the time when I would no longer be part of the family's conscious life, when they might be sitting on the front porch on some soft summer evening listening to a light rain sizzling on the tin roof and one of their number might start a conversation with "I wonder what Harry Trueman is up to right now," or even further in time: "remember that guy, what was his name? One of the presidents, wasn't it?"

I was, to Della, the same as a customer who came through her gift shop — someone who deserved all of her courtesy and a slice of her time, but whose transience made their interaction necessarily disposable. Her hope was that I would do as little lasting harm to her family during my stay there as possible, that I would be a pebble dropped in a pond: swallowed and forgotten when the water's wimpling smoothed.

It was this Della who stood laughing at me now, and as she laughed, I could see why Daylon, who on the surface seemed so mismatched with her, had fallen in love with her and why they were in fact so inextricably suited to one another. Her earnestness gave his work purpose; his joy gave her cares a balance.

I had once thought — and in moments of passion fueled by good wine, expensive dinners, a cinematically hazy, candlelit version of the perfect romantic evening, had told her so — that Corinne and I were chosen by destiny, precisely because we were so self-sufficient that neither of us "needed" another to fulfill some perceived missing part of ourselves. Neither of us would have died, either literally or figuratively, without the other, so plenary were we. Ours was a love at its most evolved.

Why, then, had I mourned my loss in those empty hours under the bridge? Why, then, after months of silently mocking these small town high school sweethearts, did I now envy them to the point of pain?

More important, why was I standing in the middle of the Hundley kitchen wearing a white lace apron, which to my chagrin read, "Don't forget to kiss the cook"?

I maintained my poker face and asked with all the gravity I could muster, "What can I do to help rustle up some supper?"

Within minutes I had flour on my cheeks from scratching an itch while dusting the pork chops. My apron front was streaked with the sticky juice from the apricot preserves I spooned into bowls for use on Della's biscuits, which she let me roll out and form by pressing the same water glass into them that she always used. The whole process was a bit more complex than I had thought, involving as it did a continual redusting of both the pastry board and my hands and the dipping of the glass's rim into water. She oversaw my efforts with glee and I could feel the unalloyed satisfaction in her voice when she chided, "Goodness sakes, Harry. Tessie does a neater job than you, and she's got the patience of a buzzy bug."

Dinner was well under way; pots and pans sizzled or bubbled on the stove, and I couldn't resist opening the oven door to check on "my biscuits," but each time I did, Della flicked me with a dishtowel. "I'll tell you when they're done by smell," she chastised.

She handed me a glass of tea. "Sit down a spell," she invited from her place at the kitchen table. She pushed my chair out with her foot. "Supper's on auto-pilot light. Nothing needs tending right now."

I did as I was told and welcomed the break. The work was not hard; in fact, it was both interesting and, I admit, satisfying. I had never cooked with my mother, had never been asked to. I suspect that the few times I can remember her cooking rather than simply reheating a meal had been traumatic, even tragic, experiments for her, and so her rare incursions into the kitchen were adventures best undertaken in solitude. From our living room, where I sat watching afternoon cartoons, I could hear muttered curses and the cracking of ice cubes more than the sounds one might associate with the adroit preparation of food.

Dad grilled often, even in rain or snow. He was, he said, the keeper of the flame, but he was a one-note chef. I can remember many meals that consisted solely of a perfect steak: perfectly seared on the outside and perfectly bloody once I cut into it. "Rare, boy, like the caveman liked it," Dad would growl. The only side dish might have been the slices of white bread we used to soak up the steak's juices.

Once I attained wealth, I developed a more sensitive palate, and discovered the subtlety of spices, sauces, and techniques. Pun very much intended, I devoured new restaurants, new cuisines, new and buzz-worthy chefs. I hosted wine tastings and tasting menu dinners new with each season. It was as if I had discovered a new land.

In Cincinnati, I ate first with my eyes and nose, the flavors appealed to various sections of the tongue. Perhaps Sinking Creek's food assaulted rather than enticed, but the people ate it with their hearts. Here in the Hundley house, I was discovering the joys of gravy. It's a big world.

I was anxious for the Hundleys and whatever roughhewn characters Daylon was hauling home to taste a dinner that I had literally had a hand in.

I took a long drink from my tea. The kitchen had gotten hot. "Who's Daylon bringing home for dinner?"

"Don't rightly know," she said, then fretted. "I just hope we fixed enough."

I turned to look at the stove, each burner cooking something: pork chops, stewed tomato dumplings, corn on the cob, home-canned green beans. She had already put dishes of cold

corn relish, cucumbers and onions in vinegar and sugar water, pickled zucchini, and slices of some of the last of their backyard tomatoes, as big around as compact discs. She had
stretched an already bounteous dinner for five into a feast that
eight would not dent.

I rolled my eyes. "I think there's plenty, Della, no matter how hungry Daylon's mechanic friends are."

"You didn't hear me, I guess," she said. "They're not
mechanics; I know everybody down at Smoky's or any young
guy in Sinking Creek who wants a job there. Daylon said these
people was from out of town and was here to talk to Daddy on
some business."

"Business?"

"Oh, I don't get my hopes up. It's probably somebody
else from Wal-Mart, or maybe some developer wants to buy
some of the property to put in houses. I don't see anything
wrong with getting rid of some of it, but Daddy's not going to
part with a blade of grass for either of those, long's he's drawing breath."

I told her that Daylon had mentioned that to me.

"We've both tried to talk some sense into him, but he
just won't listen. Says he wants a Hundley, or some version of
one, to always own this land. Carving chunks out it, he says,
is the first step to letting it all go." Della sighed. "We'll stay
here, me and Daylon. Tessie, too, I suppose. And whatever
kids God sees fit to give us, we'll raise here, too. But I'm already thirty-three, so's Daylon, so I'm not going to have the
kind of brood we'd need to take care of this place." She stood,
went to the stove, stirred the pots, and turned the pork chops.
"And, though it'll break my heart to tell Daddy this, we aren't
going to make our kids stay true to this place if it ain't in their
hearts. Our kids want to leave, get away from this farm, from
Sinking Creek entire for that matter, that'll be okay with us.

Farming can be soul-breaking work. Small towns ain't for everybody."

"What would you say if there was a way to keep this farm without relying on it for your living?" I said.

She narrowed her eyes. "What are you saying? No offense, Harry, but there are more than a thousand acres to this farm. We don't keep it for fun. Do we look like that computer guy, that Bill Gates?"

"Well, you do a little bit," I teased. Della twirled the dishtowel as warning. "I've done some thinking, and I've got an idea I'd like to mention to your Dad. And you and Daylon, too, of course."

"'S'not going to fly if it involves changing one inch of the land from something it is to something it ain't."

I was not in the habit of revealing business plans while in the incubation phase, and I have to admit that I had given this idea only preliminary thought, but this family needed some hope that they didn't have to invent or a hope that didn't rely on the vagaries of economic forces they couldn't control. I still could not imagine that they had been so fooled by an unsophisticated Internet email phishing scam that they had constructed a future bright and tangible enough to make vacation plans. They needed hope they could hold in their hands. The irony was the internet, that most fluid and intangible of storefronts, might hold that hope for them.

Della sat back down. "I'm listening."

"What's the one thing the folks of Sinking Creek produce in abundance?" I said. Wrong question, I realized immediately because Della did not understand the concept of rhetorical questions.

I decided to spare us both the pain. "Quilts, Della, quilts. Your beds are covered with some of the most beautiful quilts I've ever seen and you claim that everybody in Sinking Creek makes them."

She looked at me as if I had just said that water was wet. "So?"

"Summerset is always gathering up a load from the women at your church and taking them to the plaza gift shop, isn't he? What do they sell for there?"

Della laughed. "Too much, I always thought, for something so plain as a bed cover, something we all piece together out of scraps."

"Who gets the money?"

"Well, the ladies who made them get some. The state gets its share, too. Seems fair to me, we probably don't have ten dollars of material in them. Like I said, they're made from scraps, like quilts have always been made from." Della seemed frustrated to be forced to explain something so simple. "You act like you don't know nothing about quilts, Harry."

"That's just it. I don't. I don't know how hard they are to make, how much work goes into one. What I do know is how much people from big cities are willing to pay for the good ones, the ones made by hand by people who know not just *what* they're doing, but *why* they're doing it." Corinne had taken me to quilt exhibitions at tony museums. I had thought of them as Della did—bed coverings. Corinne, however, and the great many other oohing and aahing people at the exhibit saw them as art. Their prices—for those that could be bought—indicated that, too. "These quilts would sell for several hundred or more in Cincinnati. Maybe a thousand in New York or Chicago."

Della's face demonstrated the struggle between disbelief at what I was saying and the reverence she owed to the mention of such glamorous and cosmopolitan cities. Her mouth contorted in an attempt to say something that could reconcile the incredulity and awe, but finally emitted something that sounded like "fiddlesticks."

"I'm serious, Della. People think that owning something like this is akin, somehow, to having made it themselves. They'll show them off to their friends, they'll admire the stitching, the colors. They'll tell stories about what the patterns represent; they'll imagine what it must be like to do something that intricate, that time-consuming, that skillful, themselves." I thought quickly of watching with admiration many of the simple chores I'd seen Daylon, Tessie, and Summerset do around the farm; I thought of Della's preparation of today's dinner. "Most of those people will never sleep under those quilts, but they'll become one of their most prized possessions."

"They're just quilts," she protested.

"I don't think you mean that," I said. "You remember telling me about the closetful of quilts you have?" She nodded. "And you told me, insisted in fact, that you wanted me to have one? Well, why a quilt and not a…" I looked around the kitchen for an example "…a dishtowel or a pan or an apron?" I said, running my fingers across my Don't Forget To Kiss The Cook embroidery. "Why not a spare sweater of Daylon's or a jacket of Summerset's? Because there's something special about a handmade quilt. Otherwise you wouldn't necessarily remember which ones your mother made. There'd be no need to cherish them."

"But why would some stranger want something my mother made? Or me? Or Mrs. McCurdy, Mrs. Oliphant, old Miss Perry, or any Sinking Creek woman 'less they know them?" Her question was reasonable, innocent.

"You're not selling a quilt," I said.

Exasperated, she stood. "I got no more time for word games and trifling, Harry. I got dinner to finish. The biscuits ought to be browned up by now. Smells like it."

Quiet might be my best bet just now. I was flying by

the seat of my pants anyway. The idea had germinated but hadn't sprouted. Production, distribution, marketing, and a multitude of real world business issues had not been thought through. Like Della's cooking, my plan needed time, needed marinating and seasoning, before it would be ready. I had been hasty in revealing it to Della, but I had sought her approval for something, anything, and that was all I had to offer.

But I could see by the movement in her face, like ants below the skin, that I had disquieted her.

She closed the oven door and dusted her hands. "Biscuits need to cool a minute or two," she said. "Okay, first I'm selling quilts, then you say I'm not selling quilts. What in the Sam Hill am I selling then, Harry?"

"What I meant to say was you're selling more than just a quilt. You're selling heritage. You're selling what that quilt represents: a sense of home, permanence, cozy nights in front of the fireplace. You're selling a postcard of a log cabin snuggled in snow."

She looked as quizzical as a beagle. "Why would somebody buy a heritage that don't belong to them or their kin?"

"Doesn't matter," I said. "People don't care. Not that many people have one anyway, so buying one is as good a place to start as any." I said this and I knew that for me, at least, this was as true as anything I had ever said to her. Maybe to anybody. I could not claim theirs as my heritage, but thinking back to my suburban childhood and my many travels since then, I knew that I could have grown up on the burgeoning rim of any mid to large city in the United States. The strip mall shops, the chain restaurants, the identical kid-friendly, rubberized, mulched playgrounds bore nothing distinctive, nothing that shouted *Here, and no place else!*

There may have been other Sinking Creeks, and I'm sure there were. There may have been other places where the

Hundleys would fit comfortably, where their language, and values, and tacit philosophies would not only be shared but emulated, but it would have been like buying new shoes identical to your favorite old pair—same style, brand and size—they just don't feel exactly the same. In time, they may suffice, may even make you put the old ones away as too worn, but there will always, always be a difference. The Hundleys were Sinking Creek and vice versa. That's what Della was trying to tell me.

But what she wasn't getting was that I knew that, and, in my way, I was telling her so. And that it didn't matter. If this were successful, ultimately we'd have to procure quilts from many mountain seamstresses, some from well outside of this singular community. Selling Sinking Creek quilts was selling the *idea* of Sinking Creek, not its soul, and what could be wrong with that?

Della's interest was piqued but tempered. "Still don't think Daddy'll let us put a store here. Even if we're selling quilts," she said.

"The store won't be here. It won't be anywhere, at least not in the traditional sense. The store will be virtual, on the web, the internet." I could feel the pace of my speech quicken, my ideas racing just ahead of my words. "You establish an attractive, user-friendly interface, manage and update it regularly, and let the quilt sales begin."

Showplace.com had begun with a similar conversation between Richard Rice and me. The enthusiasm for the task, the unrestrained dream, the sense of destiny and perfect timing—it all felt so eerily similar that I could have been reliving those heady moments all over again. Difference was that conversation had been like a tennis match—for every idea I offered, Richard suggested a refinement, an enhancement, a viable alternative. We had pushed one another's natural creativity beyond the singular bounds of each of us and showplace.com had become that most tired of clichés: an entity greater than the sum of its parts. Just now, my time under the bridge felt like nothing more than a necessary, though uncomfortable, larval stage for my next incarnation.

Della did not elicit that same soaring sense of possibility from me, but her challenge necessitated that I become not just Duncan Post but also Richard Rice. With her I needed to perform as both innovator and personality. She required clarification and practicality, two facets that more properly belonged to the partner I had killed.

And then I felt a competing emotion, one that required a full attention that I had heretofore refused to give it. Guilt. I had felt many things since my discovery of Richard and Corinne's betrayal, and I suppose guilt was the underpinning for each of those emotions, but I had never yet faced it without the armor of either denial or equivocation.

I had killed a man.

It did not matter that I had been enraged; it did not matter that I had felt justified. I had taken a human life and did not deserve to feel the joys of creation. A new website devoted to the selling of homemade quilts, even to help save the Hundley's land, was not the karmic equivalent of recompense. I cringed at the inequality of my assumption.

None of this, of course, mattered to Della just now. She had company, unwanted or not, to prepare dinner for. She busied herself stirring sugar into a fresh batch of tea. "You've give me a bunch to think about, for sure. After dinner, what say you and me and Daylon sit down with Daddy? He'll have a better way of figuring all this than I ever could." She pointed toward the refrigerator. "Crack some ice, if you would, please. I hear the four-wheeler coming in from the barn. Means Daylon won't be far behind."

## CHAPTER 22

Tessie and Summerset came through the back door, Tessie's tangerine hair wind-tousled and Summerset's tonsure swept back. She looked me up and down and snickered when her eyes finally lit on the apron.

"What?" I said.

She stepped to the sink and began washing her hands. "Never see Daylon wearing one of those," she said.

"Harry's been a real big help," defended Della.

Tessie wiped her hands down the front of her jeans. "Didn't say he wasn't. Just said you'll never see Daylon in one." She grinned.

I turned to Summerset to see if I'd made him smile, too, but I hadn't. His color had returned; there seemed no vestige of last night's fainting spell. The dirt on his overalls indicated a day's work in the barn, a return to normalcy. Yet his face wore an expression that bordered on — what could I call it? — not fear, really, but apprehension, and he looked only at me. He was as detached from the repartee between his daughters and me as if he were watching television with no sound.

And as his clear gray eyes bore into me, I felt the weight of his look. And what it meant. I wanted then to run, to break past all of them, out of the house, down the painted porch steps and broad front lawn to Sinking Creek. I wanted to splash in its cool water all the way back to my bridge, climb the steep bank past my sleeping platform and emerge from the woods onto the berm of that highway that had led me here. I'd go either direction just now, north or south, didn't matter, and simply run until I fell from fatigue. Then I'd crawl and take perverse pleasure in bloodying my hands and knees on the knobbed pavement. And when my hands and knees would become too raw to bear weight, I would squirm on my elbows and stomach, rubbing first my clothes to threads then my skin away in strips and chunks until, when morning would break, loud as the scream of failing brakes, I would be nothing more than a dark smear under the fluttering tatters of my clothes, on the unnoticed verge of the highway, not worthy of regard even by scavenging, squawking crows.

We heard the front door open.

Della sprang into immediate action, straightening silverware and glasses by moving them a quarter of an inch.

"I like it when Daylon brings people home," Tessie squealed and pulled apart the first of three folding chairs to sit beside her place at the table.

"Well, of course you do," said Della. "You don't do none of the work."

Within seconds, their conversation descended into a series of half-hearted "do, too's" and "do not's." Tessie stopped first when she heard the low voices in the living room.

Around me the kitchen seemed a swirling, dangerous place. I was afraid to move, afraid I'd burn my hand on the hot stove, or knock over the table crowded with its dinnerware, afraid of slipping on the suddenly icy-slick linoleum floor. I would not move because I did not trust gravity to be constant throughout the room.

Della pushed past me to empty pots into bowls, and Tessie hurried down the hallway to greet Daylon and whoever else was coming.

I caught Summerset's gaze in the web of my eyes and

in the gaping hole in my chest. He spoke in a voice that, although steady and distinct, sounded like it was coming from not just a distant place but also another time. His voice was where the room's gravity had gone. "I'm sorry, Duncan. When I got the call, you and Della were already on the way home. I couldn't reach you in time to tell you they was coming."

If Della noticed that her father called me by my real name, she didn't show it. She simply continued dinner preparations.

So. This was how it would end. Daylon could not know he had played Judas, and I would not think Summerset played much of a role in this either. They were nothing more than innocent pawns, bringing the Virginia State Police, or detectives from Cincinnati, or, for all I knew, since murder was decidedly a federal offense, the FBI, into this house to arrest me, not because they wished me harm, but because they abided the law. It would never occur to them to do otherwise.

In many ways, this felt like witnessing the inevitable death of a terminally ill patient: the sense of relief mixed with the feeling that no matter how painful the suffering was, those left behind are never quite ready for the finality.

Della could not know that this dinner, the only one that bore some part of me, was my last as a free man. I hoped the authorities would let me eat it. I hoped they'd allow me to walk to their waiting car without handcuffs, though I did not deserve that consideration. I hoped above all things that Tessie would not find out the extent of my evil.

Into the kind hands of the other Hundleys I placed that last hope.

Something struck me as odd, however, as I heard Daylon's voice in the front of the house. His conversation did not seem serious or subdued, hushed or intimidated by the authority of law enforcement. In fact, they had paused in the living room, and I heard him say that Tessie, who had just chirped a greeting to them, was the only Hundley who could do justice to that marvelous grand piano they had apparently stopped to admire.

And I heard something else, something that made me feel demeaned for just an instant. The voice that responded in tones too low for me to fully understand was female. I didn't even warrant a gruff and burly man to bring me to justice, even after all this time as a fugitive.

And then I heard the piano stool scoot and Tessie began playing.

In the kitchen Della wiped her hands on a dishtowel and said, "Dinner's going to be ice cold if Tessie puts on a concert. She can play after we eat." She straightened her hair, or at least patted the top of her beehive, and strode down the hallway to summon everyone to the table.

Summerset and I faced each other across the kitchen. His posture remained erect, stiff. I no longer wanted to run; I felt heavy, tired. I just wanted to sit.

Summerset's standing, however, demanded that I do the same, though my legs felt like stilts of sand. "How long have you known?" I asked him.

"A pretty good spell."

"Della, Daylon, and Tessie?"

"Still don't."

I started to tell him that Tessie did know my real name, but he was right, of course. Knowing my real name was only an angstrom of my story, so in essence, she was as blind about me as Daylon and Della.

"Why, Summerset? Why haven't you turned me in?"

His rigidity softened, his shoulders relaxed. "We talked about that, but it's like I told Mr. Daugherty: a man don't live his life in one day." He leaned against the counter. "Other than that, I can't rightly say."

That was his answer, that a man don't live his life in one day? I was supposed to figure that out? I supposed the Daugherty he referred to waited in the living room with the female officer and that he'd be a bit more direct with me. I would have plenty of time to ponder whether Summerset referred to himself or me, or man in general; for now, though, I let it pass.

But something else bothered me, too. "How could you let me sleep under your roof? Why would you trust me alone with your family?" I could not think he was either this magnanimous or this negligent.

He gave me a confused look, and I thought, *well, it's a little late to be puzzled by that fact, now isn't it?*

His bewildered expression deepened. It would be difficult to justify that action, no matter how kind a man he was. I was immediately sorry that my question caused him to challenge his judgment, though. "What do you mean?" he said.

But before I could answer, Tessie's piano playing stopped, and the ensuing silence kept me from saying anything. The kitchen's acoustics would have caused at that moment, my voice to reverberate as in a concert hall. The authorities coming down the hallway knew my crime, Summerset too; there was no need to announce it. I pulled back the chair to my accustomed place at the table and sat down heavily.

Della was first to enter the kitchen, smiling and jabbering on about how we were just having pork chops, just any old weekday dinner, really, and she could just kill (I cringed at the word) Daylon for springing guests on her without time to fix a proper company supper, and that maybe tomorrow, if she could convince them to stay, she'd do a Sunday pot roast with some special sides and her mother's mushroom gravy and yeast rolls instead of these old common biscuits and peach cobbler because Mrs. Grayson up the holler had some juicy ripe peaches just now and ....

And following Della into the kitchen was Daylon, but following Daylon was not Tessie. Nor was it a law enforcement officer. Corinne's best friend Ariel appeared. She had a single braid like a filament threading down through the rest of her straight and gleaming blonde hair, like a stream coursing through a wheat field. Her hair was very much the color of Corinne's. Uncharacteristically, she walked tentatively as if she picked barefoot over unknown terrain. As soon as she stepped into the kitchen she stopped and looked at me.

I thought I should probably stand up, do the polite thing, but a force like a giant hand kept me pushed firmly into my seat. Before I could do anything, and before Ariel could acknowledge me, Della, oblivious to the looks of recognition that crackled between Ariel and me, continued her discourse.

"This is my father, Summerset Hundley," she said and stepped aside as if presenting him. "I know you all have business, but it can wait until after we've all had supper, can't it?"

Something wasn't right, though. Something about the way Della, and Daylon too, kept looking back down the hallway gave the moment a sense of incompletion. Tessie had not yet appeared, but Della would not need her to complete the introductions, nor for her to begin assembling everyone around the table. Ordinarily, she would have expressed impatience, loudly, to her sister.

Summerset moved toward Ariel and shook her hand warmly. She gave her hand and her name, then turned to me and paused.

Don't do it, don't do it, please, Summerset, don't do it, I thought. He didn't.

Ariel sensed this. She came to me and languidly offered a long-fingered hand. "It's good to see you," she said, and her eyes confirmed this with a flash of somber relief. I appreciated her ambiguity in front of Della.

I held Ariel's hand a beat longer than an introductory handshake to a stranger would have demanded, but I was trying to process what I was seeing, what was happening. What did the arrival of Corinne's best friend in the company of authorities mean?

I suddenly wanted this moment to reveal its conclusion. No dinner, no more veiled small talk. Have Daugherty get his ass down the hallway, cuff me, call the photographers, and spirit me out of Sinking Creek with sirens wailing and cameral lenses clicking.

At that moment Tessie's tangerine hair came into the kitchen. She walked backwards, entertaining Daugherty as he followed. I stood.

I should not have.

I should not have stood because as soon as Corinne came around the corner, I needed a support that even the kitchen chair did not offer.

She stopped the instant she came around that corner, though Tessie kept talking and walking backwards. But even Tessie, absorbed as she was in her conversation, finally halted when she saw the look on her guest's face.

Corinne wore beige shorts and a white sleeveless top. She looked like an Olympic swimmer. Her arms and legs were long, tanned and toned, and even when they were completely still, frozen in an attitude that suggested imminent flight, they exuded a grace that belied their lack of motion. Her white sandals were flat, yet she seemed taller by an inch or two. I had the ridiculous and fleeting notion that maybe I had shrunk.

All the Hundleys sensed an import to this moment; only Summerset, though, grasped its true significance because he looked away humbly. I felt everyone around me stop, realizing the next move, whatever it was, or why, would be mine.

And, dammit, I just didn't know what to do. I had no idea this reunion was what Summerset had apologized for only moments before. And why did he intuit that an apology, rather than excitement, was necessary on his part?

Tears formed in the corners of Corinne's eyes. That slight glistening was the only movement in the kitchen. I slid out from behind the table and went to her, but it was less an act of will than some molecular force. "Corinne," I said. I said her name for the first time in six months or more in the presence of other people, though I might have said it countless times under the bridge. Her name did not come out as a foreign sound, yet I can't say it felt entirely natural either.

She tilted her head slightly, placed both hands upon my chest and smiled. When, after what seemed like minutes, our eyes unlocked, she used those hands to trace the writing on the apron I had forgotten I still wore.

"Do you care?" she said, her voice music.

Now, there was a question fraught with opportunities for misunderstanding. Did I care about what? Her? Her betrayal? That she had come to Sinking Creek? I cared about all of that, and more.

So I just smiled. It seemed like the safest thing to do.

"Okay, then," she said. She took her hands from my chest and placed them like parentheses on either side of my face, and like those constraining punctuation marks, did not allow me to move my head, to look either left or right, but to look only in her still glistening eyes.

She kissed the cook.

I did not lose myself in the kiss, no violins swirled, no choirs swelled. I don't think I even closed my eyes all the way because I knew that Corinne did. It was an enveloping, charitable kiss, giving more than it asked in return, and when it was over I thought I should initiate a second one. But I didn't. This was like food to a starving stomach — it is unsure how to digest it, and too much too soon will only make the stomach revolt.

Daylon broke the silence. "Well, I guess you two don't need to be introduced after all."

"Daylon, why don't you and Della and Tessie come out back with me," Summerset offered. "Maybe I can explain some things."

"You don't care, I'll go with you folks," Ariel said.

Della turned the knobs on the stove off.

"Okay, but don't forget the guy out in the front yard," Daylon said.

At that, Ariel and Corinne looked at each other as if blaming the other for forgetting something.

Corinne spoke first. "There's someone else who needs to see you."

"I figured," I muttered and knew for sure now that this Daugherty had at least a streak of kindness, allowing a reunion, however brief, before arresting me.

Ariel and the Hundleys went out the back door.

Corinne held my hand tightly and led me down the hallway that by all logic I should have been leading her down. I had, after all, lived here for months; she had just arrived. Some small part of me resented this.

"I know this is all so sudden for you," she said. She couldn't know whether it was all so sudden or not. It had only been minutes. It had been years. And now she was escorting me, rather blithely I thought, to a lifetime sentence.

It's funny when you've anticipated a moment for so long, that it could turn out much differently than the dream version. I had rehearsed a reunion with Corinne many times, but none of my versions included my wearing an apron or peripheral bit players like Ariel or a policeman waiting at the end of a long hallway. I stopped short, like a led mule suddenly and arbitrarily deciding that here, not there, was where he wanted to be. I wasn't refusing my fate, just delaying it. I wanted to take this moment, uncomfortable as it was, and expand it, allow it to fill the universe. Behind us light from the westering sun filled the kitchen with gold. Before us the hallway would lead to the front porch, the light there would be watery and purple.

Here in the middle I had the best of both lights. Corinne was beautiful in either. There had been no change in her that I wouldn't have expected. Stress showed in her face, but I couldn't point to specific new lines or permanent furrows or deepened creases. Her long blonde hair, as long as Ariel's, did not lack remembered luster. Yet, there was something in her aspect that denoted worry, a sadness in her eyes that prescribed and limited the size of her smile, the breadth of her expectations.

For my part, I attributed the muting of our reunion to guilt on both ends. Our essential world had been transfigured in that instant in my office so many months ago. A slow motion run toward each other's arms—unlikely in any reality outside the movies, anyway—was not possible for us, would not have been tasteful. Eden had been pillaged.     Still, it was beyond good to see her, to know that she was well and didn't, apparently, despise me. It was just as good to know that I didn't despise her either.

When I stopped short in that hallway assessing the light at either end and assessing, too, Corinne's unforeseen installation into that light, she didn't insist on dragging me forward or on an explanation, or in fact, on any words at all. And we at last had that moment when all that had passed, and all that would, did not matter. The entrepreneur, the murderer, the fugitive, the near-dead, the revived, the farmhand, and the cook held his wife, the artist, the tour guide, the adulteress, the seeker, and the finder, in an embrace that felt like conspiracy.

When I opened my eyes again, the light had shifted. Gone was the brilliance from the kitchen, replaced by the ordinary light of the setting sun filtering through autumn leaves; the light toward the hallway's front opening had deepened, the purples had grayed. And by unspoken consent we unlocked and walked abreast, tight-fitted, down the remaining hallway.

The wooden front door was open already, but through the screen door I saw the cruelest joke fate could ever play upon any man. Daugherty stood at the bottom of the porch steps, half-turned from us. In profile, through the screen, in a light that was losing its certainty, he was a dead ringer for Richard Rice. I could only assume my guilt was transferring itself onto the detective. I deserved this, but I wondered if Corinne had lived with this resemblance during their trip here. Maybe she, too, merited a little knife-twisting.

As I pushed the screen door open with the squeak I had grown accustomed to, he turned to face me. He spread his arms out, grinned and, in a voice just a bit too forced, shouted, "Post-Man! Come and give me some love!"

Corinne stepped from behind me and took a position off to my side near the porch swing. She was between us but not directly. I was aware of her presence in the most tenuous of ways, like I might or might not take note of my shadow. I was concretely aware, really, of only one thing.

Richard Rice was not dead.

I told him so. "You're not dead."

This seemed to take him by surprise. He dropped his hand to his sides with a thwack as if testing his own solidity.

"You're not dead," I told him again.

He looked at Corinne. Then I did, too.

"Is he supposed to be?" she said.

"Yes," I said and wondered when my voice had changed, had suddenly been hijacked by a bad ventriloquist.

Corinne patted the swing beside her. "Why don't you sit here a second and let's sort this out."

It occurred to me that she didn't need to sort anything out. That whatever this was—a ghost, a look-alike, or (and this was becoming, however irrational, the most logical choice) really Richard Rice—she had already sorted it out. And that was simply not fair.

From around the corner of the house, the Hundleys and Ariel appeared, their footsteps hesitant as if they were testing pond ice.

"Everything all right out here?" one of them said, might have been Ariel.

Only six feet of porch and three stairs lay between me and the man I had killed for screwing my wife. Only it turns out I hadn't killed him, so that was the distance that lay between me and the man who had screwed my wife. If he had done even that.

On the porch swing to my right sat that wife—if, in fact, she still was—who had become that cliché.

Six months had to be accounted for. There was a bill to be paid for them, but I didn't know who owed whom.

From the bottom of the steps, Richard held his arms out again. "Come on, Duncan," he said "how 'bout a hug."

In my mind I saw it happening. I saw myself burst forward two steps and rocket off the top stair, my shoulder thudding squarely into his chest in a picture-perfect football tackle. I heard the wind whoosh from his lungs like stomping on an empty milk carton. I saw us rolling in the Hundley's front yard, my fury and my new country-toughness subduing him easily despite his outweighing me by thirty pounds. I felt my knuckles tunnel first into his soft midsection then shatter his cheekbone. I felt Corinne's thin hands pulling like flimsy plastic forks at my shoulders, desperately and futilely trying to pry me off a defeated and defenseless Richard Rice.

In my mind I saw that take place. But I didn't do it. The knowledge that this would take place if I chose it was enough. I suppose the imagined fight was as real as virtual sex.

I looked over to Della, standing with the rest of her family, stunned, as I'm sure they all were, by the revelations that Summerset had given them, and said, "Dinner still warm?"

## CHAPTER 23

Dinner began in strained formality. Bowls were passed haphazardly, some clockwise, some the reverse, others diagonally across the table, always with apologies. Daylon and Ariel led the conversation, such as it was. At my end Corinne sat beside me in a folding chair squeezed in at the table's corner. I felt her looking at me often.

Richard, seated between Summerset and Tessie, picked at his food at first, shoveled it within minutes. I think he had the sense out in the front yard that something precarious had been avoided, but he didn't know what. And that whatever had been averted had been carried inside in reduced form. He didn't know what to do to dissolve it completely, but ignoring it was his solution.

I had come down the porch steps and shaken his hand, though Richard's arms were still outstretched for an embrace. That was a start. That was all I could give him just then.

At dinner, Ariel could have been a Hundley to an outside observer. She dipped into the steaming bowls, ate heartily, loved every bite, praised every dish. Della obviously loved her immediately. The way to a cook's heart is through her ego.

I returned some of Corinne's glances, but neither of us gave sly, romantic ones; no, these were more akin to the early rounds of a boxing match, each fighter testing and teasing the opponent with jabs not meant to deliver real damage but to elicit a response, to establish a proclivity. *Who are you*, these glances asked. *Who are you now?*

Maybe Summerset knew their subtext, or maybe he had too much else to think about because, aside from every proper, polite response, he remained uninvolved in the dinner conversation once it picked up some momentum.

Daylon laughed about the sea-shift on Smoky's lot as the girls walked around.

Ariel spoke of Sinking Creek's beauty and of wanting to learn how to cook like Della.

Richard answered Della's questions about Cincinnati, about computers—she probed, I knew, because of our quilt conversation.

Everyone else laughed at how I came to be "Harry Trueman," though I was not amused by my own deceit...and how easily it had come to me.

Tessie may have been overwhelmed by the visitors, by the exotic nature of their conversation and its point of view. She may not have known where to insert herself into their prattle, but something took its toll on her appetite.

Summerset noticed; so did I. We kept offering bowls to her, to put another pork chop on her plate, though the first one sat there with only one bite cut from it. She looked like a woman drowning.


Everyone helped clean up the kitchen, insisting that Della sit down with a glass of tea and relax, as the feast's author deserved to do.

Ariel washed the dishes, pushing back strands of loose hair with the backs of her soapy hands, Corinne dried and handed them to Richard who asked where each one went, even dishes that mirrored one he had just put in the cabinet.

Summerset, Tessie, and I pointed to the appropriate drawers, shelves, or hooks.

There was laughter. But there was tension and caution, too, and after the last dish was put away and the dishtowels folded up, a silence settled in the kitchen.

Richard broke it. He leaned forward as if looking at his knees then parted the hair on the back of his head. "Anybody want to feel my pump-knot?"

Before anyone could respond, he straightened and laughed heartily. "It was just a love tap from my best friend," he said rapping his knuckles lightly against his temple. "Nothing some surgery and a couple of weeks in the hospital couldn't repair."

No one else laughed, unsure of the appropriateness of levity just now.

"Damndest thing, though," Richard went on. "Every morning I get the urge to press Control-Alt-Delete before I can get out of bed."

And there it was: Richard's true show of public forgiveness. Even Ariel, who ordinarily would chastise him for bad taste and worse timing, let it go and offered a weak *what-a-jerk* smile.

But I had to feel it for myself. I did so gently, feeling the knot that Richard's fingers guided him to. Then curiosity got the better of Daylon who did the same and who then launched into a story about a fight he got into with his best friend in high school, and soon we were comparing scars and tales of boyhood injuries.

All around, questions were asked, answered. Eventually our story emerged; half of it was new to me, half new to Corinne, nearly all of it was new and startling to the Hundleys. It was, as Della pointed out, like piecing together a quilt — as much of the story is told in the details of the stitches that hold it together as in the squares that everyone notices. And then she winked at me as if to say: remember, we're all going to talk about this quilt business tonight.

If they were appalled or amused at my past, at the disclosures of wealth and indiscretion, the Hundleys didn't show it. They showered Corinne with the attention they might show the wife of a visiting monarch. For my part, I left out any mention of sex, real or virtual, instead calling everything a gross misunderstanding. Corinne and Richard took their cues from me.

Through it all, Corinne kept a physical distance from me, but it was a distance like that allowed by a rubber band, and her attention was focused on me always, wherever I was in the room. She told me she didn't think I had lost any weight but felt I had been stripped of it somehow, then had it reapplied in a firmer fashion. Now I seemed to have edges and corners; my angles were more acute. Beneath my clothes she detected a capacity for quicker, easier movement than she recalled. She liked the look of my jawbone. I liked her use of the adjective "athletic."

And because I was altered, she wanted to impress me. She turned to Tessie and said, "Would you care if I played your gorgeous piano?"

I divorced myself from the side conversation that had developed between Richard and Daylon to evaluate Tessie's answer. Her silence throughout dinner would have masked her childlike demeanor and the depth of its hold on her to strangers. Her brief and bubbling opening conversation may have seemed nothing more than insecurity or immaturity, certainly not instability; and I had not had the opportunity to tell them her backstory. I wished there were a way to call a time-out, gather them on the front porch and fill them in.

From his seat at its head, Summerset leaned toward the

table and set down his coffee mug. Tessie's eyes narrowed, though she seemed able to look only at that mug when it clacked on the table. She did not meet Corinne's expectant face. Seconds passed while a mighty struggle was fought behind her eyes.

Corinne looked to me for reassurance, but instead I reached across the table to touch Tessie's hand. This brush caused her to flinch but not recoil, and she allowed my hand to rest on hers.

Maybe in that moment Corinne knew. She couldn't have articulated all that she knew, but she was aware that, while her husband held the hand of a beautiful woman, that touch was neither sexual nor romantic, and that red-haired beauty was the damaged reason I had stayed in Sinking Creek rather than finding my way home. She didn't need to know more than this. Other details, other explanations may come in time, if and when I choose to divulge them in a future that is far from assured for us as a couple, but for now, she would have to trust the honesty of my touch on Tessie's hand.

"Tell you what," Corinne said. "I think I'd rather hear you play it. I'm so out of practice, I couldn't even manage Chopsticks just now."

Relieved, I lightly squeezed Tessie's hand. Her eyes fluttered twice, returning from a cell just before she could close the door behind her.

"You want to hear me play, Harry?" she said, then laughed. "Can't get used to calling you Duncan...in front of everybody, at least."

"I do. I think we all do," I said.

\* \* \*

Tessie played songs that I had heard her play before and many I had not. I had the feeling that some were her own compositions. After a while, Ariel stood behind her, marveling at her musicianship, and in the middle of a plaintive, haunting piece began mindlessly braiding strands of Tessie's hair and allowed her own long hair to sway with the music's rhythm. Tessie did not respond to Ariel's spoken compliments, but Summerset and Della smiled. Daylon's reply was always "you should hear her play…" And Tessie's next song would be her brother-in-law's suggestion.

Between songs, the conversations picked up from where they'd been interrupted in the kitchen, and Della obtained the Cincinnatians' promise to spend the night.

"Miss Ariel, you can stay in the little bedroom," she said, and I knew she meant Andy's room, and I knew, too, that some day I'd have to tell her what a compliment she'd been given. "Mr. Rice, we got a real comfortable sofa in the TV room, if you don't care. Harry — well, Duncan…" she shook her head and grimaced, "already knows where he sleeps, so I suppose you'll want to go there, Corinne. Everbody okay with that?"

Tessie stood up from the piano and stretched. "Mr. Rice can use my room if he wants. I'll take the couch."

I suppressed a burst of laughter, trying to make it sound like a cough instead. I knew Richard did not envision being led to the barn to sleep for the night, and, as comfortable as Tessie's room there was, I also knew that any noise besides the cycling of an air conditioning unit would be odd and frightening to him. A sudden, middle-of-the-night bawl from a cow would scare the shit out of him. The room's paucity of color alone would disturb him. He was in for a sleepless night.

Richard's half-hearted "Oh, I couldn't," was met, predictably, by the other Hundleys' "we insist's."

With this, Tessie left to straighten her room and get Flopsy out so his scrabbling in the cage wouldn't disturb the guest. Before she left, she turned to face the room. "How many nights will they be staying, Harry?"

"Well, just the one, I suppose," I answered. Then I looked at Summerset. "If you're not too tired, I'd like to talk to you—to all of you, really, even you, Richard, about a business proposition. I've already mentioned it to Della."

Della enjoyed her moment of importance, having been the first to know. "It's worth a listen, Dad."

"Sure, then," Summerset said. "I've got the ears and the time. Tomorrow's Saturday. Only Daylon's working, but you're a young buck, ain't you?"

Daylon agreed.

Tessie leaned a shoulder against the doorframe, crossed her arms, and placed her right foot on the inside of her left knee to form a triangle. She cleared her throat. "So, they'll be leaving tomorrow? That right, Harry?" Her voice was infused with a frantic energy.

"We'll be on our way whenever we get up," I said. "It's not like I have a lot of packing to do."

Everyone laughed, but before the laughter died down, Tessie said softly, "Why are you packing?" No one heard her…but me.

Her freckled faced turned to each person in the room in succession. She tried to smile, too, but finding that not possible left her ultimate expression blank.

"Why are you packing," she said again, just a bit louder. This time Summerset heard, too.

He stood and went to her. I didn't know how to answer her, so I entrusted Summerset with the task. Then I explained to the others the story of Henderson S. Turner, and my resolve to not only return Turner's luggage but to make overwhelming restitution.

"Why is Harry packing tomorrow, Daddy?" she said below the volume of the others' conversation. I listened to her while the others picked up and extended my conversation.

"Baby," said Summerset.

"Why?" her lower lip quivered. Laughter at something Daylon said about my questionable clothing choices split the room.

"He has to go home."

"What's wrong with this home?"

"It's a long story. We'll talk about it tomorrow."

Della excused herself to go tidy the little bedroom.

"Tomorrow he'll be gone."

"It'll be all right, baby girl."

Summerset reached to pat or hug or just touch his daughter. But it didn't matter. By the time his hand got to her, she was gone.

# CHAPTER 24

I saw it happening, but I had as much ability to stop it as I might a train wreck.

Tessie had been quiet throughout dinner and had perked up only when Corinne asked her to play the piano. I had gotten so caught up in the arrival of my past, I had ignored her, too. Yet, even then I knew we were headed for this.

Summerset assured everyone that she would be fine, that he couldn't be sure if she was upset by all the day's excitement or by the news that I would be leaving tomorrow, but it didn't matter, she'd get over it.

"She's known all along that you'd be going some day, Duncan, but it's like dying, I guess: we all say we know we're going to, we just don't believe it. It'll still take us by surprise," he said.

Summerset excused himself, promising to talk to her while she got Flopsy and some other things from her room.

"Will she be all right?" said Ariel once Summerset, too, had left the room. "Should I go talk to her?"

Della, who throughout the evening seemed to feel a connection with her that was both instant and irrevocable, patted Ariel's knee. "Bless your heart. She'll be all right. She will. May not seem that way to you if you don't know her, but she will." She enlisted me with a look that said, *Won't she, Duncan?* She was entrusting me to tell the Cincinnatians of Tessie's—in fact, all the Hundley's—tragedy. Buried in that look was a request to tell it gently. And to tell it later, out of the family's hearing.

I nodded.

When Summerset returned, he told us he had done what he could to soothe her. "She'll be back in directly," he said. "If you could maybe just not talk about leaving tomorrow, I'd appreciate it. We'll handle that when the time comes. Tess don't have a lot of luck looking forward to things. It's enough to tend to the right-now part of life for her."

Like most things he said, I'd have to think about his words when I could devote the time. There was always something to mull over.

Richard, though, concurred instantly. "Here, here. I know what you're saying."

Well, maybe he did and maybe he didn't, but I suspected not. And I wanted to throttle him for treating Summerset's words as if they were facile and superficial. Richard had, after all, given me a look just after Tessie left the house that I knew all too well. *Chick's got a thing for you, doesn't she?* it said. There was a time I would have thought that roguish, found him funny.

But Summerset appeared satisfied that all was as well as it could be just then, and his relative serenity assuaged Daylon and Della. Me, too, I suppose. For the others, who had no real investment, the matter was settled.

"Now, then, let's talk business," Summerset said, sitting and slapping his legs, a show meant to illustrate his certainty that Tessie was indeed okay.

Della, I swear, gave the slightest squeal and sat forward in her high-backed chair.

We found ourselves pulling both of those uncomfortable formal chairs, the small divan, even the piano stool, into a makeshift circle, and in that sacred shape, we schemed and dreamed deep into the night.

The first thing I noticed when I opened the door to the bedroom I had come to think of as mine (but which, of course, belonged to Tessie though she had never slept in it and probably never would) was the flower that sat on the pillow. It wasn't a banal long-stemmed rose; Della's roses that rimmed the front porch had last bloomed in August. This was a rust-colored mum from a pot she had recently put on the back steps just off the door from the kitchen. Della put flowers in unexpected places, and after a while they just became a part of the household's daily surprises, both inside and out, so much so that they were no longer surprising. She transplanted wildflowers from the woods into niches in retaining walls, put single potted flowers in windowsills, others that could withstand shade she'd find a home for under the yard's many trees. She did not have a formal garden as such, it was as if she maintained a home for wayward flowers.

This single rust-colored mum was the only cut flower I had ever seen around the Hundley house, and it meant all the more because she never liked to cut a living flower.

Its presence on the pillow gave me a reason to approach the bed. I picked it up gently and instinctively held it to my nose.

"It's beautiful. Thoughtful," Corinne said. "When did you..."

"I didn't," I interrupted. "Can't take credit for this little touch of romance. Must have been Della."

Corinne sat down on the foot of the bed. "These people, Duncan. These people are so..."

She paused so long I thought she might be crying. When I looked at her, though, she wasn't. She was simply searching for vocabulary. I couldn't provide it either.

"Will you tell me about them. Some day?"

"I'll tell you about them now," I said, surprising my-self.

"Not now, I don't think. I'm sure they deserve more time." She took the mum from my hand and twirled it in her fingers then handed it back to me. "Duncan, do you know what my favorite flower is?"

I didn't, of course. I sent her flowers for every impor-tant occasion. I ordered flowers, arrangement after arrange-ment, whenever we hosted a party. But I had done so by pick-ing up the phone and leaving the selection up to the florist. *Living room's red,* I'd say, or *the patio furniture is green and white striped,* or *make it something Christmasy.* Corinne would gush at my consideration.

"That's easy," I said. "Yellow roses."

She laughed as if I were a small boy pulling a prank on her. "You don't know, do you?"

I admitted not.

"That's your homework, then. Find out my favorite flower. I've told you before. You just don't remember."

She slipped off her sandals by using her feet and crossed her ankles. I always loved her slim ankles, their attachment to her Florida-shaped feet. I still stood facing her, an arm's length away.

"How do you want to do this? I said.

"What?"

"Sleep. You can have the bed. I'll take the little couch," I said, pointing toward the love seat under the front window. I knew it was called a love seat, I just couldn't say it. When I first found myself in this room and before I learned that Tessie had never slept in it, I had envisioned her curled there reading books on rainy afternoons.

"I couldn't ask you to do that. This is your room. Besides, I'd fit better on the love seat than you." She stood and stretched. "Are you tired?"

I was still jazzed, though we'd been up almost all night. Something was not going to let me sleep, and I couldn't suppress it any longer. "Did you and Richard ever..." I started then stopped. I didn't hesitate because I thought I shouldn't ask; I hesitated because, like Corinne a few minutes before, I wasn't sure what word to use. *Make love* was all wrong. *Have sex* too clinical. *Fuck* was too harsh, I saw now, though that's certainly the verb I would have chosen five months ago. Every other euphemism screamed juvenile.

She put her arm on my wrist. "No. Not really, anyway," she said. "It was all so stupid, Duncan. It was like some strange new way of flirting. To this day, I don't even know if there's a category for what we did. It never seemed real to me, though I knew you'd think so because computers are such a real world to you. The line was blurred because, whatever it was, I liked it. I won't lie. I'm not going to blame our lifestyle or your long hours or any other of the trite 'reasons' someone might find for it. It happened. In a manner of speaking."

It was my turn to sit on the edge of the bed while she stood.

"But not in the way you're thinking," she added quickly. She knelt before me but didn't touch me. I wanted to say *get up – you're not chastising a child*. "It seemed like a big joke, a slightly naughty one for sure, but nothing more."

"Didn't feel like one to me," I said and hoped that didn't sound as petulant or peevish to her as it did to me. "The two of you weren't sitting there laughing when I came in."

And they weren't. I had come into the office of showplace.com late one evening to retrieve something I can't even remember now. The lights were off in the outer office and in mine, too, except for the blue aura of the computer screen in the demo area. There sat Richard operating a game's joy stick — hell, that alone sounds like sex — and Corinne sat next to him very closely with the dual controller. They weren't talking, yet they were so engrossed in manipulating the characters — themselves — on the screen that they didn't hear me come in. I watched their virtual doubles have sex on a 19" monitor in ways more graphic and more barbarous than Corinne and I ever had. Meanwhile, their real bodies twisted with effort, though it would take only their thumbs to move the controllers. Body english.

Their silence while they did this, their absorption, was the true betrayal.

"Duncan, it may well be that if you hadn't come in that night, I may eventually have made *the* mistake. I don't know. I could have fooled myself into thinking that the way Richard makes everyone laugh was a kind of seduction. I never knew him as well as you do. I know better than that now." She sat back onto the floor and hugged her knees. "I know that because, as you ran out the door and he lay bleeding on the floor — dead, I thought — I went after you."

There was no way, of course, I could have known this. And if I had, I don't think it would have made a difference at the time. I had assumed they had sex, that actual bodies had touched, trembled, sweated. I knew for sure Richard was capable of all that. He would not have seen the act as anything more harmful than pirating software: *who really gets hurt? What the hell are you worried about?*

But Corinne. Corinne did not have the capacity for such amoral duplicity. I could only think that she had determined a course of action, that there would be no return from it, and that she would try to find the right moment to tell me she was leaving me for my partner. Yet here she was, sitting on the floor before me, telling me that what I thought I knew about her was wrong.

In business and psychology, the trendy term for that is a paradigm shift.

Right here, right now, I had no term for it, trendy or otherwise. I could hear Summerset say "son, things ain't always what they seem." That would have been succinct, and correct.

"So you and Richard never actually…?"

"Never."

I wanted to ask again what might have happened had I not come in that night, but she had already said she didn't know. That would have to do. I most wanted to ask what about me made her even think such flirtation was necessary. What about me had been incomplete?

I didn't ask either of those questions, though, because the first person to know such things should be me. Until I could answer them, it was unfair to expect her to know.

She patted my knees like bongo drums, stood, and plopped on the bed beside me.

"What does it say about me that I want to ask you about you and Tessie?" she said, looking straight ahead.

"Only that you don't know anything about her."

She let that suffice. I was glad.

"I'm so tired, Duncan," she said finally.

I went to the bedside lamp and switched it off. The room didn't darken much; the sun was already climbing. Corinne pulled her top over her head sluggishly like a sleepy child. She tugged at her shorts without standing, first one cheek then the other, and let them fall to the floor. Seeing her body somehow didn't feel right. Good, but not right.

"Get under the covers," I said. "Get a little rest."

She did so. "Are you coming home with us?"

"Yes."

"Our home?"

"I don't know."

Her blonde hair splashed across the pillow and into her drowsy eyes. "I want you to."

I was getting tired now, too, and that conversation could have gone on forever. I let it die, or rather I let it remain open.

Corinne's eyes blinked more often, each blink lasting longer. She stared into nothing. Under the quilt her body assumed the z-shape she always fell asleep in. I went around to the other side of the bed and lay, clothed, on top of the quilt. I alphabetized my body to fit her angles but I did not drape my left arm over her. She rustled and nestled backwards into me.

We lay quietly that way for some time under and on the quilt Maude Hundley had made until I thought Corinne had fallen asleep. Tired as I was, however, something still nagged at me. I rewound the memories of our first few dates until it came.

"Astilbe," I whispered into the back of her hair. "Your favorite flower is the astilbe." I had overheard her tell her tour group that the first day I met her at Krohn Conservatory.

She was not asleep. She pulled her arm from under the quilt and reached behind herself to touch me.

"Thank you," she said, and after a moment: "You know what's not fair? I don't know what yours is. Or if you even have one." Her voice was thickening with weariness and thinking of astilbe was going to allow me to sleep, too.

"I'll have to think about that," I told her, though I already knew the answer. *That one*, I thought, looking at the rust-colored mum that lay atop the quilt.

I never slept well the night before any trip, especially one laden with the uncertainties of this one. I suspect Corinne did not sleep well either. My weight on top of the quilt confined her movements; and each of her rustlings, accustomed as I now was to sleeping alone, roused and aroused me. It was an uncomfortable dance, even in its echoed familiarity.

Yet, when we got up and made the bed together at noon after no more than five or six hours of such fitfulness, we both felt that false sweep of energy that adrenalin provides. The household had slept in, too—how could they not?—but I had heard them rustling downstairs a full hour before we came down.

In the kitchen Della was frying eggs. "How do you like yours, Corinne?"

I knew how she would answer: *oh, I'll just have a bagel and some cream cheese.* I also knew that was not on the menu here. "Over easy," I said for her. She did not dispute me.

Seven places were set at the table. Daylon had gone to work. "I appreciate your fixing breakfast for us, Della. You didn't have to do that."

She answered with her back to me, curtly. "Not a problem."

I pulled out a chair for Corinne to sit.

"Before we go, I want you to give me directions on how to get to Smoky's. I want to say goodbye to Daylon."

"Daylon's on his way home. He'll be here directly."

Stupidly, I counted the place settings again. Still seven. "Tessie?"

I went to Della and put my arm around her shoulder.

She nodded, still moving briskly among frying pans, sinks, ovens; her comfort zone. "It's no big deal. You know that by now."

From the kitchen table, Corinne caught my eye and

mouthed: *where is she?*

"Is it because of last night?" I said.

Della turned, spatula in hand. "Of course it's because of last night, Harry. And because of a million other nights. Days, too. But some broke things can't be mended." She looked at Corinne. "I'm sorry to be so short, Corinne. I don't know what Harry's — Duncan's — told you about Tess, but we're not worried. She does this. She'll be back." Again she faced the frying food.

Corinne looked to me for confirmation.

"You still have no idea where she goes?" I said.

This time she didn't face us. "I knew that, she'd be sitting at the table sopping eggs." When she turned back around to put a plate of fried eggs on the table, I thought her eyes were a bit red. "You want to get your friend from the barn? And Corinne, could you go wake up Miss Ariel?"

"Della, two things: can I borrow the four-wheeler, and will you keep our breakfast warm?"

Before she could answer, I grabbed Corinne's wrist and pulled her out the back door.


I won't pretend I drove the creek and its parallel path with the same proficiency or speed that Tessie had. The rough trail almost bounced me off even at our slow pace, and I felt Corinne's hold around my waist tighten after I thought it could be no tighter. But there was the same sense of liberation, of license, that driving through the thick woods unsurrounded by a climate-controlled cockpit gave me. I missed Tessie's loud whoop. It was replaced by Corinne's frightened silence.

My other joy was that I was certain I knew where Tessie was, and that my gift to the Hundleys would be her return. I had asked her if she retreated to the church during her disappearances; she had told me no, but I didn't believe her. Her traveling via the creek would have foiled her trackers; even dogs would have had difficulty following the false leads Tessie would have left them. I suspected she even traveled by trees for several yards to leave the hounds scrabbling and baying up their trunks and her pursuers scratching their heads.

The church would give her comfort. Her window Jesus would befriend her, and, though I didn't think she went out back to Maude and Andy's graves, I think her proximity to them was a good substitute when she simply could no longer abide the living and their troubles.

Yes, I knew where Tessie was.

At length, I burst — okay, I didn't burst, I sputtered — into the opening where the little church sat. I pried Corinne's arms from around me. She was as yet incapable of full speech, substituting susurration instead.

The early afternoon light was dimmed by a full cloud cover that nevertheless did not promise rain. I had seen this church in full sunlight before and recalled the clearing that held it as feeling like a chosen spot. I wanted to think of it as a wonder in the middle of the woods, something from a fairy tale; or something abandoned but which had not given in to forces of decay or the creepings of nature and time. Had it not been for the gravel road that led to its front door, it would have been possible to think so, to think that its only ingresses were paths through the woods.

But the lack of a more halcyon light did not diminish its serenity. Had I been Tessie, this is where I would have come.

But Tessie would have heard the approach of the four-wheeler's whine. In fact, she would have heard it if I had cut the engine a mile back up the path and walked here; and if she hadn't heard the engine, she surely would have heard our footsteps. I learned a little about the difficulty of stealth during my time under the bridge. Every sound is magnified, every movement invites attention. Tessie's senses were infinitely more acute then mine.

But here's what I thought: Tessie would respond to me. If she did hide when she heard us coming, she would answer if I called. I walked across the church's side lawn, straight to the cinder blocks that constituted Tessie's pew each Sunday. There were no fresh footprints in the damp grass.

"Wait there," I called back to Corinne who still stood beside the four-wheeler. Before she could ask why, I went around the front of the church to the other side to check that window. Nothing.

"Tessie!" I called. Only insects sawed through the October stillness. I megaphoned my hands around my mouth and shouted her name again. The bugs stopped their sawing briefly.

At the forest's fringe a twig snapped, and I saw a flash of movement. The raised white tail of a deer bobbed into the deeper shadows, followed by two more off to its side. If Tessie had run into the woods when we came, these deer would not have been there.     When I got back to the ATV, Corinne was leaning against its front end.

"What made you think she'd be here?"

I grabbed her wrist again, let my grip slide down until our fingers interlocked and walked her across the yard holding hands like schoolchildren. This seemed the place for that.

I let go when we got to the cinder block. "Look inside," I said and steadied her on the block.

She shaded her eyes with her hands against the glass. "What a cute little church. The Hundleys go here?"

"Yes. Well, except for Tessie who does, in fact, come here on Sundays, she just stays on this block looking in."

Corinne was quiet for a long time. She scanned the

church's interior, then finally lowered her hands and hopped off. "I see why," she said. "I mean, I see why she comes here even if she doesn't go in. And why you thought she might have come here today."

"Why's that?"

"Did you see that stained glass window behind the pulpit? The Jesus in it looks like he's smiling right at you."

She got it.

I decided then that I needed to tell the heart of the Hundley's story to Corinne alone. Later she could tell Richard and Ariel if she chose. And this was the best place to tell her.

I led her around back to the small cemetery, to take her to Maude's and Andy's headstones, but before we walked to them, I changed my mind. From where we stood just behind the church and under the gaze of Tessie's window Jesus, I could see, resting in the narrow margin between their graves, a pot of rust-colored mums.

\*\*\*\*\*\*\*\*\*\*\*\*


As we came in the back door, Daylon met us wearing a smug smile of inordinate size. Before I could apologize to the Hundleys for not finding Tessie, he led me down the hallway to the front door and stepped aside.

"I should have put two and two together, but I'm no math whiz," he said and pointed at the door in an "open it" gesture. Everyone, including Ariel and a haggard Richard (he had not slept well—I was happy) gathered around me. I pulled the door open, pushed the screen door out and stepped onto the porch.

There in the front yard, shining as it hadn't since I first saw it on the showroom floor, sat my Porsche. I was stunned to see it, of course, but equally stunned that I hadn't thought of it once since I'd left my bridge. While there, I'd wondered about it often: what had become of it, what forensic evidence the authorities might have found in it, how it may have looked after being denuded. Would it have been returned to Corinne, and would she let it sit in our Cincinnati garage shouting accusations to her through the walls in the deep nighttime?

I had had no need for it for a long time. Even as I planned many times to leave Sinking Creek, I had never thought of the Porsche as my mode of transportation. Now, it sat there, its hard, bright red seemingly dangerous, virulent. I walked down the porch to it. Daylon was anxious for me to acknowledge it, but I was illogically, afraid to touch it.

"I tuned it up and detailed it first thing this morning," Daylon said, running his own fingers lightly across the driver's door. "It's a real beaut, Duncan. Smoky was sorry to see it go." He laughed. "He called Summerset just to make sure I wasn't bullshitting when I told him I knew the owner."

Finally I put my hand on it. It didn't sting, or bite, or burn me. It was just metal, still cool though the day was warming up, and I pulled the door open smoothly. I didn't sit down, though. I'd be in it soon enough. I looked at Daylon's broad, expectant face. "It looks great, Daylon, really great. I don't know how to thank you."

"Oh, I think he's already thanked himself," Della interrupted. "He drove it like a bat on fire around these mountains before he decided to bring it home." Della obviously did not approve of speed.

"You mean a bat out of hell. Or maybe a house on fire," Daylon said, unaware that he was not helping his cause with her.

"I said just what I meant. I always do," she said and folded her arms.

Daylon knew when to concede. He turned back to me.

"I'm sorry; I did cut her loose a bit, but you know she'd been sitting there all those months. Had to burn the carbon out."

I waved my hand. "Good grief, Daylon, that's what the car is for."

Della pshawed. Summerset, who had been sitting quietly in the porch swing finally spoke. "It is a pretty car. I hope it'll see these mountain roads again," he said, and I knew he was speaking to everyone there, but especially to me.

Summerset's words had been definitive: they ended the bickering between his daughter and son-in-law by forgiving Daylon's transgression in a way that my dismissive wave could not, and he established for me an open invitation to return to Sinking Creek.

There was nothing to do but sit down to Della's breakfast.

\*\*\*\*\*\*\*\*\*\*\*\*\*\*

I thought—no, I knew—that Corinne wanted to give Ariel the keys to the Land Rover and ride back to Cincinnati with me. That would have been the logical, natural thing to do. I did not want to be unkind or ungentle, and there was much we needed to discuss. I was not ready for that, however, so without explanation, I helped put her small travel bag in her car with those of Ariel and Richard before quietly telling her of my plan.

"That's okay," she said, placing her fingers lightly on my cheek like a trailing spider's web. "Take the time you need. Cincinnati will be there when you pull up. So will I. I'll get Richard and Ariel out of here so you can say your goodbyes."

She jingled her keys. Richard had already shaken hands and sat in the back seat with the door still open. "I'll get to work on the publicity angles as soon as we get home,

Summerset. I'm excited to be in the Sinking Creek business."
He was, God bless him. I'd heard him say to every client we
ever had: *I'm excited to be in the Joe Smith business, or the Tom
Jones business, or the whoever I'm talking to business.* Thing was,
he wasn't lying. He would work hard on this until it was successful. Then, he'd be on to the next challenge.

Ariel was writing down cooking tips from Della who
promised to have Summerset email her some more recipes since
she, Della, was never going to learn about computers. Quilts,
she said, were her fortress — Ariel did not correct her to *forte* —
and she would enlist all the women of Sinking Creek into this
venture. She called Ariel "honey." Ariel called her "sweetie."

Daylon checked the Land Rover's tire pressure with a
gauge he pulled from his shirt pocket and scraped bugs off the
windshield with his thumbnail.

Summerset powwowed with Corinne and I could not
hear them. That was okay. Whatever he told her was right.
Whatever he asked of her was for her own good.

With a honk and a chorus of "be carefuls" they were
gone.

My bag — well, Henderson S. Turner's bag — was in the
Porsche's trunk. I turned to say my goodbyes and met their
three faces.

I wanted to simply get in the car and drive away because I knew I would not be able to speak. How could I? What
could I leave these people with? I would be in contact with
them; after all, I was establishing a website for Sinking Creek
Quilts, and we would be in touch nearly every day by phone
or email during the start-up phase. I had no doubt this venture would do well. None. I didn't think they'd get rich, but
maybe. I knew, though, that Summerset wouldn't have to work
the farm to live and that Daylon, Della, and Tessie could keep
it.

So why could I not speak just now? Did I not have any-thing to say? Or did I have too much? I had talked for hours to clients, to media, to politicians, to the rich and connected. I had only to say one word — goodbye — just now.

Their faces waited but I turned my back to them and placed my hands on my car, and before I knew it, my shoulders shook violently and my chest caught in ragged gasps and something inside me tore.

The first hand on me was Daylon's, who tousled my hair like a little boy's. Then from behind, Della's strong arms encircled my chest, and she buried her face in between my shoulder blades and sobbed.

At length, I felt I could turn around in Della's hug and return it face to face. We composed ourselves and smiled si-multaneously. "You're the best," I said.

"Tell that to that scrawny husband of mine."

"He knows."

She grew serious. "You take care of that sweet wife of yours. I don't know how things went so wrong between you, but don't nothing get so broke it can't be fixed," she said.

"Della Hundley Monroe!" I said. "Just this morning I heard you say some things couldn't be mended." Inwardly I cringed remembering she had been talking about Tessie.

"I lied." She grinned and squeezed me again, hard. "We better hear from you soon."

"Oh, I'll be calling as soon as I get some of the software underway."

"I don't mean just about business," she snapped and stepped away from me.

I extended my hand toward Daylon. He moved past it and embraced me instead. His hug was strong, too, and I thought he'd have no trouble keeping me in it as long as he chose. When he released me, his eyes, too, watered. He put his hands in his pockets. "Won't need to change your oil for another 3,000 miles," he said, looking at the car. "But don't forget to. That's a high performance vehicle you got there."

As if it had been rehearsed, they both said "you be careful, now," and walked up on the porch to sit in the wicker swing.

Summerset passed them on his way down. His gait was a little stiff, but his gray eyes sparkled. In his hands he held a quilt.

"I owe you," I said. "And I can never repay it."

"You've been good for us, too. Don't forget that."

I couldn't think of a single positive thing I had been to or done for this family.

He handed me the quilt. "This is off Andy's bed. Maudie made it for his first birthday, so it's too small for the bed you and your missus probably sleep in. But in the winter maybe you can lay it across the top of whichever one of you gets coldest and think about us. It's made out of pieces of old shirts from everybody in the family. Lots of Hundleys you never met."

There would be no sense in telling him I couldn't accept it. Besides, just then I wanted it more than I'd ever wanted anything.

"What have I ever given you that's worth this quilt, Summerset?"

"Oh son, you taught me a valuable lesson," he said, and from anyone else I might have thought that facetious.

"What's that?"

"That a man don't live his life in one day."

"*You* told *me* that!"

"I just put the words to the lesson you taught us. That's how I put it to Dexter Daugherty. He understood. That's when he told Corinne where to find you."

"I still don't understand what it means."

"I come home after working all day at the rest stop and still have a day's work to do here. Sometimes all I wanted was to get through it, to get to the sitting down part of my day. But since you got here, I'd watch you watch me. You'd watch me milk a cow, or brush a horse, or mend a saddle, any of the dozens of things that make up my every day, and I could tell to you they felt like mysteries. Pretty soon, I paid attention too and saw them for what they were to you, saw they was the same things that Maude used to call rainy days with the kids when they was all small." He tapped the air with an index finger for emphasis, tapped something I couldn't see. "Days of granted grace, she called them."

I thought he was spent, thinking of Maude, but he sighed and continued. "Life on a farm may be different than life any-where else, maybe not, I don't know," he said. "We plant in the spring, harvest in the fall. In between there's a lot of hard work, but somehow that all gets lost in the piling up of days. I'm there when the piglets are born and when the hogs are slaughtered. I never took much note of what happens after the beginnings and before the endings. Even Maude's and Andy's deaths didn't teach me to. Probably, they made me pay less attention, so I could get through them. Since you, I watch things grow instead of seeing them grown. My thanks are to you for that."

I still didn't think I'd given enough.

"I'm sorry I couldn't find Tessie this morning," I said when he was drained of speech. "I was sure she'd be at the church. Maybe she had been. I think she put a pot of flowers on Maude's and Andy's grave."

He shook his head. "No, I'm afraid not. I put those mums there at first light. That color was her favorite."

I wound my way out of Sinking Creek toward the intersection with I-81 following the landmarks I'd memorized yesterday with Della.

The Porsche felt at once novel and familiar. I babied it around these roads though it was engineered to smooth them, to divorce its occupants from the discomfort and severity of their turns. If our new business venture went well, I had no doubt I'd drive these roads again some day to discuss things with the Hundleys. I wouldn't have to, given the forms of communication designed to eliminate the need for face-to-face discussion, yet I knew I would anyway.

But I would be a different person then. Corinne and I might be together. We might not, and I'd have to either explain or obfuscate that fact to the Hundleys. Probably explain— they'd see through any other attempt. Theirs would not be my only business, either, so obeisance to other masters would foment changes that had a funny way of moving from the external to the core. Knowing that did not always prevent its happening.

And maybe they'd be different, too. I tried to imagine Della behind a desk, barking orders, or Daylon wearing anything except jeans. Summerset contending with distributors or exhibiting the righteous anger so often needed in business.

I tried to imagine Tessie changing, too, and couldn't because I had no idea in what direction she could go. And because it broke my heart to think of a world where even meaner things could happen.

No, I concluded that the Hundleys would be no different. They were the North Star, or if not as unreachable, as permanent, as that, then they were the mountains: evolving so slowly as to be imperceptible, constant, at once new and ancient.

I reached the entrance ramp. Two miles north would be the travel plaza, but only one mile ahead I would cross the bridge under which I had lived for three months. I was glad again that I had sent Corinne ahead because how could I explain that I was going to stop there? How could I show her my temporary home?

I went slow to make certain I would not miss the bridge, enduring the impatience of drivers whizzing past me. To a person they looked at me in passing, some with theatrical pity — *you don't know what kind of car you're driving?* — others with raw intolerance, one with a raised middle finger.

Was a time I'd have flipped mine back, zoomed past him, and cut him off before leaving him behind.

And then there was the small green sign, the kind that only tourists or bored kids who collected unusual place names have a need for: Sinking Creek. As if someone driving 70 miles per hour has more than an instant to ponder the name of a shriveled stream a hundred feet below. Why waste taxpayers' money on a sign of no consequence?

I could have told them it deserved a bigger sign.

I maneuvered to the shoulder and stopped. I got out, hoping that no trooper would drive by and offer help — I was fairly certain no ordinary motorist would.

It was easy enough to slip over the guardrail and under the wire fence, and within a minute I was at the top of that muffled world that had been my home. It was less easy to grab the vines and slide rapidly down the steep embankment, past my sleeping platform in the bridge's underside concrete V and to the creek where I sat out so many hours. The path I had made was still there as were the stones and logs I had sat on.

The surrounding forest had thinned considerably, most

of the leaves having already fallen. It was still noisy, though, with cicadas' high whines and the drowse of horse flies and bore bees. Nature was furiously preparing for winter.

I sat on my most comfortable log, one that had a built-in niche that perfectly fit my back, and stretched out my legs. Stuffed in the log's hollows were some of the brochures I had pinched from the rest area and which had both placated and educated me. They were yellow and warpy, water-swollen, their pages stuck together and stained.

I pried one of them—Preserving the Chesapeake Bay Watershed—apart with a ripping sound. I hadn't gotten around to reading this one, or if I had, I didn't remember it. I would have read it voraciously then; it didn't interest me now. But I stuck it in my back pocket to take home anyway. Never know.

The air lacked the thickness I remembered from June and early July, that lush vegetable humidity. Deep breaths were possible and pleasant. The forest floor was visible, nothing that desired concealment could move now with impunity. I had been frightened many times then. If I lived here now, I wouldn't be.

But then I did hear a movement, and what made that unsettling is that it occurred in my old sleeping platform. I had slid down past it so fast, I hadn't taken notice of anything there.

I looked up into its gloom from my log by the creek. It moved again and I realized that, whatever it was, it was big, and it would block my access back up the bank and to my car.

But it was Tessie who waved from those shadows. Beyond my relief that I wasn't potential bear food rang a delight at seeing her before I left Sinking Creek.

I grabbed vines and scrambled up the embankment to sit beside her. Flopsy lay between her feet.

"So, this is where you come to be alone," I said.

Tessie's eyes were fixed on Flopsy. On the other side of her body, in shadows, her right hand held a long nightcrawler.

"Till you came along," she said.

I thought my proper response should be "I'm sorry," but I'm not sure why.

"But now I get it back. You won't tell nobody?" She phrased it as a question, but her tone made it a flat statement.

"Not if you don't want me to."

We were quiet a while. Her movements told me she was setting the nightcrawler down and when it began to wriggle away, pulling it back by its tail.

"Why're you going, Harry?"

"I can't stay. I've got work to do in Cincinnati." I knew for her that this wasn't a reason, wasn't even an answer.

"There's plenty of work to do here. You don't like us?" Her voice was not plaintive or complaining. It wasn't pitiable. But it expected an explanation that I hadn't given and that hadn't been necessary for the other Hundleys.

I was about to make up some bullshit because I was sure that telling her just how much I liked them all, loved them, in fact, especially her, would not add up on her ledger sheet. Fact was, I liked them—I was leaving them. How *could* she reconcile that?

Before I could begin my dissembling, Tessie lifted the nightcrawler from the deep shadows and I saw with horror that it wasn't a worm at all. It was a vividly patterned snake, a juvenile probably, judging by its length—eight, ten inches.

Tessie's fragility made me dig for a calm I didn't feel. "Whatcha got there?"

"A snake, silly."

"I see that." She held it up and let it play through her fingers for a moment then set it down on Flopsy's back. It lay still for a few seconds but soon slithered up the motionless rabbit's spine. Each time it reached Flopsy's head, Tessie pulled it back to his tail and the cycle repeated.

"What kind of snake is it?" I said with a breeze I didn't feel. I hated snakes, had read the brochure about native Virginia species many times, and now cussed myself because I didn't remember all the identifying features.

"Corn snake," she said, and I felt some relief. "Or a copperhead. Hard to tell them apart when they're babies."

Shit, shit, shit, I thought.

"Why don't you let it go? Set it down over in the weeds and let it wander away? I don't think Flopsy likes it being on his back."

"Flopsy'll have to get used to it," she said, and there was a flash of malevolence in her voice I'd never heard, a hissing I'd associated with snakes. And I saw that she'd rather have put the snake on my spine. Let it crawl up and down my length.

"Why's that?"

"I'm going to take it home and raise it. Flopsy will have a friend. He'll have to learn to get along with all kinds of critters. Hard lesson to learn."

The snake was becoming agitated with having its progress thwarted each time it tried to get to Flopsy's head and slink off. The next time Tessie tugged it back it opened its tiny mouth and bit at the rabbit's back. It was so small, however, and Flopsy's coat so thick that it just bit fur. Still, just a nick from a copperhead, even a juvenile, would be enough to kill the rabbit.

The snake struck with greater vehemence, several times. Tessie watched placidly, eyes flat, themselves snakelike.

I became angry then. My voice trembled under bare control. "Tessie, stop it! Let the snake go. They won't grow up to be friends. It doesn't work like that, and I think you know it. Even if it's just a corn snake, it could grow up to swallow Flopsy, and I'm not going to let that happen to him."

She finally looked up from the lethal pageant of snake and rabbit, and I expected a returned anger in her eyes. I preferred it to the resentment I saw. "What do you care about Flopsy, Harry?"

Then it came. I could not coddle her just now. I had ownership in that damn rabbit, if in nothing else in Sinking Creek. "I saved that rabbit's life, Tessie!" I shouted, and in an undammed torrent spilled the story of Flopsy's capture by the hawk, of the storm that had frightened me, of my helplessness and Summerset's intervention, of my impotence and how I'd almost been reduced to tears thinking I was going to be responsible for the death of her beloved rabbit, a stinking rabbit.

"I caught Flopsy after the hawk dropped him, Tessie. And nothing I have ever held has felt so good in my hands."

Tessie's eyes had widened and become animated during my telling, and I knew her malleable face was simply reflecting the mutations of mine. I was not masquerading to appeal to a client; my face revealed the truth of what I felt as I told Flopsy's and my story. I knew this as I saw Tessie mirror it.

When I finished the tale that would not have been believed by anyone else I knew, Tessie's face had lost its austerity. She would be angry with me for leaving, and that anger would last a while, but she would not hate me, would not hold it against me as she might hold onto that snake, as protection against further hurt.

All she could say, in a voice that was full of awe was: "Flopsy flew?"

I nodded.

She looked down with new eyes at her wondrous rabbit, at her pet that had been places she could only dream about, and whose muteness she now regarded as holy. "Flopsy flew," she said again.

She plucked the wriggling snake from Flopsy's back and set it down in the vines on the steep embankment. We heard its slight rustle, saw leaves shudder at its passing, then lost its progress. Tessie stroked Flopsy's back from head to tail. I reached over and scratched the rabbit's ears; he leaned his head into my touch.

"Can I put some hug marks on you?" I said, stealing the line Daylon always used on Della.

Though she didn't return my embrace, Tessie smiled and allowed me. The only sounds were the slow gurglings of Sinking Creek far below and those of that hug. For once, at least under this bridge, the universe had nothing to say.

I emerged again from the coolness of the shade under the bridge into the late afternoon light. No one had stopped to see if the car or its driver might need help. I hadn't expected anyone would. I headed north, driving on the shoulder for hundreds of yards, almost all the way to the plaza, because I had trouble gaining enough speed to merge into the traffic. It had been a long time since I had accelerated.

2608226

Made in the USA